A

Comfortable
Alliance

A Regency Novel

CATHERINE KULLMANN

Willow
Books

Cover images antique engravings from the author's private collection.
Cover design by BookGoSocial

ISBN: 978-1-913545-67-3

First published 2021 by
Willow Books
D04 H397, Ireland

Regency Novels by Catherine Kullmann

The Duchess of Gracechurch Trilogy   **The Malvins**

The Murmur of Masks

↓

Perception & Illusion →   →   The Potential for Love

↓

The Duke's Regret

Stand Alone

A Suggestion of Scandal

A Comfortable Alliance

Novella

The Zombi of Caisteal Dun

For my sister Mary, with love and special thanks for Mr Harry Hall's couplet in Chapter Six. Also, in loving memory of our brother, Denis.

Main Characters

HELENA DOROTHEA (Nell) SWIFT

In Brussels

Captain Richard Harbury	Helena's first love
Lord and Lady Harbury	Richard's parents
Michael Harbury	The Harburys' eldest son
Mrs Caroline (Caro) Thompson	The Harburys' widowed daughter
Captain Jonathan (Jonnie) Swift	Helena's brother

At the Dower House, Swift Hall, Wiltshire

Dorothea, dowager Lady Swift	Helena's mother
Lennard	Helena's maid

At Swift Hall

Sir Augustus (Gus) Swift	Helena's brother
Rosamund Lady Swift	Gus's wife
Tom and Sally	Gus's and Rosamund's children

At the Rectory

Frances (Fannie) Richardson	Helena's sister
Rev. Harold Richardson	Fannie's husband
Molly	Fannie's and Harold's baby daughter

WILLIAM HENRY (Will), 8th EARL OF RASTLEIGH

At Rastleigh House, London

Stephen Graham MP	Son of the rector of Rastleigh and Will's oldest friend
Harry Hall	Will's distant cousin and heir
James Thornton	Will's secretary
Emmett	Will's valet
Blaines	Butler
Mrs Murray	Housekeeper

At Walton Place, Wiltshire

Lady Amelia Walton	Will's aunt
Sir Humphrey Walton	Lady Amelia's husband
Edmund Walton	Sir Humphrey's and Lady Amelia's elder son
Kathryn Walton	Edmund's wife
Hugh Walton	Sir Humphrey's and Lady Amelia's younger son

Anne, Lady Philip Martyn	Sir Humphrey's and Lady Amelia's daughter
Lord Philip Martyn	Anne's husband
Amelia Martyn	Anne's and Philip's daughter

At Colduff, Co. Wicklow Ireland

Phoebe, Lady Malcolm	Will's mother
Sir John Malcolm	Will's step-father
Jack, Kate, Alexander and Emily	Will's half-brothers and -sisters
Miss Bowen	Kate's and Emily's Governess

At Rastleigh Castle, Dorsetshire

Dr Charles Thornton	John's uncle, former secretary to Will's grandfather and now Castle librarian
Hannah Thornton	Former companion to Will's grandmother; married to Dr Thornton
Anne Hall née Lambert	Harry Hall's mother
Rachel Hall	Harry Hall's sister
Mr Hancock	Land Steward
Jenkins	Butler
Parker	Underbutler
Mrs Miller	Housekeeper

Mr and Mrs Higgs	Previous butler and housekeeper, now retired
Mrs Hope	Cook
Susan Smithson	Head housemaid
Smithson	Susan's father; Head groom

Members of the ton

Lady Georgina Benton	Harry's and Rachel's great-aunt, sister of their paternal grandmother
The dowager Lady Neary	Stephen's godmother
The dowager Lady Needham	Old friend of Will's grandmother
Lady Westland	Dashing widow with designs on Will and his heir

Note: Characters are grouped according to their connection to Helena or Will. Locations are those where we first encounter them.

Prologue

Brussels, July 1815

Nell lifted her hands from the pianoforte, letting the last notes fade in the still air. Richard had fallen into a restless doze. The slanting evening sun lit his fair hair, now dishevelled and darkened by perspiration, and accentuated the angles of his jaw and cheekbones, his face almost haggard. It was three weeks since they carried him in, gravely wounded, from the field of Waterloo. Since then she had lived between despair and hope.

As if he felt her gaze, he opened his eyes. "Nell?"

"My love."

She dipped a cloth in the bowl of cool lavender water on the bedside table and tenderly wiped his face and neck. His wavering hand found hers and pressed it to his mouth.

"Would you like a drink?"

At his nod, she poured him a glass of lemonade, then slipped her arm under his shoulders to help him raise his head. He sipped, then pushed the glass aside, wincing as he lay down again.

"What is it?"

"Just another bit of shrapnel making itself felt, I suppose. That deuced shell must have shattered into a hundred parts and most of them seem to have arrowed straight into me."

"The surgeons think they have removed most of them and the fever is not as high now."

"Thanks to your nursing, Sweetheart."

"And your Mamma's."

"I am more grateful that she permits you to spend so much time alone with me. But I'm as weak as a cat and I suppose she considers you to be safe from my wicked intentions." A ghost of a smile curved his elegant lips, reminding her of the dashing officer who had first charmed her, then wooed her. "Another day or so and I hope to prove her wrong."

"I hope so too." She bent to kiss him. "Are you tired? Shall I play again?"

"No. Sing to me, Nell, please. But first—do you know where my uniform coat is? The one I was wearing?"

"I think it is in the dressing room. Stubbs was going to see if anything could be done with it."

"Can you find it, please?"

"Now, Richard?"

"Please, Sweetheart? It's important."

As Nell crossed the room, Captain Richard Harbury's gaze followed her longingly. The setting sun struck ruby flames in her dark auburn hair. He tried to move onto his side so that he could watch her further but was arrested by another sudden, stabbing pain. "Devil take it!" His breath caught and he closed his eyes, opening them only when he heard Nell's soft footsteps returning and the rustle of her skirts as she neared his bed.

"Would you see if there is anything in the pocket?"

She slipped her fingers into the pocket of the dark green jacket and removed a small packet. "Is this what you are looking for?"

"Yes." He took it from her and opened it carefully. It held a pearl and diamond ring.

"I saw this in a shop window in one of those little streets near the Grand Place and bought it for you. I was going to give it to you after the Duchess's ball, but we were called away so suddenly. Afterwards, I was glad I had it with me—it was like having a little piece of you in my pocket to bring me luck—a promise for the future. Will you wear it now, my dearest love?"

Tears in her eyes and a trembling smile on her lips, Nell held out her left hand. He slid the ring onto her finger and raised her hand to his mouth. "We'll be married just as soon as the leeches pronounce me fit." He kissed the finger that now wore his ring and turned her hand to caress her palm. "But, Nell, I am not yet out of the woods. If I shouldn't make it, don't mourn too long for me. I'm not such a selfish brute that I would not wish you to love again and find happiness with another man. I've had time to think while I was lying here these last weeks and I cannot bear the thought of leaving you to a long, lonely life, if leave you I must. Will you promise me?"

She brushed his hair back from his forehead. "You are not going to leave me. Once you are recovered, you and Jonnie will sell out and buy neighbouring estates so that you can breed horses together. We'll find a bride for Jonnie and our children shall play together."

"I hope so indeed, my darling." But weak though he was, he would not yield on this. "Promise me, Nell."

"I promise," she whispered. "But I want to lead a long, happy life with you."

"I too, Sweetheart." He rested his cheek against her hand. "Will you sing for me again, please? One of Tom Moore's melodies."

Richard closed his eyes as Nell began a soft song full of yearning. Soon she felt him relax into sleep. When the song was over, she smoothed the bedclothes over his shoulders and moved back to the pianoforte. His mother, Lady Harbury, had had the instrument moved into his room when they had realised that music soothed him when he was restless with fever. She had just begun one of his favourite pieces when a soft knock on the door heralded the arrival of her ladyship with the army surgeon.

"Good day, Miss Swift. How does the patient?"

"Still improving, Mr Gillespie, but another piece of shrapnel seems to be making itself felt."

"Aye. Some of them may have gone quite deep and are lodged at the ribs. If you will leave me with him, ladies, I'll take a look."

It was a damn shame, the surgeon thought, as he moved towards the bed. The lass had nursed him so devotedly despite the house being in disarray; her brother wounded too and the lad's sister losing her husband. A fine officer, Major Thompson. Lady Harbury had had her hands full, with her daughter in a delicate situation and her son so grievously hurt. Miss Swift had shown herself to be extremely capable; not at all missish, supporting the stricken family as best she could. Mr Gillespie regarded the young captain's face. His colour did not please him—it was sallow, almost green in its pallor. He folded back the bedclothes, noticing the pain on his patient's face as he tried to turn. Suddenly Captain Harbury gasped, groaned on a long sigh and was still. As the surgeon had feared these past weeks, a splinter from the shell had pierced the heart.

~ ~ ~

Three weeks later a sad convoy left Brussels for England; Lord and Lady Harbury, their newly widowed daughter Mrs Caroline Thompson with her daughter Amanda, Miss Helena Swift, whom their dead son had planned to marry, and her brother Captain Jonathan Swift. Captain Swift had neglected a sabre cut to his right forearm, returning to duty too soon, and now had difficulties in using his right hand. They left behind them two graves that told simply of lives cut short and other lives changed for ever.

Book 1

Chapter One

London, 19 July 1821

"A hit!"

The Earl of Rastleigh stepped back, raised his foil to salute his opponent and then went forward to shake his hand. "A good bout, Stephen."

"Have you been taking extra lessons from Angelo, Will?" his lordship's oldest friend, Stephen Graham MP enquired. "That last was a neat trick."

"Not directly. A visiting French master called here last week. He demonstrated some new moves."

"Which you are going to share with me, I trust?"

Will laughed. "Only one at a time. I'll not sacrifice my advantage so easily."

"But you can at least demonstrate that last one."

His lordship obliged, slowly going through the movement and then engaging with his friend as he tried it out. He stretched. "I needed that after so much sitting yesterday. Now for a beefsteak and a tankard of ale."

Settled at a quiet table in The Blue Posts in Cork Street, Mr Graham raised his tankard of Burton Ale to his friend. "My parents desire me to convey their compliments to you. I went home briefly after Parliament was prorogued and they—and my sisters—were eager to hear how you went on. Do you plan to be at the Castle this summer?"

"I don't know. I must stay in town until next week's levée at Carlton House, but then I'm committed to my aunt Walton in Wiltshire. Perhaps I can spend some days at Rastleigh before I go to Ireland. My visit to my mother is late anyway this year; another week or two should not matter."

"You have a summer of dissipation ahead of you, I see," Mr Graham said solemnly. He grinned at Rastleigh's raised eyebrow. "It might be better for you if you did, Will. You know what they say about all work and no play. If you ask me, you need to shake off the old Earl. He still seems to whisper in your ear. You have been Rastleigh for almost five years. It is time you set your own mark on the Earldom."

"And set up as a rakehell, you mean? How unfortunate that Byron has never returned. He would be an entertaining guide to the various circles of hell."

"No need to go that far!" Mr Graham protested, laughing. "Why, you might be refused entrance to Almack's."

"You have convinced me, Stephen. Dissipation it shall be, if it spares me that evil nest of husband-hunting minxes and their even more predatory Mammas."

"Not so fast. For every young miss who is warned to avoid you, you'll have a Caro Lamb seeking your attentions in the most importunate way."

"Ah, the sirens of the *ton*! I shall continue to cling to the mast of duty."

"Not too tightly, I trust," his friend replied knowingly. "Is pretty Mrs Blake still in town?"

"No, alas. But let's be honest, Stephen. You know that these little affairs run their course and in the end are not very satisfying."

"I agree. I never thought to hear myself say this, Will, but maybe 'tis time we considered matrimony."

"Perhaps you're right. But I confess that that is where my grandfather's voice rings loudest in my ear. He was never tired of preaching that, as the only son of an only son, it was my duty to marry and sire heirs."

"Whatever about the second, you would have no problem in achieving the first. I cannot imagine any house refusing to entertain an offer from Rastleigh."

"And that is why I have held off so long. I have no wish for a grand alliance with a dutiful bride who will go her own way once she has presented me with a son or two. I want something more comfortable."

"Comfortable! You don't choose a wife the way you engage a mistress."

Will grinned. "Perhaps there would be fewer unhappy marriages if you did. I would want to be sure I was welcome in my wife's bed and in her life. But enough of that. What news of your family and of Rastleigh?"

"All is well with the family. My father thinks of retiring in favour of Paul, if you are agreeable. The living is in your gift, is it not?"

"Yes, and I should be happy to have your brother returned to us. Your parents would remain with us, I hope?"

"I think they would like to if a suitable house may be found. They cannot remain at the Rectory if Paul is to establish his authority."

"I agree. I shall consult with your father when I am next at the Castle."

"Better talk to my mother too, if 'tis about where she will live," Mr Graham recommended. "She's by far the more practical of the two. And that reminds me—she feels all is not well at the Castle. Couldn't put her finger on it—just a feeling you know, but time you went down again, she says."

Will sighed. "It has never really felt right to me, either, Stephen. It is my principal seat, I know, but not my home. However, I shall try and spend some weeks there once I return from Ireland. I rarely last longer than a fortnight except over the Christmas period, and even then, I leave as soon as I am able."

William Henry, 8th Earl of Rastleigh, celebrated his sixth birthday two days before his father died from a fall while out riding. He had a handful of memories of him; a laughing face looking up at him as he was thrown towards the ceiling, shrieking with delight and safe in the knowledge that strong hands would catch him; a patient hand on the bridle as he was put on his first pony; an imposing man on a tall horse beside him as they trotted around the estate once Will was allowed to ride without a leading rein; a splendid figure leading his glittering mother out to the carriage as they left for a ball; a voice explaining why the moon looked different each night; the smell of tobacco and wine, horses and dogs; a burst of laughter; comforting arms lifting him when he fell. And then the hush in the Castle, the slow tread of men carrying a heavy burden; his mother weeping, telling him Papa had gone to heaven; his grandfather's white, frozen face; his grandmother's sobs. Then all was busy for some days and he must remain in the nursery and schoolroom. And afterwards, the silence that settled over Rastleigh—everyone, including the servants, dressed in mourning, no one called and no one went anywhere.

Although he did not fully understand what had happened, Will's life had changed forever. He was now the Heir to the Earldom. His grandfather called him "Hall," but that was his father's name; the servants and even his governess now called him "my lord." Only his mother and grandmother still said, "Will." And the Graham children; Stephen, his own age, couldn't understand that his friend's name was no longer what it used be and nor could his younger sister Faith, who always waited for them to emerge from their lessons with her father, the rector. Stephen's mother, a sensible woman, had advised her husband to "let the children continue to use his Christian name, my dear. The poor child must be feeling utterly lost and at least here at the rectory he should find things unchanged."

Now, twenty-four years later, Will was Earl. He had dutifully pursued the course of instruction and intensive training set down for him by his grandfather for whom the greatest worry after his son's premature death had been that his grandson would succeed to the title at too young an age, unprepared for his new responsibilities. His only failure had been in arranging a suitable marriage for Will, who had refused even to consider it. And yet, now that he was thirty and his grandfather dead five years, Will was uneasily aware that this, too, was a duty he must fulfil.

Sitting in his library at Rastleigh House, he shifted restlessly as he looked out into the summer evening. Perfect light for fishing! Taking down a volume of Marvell, he leafed through it looking for distraction and gave a short laugh:

But at my back I always hear

Time's winged chariot hurrying near

And yonder all before us lie

Deserts of vast eternity.

....

The grave's a fine and private place

But none I think do there embrace.

'Tis not the embracing I object to but the matrimony, he thought as he left the room. If only there were some alternative to the demure debutantes or the dashing widows. I wouldn't know how to deal with the one and have no wish to shackle myself to the other.

~~~

Three days later, a bored Will surveyed the dancers at what, he was resolved, would be his last ball of this interminably long Season.

"Might I tempt your lordship to a little distraction?" a sultry voice murmured in his ear. Turning, he nodded coolly to Lady Westland, a luscious, vivacious female, the edges of whose beauty had started to harden. Rastleigh, then Lord Hall, had shared a brief dalliance with her some years previously. Widowed since then, on coming out of mourning she had not too discreetly made him aware that she would have no objection to resuming the relationship on whatever terms he chose. She had ambitions to be a countess and seemed confident of achieving this goal if she could once again entice him to an intimate encounter. For his part, Will had quickly seen past the attractive facade to the shallow woman behind and had no intention of revisiting what he considered to have been a youthful folly.

"I regret, my lady, but I must pay my respects to Lady Needham. She was a great friend of my grandmother's and I have not seen her this age."

A brief inclination of his head, and he proceeded across the floor to bow over the hand of an elderly lady, who sat enthroned in an armchair at the side of the ballroom. She favoured him with a smile and nodded to where Lady Westland accepted a glass of champagne from a slight young man, dressed in the very height of fashion.

"A hussy if ever I saw one. I see she has her eye on your heir."

"What, Harry Hall? She would have two of him for supper."

"Indeed? It is high time you found a nice, sensible girl and set up your nursery. You cannot want that fop to step into your shoes."

"I fear you are right, ma'am, but pray do not speak of it here or I shall never escape alive."

"Afraid of the Mammas, are you? Well, I can't say I blame you. I daresay even Wellington would quail before their massed ranks."

"On the contrary, his Grace would most likely decimate them."

"Reprobate!" Her ladyship rapped his knuckles with her fan, but could not quite stifle a chuckle.

"By all accounts, you were a dab hand at match-making yourself. My grandmother was used to mention admiringly how you had fired off your own daughters quite easily and to very acceptable *partis,* too."

"They were pretty, well-behaved girls with heads on their shoulders. I never held with not educating girls, for how are they to converse with their husbands if they are silly ninnies, as so many are today. They married good men, as did my granddaughters. It is a pity they are all wed, or I might try my hand at a last bout of matchmaking on your behalf."

"Perhaps I may seek your services next year. I am off to visit my aunt Walton once I have done my duty at the levée. Sir Humphrey will be seventy and there are to be great celebrations."

"Pray give him my felicitations and Amelia my dear love. And remember, you may call on my assistance at any time."

"Heading home, Will?"

"Had enough of it, too, Stephen?"

Before they could make their escape however, they were accosted by Mr Hall. "Do you leave already, Cousin? I had hoped to have a word with you."

"Not tonight," Will said curtly. "If you wish to see me before I leave town, you may call on me tomorrow morning at eleven o'clock."

"Eleven o'clock? Surely you jest! Who in the world is about at that hour? I would have to leave my bed at nine, for it takes my valet quite two hours to dress me."

Will eyed the clinging coat of superfine, fashionably nipped in at the waist, the extravagant silk waistcoat, the intricately tied cravat, and the pomaded locks falling artlessly, yet carefully. "I can quite see that."

When Will said no more, Mr Hall said sulkily, "If you leave me no choice, I suppose I must agree."

~~~

"Mr Hall, my lord."

Will looked up from the *Morning Chronicle*. "Show him in, Blaines."

"Good morning, Cousin."

"Ah, Hall! May I offer you some breakfast?"

Mr Hall shuddered. "No food, if you please. A cup of coffee would be most welcome, I admit."

Not unsympathetic to his visitor's apparent need to revive himself, Will joined in a desultory discussion of such interesting topics as the Queen's vain attempt to attend the coronation until, judging Mr Hall to be enough restored, he said, "How may I serve you, Hall? It must have been of some import to bring you here so early."

"Why, no. I thought merely to pay my respects. Now that I am your heir, I feel we should know one another better and, as the Season is nearly over, thought to seize the opportunity to call."

"My renewed condolences on the death of your father. He belonged to the Regent's set, didn't he? He would have been sorry to miss the coronation festivities."

"They were old comrades-in-arms, as one might say. It's a damnable thing. He talked of arranging for an appointment of some sort for me, but I have no hope of that now."

Will observed him over his coffee cup. "Feeling the pinch? I had thought my cousin had left you tolerably comfortable."

"Oh, as to that, I suppose he did, but a man can always use a little more. Apart from that, it would have been something to do. He kept me hanging on with the promise Prinny would do something for me, but it was all to no avail."

"Feeling a trifle jaded, are you? Well, I can't help you there."

"No, no, I didn't expect you to," his cousin exclaimed, flushing. "But that reminds me—I could find no evidence of the heir's allowance in my father's papers. That should come to me now, should it not?"

"You found no evidence because no allowance was made. My grandfather apparently did not consider it necessary and I saw no reason to change that when your father approached me about it. I trust that, despite the extravagances of the Carlton House set, the reserves have not been too depleted?"

"No, no. But surely my position as your heir—?"

"Does not entitle you to make such demands on me. If you are in difficulties, you may furnish me with details and I'll see how I might help you. But I warn you now that I am not prepared to support you in a life of gambling and excess. You might also recall that your position as heir is tenuous at best. If you will take my advice, you will retire to your estates for the summer and take more of an interest in them. There are great strides being made in agricultural management and you may improve the yield from your acres if you familiarise yourself and apply them."

Mr Hall flushed. "If that is your best advice to me, Cousin, I'll take my leave of you." At the door, he turned and said, "We have not all had your advantages, you know."

He had crossed the hall before Will could ask him what the devil he meant. Shrugging, he turned his attention to the papers on his desk. If the pup had a grievance, he need not lay it at his door.

Chapter Two

Dressed for riding in buckskin breeches and gleaming top boots, Will hurried down the stairs of Walton Place.

"There you are at last, Will," his cousin Edmund exclaimed. "Let's be off. The ladies have decreed that there is no place for men on the day before a ball. If we're wise, we'll escape while they are still of that opinion as otherwise, they are sure to discover some tasks for us. Hugh and I thought we might ride over to Swift Hall. Do you remember Sir Augustus?"

"Tall, dark, some years older than Hugh and I? I run into him occasionally in town. Wasn't there a younger brother, nearer to us in age?"

"Jonnie. He was wounded at Waterloo—they feared for some time that he had sustained a lasting injury to his right hand, but he made a full recovery, due in no small part to his sister. Miss Swift is esteemed here for her knowledge of salves, potions and simples, and her way of treating injuries. Many hereabouts will call on her sooner than see a surgeon."

"Is Jonnie still in the army? Where is he stationed now? I should like to meet him again—I think the last time I saw him was in '14, after Napoleon was safely on Elba."

"That would have been when Miss Swift made her come-out. He sold out after Waterloo, but subsequently took a new commission in India. He said he didn't want to remain in a peace-time army, but I think he found it hard to settle back into a non-military way of life. He hasn't been home for several years."

Following Edmund's lead, Will swung into a shady lane that led to paddocks and, behind, the stable block of a neat estate. As they approached, they saw that a small boy was being encouraged to try the first simple jumps on his pony. Outside the paddock a woman leaned on the fence, her arm securely around a small girl not long out of babyhood, who was balanced precariously on the middle bar. At the sound of horses, they both looked in the riders' direction.

"Good morning," Edmund called. Rounding the paddock, he reached the lady's side and dismounted. "Your servant, Miss Swift. My wife and mother have made it clear that any male presence is an irritation not to be borne the day before a ball, so we thought to see how you and Gus were doing."

"Now, Edmund," she replied, eyes dancing. "I think any book of etiquette permits a gentleman to use the Christian name of a lady he has not only rescued from a tree but also fished out of a pond. Since when have I been Miss Swift to you?"

"And what of me?" Hugh protested plaintively.

"Why, Mr Walton, as I recall it was you who pushed me into the pond and also found my predicament in the old oak most amusing."

Hugh laid his hand on his heart with a theatrical flourish. "You wound me, Helena. Can you possibly have forgotten all those times I was your devoted, trusty knight? Only remember all the dragons I slew for you."

"Or were devoured by, Hugh. Jonnie could never agree to be defeated when he was the dragon. How is everyone at Walton Place? We're all looking forward to the ball tomorrow."

Will observed the little scene with interest. She was an attractive woman, a little taller than average, with a striking face. Her buttercup-coloured muslin dress floated lightly around a delectably curved figure. In another woman her manner could be described as flirtatious, but in her it was more sisterly in nature and indeed his cousins treated her much the same as they did their sister. As she lifted the little girl down from the fence and came towards them, her straw hat lifted in the breeze, revealing dark hair of an unusual hue. It is almost like port, he thought and with that he remembered her. With her unusual colouring, she had stood out among the more insipid girls of her year. She had usually been surrounded by a court of officers, courtesy of her elder brother, he supposed, whom she had managed with the same sisterly attitude. Will had kept away from her. It had been his policy at that time to avoid well-born young virgins like the plague for fear that his grandfather's eagerness to see him hitched would get the better of him.

"Do you recall my cousin Rastleigh?" As Edmund spoke, he gestured towards Will who had dismounted and was now looping the reins around one of the fence posts. "It's some years since he has visited here. Will, may I present Miss Swift, and Miss Sally, of course," he added, smiling at the child.

Miss Swift held out her hand with a pleasant smile. "We have met, my lord, but it was many years ago."

"During the false peace, I think."

When the little girl offered her hand in imitation of her aunt, Will took it gently and solemnly repeated his bow. Sir Augustus and his son Tom had joined them by now and together they made their way towards the house. Walking beside Miss Swift and her niece, Will was surprised to find a small hand slipping into his but instinctively closed gentle fingers around it.

"Swing me!" the child commanded.

"Oh, Sally," her aunt said. "You cannot expect Lord Rastleigh to play with you."

"Swing me!" The demand came again as she pulled at his hand.

He looked at Miss Swift. "I should be happy to oblige her, but what does she expect me to do?"

"It is quite simple. We swing her arms back and forth, counting to three and then we lift her and swing her forward." She demonstrated, he followed her actions and the child flew through the air crowing with delight.

"Again!"

"Three more times, Sally," Miss Swift decreed.

Will found himself laughing with the child as, together with her aunt, he counted and swung. Such a simple pleasure, he thought.

They reached the stables and stopped in the yard to let the grooms take the horses. The children went on ahead, running to their mother who had come out of the house to meet them. After hugging them, and listening to Tom's report of his prowess on his pony and Sally's description of how Aunt Helena and the man had "swinged" her, she sent them off with their nurse for their nuncheon and turned to greet the visitors.

"May I present my wife, Lady Swift?" Gus said proudly. "Rosamund, the Earl of Rastleigh, Lady Amelia's nephew."

"Welcome, my lord," she said, curtseying, "and Edmund and Hugh, as well. You will take a nuncheon with us?" She gestured invitingly towards a table that had been set up on a shady part of the terrace.

This is a happy home, Will thought, as he helped himself to some cold salmon and a variety of salads, charmed by the easy interaction between husband and wife, and parents and children, and admiring his hostess's golden hair and blue eyes. Swift is a lucky fellow.

Lady Swift and her sister-in-law were asking Hugh about the other guests expected at the ball and, his attention caught by a reference to Coke of Norfolk, Will joined in a detailed discussion of agricultural reforms with Edmund and Sir Augustus.

"We must be getting back," Edmund said at last. "But I almost forgot, Helena, Kathryn was wondering if you have any more of the salve you made up for her last month. She finds it most beneficial."

"Of course. I'll bring it tomorrow or, if you prefer, I can run down now to the Dower House and get some."

"Thank you, my dear, but that is not necessary. I would not have you rush back and forth in the hot sun."

"I must go there in any event, for Mamma will be wondering where I am."

"May I escort you, Miss Swift?" Will said. "I should like to stretch my legs before we leave and I would be able to save you having to return here."

"If you wish," she said, rising. She touched cheeks with her sister-in-law. "Thank you, Rosamund. That was most refreshing. This way, my lord."

She smiled at the other two men who had risen with her and led the way down the steps into the garden.

"You and your mother live in the Dower House?" Will asked, looking down at the hand resting on his sleeve. He liked the fact that she did not feel the need to wear gloves while in her brother's domain. Squarish but well-proportioned, with well-formed shell-pink nails, it was a hand you could trust. She wore a pearl and diamond ring on her right hand.

"Yes, we removed there three years ago, after my sister married. We felt it was time Gus and Rosamund had their home to themselves. They had had their own apartments, of course, since they were married in 1814. The following years were eventful between my brother's injury at Waterloo and my father's subsequent illness. I think we were all glad to stay together in those times. There is a support that only family can give one another in such circumstances."

Will wondered what that support might be but dismissed the fleeting thought with an inward shrug. "I understand from Edmund that your brother is fully recovered now?"

"Yes, thank Heavens."

"He also mentioned that you had some knowledge of healing," Will said curiously. It seemed an unusual pursuit for a gentlewoman.

"I took an interest in it after Waterloo. Some of the surgeons were no better than butchers and I could not understand why it should be thought to be advisable and even beneficial to bleed a man who was already suffering from loss of blood from his wounds. And then my brother's arm was neglected. It was partly his own fault, of course, for he would return to his duty too soon, but Jonnie insisted that if he could walk, he must report back, especially as there were so many casualties. The wound became inflamed and before he knew it, he could not grip properly—not his reins nor his sword nor anything at all." She paused and sighed as if looking back to that time.

"When we returned home, I consulted the midwife and some of the local women who were known for their still-rooms and healing abilities. We were able to check the inflammation with hot fomentations, but it left a weakness. Between us, we developed a salve to massage into his wrist and one of the women suggested he try a series of movements with different grasps and holds that she had devised for her son when he had sustained a similar injury from a sickle. It took some months, but eventually Jonnie regained the full use of his wrist and hand."

"And re-joined the army, I understand?"

She nodded. He thought he glimpsed a hint of sadness in her eyes.

They had arrived at the Dower House, a pleasant two-storey building, with three windows either side of the front door. She ushered him into a sunny parlour.

"If you would be pleased to wait here, my lord? Mamma must be resting. Pray be seated while I fetch the salve for Kathryn. I shall be just a moment."

Will looked around at the comfortable sofa and chairs, the bookcases either side of the fireplace. Watercolours and a group of charming silk pictures hung on the walls. A painting of a middle-aged man in the costume of the last century hung over the mantelpiece; below it were miniatures he recognised as being of Lady Swift's children and grandchildren. An elegant writing table was placed at one of the windows; at the other, one of the ladies had arranged a table and chair so as to have the best light for her embroidery. A vase of roses on a centre table lent their soft scent to an attractive room.

Miss Swift returned soon and handed him a small package. "Thank you, my lord."

"It is my pleasure, Miss Swift. I look forward to meeting you again. May I request a dance tomorrow?"

The lady's eyes flew to his in surprise. It was the first time he had seen her calm demeanour ruffled. She recovered at once and dipped a small curtsey. "I should be honoured, sir."

"Then I will take my leave for now. Your servant, Miss Swift."

Helena walked with him to the front door and watched him stride down the drive. An interesting man, she thought. Reserved, but not too stiff-rumped to play with a child, although it had been obvious that it was not something he was accustomed to doing.

This was the first time in recent years that she could remember him visiting his aunt. Perhaps they had previously met in town. He seemed to be on good terms with Hugh and Edmund, at any rate.

Chapter Three

"Are you ready, my love?" The dowager Lady Swift hurried into her daughter's room. "Oh, Helena! I knew that sea-green silk would become you admirably. Let me look at you."

She stood back to admire the sheen of the fabric that fell gracefully from where it was caught beneath Helena's full breasts by a pearl ribbon. Creamy lace adorned the bodice, the hem and the short sleeves of the dress. "Your grandmother's pearls are perfect with it and they set off your hair beautifully. I always thought she left them to you because you have her colouring. Of course, by the time I knew her, her hair was white, though as she always wore it powdered, I do not suppose it would have mattered."

"You look beautiful yourself, Mamma."

Lady Swift knew to perfection how to dress to set off her petite, fading prettiness. Not for her a dowager's purple and imposing turban. A gown of shimmering dove-coloured silk shot with delicate shades of lavender was trimmed with silver lace and a matching artful little confection of silk and lace was set atop her silvery curls. Around her neck she wore a delicate diamond necklace, a bridal gift from her husband, and matching bracelets gleamed on her long gloves.

"I love a summer ball," Helena said as they descended the stairs. "Especially on an evening like this when you do not need a heavy cloak and must not worry about ruining your shoes before reaching your destination."

"And they will be able to leave the doors to the terrace open so it will not be hot and stuffy and we can spill out into the balmy evening."

Gus was waiting at the carriage door to hand his mother and sister in. "I shall be the envy of every gentleman there tonight, arriving with three such beautiful ladies," he quipped. "Each of you must be sure to save me a dance."

"I did not think to dance," his mother protested.

"Indeed you must, Mamma, for you know you always love it. And you, Helena? Will you also dance with me? Rosamund has already promised me at least two waltzes," he added, smiling at his wife.

"You honour me, Sir Augustus."

Helena sketched a teasing bow to her brother, thinking that the more she danced, the less singular it would appear if she were to stand up with Lord Rastleigh. She knew everyone in the neighbourhood and, while she was popular, it was generally accepted that she had no interest in marriage. "Miss Swift is on the shelf and quite happy to be there," one matron had uttered in her hearing last winter. "It is such a pity because she is a lovely girl and I understand that Sir Thomas left her well dowered, but she will have no man."

But there would be other strangers there tonight, come to celebrate Sir Humphrey's birthday. Helena resolved to keep to her old friends and neighbours where she would be safe from any importunity.

~~~

Helena's plan worked well. Although Lord Rastleigh had immediately reserved *La Boulangère* "which my aunt assures me is the supper dance. I hope I may also have the pleasure of taking you in to supper, Miss Swift", Helena was able to enjoy the ball, dancing with her usual selection of very young men and older ones such as her brother, Edmund, Hugh and even Sir Humphrey, as well as neighbours who enjoyed her company but would never think of paying any sort of addresses to her. She was a little perturbed when she noticed an elegant stranger come towards her, accompanied by Hugh Walton, but managed to take refuge among the older ladies on the pretext of enquiring whether her mother wished for any refreshments. From there it was easy to slip through an ante-room into the hall and re-enter the ballroom where she saw the stranger dancing with another lady.

Lord Rastleigh, she noted, did his duty by his aunt, his cousin Anne, her daughter Amelia, whose first ball this was, Edmund's wife Kathryn and various senior ladies present, including Rosamund and, to Helena's amazement, her mother.

Will noticed Miss Swift's neat evasion of Mr Geoffrey Walton, Sir Humphrey's nephew, and smiled to himself, looking forward to Walton's chagrin when he saw who had gained this prize for the supper dance. For there could be no doubt that Miss Swift was the most interesting and attractive female present. She did not want for partners, but apart from Hugh, whom she clearly saw as another brother, did not dance with any gentleman who could be considered eligible.

At last it was time for the supper dance. He glanced around. Miss Swift was among a group of neighbours discussing, he discovered, the forthcoming Lammas Fair. She did not demur when he said, "I believe this is our dance, Miss Swift," but placed her hand on his arm and let him lead her onto the dance floor where sets were forming. Will's cousin Anne, Lady Phillip Martyn, beckoned him to join her and, to his annoyance, he found himself standing opposite Geoffrey Walton and an unknown lady. Anne was partnered by her husband and the set was made up by Hugh and Miss Phillips, the daughter of Sir Jonas Phillips, a neighbouring baronet.

La Boulangère was a lively dance, with frequent changes of partner. Miss Swift was quick and light-footed but there was hardly any opportunity to talk privately to her. When the music stopped, the group moved as one to the supper room where tables had been set for eight.

Will sighed inwardly as Hugh led the way to a round table. Once the ladies were seated, Hugh instructed his two cousins to entertain them while he and Lord Philip Martyn procured a selection of the dishes laid out on the supper table.

"Pray present me to your charming partner, Rastleigh," Mr Walton said with a glint in his eye.

"Miss Swift, may I present Mr Geoffrey Walton, nephew of Sir Humphrey?"

"How do you do, sir."

"Cousin, perhaps you would be so good as to introduce your partner," Anne said to Mr Walton.

"You do not know each other?" he asked, surprised.

"No indeed, I collect she is new to our society."

"Ah, may I present Mrs Diana Logan. She is at present visiting friends here, I understand."

Introductions completed, the party fell into animated conversation, the topics ranging from local to national, from personal to matters of more general interest. Miss Swift was eager to enquire how the Martyn children did, Mrs Logan wanted to hear the latest London gossip, and the gentlemen were keen to find out all the details of Lord Philip's new team of bays. Mrs Logan, seated on Will's left, tried to attract more tempting prey without frightening away the bird in hand, but Will skilfully parried her sallies and attempts to lure him into a more personal discussion.

When the supper room began to empty, Miss Swift rose. "I must see how my mother does—if she is not too tired."

"May I escort you to her?"

"Oh no, my lord. Indeed, it is not necessary."

"Then let me thank you for the pleasure of your company."

Reluctant to seek another partner, Will sauntered out onto the terrace.

"A most appealing filly," Geoffrey Walton said behind him.

"Of whom do you speak?" Will asked coldly.

"Why, your Miss Swift, of course."

Will was surprised at the urge to smash his tightening fist into Mr Walton's face. "I trust, Walton, that you will refer to—and treat—all my aunt's guests with respect."

"No offence, Rastleigh. It was just a stray comment, of no import."

"Then you will not repeat it."

"Wouldn't dream of it."

"There you are, Will. If you are free, come and dance this next with me."

He obediently offered Anne his arm and walked with her to the bottom of the nearest set.

"I don't know what made my mother suddenly decide to give a ball this summer, but I am exceedingly glad she did," Anne said as they waited for their turn to dance the figure. "Thank you for standing up with Amelia earlier."

"She is a charming girl. Will you bring her out next year?"

"I think so. She will be eighteen in November and if she gains some experience at smaller parties like this over the winter, she will be more at ease. I may rely on you to support us, I hope."

"In what way?" Will asked cautiously. "I tend to avoid the debutantes. I am too old for them."

"I'll wager their mothers don't think so. I daresay you are still trying to avoid parson's mousetrap."

"True, especially when it is baited with a girl just out of the schoolroom who very likely would have no say in whether she wished to accept me or not." They were separated by the dance but she returned to the attack later.

"To return to Amelia's come-out. Lady Martinborough has offered to give her a ball at Martinborough House."

"Obliging of her."

Anne shrugged. "Amelia is their niece, after all. Besides, she feels she must give one ball each Season and better in a good cause, she said."

"I suppose she is right. I'll come to the ball, Anne, but that will be all," he said firmly. He had met Miss Amelia for the first time tonight and he would be just as cautious with her as he would with any other young lady. The prayer-book did not forbid marriage between cousins and he was too used to being one of the biggest prizes on the marriage market to let down his guard.

The dance over, he escorted his cousin to where a flushed Amelia chatted to a young officer. After a few minutes, he made his excuses. Restless, he headed for the library which had been turned into the card room for the evening. To his surprise, he found Miss Swift there, partnering her mother at the whist table. She played quickly and decisively, he saw, taking the final trick with aplomb.

"And that's the rubber," the elderly gentleman at the table said, making a note on the sheet of paper at his elbow. "We should have known better than to challenge you ladies, should we not, my dear?" he added to the lady sitting opposite him. He beckoned a footman. "You will take a glass of wine with us, I hope."

"I shall, with pleasure, Sir Jonas," Mrs Swift said, "but I think my daughter is looked for in the ballroom."

"Yes, we mustn't detain you, Miss Helena," Sir Jonas said. "Well, ladies, as we are only three, shall we play ombre? Or what about you, sir? Do you fancy a hand of whist?"

"I'm afraid I, too, must return to the ballroom," Will said smoothly. "May I escort you, Miss Swift?"

She looked surprised but took his arm quite naturally. "You are wise to escape, sir," she said quietly as they left the library. "Once Sir Jonas and his wife have you in their coils, you are doomed for the night. But they will settle down comfortably to ombre now. The ballroom gets too loud and too hot for them as the night goes on. The card room is quieter."

"Do you enjoy cards, Miss Swift?"

"I like to play a hand now and then, but I find an evening of it becomes tedious, especially with people like Sir Jonas who take it so seriously. At least he plays for the love of the game, and is happy to play with my mother for a penny a point. He was a great friend of my father's and the two couples used meet once or twice a week to play cards. I am grateful that the custom continued after my father's death."

Tell-tale strains stole from the ballroom. No one had come to claim her hand. "Do you waltz, Miss Swift?" Will asked impulsively.

"Yes,"

"Then may I have the pleasure?"

The first waltz with a lady was always revealing. Would she instinctively respond to the music and his lead or attempt to reproduce Mr Wilson's nine positions in the prescribed order, regardless of what the space permitted? Miss Swift was happy to deliver herself up to him, Will discovered, reacting to the most subtle of touches.

"You waltz delightfully," he murmured in her ear as he guided her into the turn at the end of the ballroom. "Now, one, two, three, swing!"

As he spun her round the corner, she looked up at him, astonished, and a delighted chuckle escaped her. "You learnt your lesson well, my lord."

"Your niece is an excellent teacher. She is a charming child."

"Do you have nephews or nieces of your own?"

His lips tightened. "No, I am an only child. That is, I have four half-brothers and -sisters from a later marriage of my mother. They are much younger, so it will be some time before they make me an uncle, I hope."

"It is aging, is it not?" she teased. "But rewarding too."

He was tempted to ask did she not hope for children of her own, but decided not to rush his fences.

"Do you see a lot of your mother and her family?" Her question broke the comfortable silence that had fallen between them.

"No, they live in Ireland. My mother married Sir John Malcolm in 1803. They live at his home in County Wicklow. I try to visit them every summer. Between the Coronation and my uncle's birthday, it will be quite late this year. I must go home to Rastleigh before I head for Ireland."

"You must have been quite young when you lost your father."

"I was six," he replied shortly, wondering at himself in providing someone he had met only the previous day with such personal information. It was her genuine sympathy, he thought as she looked at him with gentle eyes and murmured, "Poor boy." It was ridiculous, but Will felt comforted, as if she had somehow reached back through time to console his younger, bereft self. He smiled at her and said an equally quiet "thank you" as the last bars of the music died away.

Both the Swift and the Walton ladies rested the day after the ball, but on the following day Lady Swift, accompanied by her mother-in-law and sister-in-law called on Lady Amelia to express their appreciation of the festivities. This was no formal call of thirty minutes duration. The two families had been close since Lady Amelia had befriended the elder Lady Swift when she had come to Swift Hall as a young bride and the assembled ladies soon settled down to an exhaustive review of every detail of the proceedings. Helena was not much given to chatter of this nature and, once she had paid her compliments on the success of the occasion and described her enjoyment of the entertainment offered her, she sat silently, gazing out at Lady Amelia's beautiful gardens.

She was recalled to her surroundings by her ladyship's exclaiming, "Why, Will, I thought you were going out with Edmund!"

"Not today, Aunt. I plan to take a rod out later."

"Well, sit down," Lady Amelia commanded, "and tell us what you think of Geoffrey and Mrs Logan. It is not a connection I would welcome, but I was more or less forced to issue an invitation as she is staying with the Forbes' again this year. I did not want to offend Mrs Forbes by excluding her—they are cousins, I understand. I saw that you had supper with them."

"As did Miss Swift. I think we should hear her opinion first, as you ladies are generally held to be more astute in these matters."

"They seemed to deal perfectly amicably with one another," Helena replied shortly.

"Of that I have no doubt," Lady Amelia exclaimed. "They appeared very amicable indeed when they returned from viewing my shrubbery."

"Are you a keen angler, my lord?" Helena enquired.

"I enjoy it, especially on a perfect summer evening, and your Wiltshire chalk streams are most tempting, but at home I am always torn between the river and the sea."

"To fish, you mean?"

"No, no—to sail. I keep a yacht and know no greater pleasure than to be out on the waves, the wind in the sails, the sounds of the sea and the cries of the birds in my ears. There I feel free of all duties and responsibilities."

She heard the longing in his voice. "Do you sail along the coast or go out to sea?"

"It depends. Sometimes I can just take her out for a day, but other times I have taken her to Ireland, to Jersey, even to France."

"It must be quite large, then."

"She, Miss Swift, she," he admonished her. "Boats are always female—perhaps because they are such beautiful, temperamental creatures, responsive to every touch and so must be treated with care."

"What do you call her?" she enquired, ignoring the glint in his eye as he made this rather audacious pronouncement.

"The *Sweet Mary*."

"After your first sweetheart, perhaps?"

"No, after my grandmother. We, that is my grandfather, had the yacht built the year after she died."

"What a lovely tribute. Now she is with you when you are at your happiest."

"How long do you remain with Sir Humphrey and Lady Amelia, my lord?" asked Helena's mother.

"For some time, I hope," his aunt replied. "You are surely not going to rush away, Will."

"Of course not, Aunt, although I will excuse myself shortly to attempt the evening rise."

"Perhaps you would like to try our stream one day, my lord," Helena's sister-in-law said. "You would be welcome any time. Edmund and Hugh know that if they seek variety, they may come to us, for my husband has no real interest in angling and they consider it a shame that the stream goes unfished for most of the year."

"I should be delighted." He hesitated for a moment and then went on impulsively. "May I request another favour? My family is small—it is really only in this house and my mother's home that I am anyone other than 'my lord'. I hate to hear it here. Would you not all call me Will or at least Rastleigh if Will is too informal for you?"

"You poor boy," said Helena's mother, "of course we shall, Will." She gave him a maternal smile.

"And you must call us Rosamund and Helena," Lady Swift added.

"May I?" He looked at Helena.

Not quite sure how this had happened so quickly, she nodded her consent.

"Thank you," he murmured, holding her gaze and ignoring his aunt who sat looking at him as if he were a stranger to her.

"I don't know what has come over Will," she said after he had departed. "I have always thought him to be almost as stiff as my father was, and he, you know, was very much the Earl as they knew them in the old King's hey-day."

"I think he's lonely," Kathryn Walton replied thoughtfully, "and apart from us here he has no family or even a proper home. Oh, he has plenty of houses to live in, but he seems merely to visit them in turn. Has he changed any of them since the old Earl died and he inherited? He hasn't mentioned any refurbishment and, as I recall, the House and the Castle remain exactly as they were in his grandfather's day. Of course, he is a man and they tend not to think of these things."

"You're so right," her mother-in-law said. "We must see how we may help him while he is here."

Chapter Four

Helena sighed wearily as she turned the gig into the lane and set the mare trotting towards the bridge over the stream. The purling stream widened here, forming a pool bordered by a grassy bank shaded by willows whose low branches formed a pleasant seat beside the water. She steered her equipage off the track and drew to a halt. She would have ten minutes' peace before continuing on to the Dower House.

"Helena! I hadn't expected this pleasure."

She jumped at the sound of Lord Rastleigh's voice. He strode towards her, clad in top boots, snug-fitting buckskins and the most disreputable coat she had ever set eyes on. She knew poachers who would be ashamed to be seen in it. A Belcher handkerchief was knotted casually about his throat.

"My lo—"

"Will," he interrupted with a teasing smile. "I thought we had already fought that battle." As he spoke, he reached to lift her down from the gig and for a fleeting moment she rested safe in his strong hands. A sigh escaped her. Frowning, he put a finger under her chin to lift her head so that he could see her face.

"My God, Helena!" he exclaimed. "You look as if you have been up all night."

"I have. My little niece was running a high fever and her parents were distraught. It had broken by midnight so I told Fannie and Harold I would sit with her while they got some rest, for I can lie down on my bed during the day but a rectory is always busy." She swayed and he slipped his arm around her waist to steady her.

"Why do you stop here?"

"To gather my strength before I go home," she said frankly. "They will all fuss so at the Dower House, Mamma and Mrs Dobbins and the rest of them, and at times I find it trying."

"I have no doubt of it," he replied in amused sympathy. "Have you had any breakfast?"

"A cup of tea at the rectory. I did not want anything more."

"Then might I invite you to join me, Miss Swift?"

With a flourish he indicated the small fire he had lit near the stream. Beside it, spitted on twigs and waiting to be roasted, lay two fine trout. "I am recapturing my boyhood," he explained, leading her to where two willow branches had formed a natural bench. He stripped off his coat and folded it to make a cushion for her.

"Sit here and close your eyes while I prepare our feast. I purloined some fresh bread and butter from the kitchen at the Place on my way out. Believe me, it will be a breakfast fit for a queen."

The willow seat was surprisingly comfortable. Helena dozed, enjoying the warmth of the early sun on her eyelids, lulled by the gentle sound of the brook as it made its way through and around the stones and pebbles. Her thoughts drifted and dissolved along with the babbling of the stream. She slipped further and further into sleep, but was drawn back to the surface by the most tantalizing smell.

"You are served, Helena."

She opened her eyes to see the crisp trout laid out on broad leaves with the bread and butter. "I had a knife to cut the bread and spread the butter, but otherwise we must use our fingers," he said as he offered her the plumpest fish.

She lifted a filet off the bone and tasted it. "Mmm. This is delicious. What an unlikely skill for an earl to have."

"I learnt it from an old rogue of a poacher at Rastleigh. He used to call at the rectory for alms and Stephen and I made friends with him."

"Stephen?"

"Stephen Graham, the rector's son. We are of an age and his father tutored us both in the classics. Old Barnes taught us both how to tickle trout—catch them with our hand," he wiggled his fingers as she looked an enquiry, "and clean and cook them like this. He took special delight when our gamekeeper came upon us, for he could hardly be punished when the young master was sharing the catch."

"And you? Were you punished?"

"No, though not long after, the gamekeeper began to teach us how to cast a line. No doubt he thought it more prudent to divert our activities into more legitimate channels."

"Was he successful?"

"Let's say I became more adept at avoiding him," he replied with a boyish grin. "But I did enjoy the lessons as well."

"Do you still see the Grahams?"

"Oh, yes. Stephen's father is still rector, although he hopes to retire soon in favour of his elder son. Stephen is my closest friend. He inherited a snug estate from his godfather and is now also a member of parliament. We meet regularly and frequently consult together on political matters, but I am attached to all the family. They also call me Will, for Stephen and his younger sister Faith could not fathom why they should say anything else and their mother is a wise woman and did not insist."

"Did it mean so much to you?"

"I think it did," he said slowly. "As I told you, I was six when my father died and losing my name as well; I would not have put it so then, of course, but looking back it was as if I had lost my sense of self."

"And the Grahams gave it back to you?"

"They did. And more, they did not suddenly treat me as a viscount or as a future earl, but as any other small boy. If Stephen and I got up to mischief, Mr Graham thrashed us both. I preferred it to my grandfather's lectures on how I had failed to live up to my duty to my name and station."

"I can sympathise. Papa took a switch to my brothers but he left disciplining us girls to my mother. She could not bring herself to use corporal punishment, so her preferred method was to make us sew samplers with mottoes suitable to the offense."

"Young ladies must not climb trees or it behoves young ladies to avoid ponds and other waters?"

"I have a fine collection stored away."

"To serve as an awful warning for your own daughters?"

"I do not think so." She brushed crumbs from her skirts. "Thank you for my breakfast. I feel much restored."

"I am glad." He offered his hand to help her rise from her rustic seat, then checked the fire to make sure it was completely extinguished and went to gather his belongings.

He was still in his shirt sleeves, and his leather waistcoat and buckskin breeches, together with the hint of a beard, made him look like a pirate, Helena thought fancifully. "Your coat, my lord," she said, shaking it out and holding it for him to put on.

He shrugged into it and turned to look down into her mirthful eyes.

"Helena, if you 'my lord' me one more time I'll…," he said menacingly.

"Yes, my lord?"

"Exact a forfeit," he finished, and bent and kissed her swiftly. "In fact, now that I come to think of it, feel free to say 'my lord' whenever you like."

"Indeed not, Will."

It was six years since she had experienced a man's kiss, if Will's fleeting caress could be dignified with such a name. Certainly, it was not worth making a pother about. She was no green girl, after all and a kiss was quite a usual forfeit.

"Why does Helena Swift remain unmarried?" Will asked his aunt abruptly that evening as they strolled through the gardens of Walton Place.

"I really don't know. It's such a pity for she is a lovely girl and so capable with a good head on her shoulders. For all that she was so young, it was she who kept the household going when Sir Thomas took ill."

"Was there never any talk of a suitor?"

"Oh, suitors there were plenty, but she has a way of keeping them at a distance or turning them into friends."

"Or brothers," he interjected. "She is quite sisterly in her attitude to men, I noticed."

"You are right. I seem to remember hearing mention of a young officer, a friend of Jonnie's, after she came out, but there were so many and if she took a more special interest in one, well it obviously came to nothing. It cannot have been too serious, for there was no more talk of him."

"Who was he?"

"I really can't recall the name." His aunt stopped walking and looked at him. "Why these questions, Will? Are you interested there yourself?"

"I'm becoming increasingly interested," he confessed. "Since my thirtieth birthday I have been more and more conscious of my duty to marry and have children. You know our cousin Anthony died last year? I didn't know him well, for he was not on visiting terms with Grandfather, and the odd time I ran into him he was as inclined to ignore me as I was reluctant to speak to him."

"You didn't miss much. I once heard Papa describe him as an arrant scoundrel," Lady Amelia said trenchantly. She sat on a bench, gesturing him to sit beside her.

"His son Harry doesn't seem to be much better. A dandified wastrel if ever I saw one. He parades around town puffing himself off as my heir, which he is, of course. He had the impertinence to call on me recently to request 'the heir's allowance' as he put it."

"Not unreasonable, I suppose."

"Perhaps not, but I am not going to frank his gambling. And if I don't wish him to succeed me, I must marry and really the sooner the better. I don't want him to feel secure enough in his position that he thinks to cover his losses by means of a post-obit bond."

"Surely he would not," his aunt replied, shocked. "You're still a young man, after all. But I agree, it is time you thought of marriage. I have known Helena all her life and am very fond of her. I also have a great admiration for her. She has made a good life for herself, with which she appears to be content. She keeps herself usefully occupied and is highly regarded in the area for her knowledge of healing. She is not above advising the local women and their families, and has trained many of the girls in the still-room. She is a devoted daughter, sister, and aunt and I have no doubt but that she would make an exceptional wife and countess. She would be an excellent choice for you."

Will was surprised but pleased by this measured panegyric, which was delivered by his aunt in her most stately tones.

"I am coming more and more to think so. She is attractive, not only in her appearance but also in her manner and her way of dealing with others. She is intelligent and interested in matters beyond her own parish boundaries. She is not missish and, as you say, seems extremely capable. I think she would be faithful, not only to her husband but also to her children. I want a wife who would defend them if she were widowed and not abandon them for another marriage." He stopped suddenly, feeling he had said too much.

His aunt pressed his hand but all she said was. "I will see about arranging some outings—a picnic perhaps, but I think you might

also suggest she accompany you, say to Salisbury, to see the cathedral. There could be no objection if you were to go in your curricle. Or, if you don't wish to appear too particular as yet, for it might be wiser not to put her on the alert, you might offer to take her mother and me as well. I will engage to occupy Dorothea for enough of the time to give you the opportunity to be private with Helena."

~~~

The following day Will called to the Dower House to enquire after the welfare of Helena's niece and also to deliver his aunt's invitation to the ladies to visit Salisbury with her. He found them in their sunny parlour, Lady Swift attending to her correspondence while Helena sat at the window with her embroidery.

"Been climbing trees again, have you?" he murmured while Lady Swift rang the bell and ordered refreshments served on the lawn in the shade of the oak tree.

"Indeed not," she said repressively, but was unable to hide her smile. "I have long since come to enjoy it."

"You two go on ahead," Lady Swift said, "while I finish this note to dear Amelia. You might be so kind as to take it for me, Will."

"What magnificent trees you have," Will said as they strolled through the gardens. "I can see the temptation."

"I daresay Jonnie and I tried to climb most of them. Gus too, of course, but he was so much older and ceased enjoying such pastimes before we did."

"Surely you must have found your skirts an inconvenience?"

"Until I was twelve or thirteen, Jonnie's old breeches were most useful."

"And your mother didn't object?" he asked incredulously.

"We became adept at creeping out early in the morning on our adventures. It was mostly over one or two summers; then the attraction palled."

"What did you turn to then?"

"Oh, Gus taught me to drive, and I used to go riding with him and Jonnie as well. Then there were the usual young lady pursuits—pianoforte, singing, dancing, sketching and watercolours. You know the sort of thing. It was from watercolours that I learnt to enjoy embroidery, for I took the notion of making silk pictures from my sketches and found that much more interesting than sewing mottoes and samplers."

"Aunt Helena," a voice called and Tom and Sally ran across the lawn to her outstretched arms, followed more sedately by Rosamund with her mother-in-law.

"Children, make your bow and curtsey to Lord Rastleigh," their mother commanded and watched proudly as Tom executed a creditable bow. Sally's curtsey wobbled slightly and Will gently took her hand to steady her.

"Master Tom, Miss Sally," he said formally, bowing to them as best he could, for Sally had retained his hand and was tugging at it. "Up!"

"She has no sense of decorum," her mother sighed with a rueful smile.

Will caught Helena's eye over the child's head and grinned as he lifted her to sit high on his arm. "I find her delightful,

Rosamund. Now you are taller than your aunt," he told Sally, as he carried her across the grass to the seats under the oak tree. Sitting there, watching Helena hold a glass for her niece and later play ball with the children, he could not help picturing her at Rastleigh with his, no their, children. He had always thought of his future offspring in abstract terms of an heir, an obligation to the title, but now he realised that a man could enjoy the company of his children, be proud of a son and indulge a daughter. He froze for a moment when Sally got tired of playing and came to climb onto his lap, but carefully put his arm around her so that she would not fall. She chattered away to him for a couple of minutes before yawning and resting her head against his chest.

"She is getting tired," Rosamund said, "just lay her down on the rug here, Will."

Holding his breath, he carefully lifted the child and placed her in the little nest of cushions. "My aunt will be wondering what has become of me," he said as he straightened up. "What time may we call for you tomorrow, ma'am? Would half past eleven be too soon?"

"Of course not."

"Why, where do you go?" enquired Rosamund. On hearing of the proposed outing, she said, "I hope you won't find it too dull. I would rather have suggested riding out to Stonehenge for I consider the view of the vast stones as you approach them to be truly awe-inspiring and it's most pleasant to wander among them. But that might be too strenuous for the older ladies," she corrected herself. "Perhaps we could arrange such an expedition with Edmund, Kathryn and Hugh on another day."

Chapter Five

Helena mentally ran through the remainder of her morning list. Visit the blacksmith's wife to admire the new baby—a basket of useful gifts lay ready beside her—and then look in at the rectory to play with her niece.

Two hours later she turned for home. As she crossed the bridge over the stream, she thought of her *al fresco* breakfast with Will. Not exactly what the *ton* hostesses meant when they sent out their invitations for such events but nothing they could ever serve would compare with the delicate, fresh flavour of Will's trout. And if the debutantes—or the matrons—had been privileged with a glimpse of him *en déshabillé* and unshaven; why they would have swooned in his arms in shock or admiration.

Smiling to herself, she relaxed her grip on the reins and the black gelding picked up speed. She had enjoyed yesterday's outing to Salisbury. The party had naturally split into two couples, with the older ladies moving at a slower pace. Helena had felt comfortable alone with Will, although there was a certain unsettling awareness of him that she did not feel with other men. No doubt because he was a new acquaintance and she was not used to being on such friendly terms with a gentleman who, when all was said and done, was still a stranger. It was obvious from his conversation that he took his duties and responsibilities seriously. Perhaps too seriously? How often did he manage to get away on his yacht?

He had seemed to be flirting with her—there was a note in his teasing that made it different to that of Edmund and Hugh. He never went over the line—she did not feel wary of him as she had of Geoffrey Walton. But he kissed me there by the stream, she remembered. Although it was most improper, she could not regret feeling a man's lips on hers again, if only for a moment. Wistfully she thought of Richard and the kisses they had stolen on a terrace or garden, or daringly in a quiet room they had found during a ball. Helena shook her head and squared her shoulders. The gig had slowed again and she snapped the reins to encourage the horse into a trot. There was no point in repining about the past and love was dangerous—too dangerous—for, in the end, you were left behind and alone.

She had made a new life for herself; it may not have been the one she had anticipated after her come-out, when she had fallen in love with Richard Harbury, now no longer Jonnie's schoolboy companion but a seasoned officer who bore the marks of five years of hard campaigning in the Peninsula. He and Jonnie had talked of selling out and buying neighbouring estates to breed horses together. Their children would grow up as one family. But fate had decided otherwise. Richard was dead and Jonnie was in India and Nell—Nell was gone too. It was Helena who lived with her mother in the Dower House. She would never again have what she had lost, but she was content with what she had.

When she looked into the morning room to say she had returned, Helena was taken aback to find Will there.

He rose immediately. "Good day, Helena."

"Good day, Will. I had not expected to see you again so soon."

"I am partly here on Kathryn's behalf. She wishes to know if half-past ten o'clock will be too early to set out for Stonehenge on Tuesday."

"No, not at all."

"In that case, I am to say we will meet you, Gus and Rosamond at the bridge at that time."

"Very good. Have you also called to the Hall?"

"No, I wished to see first if it suited you."

"Thank you." She was flattered by his consideration. It was generally assumed that she would fall in with whatever plans were made by her brother and his wife and, while she rarely objected, it was pleasant to have her wishes put first.

"I also hoped you might come for a walk with me, but not if you are too tired," he said, eyeing her hat.

"No, indeed. A walk would be very pleasant. We'll go down to the lake."

She walked easily—he wouldn't call her stride mannish, she moved too gracefully for that—but she displayed no inclination to cling to any convenient male arm. They soon fell into a comfortable rhythm and an easy silence which lasted until they arrived at a small lake half-covered in white water lilies with golden centres. A rustic bench invited the visitor to sit and admire the view while on the far bank a pretty gazebo lured him to a longer stay. A gentle breeze ruffled the trees that shaded the circling path, providing welcome relief from the heat.

"This is charming," Will said. "Is it natural?"

"Yes and no. The river always widened here, I believe. My father created the lake and then planted the trees."

"Are there trout here?"

"I imagine there must be as the stream flows out again but I don't know if anyone fishes here. You are welcome to try if you like. We can turn right here and continue around the lake. It's about twenty-five minutes until we are back at the garden gate. If you want a longer walk, we can go through the trees and into the park proper."

He shook his head. "Let us stay here at the lake. It is so peaceful."

"What is your home like?" she asked as they continued on.

"Do you mean the house in London—I suppose I spend half the year there at least—or Rastleigh Castle?"

"Oh, the Castle. How old is it?"

"We have held the manor through the female line since before the conquest. One of William's knights was awarded the Saxon manor and married a daughter of the house. They built the first keep beside the old hall. The old keep was rebuilt in its present form around fifteen hundred. In Queen Anne's time, the then Earl wanted more space and he added two wings, one east and one west, with a wide passage connecting them across the north front."

"So, one might think they were two different buildings depending on whether one approached from the north or the south?"

"Except that the only entrance is on the north side. The Castle stands on a headland looking south to the sea, guarding the coast. A beacon was lit there to warn of the approaching Spanish Armada."

"Did you maintain a watch there during the recent wars as well?"

"Our local yeomanry did. My grandfather raised a small corps in 1803."

"Did you join?"

"As soon as I was old enough. My father was dead and I am his only son, so there was no question of my being allowed to buy a pair of colours."

"Would you have liked to?"

"As much as any patriotic young man, I suppose, but I knew it was impossible."

"At least you could do something. It must have been exciting to see the Castle used for its original purpose, too."

"It was, but that ended in 1814 when Boney was first defeated."

"How we all rejoiced then. We never thought he could fulfil his promise to come back with the violets, and that the worst was still to come."

"He's dead now," Will said comfortingly. "There can be no fear of another return."

"Let us hope this decade will be less eventful than the last one," she said as they reached the gazebo. "Let us sit for a moment. I love to look over the lake."

"Used you swim here?"

"Jonnie did—I don't know about Gus. The lilies have spread so much now, that I don't think it would be very pleasant. Do you like to swim?

"Yes, in the sea. Have you ever done it?"

She shuddered theatrically. "Never. I find the idea of getting undressed in a bathing machine as it is towed into the water, being submerged in cold seawater by careless attendants, and then trying to get dressed again in the swaying machine as it is drawn back to land most unattractive."

He laughed. "So do I. But to slip into refreshing, cool water on a day like today, and float there, at one with the sea and the sky, or to pit one's strength against the waves is a different matter."

"I can imagine. Just, like so many other things, reserved to men."

"Do you find it irksome, to be a woman?"

She was silent for some moments. "I find it irksome to be treated as a lesser being," she said at last. "I can see no reason why women should be regarded as inferior to men. Yes, in some ways we may be physically less strong than you, but there are weaker and stronger men too. When it comes to the ability to bear pain, and to resilience and fortitude, we are your equals if not your superiors. Any midwife will tell you that. I am convinced that if girls received the same education and opportunities as their brothers, they would do just as well in life."

"I have never thought about it but, when you put it that way, I must agree with you. However, it would take a lot to change our society."

"You could say the same about any cause, be it slavery or electoral reform or Catholic emancipation. Does that mean one should not try?"

"No. If one is convinced of it, one must try," Will said, thinking of how often he and Stephen had discussed reform. But always in a male context, he had to admit. Was that because the feminine aspect was rarely considered by those who ruled both church and state?

"Ladies have a lot of power at home and in society in general, and there are the political hostesses," he pointed out. He knew it was not the same, but he was interested to see if she would argue her point. She immediately picked up the gauntlet.

"Yes, but their role is to support, to be a helpmeet. A woman cannot be a member of parliament; indeed, even if she holds a peerage in her own right, she cannot take her seat in the House of Lords. Why is that?"

"I have no answer for you, except to say that it is tradition."

"Because it always was, so must it always be? There would never be any progress if that were the case."

"That is all too true. But it has taken us centuries to reach this point—change will be slow and is bound to meet with opposition. However, you have opened my eyes, at least."

"A small beginning," she said with a smile. "We should return to the house. You still must call on the others."

"You are such a devoted sister and aunt," he commented as they continued their walk. "Do you not wish for children of your own?"

"As a girl I did, of course, but that is all in the past."

"Must it remain in the past?"

68

"Oh, I think so," she said lightly. "One cannot go back."

Before he could say anymore, Gus appeared at the garden gate and Will had to drop the subject.

"You seem distracted, my love." Lady Swift looked at her daughter who sat gazing out the window, her embroidery lying unheeded on her lap. "Is anything the matter?"

It was some moments before Helena confided, "I think Will was about to make me an offer today, just before Gus arrived. I was never so glad to see anyone."

"You would not welcome his proposal?" her mother asked in surprise. "He is a most personable gentleman and would, I think, make a good husband. I do not speak of the advantages such a match would bring you, for I know you would never make those the reason for your decision. He is intelligent and easy to talk to and strikes me as being kind and considerate."

"I don't dispute that. But you know I've put all thoughts of forming another attachment out of my head. I've made my life here with you."

"And now he comes and disrupts it. But perhaps your life is too quiet, Helena. I've never said anything, for you seem quite content, but you are only five and twenty and have, I hope, a long life ahead of you. I confess I should like to see you with your own home and family. I worry sometime what will become of you when I am gone."

"I cannot feel for him what I felt for Richard."

"Nor should you expect to, dearest, for you are no longer the girl you were then. Your experiences and the intervening years must have left their mark on you. I have become concerned that they have left you stranded in shallow waters. I should like to see you brave the stronger currents again."

"You never said anything," Helena said, shocked.

"It never seemed to be the right time. But now I would ask you seriously to consider Rastleigh as a husband. Do you not like him? You have always appeared to me to go on famously together."

"As far as that goes, yes. We can talk easily on any variety of subjects. He listens to my opinions too and with him I feel I am more Helena than a daughter or a sister or an aunt."

"I know what you mean." Lady Swift was silent for some moments. Then she said, "Do you know that I hardly knew your father when I was told I was to marry him?"

"Told?" Helena interrupted. "You mean he did not make his proposals directly to you?"

"No, he approached my father first. Sir Thomas was used to visit us frequently to discuss matters of scholarship with him. He was almost twenty years older than I, you may recall."

"I suppose I did know it, but I never really considered it." Helena was horrified. "Were you happy to marry him, Mamma?"

"Oh yes, for my parents' house was a joyless one. You cannot imagine it. Deep in his heart, my father was a puritan and our lives were committed to work and prayer. Propriety and prudence were the watchwords that governed us. My brothers 'escaped' I could almost say, for they were required to earn their livings elsewhere, but we girls were constrained to work at home. My elder sister, your Aunt Prudence, was required to be my father's amanuensis while I was charged with the household, thus saving the expense of a housekeeper. 'The devil finds work for idle hands' was a favourite saying of my father's; it ranked just behind 'honour thy father and thy mother' when it came to dealing with his children. My only consolation was that my duties permitted me to spend considerable time in the kitchen with the servants. It was harder for poor Prudence, trapped in his study with him."

"And so you did not resist when told my father wanted to marry you?"

"I thought it could not be worse that it was at home," Lady Swift said simply. "Sir Thomas often dined with us when he visited my father. He was always most courteous, making a point of thanking me as well as my mother for a good meal. I noticed too that he also expressed his appreciation to Prudence for any little service she might have rendered him—seeking out a reference or making a fair copy of something."

Helena was fascinated by this unexpected glimpse into her parents' lives. "How did you deal together? It always appeared to me that you and Papa were devoted to one another and we were a happy family growing up."

"We came to love one another dearly." Her mother smiled wistfully. "He was so good to me—I had never had pretty dresses or jewellery, for your grandfather had us dress plainly in drab colours. Your father loved to indulge me and he engaged a maid to assist me with my wardrobe and to dress my hair, for I had no notion how to do anything other than scrape it all back tightly from my face and confine it under a plain cap. He also employed dancing, drawing and music masters for me—all things my father dismissed as too frivolous. We were permitted to sing hymns, of course, but that was all. Dear Amelia was extremely kind to me too, explaining to me how to go on in society and Sir Humphrey's father, who was still alive, took Papa under his wing, for he had never been trained in estate matters. To his parents he was just the second son and once Frederick's wife had borne him two sons, Papa was of little interest to them. He was possessed of a modest fortune suitable to his needs and was able to pursue his scholarly interests at leisure."

"He was so different to his parents. He was interested in our ideas and always willing to discuss them. And think of the hours we all spent together, reading aloud, making music and playing games."

"I think we were both making up for what we had not had as children. It is my dearest wish that you should experience such a happy marriage. Much can be achieved with a fond heart, a good will and respect for one another, and I think you and Rastleigh would each bring those qualities to your union, were you to wed. If Rastleigh does make you an offer, please at least allow him to express himself, for only so can you know his reasons for wishing to marry you."

"Yes, Mamma." Helena folded her embroidery and put it away. "I'll say goodnight. You have given me a lot to think about."

Her mother smiled at her. "That is all I ask, my love. I'll go up with you."

Although the ladies went upstairs together, parting to seek out their respective chambers, Helena was too restless to go to bed immediately. After her maid left, she sat for some time at the window looking out into the moonlit night. Her world had suddenly turned upside down. It was bad enough that Will had managed to slip past her defences to the extent that he felt encouraged enough to propose, but her mother's words had disturbed her almost as much. "Stranded in shallow waters." It seemed to her to be an accusation of weakness or even cowardice, to be unable or, perhaps worse, unwilling to "brave the stronger currents".

Richard's ring gleamed on her right hand, a reminder of that last day. He had made her promise that she would not mourn him too long. She had forgotten that. Had the time come for her to keep her word? What would her life be like if she rejected Will? Much the same as it was now, she supposed; there could be no talk of her having another Season even if she wished for one. She was far too old for that. She would be an object of ridicule among the girls of seventeen and eighteen, even if she thought she would be able to support their company or indeed submit again to the strict rules governing debutantes. And she certainly could not expect to receive an offer better than that of the amiable and personable Earl of Rastleigh! He must be one of the prime catches on the marriage market.

While she had no pressing desire for the position of countess, there could be no doubt that such a marriage would take her into deeper waters. Was that what she wanted? She was not sure. But did she really want to spend the rest of her life in the Dower House, perhaps the last decades of it alone? Why had that never occurred to her before? Will would be a pleasant companion, Helena thought. And he would give her children. Her breath caught—a child of her own! She had never considered that that joy might yet be hers —even now she did not dare dwell on it.

She quickly got into bed and resolutely closed her eyes. But she dreamt of holding Will's baby to her breast and of her own child running to meet her. The sound of "Mamma" rather than "Aunt" on its lips was sweet.

Chapter Six

"I am so pleased we were able to arrange this," Rosamund murmured to Helena as they rode towards the agreed meeting place the next day. "I suspect I am with child again and once Gus knows, he will forbid me to ride. You know how protective he is when I am in a delicate condition."

"Does it not irritate you to be so cosseted and confined?"

"A little, but I know that he worries about me. He feels so helpless—I think all men do when their wife is *enceinte*. This lets him think he has some little control of the situation. But I see no need to tell him before I must, for I am perfectly well and will have enough of cosseting later."

They came up with the Walton Place party and greeted Edmund, Kathryn and Will, before Rosamund asked, "Is Hugh not with you?"

"He's joined some friends for a shooting party," Edmund answered.

"Good morning, ladies, Swift." Will wheeled his horse to fall in beside Helena's mare. She wore a dark blue riding habit, the severe cut of which served to display the pleasing curve of her bosom, her narrow waist and the tempting flare of her hips. A jaunty hat sat atop her beautiful hair. Her eyes were shielded by a light veil that drew attention to her generous mouth.

As they rode across the plain, the group fell naturally into three couples.

Kathryn suddenly laughed. "Isn't this famous?" she cried, riding ahead with a challenging glance at her husband as she picked up her pace until she had pulled away at a gallop. With a glint in his eye, Edmund followed and it soon became apparent that he was determined to catch her. She looked over her shoulder and bent lower over her horse's withers but to no avail.

"Pay up!" Her husband demanded once their mounts had slowed to a walk, and he pulled her towards him for a fierce kiss.

"And here I thought you were a staid matron now," Will teased as the others, who had been following more sedately, caught up with them.

"Most of the time I am," she replied. "But sometimes—"

"The old hoyden comes to the fore again," her husband interrupted. It did not appear to distress him; on the contrary he exchanged a secret smile with her as they rode on side by side.

Helena gasped when she first saw the pillars of Stonehenge etched against the sky. "I hadn't thought it to be so large! It's magnificent."

"Have you never been here before?" Will asked, surprised.

"No. My father and Gus made several excursions here, but more to explore and investigate than for a pleasure outing such as this. Gus must have brought Rosamund sometime later, for it was her suggestion to come here today."

Slowly they encircled the monument and then dismounted to wander through the vast enclosure, dwarfed by the huge stones, some of which stood upright while others leaned at impossible angles or lay flat on the ground.

Helena craned her neck trying to see the top of a massive block resting horizontally on two upright ones. "I wonder what the purpose of it was? It must have been a colossal undertaking, lasting years for a primitive people to erect this."

"Similar to building a cathedral in the Middle Ages, I suppose."

"What great works will we leave behind for the generations to come? There is nothing as mysterious or awe-inspiring, nor has there been for some centuries."

"Perhaps we have become too enlightened," he offered. "When we assume we can know and understand everything, we lose the need to establish a connection between this world and the next."

"And great nations devote their energies to proclaiming and defending their own supremacy," she said rather bitterly. "Why can't we live in peace?"

"We are at peace now," he reminded her.

"Here at home, perhaps, although our troops are used to suppress justified protest. Only think of Peterloo. And in how many countries around the world are our forces to be found? Do we really need to lay claim to so many corners of the earth?"

"If we don't, others will, and that would leave our merchants and traders greatly disadvantaged. But I agree that it would be desirable to deal with other countries without feeling the need to impose our will on them by means of arms."

As they spoke, they completed their turn of the great circle and came up again to the sheltered corner where Rosamund was overseeing the laying out of a picnic ferried from the Place by a groom in a gig. A variety of tempting dishes were laid out on a white cloth spread on a carpet that also provided seating for the three couples.

"It is nothing fancy—I told Cook to prepare everything so that we could easily manage it with our fingers. There is ale for you gentlemen and hock and seltzer for the ladies."

"It looks wonderful. My compliments to your cook, Rosamund," Will exclaimed, polishing off a little meat pie and reaching for a chicken drumstick. "Her services would have been greatly appreciated at the coronation."

"I thought that a splendid banquet had been provided," Gus said. "Surely there was enough for all?"

"Yes, for the banquet participants, in other words the gentlemen who had attended the ceremony in the Abbey. But their ladies, who sat above them in the galleries in Westminster Hall, were compelled to look on, famished, as those seated below in the Hall feasted. One peer, who shall be nameless, was observed tying a capon in his handkerchief and tossing it up to his family."

"I wonder did they eat it," Kathryn commented. "I think I should have been too mortified to do so, no matter how hungry I was."

Will laughed suddenly. "I don't know what was more absurd, young Dymoke riding into the Hall on a white horse he had procured from Astley's Circus so as to ensure that it was accustomed to such loud events—and flinging down the gauntlet as Hereditary Champion in his father's stead, or the Deputy Marshall swearing at his horse so that the entire assembly could hear. He had taken no such precautions with his mount and it took violent exception to the whole affair."

"Tell us about the Coronation itself," Rosamund urged as she nibbled a fruit tart. "It must have been truly magnificent."

"Magnificent and costly."

"Is it true that there were prize-fighters dressed as pages, with instructions to turn away Queen Caroline should she appear and seek entrance to Westminster Abbey?"

"It is, she did, and they did."

"She has been treated shamefully," Rosamund said. "From their first meeting, by all accounts. My mother used talk of the prince's liaison with the then Lady Jersey. And as for bringing her before the House of Lords to be tried for adultery! What is sauce for the goose should be sauce for the gander! If the Lords were to sit and listen to a list of the Regent's *affaires*, they would still be sitting."

"God preserve us from such a fate," Will said, getting up. He held a hand down to Helena. "Come for a walk with me. I need to move after that repast."

She let him pull her to her feet and then saw that the others remained seated. "Do you accompany us?"

"I intend to rest," Kathryn said, lying back to put her head on her husband's shoulder.

"And I," Rosamund agreed, following suit. "You two go on."

Four pairs of eyes watched Will and Helena as they left the little group.

"My Mamma-in-law said to be sure to give them plenty of opportunities to be on their own," Kathryn murmured.

"So did mine," Rosamund said drowsily. "I do hope something comes of it."

"I hope you have not put them off their stroke completely with all that talk of royal marriages and adulteries," Gus said severely.

"As his eldest male relative, let me assure you that Will does not have a pack of brats by an actress—or by anyone else," Edmund replied loftily, to be silenced by an elbow in the ribs from his wife.

Helena felt quite self-conscious as she walked at Will's side. While she had considered her mother's advice and was resolved to hear him out, should he propose, this did not mean that she wished to encourage a declaration. Although usually not at a loss for conversation, every topic that occurred to her now seemed too pointed. To ask again about his home might suggest that she wished to be mistress of it. Similarly, she did not wish to enquire about his family or even his pastimes. She resented the loss of her usual serenity and was vaguely inclined to blame him for it.

She stopped when they heard the bright notes of a lark. "Let us see if we can spy him. I love to watch them rising higher and higher until they almost disappear and yet their melody remains as strong and as sweet as ever. Look! There he is, no more than a speck but winging his way ever higher."

They followed the ascent of the bird until he hung against the blue sky spilling his ecstatic notes to the silent world below. When all was hushed again, Will faced Helena. "We were interrupted by your brother the last time we met. I think you know that I have something particular to say to you. May I do so, or is too soon?" He spoke gravely, his gaze focussed on hers.

"You took me by surprise the other day," she admitted frankly.

He took both her hands in his. "My dear Helena, to put it plainly, I have come to hold you in the highest esteem and I hope very much that you will do me the honour of becoming my wife. But I think that you wish to hear something more from me than a simple proposal of marriage?"

She nodded. "I hope that you are not offended, Will, for I am sure that most ladies would leap at such an offer, but I need to know why—why you are thinking of marriage and why you wish to marry me. You're not claiming to have developed a grand passion for me, I think."

"Is that what you would look for in a husband? I will not lie to you, Helena. I do not offer you that. It is not in my nature, I think. However, I like, admire and respect you. I think we would deal well together and that a deep and abiding affection could grow between us, as I saw between my grandparents, who only met on the day of their betrothal. As to being offended by your question—on the contrary it serves as an example of what I like about you." He smiled at her. "You are refreshingly candid. I know I must marry, especially as my heir bids fair to develop into a wastrel. It would be most remiss of me not to try to prevent the earldom from passing into his hands and to achieve that I must have a son of my own.

"You know the *ton*. You will appreciate that I've been the recipient of the most refined onslaughts from Mammas and debutantes alike, not to mention from older ladies ambitious in their own right, and this from the moment I came on the town. I had despaired of finding an intelligent and attractive woman who, I dared hope, would be more interested in being my wife and a caring mother of my children than in her position as Countess of Rastleigh. I think—no, I know—that in you I have found such a woman."

"But you would wish your wife to take her place in society?"

"Of course, both in town and at Rastleigh. But I don't want a tonnish marriage where society plays an all-important role and a couple mightn't exchange two words in private from one end of the week to another or see their children for weeks on end, but more the sort of family connection to be seen between your brother and his wife and Edmund and Kathryn. And you, Helena? What do you want for yourself?"

He stopped and bent down to fold back the little veil on her hat. "I must see your eyes."

They met his and then their focus changed, as if she were looking inwards.

What did she want for herself? To her own surprise, Helena realised that she did not want to remain at the Dower House as a spinster daughter and maiden aunt. She had forgotten to put her gloves on again after their picnic and now glanced briefly at the pearl and diamond ring on her right hand. She knew what Richard had wished for her. She could hear the echo of his voice as he said, "I can't bear the thought of leaving you to a long, lonely life, if leave you I must."

She had given him her promise not to mourn too long and he would have held her to it, she knew. She thought of her dream— of the baby and the little boy who called her "Mamma". Will would be a kind and considerate husband, she was sure. And he did not seek her love. That was good, for she felt none of the intense emotions she had experienced with Richard. But she liked him. If she refused him, she might never see him again or, if she did, he could be married to another woman and perhaps accompanied by their children. Would she look at them and think they might have been hers? She was astonished how that image hurt.

"Helena?" Will's voice seemed to come from far away.

"I'm sorry, Will." She took a breath and continued, "I have never wanted to make a splendid match and indeed I had put all thought of marriage aside long ago. But I confess I find the idea of a marriage as you describe, based on affectionate companionship, attractive. And I should like to have children of my own."

"Our children," he said, taking her into his arms. "Will you welcome me into your bed, Helena? For there, too, I think we could find pleasure and comfort together."

She looked up at him in surprise and he bent to kiss her, gently at first and then more demandingly, his arms tightening around her.

"Open for me," he coaxed and instinctively she did, clasping him as his probing tongue provoked a strange but not unpleasant sensation in her lower belly, one she had quite forgotten. She gasped in amazement and, at first tentatively, began to return his kiss. She felt his hands trace her curves and mould her to him and her own arms went around his neck, almost of their own accord. The feel of the short hair at his nape under her palm as she stroked it up his neck was unexpected but appealing and this response seemed to incite him to an even deeper kiss.

The kiss ended; he raised his head, then rested his forehead against hers for a long moment before tenderly smoothing wisps of hair back from her face, smiling down at her as he did so. "Helena, will you marry me?" His voice was composed, but insistent.

Helena felt as if she were poised on a cliff-edge. Would she fly or fall if she stepped off it? Suddenly, she was loath to scurry back to safety. Brave the depths, her mother had said. She took a deep breath, squared her shoulders and smiled back at him. "Yes. Yes, Will, I will be your wife."

"Helena!" He took her mouth in an ardent yet tender kiss.

She suddenly felt lightheaded and swayed dizzily. He steadied her with a triumphant look on his face. "I promise you will never regret it."

"I hope you will not, either." She picked up her hat which had fallen off during their embrace and set it on her head, pulling down the veil. "We must go back to the others."

"I suppose we must," he said reluctantly. "Shall we inform them that we have come to an understanding?"

"I must tell my mother, first."

"I'm sure that Gus and Rosamund will engage to say nothing before you have had a chance to do so."

"I suppose not. And they will probably guess that something has happened between us. Very well."

"Excellent. You will prefer to tell your mother privately, I am sure, but please tell her that I'll call on her this evening."

Their news was received with universal approval and acclaim. Apart from their happiness for the newly betrothed couple, the other four welcomed the new tie between their families, which served to formalise, as Edmund put it, a long-established connection.

"Shall we come in with you?" Gus asked as they arrived at the Dower House stables.

Helena smiled wearily at him. "No, thank you, Brother. I must change before I go to Mamma and, to be honest, I feel the need of a period of quiet reflection before doing so."

"It has been a long and exciting day, and it is not yet over," Rosamund said sympathetically. "You must rest tomorrow. Let me see. Today is Tuesday. Would it be agreeable to you if I invite the Waltons and Fannie and Harold to dinner on Thursday? Just for a quiet, family celebration. There will be time enough to discuss the betrothal announcement and the wedding arrangements. I'm sure these will be more complex where the bridegroom is an earl."

Helena was daunted by Rosamund's supposition. "That is not how I think of you," she explained later to Will, who had manfully withstood a tearful though celebratory discussion with her mother. "I thought to have a simple wedding here, similar to those of Gus and Rosamund and Fannie and Harold. Must ours be vastly different? Anne and Lord Philip had a big London wedding, I know."

He hugged her exuberantly. "That you do not think of me as an earl—I declare it is the nicest thing anyone has ever said to me. As to the type of ceremony we have—that depends on you. Do you wish for a society wedding in St George's of Hanover Square?" He laughed at the horrified look on her face. "One of the advantages of being an earl is that one need not follow fashion slavishly—rather it is we who set the fashion."

He did not seem to notice Helena's appalled reaction to this arrogant pronouncement and went on. "We can discuss all the possibilities at our ease and decide what we want. Let us take the rest of this week for ourselves. We needn't make any immediate decisions and I would like to be able to spend some time with you before I go to visit my mother. She will be delighted to hear that I am to be married, for she is always hinting that it is time I found a wife."

Later that evening Helena pensively removed Richard's ring from her finger and put it away with the other keepsakes and mementos she had of him. A tear escaped her, but somehow she knew that it was the last one she would shed for him. He would be glad for her if he knew. Perhaps, somewhere, he did.

Meanwhile, Mrs Logan, who had taken exception to his lordship's lack of interest in pursuing the acquaintance so fortuitously established at his aunt's ball, was writing to her "dear friend", Lady Westland who was disporting herself at a large and disreputable house party.

"I thought you would wish to learn that Rastleigh is still here, for I know you have an interest there, tho' I never could understand

it, for he must be the veriest icicle that not even you could thaw. Be that as it may, he continues to rusticate here and has set up a flirt— one of our country misses, tho' why I do not know, for she must be twenty-five if she is a day and has been an ape-leader these many years, or so I am assured."

Her ladyship lost no time in twitting Mr Harry Hall who was also a guest that he would soon be cut out of the succession as his cousin had found a new interest.

He shrugged. "Indulging in country matters, is he? Well, I wish them joy of each other." He headed for the stables, singing a couplet from The Lord and the Country Lass:

And when she caught sight of him on the bedding night
She fell into transports of unspeakable delight

to the sniggering amusement of his companions, who joined in the raucous chorus: "*And oh my lord, she said...*"

Chapter Seven

"Then we are agreed. The betrothal will be announced in September and there will be a family wedding here in December."

When no voice was raised in opposition, Lady Amelia continued, "Will, Helena will need to make arrangements for her bride-clothes. If I act as your hostess, she and Dorothea could stay at Rastleigh House, could they not, while they visit the modistes?"

"A splendid idea, Aunt."

Will's only other contributions to the discussion thus far had been to insist that the wedding take place before Christmas and to support Helena in her desire for a quiet ceremony at home.

"Excellent. That will also give Helena the opportunity to consider any changes she wishes to make, for the house has been sadly neglected these many years."

"I am not marrying Helena so that she can refurbish my houses, although I hope she will make any changes she wishes," Will said acerbically. He smiled at his betrothed. "You and your mother must stay for as long as you like. Just let me know when will suit you."

"What of your plans? You spoke of going to Rastleigh, and to Ireland."

"I have no plans that cannot be changed. I am completely at your disposal."

"That is extremely obliging of you, Will," Lady Swift said. "Dear me, it must be seven years since I was in town. We must find out who the latest modistes are, and the milliners. I should like some new hats."

When the talk turned to the latest styles, Will got to his feet. "I shall leave you ladies to your deliberations."

"Wait, Will," his aunt said. "It will be difficult for you to make your usual visit to Ireland this year. Why not suggest that your mother and Sir John Malcolm come here next month? They may not wish to make the crossing in December."

"That is an excellent idea, Aunt. I had been wondering how I might fit everything in this year. This is the ideal solution. I'll write to my mother immediately to apprise her of my engagement and invite her and her family to come and meet my bride." He smiled proudly at Helena as he spoke.

She smiled back at him. "I should like that above all things."

Will was stopped in the hall by his aunt's butler. "A messenger has just arrived from Rastleigh House, my lord."

He took the proffered packet with a sigh. There was apparently no escaping the call of duty. "Where are the others?" he enquired casually.

"Sir Humphrey has retired to the library and Mr Walton and Sir Augustus are in the billiard room, my lord."

"I'll join them there."

He broke the seal on the packet of papers and idly rifled through the contents as he headed for the billiard room where Edmund and Gus were in intense competition. Will poured himself a glass of port and sat down to examine his letters more thoroughly.

"Will! What is it, old man? Will?" Edmund's voice broke through Will's daze.

He glanced down at the letter clutched in his hand. "I must talk to Helena."

"Back already?" The words froze on Helena's lips. Will was white, his features taut with distress and he held onto the doorframe as if he could not stand on his own. She hurried to his side. "What is it?"

Wordlessly, he handed her a sheet of paper. She took it, then slipped her arm into his and guided him to a nearby sofa. He collapsed onto it, drawing her down beside him, and sat passively as she began to read.

"Dear Heavens," she said when she had finished the letter. "What dreadful news! And you had no idea?"

"None."

"Will, what has happened?" Lady Amelia asked urgently.

Will shook his head, unable to reply.

"May I read it to them?" Helena asked. "It would be the simplest way to inform everyone."

When he nodded, she said, "It is a letter from Sir John Malcolm, dated the seventh of August."

My dear Rastleigh,

It is with immense sadness that I write this letter, for I had hoped to spare you learning of your dear mother's condition by this means. Indeed, she has been most insistent that I should not write to you in this matter, feeling that there would be ample time for you to learn of her illness when you visited her as usual this summer.

However, due to a recent and marked deterioration in her state of health, it has become my sad duty to inform you that she has been suffering for some months from a cruel wasting disease. Please let me assure you that all that can be done for her has and is being done and that she is being attended by the best physicians in Ireland. They have now advised me that the End may only be some weeks away and therefore I urge you, if you wish to take farewell of your beloved mother, to proceed to Ireland in some haste. While she is unaware that I have written to you, for the physicians prefer to keep the seriousness of her situation from her so as not to discourage her brave efforts to combat this dreadful illness, I am convinced that she longs to be able to clasp you, her firstborn and eldest son, in her arms once more.

Pray send a letter ahead by the mail should you be able to come to her, for the joyful news and prospect of your visit will undoubtedly raise her spirits.

  I am,

    Yours etc.

     Sir John Malcolm

A shocked hush filled the room as Helena's voice died away. She sat as close to Will as she could. Her presence seemed to be a comfort to him for he released her arm and slid his arm around her waist, holding her tightly to him.

"Poor, dear Phoebe."

As his mother's voice broke the frozen silence, Edmund quietly left the room. He returned a few moments later, accompanied by his father and bearing the library decanter and glasses. He poured a stiff brandy and handed it to Will, who looked at the glass in his hand as if not sure how it had got there, lifted it automatically to his lips and then put it down untasted.

"What a dreadful turn of events," Kathryn said. "It is shocking. To go from planning such a joyful event to this sad news! It is beyond belief."

"Bridal plans can no longer be of importance," Helena said. "You will wish to go at once to your mother, Will."

He nodded, still ashen from shock and unable to speak.

"Would you prefer to be on your own?" she asked gently.

He shook his head, his arm tightening about her. She raised her hand to stroke his cheek and he turned his head to kiss her palm. "Stay with me."

She nodded and he locked both arms about her, resting his head on hers. They remained so for some minutes, heedless of the mutterings of their families who huddled together on the other side of the room.

Will drew a deep breath and raised his head. "I'm sorry. This news has sent me all to pieces."

"I'm sure it has. You will have a lot of arrangements to make. You need only tell me if there is any way I can help."

"I don't know where to start or how long I shall be away." He shivered and his hand was cold to her touch.

Helena looked over to Lady Amelia. "Might I suggest you send for some tea, ma'am?"

"Of course, my dear."

Having complied with this request, her ladyship came to sit with Helena and Will. "My dear Will, I do not like the idea of your making such a journey on your own. And this must also throw all your wedding plans into confusion. It occurs to me that if you were to procure a licence—which would be easily done— you could be married immediately. Helena could then accompany you to Ireland where I am sure she would prove to be an invaluable support."

While an expression of relief crossed Will's face at his aunt's suggestion, Helena was suddenly transported back to another drawing-room and the shocking news that Napoleon had escaped from Elba. "Now is not the time to announce a betrothal," Lady Harbury was saying, and Richard agreed.

He had died before they could marry. She knew it was irrational to suppose that if her wedding to Will were delayed, it too might not take place, but what if some harm were to come to him? She had been unable to save Richard but she might be able to shield Will from some of the distress ahead. There are wounds of the soul as well as of the body, she thought as she regarded him anxiously.

"How quickly could it be arranged? Would there be enough time?" he asked.

"I am sure my brother-in-law would go to the Bishop with you on Monday," Gus said. "We can discuss it with him after church tomorrow. As we are in Helena's home parish, once you have the licence, the ceremony may be held as soon as you wish."

They were interrupted by the arrival of the tea-tray and Helena had the satisfaction of seeing some colour return to Will's face as he drank.

"I can think of nothing better than to have Helena with me, but would it not be too rushed for her?" He looked at Helena's mother. "What is your opinion of my aunt's proposal, ma'am?"

"I think it is an excellent idea," Lady Swift said to Helena's surprise. "If marriage was indeed *ordained for the mutual society, help and comfort that one ought to have of the other, both in prosperity and adversity*, as the Prayer-book has it, then Helena should be at your side in the coming weeks."

"Thank you. I beg you will excuse us—I would like to talk to Helena in private."

Lady Amelia nodded. "Of course. Go into the music room, you will not be disturbed there."

In the music room, Will took Helena in his arms. He held her close for some minutes as if to draw from her strength before pulling back so he could see her face. "I beg you, tell me honestly if such a hurried wedding is not to your taste or if you have any other reservations about it."

She bit her lip. "It's just—I fear I would be intruding on your mother and her family, and at such a time."

"On the contrary, she will be longing to meet my bride. My sisters and brothers will also welcome you, as will their father. I am sure of it. As for me, although I am a wretch to ask you to contemplate it, your presence would be a great solace both on the journey and while we are there."

She took a deep breath and lifted her hands to frame his face. "If you indeed wish it, Will, I will marry you as soon as may be and go with you to Ireland."

He slid his hands from her shoulders to her waist and caught her to him.

"Helena!" was all he said, but it was enough.

She smoothed his hair back from his forehead. "Let us make some plans before we go back to the others; they will be full of questions and will try to take things over if we are not careful."

He even smiled at this and sat at a writing desk, drawing a sheet of paper towards him. "Your secretary awaits your instructions."

"I see you have come to a decision," Lady Amelia said when they returned to the drawing-room. She embraced them both, murmuring, "Thank you, my dear," to Helena as she held her close for a moment. To Will she said, "You are an extremely fortunate man, Nephew."

He hugged her back, saying simply, "I know, Aunt."

"There is much to be done," Rosamund said as Will's eyes met Helena's in unholy amusement. It was apparent that she had judged her family correctly. "Please tell us how we may help. We shall give the wedding breakfast, of course. How many should we reckon with? Will anyone be coming to support you, Will?"

"I am sure my friend Stephen Graham will come. I shall write to him tonight. I must also send for my secretary, James Thornton, for there is much to be arranged before we depart."

"How will you travel? Will you take the steam-packet from Holyhead?" Gus enquired.

"No. I know the steam-packet now crosses in seven hours, but the road from here to Holyhead is not good, despite the recent improvement in other stretches, and the final section from Chester in particular is still dreadful. I'll instruct my crew to bring my yacht around to Bristol."

"It is time we left," Helena's mother said. "You have several letters to write tonight, Will. It is very sad but, my dear boy," she added, going to him and embracing him, "you now have a second family and may call on us for anything."

"She is right, Brother," Gus said, shaking his hand. "We are at your service."

"Thank you all very much." Will was more than a little bemused by this aspect of a marriage to Helena. "I'll see you at church tomorrow."

"Shall you return with us afterwards or will you have too much to do?" Helena asked.

"I should be glad to stay, but there is too much to be done in so short a time. Even though tomorrow is Sunday, I wish to send a messenger to Rastleigh with instructions for the captain of the *Sweet Mary*. He will need to provision her and be ready to sail before the week is out. I must also write to my mother, my secretary and to Stephen, as well as dealing with the other matters in the packet that the messenger brought from London." He turned to Gus. "I shall instruct Thornton to have my solicitor immediately call on me here. Would you be so good as to arrange for yours to be available, say on Tuesday, Swift? I want to make proper provision for Helena before we depart, in case I meet with a mishap while we are absent."

"Yes, of course."

Will bent and kissed his betrothed quickly. "Good night, my dear, and thank you once again."

"There is no need for thanks between us," she interrupted him. "If the circumstances were reversed, would you not do your utmost to help me? As my mother said, it is what marriage is about." She smiled up at him and turned to get into the carriage.

He closed the door behind her and watched as it drew away, bemused by this view of what to him had always been more a civil contract than a personal union, yet heartened beyond measure by her unequivocal and immediate decision to be at his side in the coming weeks.

~~~

On Monday afternoon Will arrived at the Dower House to report that the licence had been obtained. "The bishop was most obliging—too obliging in fact, for he offered to assist at the ceremony. I could hardly refuse him, with Harold standing beside me. He is his superior, after all."

"I suppose not," Helena said, amused. "What did Harold say afterwards?"

"He was quite cheerful about it. I should not have thought him to be so worldly, but he went on to say that there is bound to be some talk at such a sudden wedding and the bishop's presence would serve to quell it."

"Oh, Harold is well up to snuff, as Jonnie used say. I don't think the worldliness is only on his side, however. I am sure the bishop is pleased to have the opportunity to officiate at the nuptials of an earl. I shall talk to Mamma—we had better send an invitation to his wife, in case she would like to accompany him.

We met her when we were in Salisbury, if you recall. Mamma and Lady Amelia took tea with her while you and I went on to Old Sarum."

Will smiled to himself, remembering with what ease his aunt had contrived to send him and Helena off on their own, without putting any notion into her head that her escort was in fact a suitor. "I do not like your being exposed to gossip because we married so hastily," he said aloud.

"It can't be helped, and really it is no concern of anyone but us. We have enough on our minds without paying attention to the possible speculations of ill-bred persons. What is more to the point, when will the ceremony take place?"

Will, entertained and not unimpressed by his bride's disregard for ill-natured tittle-tattle, obediently returned to the matter in hand. "Would Wednesday be too soon for you?"

"No. The sooner we can leave for Ireland the better. Have you written to say you are coming?"

"Yes, I told my mother I would bring my bride to meet her. If that doesn't lift her spirits nothing will, for she is forever telling me that I should marry."

"When shall we leave for Bristol?"

"I thought early the following morning, if that is agreeable to you. You should not be deprived of your wedding day in all this haste. We can be in Bristol before evening and put to sea at once. I thought to send our trunks on the day before. We must expect to be some weeks in Ireland if the end is indeed imminent. I should like to remain until then, if possible."

"Of course. Lennard is already reviewing my wardrobe, but I shall tell her that she is to be ready by tomorrow mid-day."

"I expect my solicitor and Thornton in the morning, and Stephen of course. Shall we walk to the Hall to let Rosamund know that we have fixed on Wednesday?"

"First I must tell my mother. If I drive with you to the Hall, you may leave me there and go on directly to the Place, for your aunt must be informed as well."

~~~

Later that evening Will joined his aunt for her customary evening stroll through her gardens. He was too restless to settle to anything, his mind oscillating between happiness at his approaching marriage and sorrow at his mother's illness. He said something of this to Lady Amelia.

"Poor Phoebe," she said. "Most beautiful women delight in their appearance and their ability to attract. She was not one of those. She was but a child when she lost her parents. When her aunt brought her out, her inheritance together with her beauty made her appetising prey for every rogue and impoverished gentleman in town. That is how she met your father—he rescued her from the importunities of a half-pay captain who had nothing to recommend him but his rather faded blue blood. When she lost him, your father, I mean, I think she was a little lost herself. She devoted herself to you as much as your grandfather would permit. But then he suggested quite strongly that she come to London for the Season once you had gone away to school."

"She married Sir John almost immediately after that first Season." Will vividly remembered the shock of receiving at school her letter announcing her imminent wedding.

"She found tonnish society even more difficult than she had before. She was now a beautiful, wealthy, young widow and I do not have to tell you how such are perceived within the *ton*. As well as the fortune-hunters, she was pursued by every rake in town. When she showed no sign of succumbing to any of them, it became a sport to attempt to seduce her. I believe bets were placed in the clubs as to who would be the first to take Hall Castle. She was on the verge of returning to Rastleigh in despair when she met Sir John. He was decent and kind and she felt safe with him."

Lady Amelia stopped and turned to face him. "I will be candid with you, Will. When she wrote to me of Sir John's offer, I encouraged her to accept it. My father would have brooked little or no interference with his plans for you. You must not forget that it was he who was your guardian, not your mother; we women have no legal right to our children. If a husband or guardian removes them from our company, we have no redress."

"Surely my grandfather would not have resorted to such means."

"He was determined that you would be ready to step into his shoes at a very early age and thought Phoebe was inclined to cosset you. The only time she stood up to him was in insisting that she put you to bed herself and read you a bed-time story. But eventually you got too old for that, of course."

Will had a sudden memory of telling his mother he was nine now and too old to be read to at night. She had smiled gently and agreed, and from then until he went away to school, he had joined her in her sitting-room each evening for an hour before bed-time. She must have been lonely, he thought. On an impulse he bent and kissed his aunt's cheek. "Thank you for telling me this, Aunt. It is salutary to view one's childhood memories through adult eyes."

Lady Amelia nodded. "Phoebe was only twenty-five when your father died—the same age as Helena is now. I considered it a shame that she should dwindle away at Rastleigh, a widow for decades longer than she had ever been a wife. She was reluctant to leave you, but in the end, she said she would marry Sir John if my father agreed that you might go to her for one month each summer. Even that was difficult for him to accept, but your grandmother, your uncle and I all spoke to him, and eventually we were able to convince him. That was why he bought his first yacht, you know. He felt you would be safer travelling privately than being exposed to the rigours of the road and the packet-boat."

"I hadn't realised that. I had my valet and a bear-leader too as long as I was at school, though that wasn't so bad. Stephen Graham's brother Paul came with me as it was during the long vacation and he had me on the lightest of reins."

"Your mother was a very faithful correspondent, I understand."

"More than I was," Will confessed ruefully. "I don't suppose she received even one letter for each two she wrote to me."

As they returned to the house his spirits felt lighter. Understanding something of his mother's past had helped him let go of his resentment at her remarriage; a resentment which, unconsidered, had been left to fester for far too long.

Chapter Eight

Helena sat opposite Gus and Fannie in the carriage, not quite sure if it were all a dream. It was her wedding day! She still couldn't quite understand how it had happened—not the wedding itself, but how Will had managed to transform himself from friend to suitor without alerting her to his true purpose. Maybe it was for the best—had she been forewarned she may well have thrown up a barrier between them. Now it was done and she couldn't regret it. It was time to look forward.

The little church was lit with a golden light by the morning sun. Her mother, a lace handkerchief raised to her eyes, smiled from the front, left pew. The bishop, flanked by Harold, stood at the altar and, at the top of the aisle on the right, Will waited for her, the Walton family ranked behind him, his friend Mr Graham at his side.

Will took a deep breath as he watched his bride approach. She appeared to float up the aisle in a cream muslin dress that flared slightly from the raised waist, the skirt decorated with four rows of soft muslin puffs. Over it she wore a spencer of silk taffeta in a deeper shade of cream, the front and sleeves of which were decorated with cleverly pleated silk and set off by little gold tassels and gold embroidery. Cream lace peeped out from the high collar of the spencer and in it she had fixed his gift, a gold brooch of cunningly chased buds, blossoms and leaves, set with emeralds, rubies, pearls and diamonds.

"I spied it in a shop in Salisbury when we called on the bishop," he had explained when he gave it to her the previous evening. "This way you will have your bridal flowers with you always."

She carried a nosegay of cream and golden rose-buds from Rosamund's garden, and more of them secured Lady Amelia's lace wedding veil to her glorious hair. She looked solemn but a warm smile lit her eyes when they met his.

You are no longer alone, she had said to him when she agreed to this hasty wedding.

Impulsively he bent and kissed her hand, savouring the slight pressure of her fingers in response. Making his vows, he felt as if he committed himself into her keeping and, as she pledged herself to him in unwavering tones, the echo in his mind repeated, *to have and to hold.*

Afterwards they followed Harold into the vestry where, for the last time, she signed her name as Helena Dorothea Swift.

"Well done, Lady Rastleigh," he whispered in her ear just before her mother threw her arms around her.

"My dearest love, I wish you both every happiness," she exclaimed, before turning to welcome her new son-in-law. There followed a confused flurry of congratulations punctuated by embraces before Will could at last lead his wife back into the church, down the aisle and out into the sunlight where children waited to cast jewel-like petals at their feet. Their progress to the waiting barouche was impeded by well-wishers.

"We'll miss you, Miss Helen," one woman said wistfully, "or my lady, as I must say now."

"It will take me some time to get used to it too, Joan," Helena replied with a sympathetic smile.

As the carriage pulled away to continued cheers and good wishes. Will slipped his arm around his bride.

"Tired?"

"No, just glad to catch my breath for a moment."

"Do you like your ring?"

"It is beautiful." She turned her hand to admire the gold band simply set with a heart-shaped ruby.

"We do not have a family betrothal ring as such that is passed from bride to bride, but I particularly wanted you to have this one."

"How did you retrieve it so quickly?"

"Thornton brought it down with him. I told him where to find it. It has been in the family for over one hundred years, ever since the fifth Earl gave it to his bride. I chose it because of the engraving." Slipping the ring from her finger, he showed her the words running around the inside: "*In thee my choyce I do rejoyce*".

"I feel as if I have opened a door into a new world," she said as he returned the ring to its proper place.

"A brave new world, I trust?"

"Why, my lord, do you think to play Ferdinand to my Miranda?" she teased, then gasped as he kissed her.

"My forfeit, remember?" he murmured and then more seriously, "How do you feel about this new world?"

"A little apprehensive, if I am to be frank. It will be so different to what I have been used to. But you will be with me."

"Yes. We are together now. You are not alone as you set out on this voyage."

She did not reply but just pressed his hand. After the hectic pace of the last days, she seemed content to sit back, her hand in his, for the remainder of the short journey to the Hall. He too relaxed, relishing the companionable silence.

At the Hall a lavish wedding breakfast had been set out on the terrace. To welcome the guests, Cook had prepared a cold wine cup flavoured with sweet woodruff and when all had been served, Sir Augustus raised his glass to toast, "The Earl and Countess of Rastleigh—my dear sister Helena and our new brother Will."

"Come, Will, you must lead your bride to the place of honour," Rosamund said after the toast was drunk with great acclaim, indicating the centre of the long table where two places had been garlanded with flowers. With a proud flourish he raised Helena's hand to parade her before the guests and seat her as all applauded.

It was a true family celebration, with none of the stiffness that pertained on more formal occasions. As the meal drew to a close, Will rose to thank the assembly for their good wishes. He spoke simply and from the heart, expressing his appreciation to his wife's family for the gift of such a treasure and to both families for their efforts in arranging such a festive occasion in so short a time. "This will not be the last time we sit together as one family and my wife and I hope to have the pleasure of welcoming you all to Rastleigh in the not-too-distant future."

"For the christening," Hugh called and was shushed by the ladies as Helena blushed and the gentlemen laughed.

"Come, Sister, on your wedding day you must dance."

Fannie seated herself at the pianoforte and, as the guests formed a circle, Will took Helena in his arms to lead her out in a waltz. No one could object if on such a day he held her more tightly than was proper and she gave herself up to the dance, delighting in the contrast between the light, swift movements, the safe cradle of his arms and the strength of his firm body against hers. One dance led to another but at last the moment came when Helena's mother, who would remain at the Hall that night to give the bridal couple privacy, took her aside.

"You should slip away now, my love, so that you can have some time together before you set off tomorrow. You have a trying time ahead of you in Ireland and must make the most of the hours available to you now."

Unfortunately, it did not prove possible to depart as quietly as her mother had suggested. They had to do the rounds of the family, taking a fond farewell with good wishes whispered for the journey ahead of them.

"Let's go around by the stream," Helena suggested.

Will was more than happy to do so. They strolled along arm in arm until they reached the clearing where he had cooked breakfast for her almost three weeks earlier. As on that morning he led her to the willow "seat" but this time he sat beside her, his arm around her waist.

"This is what I wanted to do that morning," he whispered, just before his lips met hers in an ardent kiss. "If I had been a dragon and had found such a fair maiden, I would have immediately carried her off to my lair."

"Perhaps I would have sent my knight in shining armour away again so I could stay with the dragon," she murmured. He gently caressed her face and neck, and then moved his fingers lower to unbutton her spencer, only to find his progress halted by the lace fichu that was held in place by his brooch. He contented himself with tracing and shaping her breasts over the fine muslin of her gown until Helena shivered and stayed his hand. "We should go on to the house. The path to the village goes quite near here."

"I suppose you're right," he agreed with obvious reluctance and carefully buttoned up her spencer, pressing a final kiss in the hollow of her throat. They walked on, now with their arms around each other, just like village sweethearts, Helena thought with an inward smile.

"What would the *ton* think of his lordship the Earl of Rastleigh if they could see him now?"

"The *ton* can go hang," his lordship replied contentedly. "If they had any sense, they would envy us."

~~~

Will had never been so happy in his life. He had never before been privileged to be not only part of, but the focal point of a family celebration; he had been overwhelmed by the warm welcome extended to him by his wife's family, and his wife—it was becoming clear that she was not going to prove to be a chilly bride.

A short time later when he saw her in her fine lawn nightdress, her glorious hair loose to below her waist, her smile of welcome made his breath catch. He was determined to make it easy for her. Taking her in his arms he made long, slow love to her, revealing and worshipping her body inch by inch.

"O my America, my Newfoundland!"

"Hmmmm?"

He chuckled softly. "I can see we shall have to hold poetry readings—intimate ones," he whispered back.

Soon her little moans grew longer and she started to lift her hips against him. "I'll try not to hurt you, but it will only be this one time," he said breathlessly as he positioned himself and slid into her, first a little, and then withdrawing and then a little more and back and forth until he reached her barrier and with a long stroke pushed through.

Helena, who had begun to match his movements stilled and he paused for a moment until he felt her relax. Picking up the rhythm again, they moved together almost as one. As the pace quickened, he felt her body gather itself in a strange tension which broke and quivered around him as he lay deep within her. This was too much for him, and with a groan he shuddered and clutched her fiercely.

"Helena!"

When his breathing eased, Will slipped to lie beside his wife, his head on her shoulder and his hand on her breast, idly playing. They lay quietly together for long moments, exchanging soft caresses until he rose on his elbow to look down at her

"Did I hurt you?"

She shook her head. "Only a little and it didn't last."

"And did I please you?"

She nodded. "I never imagined it could be like that. I had heard the women talking—as I am known to care for the sick, they were inclined to forget that I wasn't married and would talk about anything when I was there. And Mamma had told me there was no need to be fearful. But there is a difference between 'knowing' and 'experiencing'. And you? Were you pleased with me? Did I— do it right?"

"You were perfection herself. If you don't believe me, I shall have to prove it to you again. But rest now."

They dozed contentedly in the twilight until Will moved to pull up the bedclothes which were in complete disarray. "I don't want you to take a chill."

Helena stopped him, getting out of bed. "Let's make it properly or we shall be uncomfortable all night," she said practically. She looked for her nightdress and then saw the streaks of blood on the sheet. Automatically she removed it. "I'll fetch a fresh one." She slipped behind a screen.

Will went to his dressing-room to don a banyan. He returned to find his new wife competently making the bed.

"You seem to have some experience of this."

"You cannot look after the sick without learning these things," she replied briskly. She plumped up the pillows and folded back the covers. "Are you hungry? Mamma said that Mrs Dobbins would leave a cold supper in the dining parlour. We came straight up here, but maybe you would like something now."

"I'm famished," he discovered.

"Then let us explore." She wrapped a Cashmere shawl around her shoulders and led him to a small parlour where covered platters of salmon, chicken and ham had been left on ice together with a variety of sauces, salads and fresh white rolls, a bowl of fruit, a dish of a rich lemon cream and little curd tarts. White wine and a jug of lemonade were kept cool separately.

Will pulled out a chair. "Will my lady be seated?"

Helena glanced up at him. "Now it is my turn to exact a forfeit for each 'my lady'."

"I am at your command," he replied promptly. "What is my lady's desire?"

"I can see I shall have to give some thought to this," she said with a laugh, "or I shall make the offence too tempting."

"If I had known marriage would be like this, I would not have resisted it for so long," Will said sometime later, admiring his bride's dishevelled appearance; the candles struck ruby lights in her loose, dark hair and a richly coloured shawl slipped off one shoulder to reveal the creamy skin beneath. 'A sweet disorder' indeed, he thought, raising his glass to her.

"It does seem decadent," she agreed, yawning, "I suppose we should retire—we have a long journey tomorrow."

Retire they did, but not immediately to sleep, for once in bed he must kiss her goodnight, to kiss her was to caress her and soon he made love to her again before folding her into his arms to hold her securely as they slept.

Book 2

Chapter Nine

Will looked at his wife anxiously. She had craned her neck to see the last of the Dower House and the village but now lay back against the squabs of his travelling chariot, so pale that a sprinkling of tiny freckles stood out on her nose and cheeks.

"Regrets?" he asked gently

She shook her head. "Just a bit daunted, perhaps. I knew this would never be my home again, but leaving it makes it so final. That part of my life is over."

"You will come here again," he said comfortingly, "and it will always be your childhood home. You take those memories with you."

"Memories, yes. But what of the future? This has all happened so quickly. I don't even know where you live or how you spend your days or what place there will be for me in your life." She sounded quite unnerved. "It all seemed so simple when your aunt suggested it and Mamma approved, but now I'm leaving my family behind and there is just you."

He hugged her to him. "I hadn't thought how it must be for you," he said ruefully. "My life will be enriched beyond measure by your presence in it, but it will still be my life. You must begin your life anew. But you will not be alone and you must tell me if something does not please you."

She rested her head on his shoulder. "Tell me about your home—Rastleigh, I think?"

"Rastleigh Castle. If you're looking for an occupation, you will find more than you anticipate there, for it remains more or less as it was in the fifth Earl's time. He was my great-great-grandfather. My grandfather had the Earl's apartments decorated when he inherited and the heir's apartments were likewise refurbished when my parents wed, but that was all."

"And the town house?"

"That is newer and more comfortable. I spend most of my time there. I visit Rastleigh in the summer and at Christmas, and I must also visit my other properties."

Helena glanced at him, opened her mouth as if to say something, hesitated and then closed it again.

"What is it?" When she delayed replying, he coaxed, "Come, Helena, you must not be afraid to express your concerns or ask me questions. You don't lack for courage. What were you about to say?"

She flushed. "I know that some gentlemen prefer their wives to remain on their country estates, especially once they have children, and they continue to lead their own, separate lives as much as possible. Is that what you wish to do?"

Will looked at her, appalled. "Of course not! I have spent too much of my life alone. I should like us to be together unless," he joked, "you decide you can no longer bear my company and banish me from your presence."

"That will depend on how well you treat me," she responded sweetly. "I trust you will not turn out to be a dictatorial husband, for I am used to managing my own life, as you know."

More likely an uxorious one, he thought, tilting her face so that he could kiss her. She returned the caress happily and laid her head back on his shoulder with a sigh.

"Close your eyes and rest. You didn't have much sleep last night and these last days have been busy ones."

Helena was indeed tired. She slept through the first changes of horses, only wakening when they stopped for a longer break near Warminster.

"Welcome, my lord, my lady. All is as you requested. A room has been prepared for you upstairs, my lady," the inn-keeper's wife added to Helena, "if you will be pleased to come with me."

In the pretty bedroom, Helena washed her face and hands and attended to other necessities. It seemed odd to find a husband waiting for her in the private parlour. She had thought she wasn't hungry, but found she could enjoy some new-laid eggs with tea and fresh bread and butter. He made a more substantial meal. Less than an hour later, they were on their way again.

Will opened some compartments in the side of the coach. "How would you like to while away the time? We have cards, books, and chess, though I cannot guarantee that the chess-pieces will stay on the board if we hit a large pot-hole. Or here is *The London Magazine*. Do you know Elia's writings?"

"No, not at all."

"Then let me read you one of his pieces, for they are most diverting and quaint; simple but with a charm all his own, he leads us into the by-ways of his life. What is his subject this month? Ah—*Mackery End in Hertfordshire.*"

When he had finished reading aloud, which he did exceedingly well, his pleasantly modulated voice reflecting his appreciation of Elia's sometimes whimsical opinions, he smiled at her and said, "So you see, Helena, that even if it were some forty years until you next visit Swift Hall, which will not be the case, I assure you, for I do not intend to lose sight of my new family so quickly, you will not have forgotten it and you will be welcomed as one who belongs there."

Unaccountably reassured by this conceit and his apt allusion to their previous conversation, she smiled back, taking the magazine from him. "Now let me read to you, for turnabout is fair play. Here we have a letter from India. That reminds me, why were you suddenly talking about the colonies last night?"

"The colonies?" he repeated blankly

"Yes. America and Newfoundland. I thought it strange that you were so distracted at such a moment."

He laughed softly and caught her hand, bringing it to his lips to kiss the palm. "On the contrary it was most apt. It is a line from John Donne's poem 'To His Mistress on Going to Bed'. Someday I'll say it all to you but not now, as it is best if one starts at the beginning, just as the poet did."

~~~

Helena stirred as they neared Bristol. "Must we go directly to your yacht?"

"Not immediately if you don't wish to, but I would prefer to put to sea sooner rather than later."

116

"Have we time to purchase the latest journals and some other items that might divert your mother and her family and turn their thoughts a little?"

"An excellent notion. Let us see what we can find."

Once they had assembled a collection of periodicals and books, Helena stopped at a draper's window. "What pretty caps and shawls—your mother may welcome some variety, even if she is confined to bed."

"You think of everything," he said as they walked back towards the carriage.

She shrugged. "I am used to invalids. But what is that?" she asked, peering into an establishment displaying curios and small items of furniture. "I've never seen anything like it. Is it a type of doll's house?"

Will looked more closely at a deep, rectangular mahogany tray that had been divided up into small rooms that opened one into another. Small skittles stood at different points in the rooms while tiny bells dangled from curved brass fittings that seemed to be placed at random on the board. "It is a *table à toupie*. I've seen them in Paris. You set the little top spinning down the board. The aim is to topple the skittles without ringing the bells. You gain points for the one and lose them for the other."

"Would your brothers and sisters like it?"

"The younger ones certainly. It requires some dexterity so I think even Jack wouldn't be able to resist trying his hand." In short order the game was purchased, wrapped up and an assistant instructed to take the unwieldy parcel to the waiting carriage.

The *Sweet Mary* was a handsome vessel with a spacious cabin for the owner. Helena looked with approval at the polished wood and brass fittings and the large bed. "I see you believe in being comfortable."

"Why not? Would you like to come on deck while we set sail? Take a warm shawl—the wind will become more noticeable once we leave the shelter of the harbour." He took her to a sheltered corner of the deck where chairs had been placed under an awning. "We'll sit here as we go down the Bristol Channel and out into the open sea."

Once the travelling chariot had been lifted on board and made fast, the mooring lines were cast off and the crew set about unfurling sails that flapped and snapped as they swelled in the evening breeze.

"It's magical," Helena said as the setting sun cast a golden path across the sea. "It must lead to some fairyland, perhaps, or the home of the Hesperides."

"But we cannot go there."

"No. But there is more magic to be seen later."

~~~

"Come on deck before you retire," Will said, wrapping her shawl around her shoulders. Once outside, he positioned her so that they were facing the north-east horizon, pulling her to him so that his body sheltered her from the wind. She rested against him, relishing the comfort of this strength and warmth. "Let your eyes adjusts to the darkness," he murmured and then "there!"

A bright light shot towards the horizon and then another and another, their sparkling trails weaving a glittering web across the night sky.

"Like spangles on a gauze gown," Helena said. "How beautiful. How did you know where to look for them?"

"I have frequently observed them in that part of the sky in July and August."

"It's wonderful, like angelic fireworks, with no din or smoke."

The yacht turned slightly and the wind grew stronger.

"You're cold," Will said. "Go to bed, my dear. I shall not be long after you."

Helena smiled and went to the cabin, grateful for his tact in allowing her some privacy to prepare for bed. There were many different aspects to marriage, it seemed. He came in some twenty minutes later wearing his banyan.

"I'm using the adjoining cabin as a dressing room. I can sleep there if you would prefer to be alone."

Helena would have liked some hours to herself, but something in his eyes—a certain wistfulness—prevented her from saying so. Instead she held back the bed-clothes to invite him to her bed. He slid in gratefully and turned to her.

"It has been a long day. You must be tired."

"Yes."

"Just let me hold you then," he said, taking her in his arms and turning her on her side so that they lay together like spoons in a drawer. "Good night, Helena." She felt a gentle kiss on the nape of her neck.

"Good night, Will."

He seemed to fall asleep almost immediately but she lay awake for some time reviewing all that had happened since the previous morning. It was strange to sleep so close to someone else. Gradually his grip relaxed and she was able to ease away

---

from him, though his arm still lay heavy over her waist. Sighing, she turned her face into the pillow. Towards morning, she slept, her dreams made restless by the trotting of horses and the rocking of waves.

It didn't seem so strange the next morning to see an unshaven male face on the pillow beside her, smiling at her.

"Good morning, Helena."

"Good morning, Will."

"It is indeed, for today we are completely free of all duties," he answered with a huge smile, like a child who has been released early from his lessons. "It's one of the great pleasures of a day at sea, for we cannot be reached and may do exactly what we wish." As he spoke, he took her in his arms and began to make eager love to her.

Helena was startled by the idea of performing her marital duty in the morning and in daylight, but soon saw the attraction and reciprocated his caresses at first shyly but then more adventurously. This spurred him on to greater efforts and they finished in harmony, lying close together afterwards for a considerable time until he said, "We should get up." With a last kiss he left the bed. "Dress warmly, but not too fine. We shall spend the night at a hotel in Dunleary and go on to my mother's home in the morning."

The day passed quietly and happily. It was indeed good to spend some hours if not quite in idleness, at least without having to think of the demands or needs of others. Will came and went—she might look up and catch sight of him at the helm or aloft in the rigging or just chatting to one of the seamen. He didn't ignore her, but returned to her at intervals to admire her work, eat a late nuncheon with her or just to sit beside her, reading aloud interesting paragraphs from yesterday's Morning Chronicle as she embroidered.

"May I see?" He took the hoop from her hand.

"I wonder if you will recognise it."

He peered at the faint design on the linen. "Why, it's our breakfast by the stream."

Helena nodded. "It's my way of keeping a journal."

"What do you do with them? Do you have them framed?"

"Sometimes, and some I give as gifts. But I have the full record here." She showed him her sketchbook. "I do the sketch as soon as possible so that I do not forget the details or the—the mood of the occasion."

He leafed through the sketches. "There we are, swinging little Sally," he exclaimed, clearly pleased. "That is my aunt's ball—and here we are at Stonehenge, listening to the lark. Do you make embroidered versions of them all?"

"No, only the special ones." She looked up. "We are approaching the harbour. I had better put my things together."

Chapter Ten

Early the following morning they turned their backs on the sea and followed the road first inland and then south towards Ballymore Eustace, the nearest market-town to Sir John Malcolm's estate at Colduff. The further they got, the wilder and more desolate the countryside became, though it was punctuated by small villages and what were obviously larger estates as well as isolated cottages.

"I'll be glad to arrive," Helena said when some hours had passed. "We seem to have been travelling forever."

"Is this your first journey outside England?" Will asked.

"No. Lady Harbury kindly invited me to stay with them in Brussels in 1815. Her son, Captain Richard Harbury, and Jonnie were friends since their schooldays and her ladyship was exceedingly good to me when I made my come-out in 1814. It was she who arranged for us to have vouchers for Almack's; she and Lady Sefton are friends."

"Almack's." Will shuddered theatrically. "My grandfather constantly urged me to attend. I don't know who were worse— the daughters or the mothers! Though I am sure that you and Lady

Swift were always everything that was proper," he added hastily. "Perhaps if we had met then—but I digress. You were telling me about Brussels."

"The Harburys decided to take a house there—you probably remember how much of fashionable society had decamped there for one reason or another once it was safe to leave England. They invited me to join them as Rosalind was expecting Tom and Mamma wished to remain at home that year. I was vastly excited. It seems amazing when you consider that we live on an island, but there was never the occasion for me to travel so far and I had never seen the sea.

"And then, to be in a foreign country—to hear other languages spoken and to eat different food! It was all so interesting. Of course, there were those like the so-called Ladies in the Park who would only visit people they had known in London and in general tried to replicate tonnish society in Brussels, despite the fact that some of them had left England because they could not pay their debts, but Lady Harbury was not so narrow-minded. We went on outings by canal, to Bruges, for example and on one occasion attended mass in the Cathedral. And I bought such wonderful lace, for Mamma and Rosalind as well, of course. And a beautiful christening gown for the new baby." She took a breath.

"Then later it proved most fortuitous that we were already there, for once Bonaparte escaped and our army came to Brussels, you couldn't get accommodation for love or money. We were joined by the Harburys' daughter Caro and her husband Major Thompson, and Richard and Jonnie, of course. The gentlemen stayed at the house when they were able to get away from their duties and we ladies occupied ourselves with the social round. It was the strangest of times; gay, almost frenzied it seemed to me, for people vied with one another to host the most singular entertainments. Even Wellington himself gave three balls between arriving in Brussels and Waterloo.

"There were race-meetings and reviews of the cavalry and pick nick dinner parties. Yet all the time the talk of the coming battle increased and rumours abounded as to Napoleon's progress. By the second week in June we hardly saw our men. When it appeared that Napoleon was marching on Brussels, some families decided to return to England but Lord and Lady Harbury remained."

She paused. She was not looking at him, Will realised, but back to the past.

"Then there was the Duchess of Richmond's ball—you will have heard of it, I am sure. It was such a wonderful spectacle. Wellington was there, and the Highlanders danced for us." Her voice changed, her tone grew puzzled and more serious. "We only discovered later that Napoleon had reached Charleroi that day. But that evening we noticed that the gentlemen were disappearing; fewer and fewer of the military were left in the ballroom. Then someone, Lord Uxbridge, I think, announced that officers who had engaged partners had better finish their dance and return to their quarters. Caro, Lady Harbury and I went to see what was happening. There was such a bustle in the hall; everywhere officers were taking leave of their ladies. Our men found us—but it was a hasty farewell."

She stopped and caught her breath almost on a sob, but then continued as if once started she could not stop.

"The next days—I hope never to experience their like again. As we returned home it seemed as if Brussels echoed with marching feet. In the morning there were chaotic calls, people going hither and thither seeking news. Some ladies were trying to make desperate arrangements to leave, others gathered together to scrape lint, prepare bandages and to see about receiving the wounded." She looked at him. "It occurred to me afterwards how fortunate England is in being an island, for we have been able to prevent invasion and wage our wars on other countries' soil. Our armies may be in danger, but the people do not have to fear for their lives or properties. I know the Duke insisted his troops pay for the supplies they took, unlike the French who looted and pillaged, but what use is money if there is nothing left to purchase, or are your fields if a battle has been fought on them? And if you should suffer defeat!" She shuddered. "I once heard Jonnie and Richard talking about the sack of Badajoz—they didn't know I was nearby. It must have been horrific. And Wellington let it go on for almost three days before the troops were brought under control."

Will said nothing, afraid that if he broke his silence, she would cease her description of those terrible days. It seemed to well up from deep within her in an awful flow that should not be dammed.

She took a deep, trembling breath. "Then we heard a dull rumble like far-off thunder. Someone said it was the guns. Hours passed. The waiting was interminable. In the afternoon, when the first wounded arrived, we went to see if we could help. We went to bed that night but could only sleep fitfully and once the servants woke us crying, *les français sont ici*. Lord Harbury went then to the stables to give orders that they must be ready to put the horses to at a moment's notice and told us all to pack one bag only each. But nothing more happened. The next day the guns were still to be heard and still the wounded came. Another night passed.

"Some time the next day a cavalry troupe, German, I think, came rushing through the town crying, 'the French are at our heels.' But the French did not appear. It was the next morning that we learnt that Napoleon had been defeated. And then, more waiting. It's all a jumble of nights and days in my mind. Once the first wounded arrived in the town, we were occupied looking after them. You did what you could. And it wasn't only the English who had remained who cared for them. The Belgics helped as well and if they discovered a soldier who had been billeted with them, they took him home to nurse him there. But even with that, the streets were full of wounded lying on straw.

"Of course, if we saw somebody from our men's regiments, we asked for news. That was how we learned that Caro's husband was dead. But she said nothing and continued to work so, as she said later, that some other woman's husband might be saved. At last Jonnie arrived. He had sustained a sabre slash to his right forearm which had been roughly bandaged. He knew where Richard had been fighting and went back to the battle-field with Lord Harbury to search for him. He was severely wounded—a shell had exploded near him causing internal injuries and his right side had been blasted by shrapnel. They brought him back to the house. We did our best, but he died three weeks later—a shard that was too deep to be removed pierced his heart."

Helena stopped suddenly and rested her head against the cushioned back of the seat, her eyes closed and her face pale. Will took her hand comfortingly and they sat in silence for some minutes. At last she opened her eyes.

"I'm sorry. It was as if I were reliving it."

"No, I am sorry if my question brought back such dreadful memories." They were nearing a country inn. "Would you like to stop for a few minutes?"

At her nod, he leaned out the window and called to the postilion to pull up.

The innkeeper could only offer porter or whiskey but suggested that his wife prepare a dish of tea for the lady. While they waited for it, Will and Helena strolled up and down, glad to ease the stiffness caused by sitting so long. She tucked her hand into his arm—it seemed to him that she leaned upon him a little more than usual—and talked inconsequentially about trivialities until he was relieved to see her colour return and the haunted expression disappear from her eyes. As they returned to the inn, he said again, "I am so sorry that my question revived such memories for you. It is not always easy to be brushed by the wings of history."

"It may seem strange, but I feel better, lighter somehow for talking about it. I don't think I ever have before—not in one fell swoop, like that. Once we were at home, it all seemed unreal—almost as if it had happened to someone else—and the whole country in such a flood of patriotic fervour at the victory that they did not want to know about the cost. I suppose I just locked all the memories away."

"Could you not have spoken to Jonnie about it?"

"No. He didn't want to talk about the battle. He was blue-devilled for a good while afterwards, especially when it seemed that he would not regain the full use of his hand. I think he slept badly. So did I." She sighed. "It was better to leave it behind us. It doesn't do any good to dwell on things although, I confess, I still feel uneasy when I hear thunder rumbling in the distance." They were back at the inn by now and she said brightly, "Here we are! I shall be glad of a cup of tea. Is it much further from here to your mother's home?"

"Not too long now. Why don't you sit outside here on this bench? You are not accustomed to the smell of the peat they burn here and it's horribly smoky inside. I'll see if there is a small table that may be brought out."

~~~

At about three o'clock they turned into the gates of Colduff and followed a long, curved drive to a large house set in verdant gardens. As they approached, the door opened and a tall, grey-haired gentleman of about fifty emerged, followed by two boys and two girls. He waved the footman away and opened the door of the carriage himself. Will jumped down and turned to help Helena.

"Welcome," Sir John said, "and a special welcome to Colduff to you, my lady. Rastleigh could not have sent his mother any better news that that he would be accompanied by his bride. May I present my family? This is Jack, my eldest, Kate is sixteen, Alexander is twelve and Emily will be nine at Christmas."

"Welcome, my lady," Kate said shyly.

"Oh no, you must call me Helena," she responded with a warm smile. "Am I not now your sister?"

This served to break the ice and the two girls escorted her into the house, the boys following with their half-brother and father.

"Phoebe is resting," Sir John said. "We usually take tea together about half-past five o'clock, which is after our dinner, for we dine at four. Today, you shall see her first and we'll dine later, as we were not sure when you would arrive."

Overhearing, Kate said, "You will wish to refresh yourselves. Your rooms are ready and Cook has prepared a cold collation in case you have not had the opportunity to take a nuncheon." She spoke carefully, as if reciting a prepared speech.

"Excellent," Will said. "I'm famished."

"Then, pray come with me."

They followed her upstairs to a charming room overlooking the gardens at the rear of the house.

"It's not your usual room, Will. We thought you and Helena would like to have your own sitting-room, which is through that door. Your dressing room is on this side."

Will bent to kiss her cheek. "Thank you, Kate. We'll be down in twenty minutes."

~~~

"Her ladyship would like to see you now, sir."

"Thank you, Máire," Sir John said to the neat, middle-aged woman who had brought this news. "Rastleigh, if you and your wife would like to accompany me?" Noticing the children's disappointment, he added, "We don't want to overtire your

Mamma. Let her enjoy this reunion with your brother. You may join us later if her strength permits."

Lady Malcolm lay on a day-bed in a sunny parlour, propped up on pillows. Will was shocked to see how thin and drawn she was. She was looking eagerly towards the door and her eyes lit up as they entered.

"Will." She opened her arms to him.

Quickly crossing the room, he knelt to embrace her gently. "We are so happy to be here, Mother."

"And this must be your bride." She smiled at Helena. "Welcome, my dear." Helena carefully took the frail hand and Lady Malcolm pulled her down to kiss her cheek. "I met your parents several times at Walton Place. You remember, Will, we used visit Amelia each year in summer. Pray give your mother my fond regards."

"Thank you, ma'am. Mamma desired me to convey her compliments and regards to you."

"As did my uncle and aunt," Will added.

"Do sit down and tell me all the news." She looked up as Máire came in with a tea-tray. "Will you pour please, my dear?" she asked Helena.

"Shall I help you sit up, my love?" Sir John supported his wife with one arm while he rearranged her pillows and adjusted the soft shawl around her shoulders.

"Thank you," she said, accepting a cup of tea from Helena. "And now you must tell me everything, Will, for there was no mention of marriage in any of your recent letters."

"I should think not. If I had so much as hinted that I was looking for a bride, you would have bombarded me with maternal questions and advice. This way I have been able to steal a march on the whole *ton*." When the laughter had subsided, he went on, "The truth is, Mother, that until I met Helena my attitude towards matrimony was more 'one day I must' than 'now I will'."

"Just like St. Augustine," Helena remarked and clapped her hand to her mouth.

"What can you mean?" Lady Malcolm said. "I love Will dearly but am nonetheless surprised to hear him compared to a saint."

Will raised an enquiring eyebrow. "I must know why you have put yourself to the blush. Out with it!"

"It is from his Confessions. *Da mihi castiatem et continentiam, sed noli modo.*"

"Give me chastity and continence, but not yet," he translated with a grin. "So that is what you think of your husband, my lady?" A slanted glance challenged her to dispute his use of this address.

"Why no, my lord." And now her smiling eyes met his. "It merely seemed an apposite descant to your remark but you have assured us that your view of marriage has changed."

"Indeed, it has." Leaning forward, he dropped a swift kiss on her lips, causing her to blush anew and his mother to give a satisfied smile.

"You must have had an unusual education, Lady Rastleigh, if you can quote the church fathers so aptly and in Latin too," Sir John remarked.

"I suppose I must have, but to me it was quite normal, for I had nothing to compare it with. My father was of a scholarly turn of mind and I don't think it ever occurred to him to treat his daughters any differently to his sons. In fact, we benefited longer from his instruction, for we were not sent to school. We had a governess of course, but my father continued to read with us each day as well."

"Old Lady Needham would have agreed with him," Will said. "She commented to me only recently that she did not hold with not educating girls, for otherwise how were they to talk to their husbands. 'Silly ninnies' was how she described today's debutantes."

"What, is she still alive?" Lady Malcolm said. "How did you come to meet her?"

After Will had described the ball, his brothers and sisters were sent for and the conversation became more general. Helena listened to the chatter, watching his interaction with the young people. They treated him more like an uncle than a brother, she thought, and although he was obviously welcome in this house, it seemed in no sense to be his home. His mother had lain back again and her strength seemed to be flagging.

"It is time to dress for dinner," Sir John announced. "If we do not dine soon, Emily will fall asleep in her soup."

"You go on with the children, my love," his wife said. "I should like Will—and his wife—to stay for a few more minutes."

"Please call me Helena, ma'am," her new daughter-in-law said at once.

"May I?" Lady Malcolm's eyes filled with tears. "I should like of all things to be on good terms with Will's bride. And if you would call me "Mother" as he does, it would please me greatly."

Helena bent and touched her cheek to hers. "I should be honoured to, Mother." She and Will resumed their seats beside her bed and his mother continued, taking their hands.

"I wish you both a long and happy life together. I am in alt that Will has found such a wife. I cannot describe my delight when I read his letter and it is the greatest blessing that I am able to make her acquaintance. I do not think that I shall live to see your children. No, Will," she stopped his protest, "you see how it is with me and we must not waste the time that is left to us by pretending otherwise. Helena, although I suppose I am partial because Will is my son, in him you have found an excellent husband."

"I think so, Mother," Helena said.

Poor Will looked completely done up by this encounter, but he summoned enough strength to kiss his mother gently and say, "We shall leave you now but rest assured that we shall spend as much time with you as is possible."

"I hope that you will. John knows when I am at my best. Come in and see me again after dinner if you will."

"Should I ring for your maid, Mother?" Helena asked.

"There is no need. She has a room opposite where she can prepare things for me. She will see when you leave."

"You must find your mother much changed," Sir John said the next morning as he walked with Will to inspect the stables. "It will have been a sad shock to you."

"It was. No matter how you prepare yourself…" Will's voice trailed away. "What do the physicians say?"

"Nothing good. It is as if something is devouring her from within. They do their best to alleviate her pain, but their potions make her drowsy and so we can only be with her at certain times. I sit with her as much as I can, but she doesn't want the children to be neglected and they are so lively that they tire her even more."

"Helena and I could assist you, both in sitting with my mother and occupying the younger ones. She has considerable experience in nursing invalids," he added.

"Well, we'll see how we go on."

Helena, meantime, had received an invitation via Lady Malcolm's maid to call on her ladyship. She brought with her some of the journals and books they had bought in Bristol as well as the caps and shawls.

Her mother-in-law received these offerings with real appreciation. "How kind and clever of you to think of it. Pray ring for Máire."

She passed a pleasant half an hour trying on her new finery and consulting with Helena and her maid as to which ones she should wear that evening. "And what have we here?" she asked. "Northanger Abbey?"

"I wasn't sure if you had read it. It appeared about three years ago and is by the author of Pride and Prejudice. I thought your young people might find it amusing, for it mocks the gothick style of novel."

"Wonderful. We must read it aloud in the evenings after tea. I like to do that you know; we are all together but I don't find it as exhausting as when the children all chatter at once."

Chapter Eleven

Helena hurried down the curved, stone steps. She had discovered the walled garden some days earlier but this was the first time she had been able to slip away by herself. She was not needed for the moment; Will and his brothers were helping school Sir John's young horses and Kate was with Emily in the schoolroom. She sank onto the bench in the shady arbour and took what seemed to be her first deep breath since word had come of Lady Malcolm's illness. She smiled wryly. She may have wished to leave the shallows but had not expected to be thrown so quickly into such deep waters.

So far, she had not regretted her rushed marriage. Will was proving to be an agreeable husband. He was surprisingly passionate in private—she had not expected that aspect of her wifely duties to be so, well, interesting—and she was grateful for Kathryn's advice not to be missish but to allow him to give her pleasure as this would in turn please him.

Outside the bedroom he was courteous and considerate but once arrived at Colduff he seemed to have retreated into his accustomed role of earl. He was not as unbending as he had been when visiting the Waltons and she found this surprising given that they were now in his mother's home. He was inclined to hold himself aloof, she thought. He was however amenable to suggestion and made no bones about spending time with his step-father and brothers and, to a lesser extent, with his sisters. Though he may be reserved, he was sweet-tempered—she had never heard him raise his voice or seen him lose his temper. He took it for granted that the household would function as usual despite his mother's illness, but in that he was not different to any other gentleman, she supposed.

The days at Colduff had soon developed a pattern. The adults took turns to sit with Lady Malcolm. She liked to spend time with each of her children mid-morning, when she was at her best, and the whole family sat with her in the evening over tea.

It was instinctive to Helena to notice where assistance was required and quietly to arrange for it, so Sir John found that he had more time to deal with estate matters. Will rode out daily with his brothers and she herself spent time with the girls, who were missing their mother's attention and guidance. She did not encroach on Kate's burgeoning role as mistress of Colduff but supported her young sister-in-law in her consultations with the housekeeper so that the household ran more smoothly. The *table à toupie* had proved a great favourite with the children and, as Will had forecast, even Jack did not consider it beneath him to demonstrate to his brother and sisters how best to spin the top so as to knock down the most skittles in one go.

Helena's eyes closed. She would just sit here until it was time for breakfast.

Helena put down her tea-cup and looked across the table. "Are you not well, Kate?"

Kate smiled wanly and shook her head but closed her lips firmly, glancing at her father and brothers as she did so.

"If you're finished, I'm sure the gentlemen will excuse us."

Once they were outside the breakfast parlour, Helena put her arm around Kate's waist and led her into the neighbouring room.

Kate let her sister-in-law draw her down onto the sofa where she sat hunched over, with her hand on her lower abdomen.

"Is it your time of the month?" Helena asked gently.

Kate nodded. "It's never been like this. I feel ill and it hurts."

"I'm sure it's no wonder, with all the worry you have at the moment. Come, we'll get you into bed and I'll prepare a special tea that will help."

Some fifteen minutes later, she returned to Kate's bedroom, accompanied by a maid bringing hot bricks wrapped in a soft cloth. "You'll soon feel much more the thing," she said as she handed her a cup. "It happens to all women at some time or another."

The maid smiled in fellow-feeling. "That's right, Miss Kate. 'Tis the curse of Eve, my mother says. I've brought you more cloths as well and just ring the bell if you want anything else."

Kate obediently drank the tea, not without making a face at the bitter taste and lay down on her side, her knees pulled up. Helena tucked the blankets around her.

"I'll make sure you remain undisturbed. I'll look in on you again in an hour or so to see if you need anything else, but I hope that you will be able to sleep."

"Thank you, Helena. I didn't want to disturb Mamma."

Kate closed her eyes, utterly exhausted. She was trying so hard to take Mamma's place, but it was good to be looked after again. How would it be when Will and Helena left? She tried not to think about it, but she could not feel that Mamma would recover. What would happen to them all? How would they bear it? She smelt lavender and felt a cool compress placed on her forehead. She roused herself to ask, "Emily's practice?"

"I'll take Emily into the garden. The music room is beneath yours and you will not wish to hear her scales. Sleep now, my dear."

Her husband was in their sitting-room when Helena entered some minutes later. "You didn't eat much breakfast" he remarked.

"No, I am just going to order some more," she replied, going to the bell pull. "I wanted to look after Kate. I could see that she was out of sorts."

"It is not serious, I hope?"

"No, no. Just a female complaint. She was reluctant to distress her mother and didn't know what to do."

"But you were able to help her. That's good. I must leave you, my dear. Sir John asked me to ride out with him." With a quick kiss he departed, leaving his wife to gaze after him in mild exasperation before she turned to the maid to request tea, toast and the presence of Miss Emily.

Emily at first was happy at the idea of spending the morning with Helena, but was upset when she was told that her sister was not well. "Like Mamma?" she asked fearfully.

Helena hugged her reassuringly. "Not at all like your Mamma. Kate just has a touch of the megrims and you are excused your music practice today as the sound of the scales and arpeggios would carry up to her room, you know."

"They give me the megrims frequently as well," the child said glumly and then more cheerfully, "maybe I should stop practising altogether?"

Helena laughed. "No, you must practice harder so that they sound more musical. Just not today. Shall we go and pick some flowers for your mother and Kate?"

Emily nodded and the arrival of the maid bearing not only tea and toast but some plum tarts, "Fresh out of the oven, Cook says, my lady," completed the restoration of her good humour.

~~~

"It's not fair, I say!"

Will was nearly bowled over by Alexander who came running out of the house, a stormy look on his face. The boy was obviously in a high rage. He did not stop but with a muttered "beg pardon" went on his way leaving his brother to gaze after him with disapproval. Shaking his head, Will continued on to his room to change his clothes. There was no sign of Alexander when the family later assembled in the drawing-room before dinner and no one knew where he was.

"That boy is impossible at the moment," Sir John said.

"He needs a good thrashing," Jack said from the lofty eminence of his seventeen years. "He flies up into the boughs over the slightest thing. He has been pestering me all day to show him how to handle the ribbons—there is no holding him now that Will has taught Kate to drive the gig. I said I would, but then Mamma wished to see me so of course I must go to her."

"I asked him would he play Fox and Geese with me and he said no," Emily said sadly. "He said if no one would do anything for him, why then he would do nothing for anybody."

"The young devil!" Sir John said wrathfully. "He may go without his dinner if that is the way he behaves. Let us go in." He turned to Helena and offered her his arm, it being his custom to squire either his daughter-in-law or one of his daughters each evening. It was touching to see Emily act the fine lady when it was her turn.

At that moment the door opened and the errant son appeared. He was neatly and correctly dressed, but unusually subdued. Will thought he had been weeping, but knew better than to mention such a suspicion.

Helena must have felt the same, for he heard her murmur to Sir John, "Pray overlook his behaviour for the moment, sir. It will only distress his mother if she thinks that he is at outs with you."

Will, who was reminded by the forlorn appearance of his younger brother of himself at the same age, offered his arm to Kate and, as they left the room tucked his free hand into the crook of Alexander's elbow to take him with them. "I'm starving," he remarked cheerfully if inelegantly. "What do you have for us today, Kate?"

"Cook has prepared mackerel with a gooseberry sauce—I know you are partial to that, Will—as well as collops of beef and we have syllabubs and plum tarts, Alex," she added to her youngest brother who acknowledged her comment with a weak smile. He did not contribute much to the conversation during dinner but had sufficiently recovered his composure by the time the family paid its usual visit to his mother to be able to respond to her and to take his turn in reading aloud.

When the time came for Emily to go to bed, Kate, who was still looking pale, announced she would retire as well. Helena whispered in Will's ear, "Challenge the boys to a game of billiards when we go down. I wish to have quiet word with Sir John."

Sir John looked relieved when Will took his brothers off to the billiard room. He sat back in his chair with a sigh and shut his eyes for a moment.

"You are exhausted, sir," Helena said sympathetically. "May I fetch you a restorative? Pray do not get up," she added as he made to rise to his feet. "Some whiskey, perhaps?"

"Aye. Pour me a dram, if you please."

She gave him a generous measure and poured a glass of Madeira for herself.

After some minutes, he broke the easy silence that had fallen between them. "It is hard, Lady Rastleigh, deuced hard, to watch my poor Phoebe suffer and know there can only be one end. And what am I to do with Alexander? He cannot be permitted to go on as he is. I suppose I should thrash him, although I have always hated doing so," he added sheepishly.

"Will told me once that as a boy he had preferred the rector's thrashings—his son and Will were great friends and prone to all sorts of mischief—to his grandfather's scolds and lectures. But I do not think that a whipping would be the right answer in this case. Alexander has not been up to mischief—he is unhappy and does not know how to express it. Have you told him how grave his mother's situation is?"

"Not directly, no."

"But he will have a fair idea, I think. And in that case, it is worse if he is left to his speculations with no one to talk to about them."

"You are right, ma'am," Sir John said heavily. "But what am I to say to him?"

"I think if you give him the opportunity, he will confide in you. Explain as simply as you can that his mother will not get better. And then listen to what he has to say and respond honestly."

"Now I must be both mother and father to them," he replied with another sigh. "I am woefully ill-equipped for it, I fear."

"You will do your best, I am sure, sir. That is all any of us can do. But perhaps you could consider whether there is a lady in the neighbourhood to whom the girls, Kate in particular, might apply for advice. There are some matters where a father can be of little assistance."

"Usually they would have their governess, but Miss Bowen always spends some weeks in summer with her family in England. She had departed before the deterioration in Phoebe's condition became noticeable. She will return next week. I have arranged with my sister that the girls and Miss Bowen will go to her for a long visit when all is over. I've taken a house in Dublin for the winter. Jack will be at Trinity College and Alexander is due to go to school. It is unfortunate that his tutor's term of employment ended in July, for he will be late starting and will be behind."

"Perhaps Will and I could devise a programme of study for him when Miss Bowen returns. Jack might help too. It would serve to give their days a semblance of normality."

"That is an excellent suggestion, ma'am. Pray do not think that I am insensible of your assistance to my family and your support of my wife. Rastleigh is a fortunate man."

"Thank you, sir. I am happy to be of service to you all, you know, and you must not hesitate to say if there is anything you wish me to do for you."

~~~

"Alexander, I wish you to come with me this morning," Sir John said at breakfast the next day. "I want to inspect the work on those cottages."

"Yes, sir." His son had a wary look on his face. His father had spoken quite abruptly and it was clear that the boy was uncertain as to what might await him. They rode side by side, at first in silence, but little by little they fell into conversation about the estate.

"It's good to be away from the house for a couple of hours, is it not?" Sir John commented. The boy nodded.

"Come, we'll stop here and sit by the stream. It is time we talked."

Alexander dismounted obediently if apprehensively and took the place indicated. He apparently expected to receive a lecture, for he blurted, "I am sure I am sorry, sir, but it is not to be borne, you know."

"What is not to be borne?"

"Why, everything! There has never been such a dreadful summer. Jack thinks he is above us all since he went to Trinity, Kate has no time because she is either with Mamma or talking to Cook or Mrs Byrne, and now Helena as well. You all treat me the same as Emily, but I'm twelve now—I'm no longer a small child. And what about going to school? Who is going to arrange for that? Summer used to be so jolly, especially when Will was here, but this year is all different." His voice faltered and then in a completely altered tone he said, "Mamma is not getting better, is she?"

Sir John reached over and took the boy's hand. "No, son, she is not."

Alexander gulped. In a very small voice, he asked, "Is she going to die?"

Tears in his eyes, Sir John nodded.

With a sob, Alexander threw himself into his father's arms. For a long moment they clung together until the boy sat up and fumbled in his pocket for his handkerchief.

"I am sorry, Alex," Sir John said. "I should have talked to you sooner and not left you to muddle along by yourself. I think Emily is too young to realise what is happening and there is no need to distress her yet, but perhaps we should all sit together tonight after she has gone to bed and discuss how we shall go on for the next while."

"Will and Helena as well?"

"Yes."

"Would they look after us if something happened to you too?"

"I am sure they would," Sir John said firmly, "and there is your Aunt Cordelia also. You may be sure that you children will not be left to fend for yourselves if I should come a cropper at some fence, which I have no intention of doing."

Alexander glanced awkwardly at his father. "I tried not to think of it, but I was worried," he said simply, "and then I felt bad—"

"For even contemplating such a thing. I understand. It's as if thinking about it or, worse, talking about it, will somehow make it happen. But these matters are subject to Providence, not to our poor selves and it is left to us to make shift as best we can."

~~~

"You have a horse running in the Gold Cup at the Curragh on Saturday, sir," Will said to Sir John at dinner the following evening. "A fine animal indeed. What do you make of its chances?"

"Fair enough. It will depend on the ground on the day."

"Is that the race meeting the King will attend?" Helena enquired. "I understand it is to be a magnificent spectacle."

"As well it should be, for the Turf Club has had to raise by subscription some three thousand pounds to erect a new Royal Stand, the old Stand House being in such a poor state of repair it could in no way be considered suitable for His Majesty." Sir John laughed shortly. "Indeed, I do not know whether the club was more flattered or appalled when he expressed his desire to visit the Curragh races. Nor do I know how lasting an edifice the new stand may be, for it was constructed within twenty-one days."

"A remarkable achievement," Will commented.

"Aye, but I shall not attend. I don't wish to leave your mother for so long."

"Perhaps you could do so now that we are here," Helena said. "Is it far from Colduff?"

"Not too far, especially if you ride," Jack said eagerly. His father looked torn, as if he wished to go but felt he should not.

"You may safely leave Lady Malcolm in our care," Helena said. "Indeed, if Will and Jack were to accompany you, I assure you we four," she smiled at the other three children, "will cope admirably."

It was almost painful to see the look of expectation and hope on Jack's face.

"Do go, Papa," Kate urged. "It will be good for you to have a change of scene."

"What say you, Rastleigh?" Sir John asked. "I confess I should like to see my horse run."

"Why, if it can be accomplished in one day, sir, I see no reason why we should not go."

"And I? May I not go too?" Alexander cried. "Why must I always stay at home with the girls?"

"What do you think, sir?" Will asked his step-father. "Would the ride be too much for him?"

"I'm afraid it would," Sir John said, having given due consideration to the suggestion. "It is not that I would not like to have you with me, Alexander," he added, "for it would give me great satisfaction to show off my two sons, and my stepson of course," this last with a nod at Will. "But if we are to do it in one day we must ride hard. It will be a year or two before you are up to it."

It was clear that the boy was disappointed, but to his credit he managed to swallow his chagrin and mutter, "I understand, sir."

~~~

"Have you met the King?" Will asked Sir John as they rode cross-country on Saturday morning. "I should be happy to present you if the occasion arises, for I must pay my respects."

"I was presented to him many years ago, when he was still Prince of Wales. I daresay he will not remember."

Jack looked horrified. "Shall you present me as well, Will?"

Will nodded. "Yes indeed, for you are my brother are you not?"

"But how should I behave?" Jack blurted out. "I'm not used to kings and princes."

"Just make your best bow and don't turn your back on him. If he should speak to you, reply simply and directly, but do not attempt to change the subject. Follow my lead if you are unsure."

Arriving at the Curragh, they first went to check on Sir John's horse and then set off towards the new stand. It was a slow progress. Between neighbours and friends of Sir John, the Irish nobility and other members of the *ton* who had travelled because of the royal visit, Will found he recognised many of those present. Some of these expressed their surprise at his presence there, for he was not known to be a devotee of the turf. Not least among these was the King himself who, on catching sight of him in the viewing room exclaimed, "Why, Rastleigh, We did not expect to see you here."

Will bowed. "Your Majesty, I am in Ireland to visit my mother and her family. May I have the honour of presenting my step-father, Sir John Malcolm of Colduff, County Wicklow and my brother, Mr Malcolm? Sir John has a horse running in the race for the Gold Cup," he added.

Sir John and Jack bowed deeply.

"Malcolm, Malcolm," the King said. "Why, you are the villain who captured the charming Viscountess Hall from under all our noses. Lucky dog, eh!"

"I have that honour, your Majesty," Sir John said stiffly, bowing again.

"Pray give your lady Our compliments," the King said jovially and passed on to the next group.

"Hurry," Sir John said. "We must be down at the rails before the Gold cup starts."

"Would you not have a better view from here?" Jack asked.

His father shook his head. "To fully experience the exhilaration, you must be down there, where you have the sight, the sound, even the smell, and the sense of speed as they rush past, the cries of the jockeys urging on their mounts."

He was disappointed in his own runner, however, for although starting well, Black Velvet could not stay the pace and finished well at the back. Sir John was philosophical in defeat. "Well, next year, maybe. Now that we have met the King and watched our race, I think it is time for us to return home."

"Not without having something to eat," Jack protested.

"Just a pie and a glass of ale, then. Your mother will be looking for us."

~~~

Lady Malcolm did not appear to be overly flattered when the royal compliments were conveyed to her and later, when he and Helena were alone with her, Will said, "Mother, my Aunt Amelia mentioned that when you went to London for the Season after I went to school, you had been the recipient of some unwelcome attentions, and that your admirers included one of the royal dukes."

"Oh, pray do not remind me of that time, Will," she exclaimed. "I was never so miserable in all my life. Your grandparents had convinced me it was time I returned to town, but I was without the natural support of family and friends that makes a Season supportable."

She looked at Helena. "I was orphaned young and have no brothers and sisters. The uncle and aunt who brought me up did not move in fashionable circles and, once in London, the old Earl retreated to the Lords and his clubs while his wife rarely went to a ball. Dear Amelia did not come to town that year, for little Amelia was a sickly baby and she wanted to support Anne. It seemed to me that I was the chosen quarry of every rake and roué in the *ton* and I came to dread the evening round of balls and routs. When Sir John began to pay his addresses to me, honest and sincere as he was, he appeared to me as a knight from the tales of old."

She paused, gazing into the firelight. Although it was only the beginning of September, a fire burnt in her room day and night, for she felt the cold more and more. "I hope you do not think too harshly of me, Will. Sir John would have been happy for you to come with me and he would have been a father to you, but your grandfather would not hear of it."

"Do not distress yourself, Mother," Will kissed her cheek gently. "I understand."

"I would ask you, both of you," his mother continued, "to stand friend to your brothers and sisters, particularly if they should make their bows to London society. Kate bids fair to be very pretty in a year or so and I should not like her to suffer as I did."

Helena hastened to reassure her, "Pray do not worry, Mother. They will always be welcome in our home and we should be pleased to sponsor them into society. Is that not so, Will?"

"Of course. I shall talk to Sir John about it and I know my Walton cousins will welcome them as well. Their children are of similar ages. Indeed, Anne's Amelia will come out next year."

"That is a relief. I fear that my poor John may be overwhelmed by the demands of bringing out two daughters. They will be well-dowered too, and in some ways that will make it more difficult, for you do not wish them to fall foul of fortune-hunters."

Chapter Twelve

Will helped Helena dismount and looped the horses' reins over a branch. "We'll walk from here. This way, we go upstream."

About them leaves rustled, birds twittered and called, and the elusive tang of early autumn scented the air. After some time, the way grew steeper and narrower and the stream rushed faster and louder until they came to a steep, wooded gorge down which it spilled, white-flecked, in a series of cascades.

Helena's tired face lit up just as it had at Stonehenge and Will was pleased that he had taken advantage of the return of his sisters' governess, Miss Bowen, to suggest this excursion *à deux*. They had been confined to the house for some days due to a severe autumnal storm and it was good to escape, if only for a few hours.

"What a wonderful place," Helena said. "What is it called?"

"Poulaphuca. It means the hole of the Puca—some local daemon, I believe."

"I can well believe such a being at home here. I am so glad that they left their improvements below. It is pleasant to be able to stroll undisturbed, and the plantations are pretty, but I prefer this wilderness."

"I agree." Will drew her down onto a conveniently-sized boulder to sit within the circle of his arm.

She rested against him in the autumn sun. After some minutes, she sighed. "How wonderful to sit and just be."

"Yes. I thought I was used to this from my grandparents."

"I don't think you ever get used to it. Yet, somehow, it seems more natural when it is an old person who is mortally ill. Your Mamma is not yet fifty."

"I don't know what is worse—the sudden shock, as with my father, or this lingering."

"She is so brave. When I see her with the children, especially with Emily, I am in awe of her courage."

"I know. I can't tell you how grateful I am that you are here." His arm tightened. "When I imagine living through these weeks without you! We all benefit from it. You have a way of bringing calm and serenity to all with whom you come in contact. Sir John remarked upon it to me the other day."

She pinked, as if embarrassed by the compliment. "I'm glad to be of help to you and your family." She turned to look at him. "It is much better than sitting at home in the Dower House, wondering how you go on. That would have been truly dreadful."

~~~

With Miss Bowen's return, the children were occupied with their books for some hours daily, Jack and Alexander also applying themselves to their studies.

"Why must I read about stuffy Greeks and mouldy Romans," Alexander demanded that evening.

"It is part of a gentleman's education," his father replied.

"I must see if my step-father has anything more interesting than Caesar in his library," Will murmured to Helena.

"Surely Alexander is too young for that?"

"Why, I was thinking of the Odyssey," he replied in surprise. "What was on your mind?" He raised an eyebrow when she blushed. "Perhaps the *Ars Amatoria*? I gather your father had an extremely liberal opinion of what his daughters might read."

"He did, of course, and after he died, I was free to roam his library at will."

"And? What did you find?" He manoeuvred her to the window, turning their backs to the room. "Come, confess."

Helen blushed. "Well, they were talking about Aristophanes and that reminded me of *Lysistrata*."

"You are not planning to emulate her?" he asked, horrified.

"No, but," she paused and then said in a rush, "I have always wondered what was meant by *the position of the lioness-on-a-cheese-grater*."

Will looked down at his wife, his body tightening almost painfully. "Have you, now," he purred in her ear. "I think we need to further your knowledge of the classics. Immediately!" With that, and an indistinct murmur of explanation, he whisked her out of the parlour and up to their rooms, where he at once ensured that all doors were safely locked before advancing on her. "Now" he said, backing her towards their bed, "just remind me again what it was you wanted to know."

Later, sated, he pulled her into his arms. "You have the most deliciously unruly mind behind that calm, ladylike appearance."

Helena yawned and pillowed her head on his shoulder. "Do you mind? I usually keep my thoughts to myself, but with you—"

"Mind? On the contrary! I shall like to look at you at a ball or across the dinner table and know that only I will be privy to whatever wicked thoughts you may be hatching." His arm tightened around her and, exhausted, they both drifted into sleep.

~~~

The next time they visited Will's mother, Helena brought her sketch book.

Lady Malcolm was in alt as she turned the pages. "Now I can picture you and your family. And there are dear Amelia and Sir Humphrey. It is so long since we met and now, we shall not see one another again." Her smile dimmed. "Will, never assume you have all the time in the world or fall into the trap of constantly saying 'one day, I shall or I must.' If there is something you wish or need to do, do it as soon as possible. And this goes as much for pleasures as for duties. Sometimes we get so immersed in our obligations that we forget to cultivate our joys."

"I'll remember, Mother, I promise."

"Good. Now, I had Máire bring up some of my jewellery. It's over there on that tray. Would you bring it to me, please?"

When he had complied, she said, "Dearest Helena, I cannot tell you how happy your visit has made me. I have worried about Will. I think that he has often been lonely and I was afraid that he might get used to this and would become too remote like his grandfather, but I feel now I shall leave him in good hands. In the short time we have known each other, you have become like another daughter to me and I want you to have the jewellery that Will's father gave me. I hope you will think of me when you wear it. I have pieces from my parents as well as Sir John's gifts for Kate, Emily, and the boys' wives."

She opened a case to display a parure of tiara, necklace, earrings, bracelets and ring made of diamonds and sapphires. "This was Hall's wedding gift. Your eyes are darker than mine, but the sapphires should still go well with your colouring and, with the diamonds, they will be superb in your hair." She lifted a ruby bracelet. "This was a gift from the old Earl when Will was born. It is only right that his wife wears it, and these are other gifts from Hall. They are not family jewels—they are all still at Rastleigh, but are my own, and now are yours, as a gift from me to you and you in turn may dispose of them as you see fit."

Helena stared at the glittering array. How generous of her mother-in-law. There was something special about receiving the jewels this way, directly from her hand. She stooped to embrace the older woman. "Thank you, Mother. I shall wear them gladly as a reminder of you, and of these bitter-sweet weeks at Colduff. I hope that one day they will be worn by granddaughters who look like you."

Her mother-in-law's eyes filled with tears. "Think of me then."

Helena pressed her hand. "I promise you we will tell them about you."

"Your grandchildren will know you too, Mother," Will added gently. "Remember your portrait by Lawrence? It still hangs at Rastleigh."

Lady Malcolm was clearly pleased by this reminder. "I had forgotten that I was wearing the sapphire set when that likeness was taken. Now, Will, these miniatures of you and your father have stood on my dressing table all these years. Sir John understood—he never requested me to put them away. You should take them now, and here," she opened another box, "are some pieces that belonged to my father. Please select one so that you have a remembrance of my family as well. I do not know—it is all quite old-fashioned now, of course—but maybe there is something you will like."

Will, immensely touched by his mother's revelation that he and his father had never been out of her sight, looked carefully at the jewellery and chose a cravat pin set with a sapphire. "It will remind me of your eyes. Thank you, Mother."

"She feels her time is drawing close," Helena said sadly to Will when they were back in their sitting-room. "She wishes to order her affairs."

"Yes." He looked at the two miniatures. "She never forgot me."

"Did you think she had?" Helena asked, surprised.

"Sometimes I wondered, but at times I forgot her too, or at least she was not in the forefront of my mind."

"That is only natural, but love is a flower with deep roots. We do not love someone less when we are not in their presence. I'm sure she was always in your heart, and you in hers."

~~~

The periods when Lady Malcolm was awake and alert were now noticeably shorter. She had to be lifted to her day-bed and the close-stool, and a nurse had been engaged to assist Máire. She ate very little, although she still took tea with her family each evening. She no longer received callers except for one or two ladies, old friends in the neighbourhood, whom she had known since she came to Colduff as a bride. Sometimes they were accompanied by their husbands who sat with Sir John or rode out with him to inspect the harvest.

"It is all gathered in now," Sir John said one evening after his children had gone to bed, "and my poor Phoebe will be gathered soon into God's granary, as they say here." He stared into the flames, a glass of port in his hand.

"I must thank you, sir, for your care of my mother." Will felt awkward in broaching this subject but was uneasily aware that he had never really given his step-father his due. "She has but recently told me of the difficulties she encountered when she returned to society some years after my father's death."

"Society! Pah!" Sir John exploded. "A pack of rakes, wastrels and so-called ladies that claims for itself the designation of the *bons tons* and sets itself above God and all other men. They hounded my gentle Phoebe for sport, and she only a sweet, shy doe. It was an honour and a privilege for me to shelter her as best I could. The day she accepted my suit I was the happiest man alive."

"Indeed, she told us you seemed to her to be one of the knights in the tales of old," Helena said with a smile.

"Whatever about that," Sir John answered, clearly not displeased by this tribute, "I was happy to be able to take her away from a life that was truly distasteful to her. Her only sadness in leaving London was in being deprived of her son for so much of the year, but there was no talking to your grandfather. Well, he did his best for you according to his lights, I suppose, and he would be proud of you, I have no doubt, were he still alive. You have an earnest turn of mind and take your responsibilities seriously."

Will looked astounded at this accolade. "I was born to a position of great privilege," he said simply, "and feel it incumbent on me to strive for the good of all. I have been influenced by our old rector, Mr Graham who tutored me before I went to school and his son Stephen, who is now a member of parliament and works assiduously for reform."

"And an uphill struggle he has of it, I warrant," Sir John said. "Reform would not be necessary if there had not been such an abuse of privilege. And when something is achieved, it is always too little. How long did it take us to abolish the slave-trade? Years, if not decades. And yet slavery is still legal within the British Empire. Why? Because so many of the rich and powerful in our society continue to enslave men, women and children on their overseas estates in order to fund their excessive way of life at home.

"And look at Ireland," he continued. "The majority here supported King James who was defeated at the Boyne in 1690. Was there any attempt to heal the wounds? No. On the contrary they enacted law after law that could only serve to alienate further three quarters of the inhabitants of this country. A Catholic could not sit in parliament or vote in parliamentary elections, keep a school or send his children to be educated abroad, though of

158

course many ignored this last. And worse, if a son converted to the Anglican Church, he could supplant his father in the management and disposal of his property. Some similar restrictions applied to us dissenters too, of course. Without disowning our beliefs in the so-called sacramental test, we could not obtain military or public employment." Sir John sighed. "And when enlightened men achieve a change, they do not go far enough. Catholics now have the franchise such as it is but remain excluded from parliament."

Will was surprised by this vehemence but pleased to see Sir John distracted for the moment from his overriding concern for his wife.

"There are many loyal members of the Church of England who do not have the franchise," he said wryly. "The property restrictions together with the so-called rotten boroughs leave Parliament in the control of the élite."

"If only the Union had been accompanied by Catholic emancipation, as we had hoped. But here I am, riding my hobby-horse again. Perhaps the new king will do more for Ireland. He was greatly flattered by the warm welcome he received."

"I would not rely on it, sir. Especially when you consider that the Coronation Oath was considerably tightened compared with the one his father took. This was due to *the hydra of Catholic Emancipation having raised its head so high,* as one gentleman put it."

Sir John frowned. "That does not bode well for Ireland."

"If we are talking about the disadvantaged, do not forget women," Helena interjected. "We have no vote whatsoever. The most educated and intelligent woman is as naught in the eyes of the law once she is married. Her property becomes her husband's and she loses whatever voice she may once have had. It is no wonder that heiresses are so sought after by fortune hunters and wastrels."

"I have married a blue-stocking, I see. Well, it has its advantages, I suppose," Will said.

"You may be sure it has disadvantages as well, my lord, as you will find out if you continue to smirk at me in such an odious fashion."

"Peace!" He held up his hand, laughing. "In fact, I agree with you. Apart from natural justice, it makes women too vulnerable if they are completely at the mercy of their fathers and husbands. And that reminds me, sir," he turned to his step-father, "we have assured my mother of our support and assistance for my brothers and sisters should they ever require it. She was concerned that Kate may be the target of fortune-hunters when she makes her come-out. I should like to maintain my connection with Colduff and perhaps you will bring them to visit Rastleigh as well. I am ashamed that I never thought before to extend an invitation to you and your family. My only excuse is that without a wife I have not been given much to entertaining guests there."

"We should be honoured," Sir John said. "It has been on my mind to appoint you as guardian to my children should I meet with any mishap. This was one of Alexander's concerns—what if they lost father as well as mother? Should you have any objection, Rastleigh? I would value your promise to protect them."

"I pray it may never come to pass, but I should regard it as a sacred trust. You have my word on it," he added offering his hand to his step-father who clasped it strongly.

"My sincere thanks." Sir John smiled. "Jack was so proud when you presented him to His Majesty simply as your brother, with no quibble or roundaboutation."

"Why, how else should I have introduced him?" Will asked in surprise. "He is my mother's son. To deny him would be to deny her."

Chapter Thirteen

"It will not be long now," the doctor said quietly to Sir John, who waited with Will and Helena in the hushed library. Lady Malcolm had not left her bed for the last days and was refusing all nourishment except for some sips of barley water. She appeared to sleep all the time. "See if you can get her to take the medicine and keep her comfortable."

"How long does she have?"

"It is always hard to say, but I think not more than forty-eight hours. You must endeavour to keep up your strength, sir. I know you will not feel like eating, but it your duty to stay strong, also for your children. You may send for me at any time."

After he had left, the three left behind looked at one another.

"No matter how prepared you think you are, it always comes as a shock," Helena said softly.

"What am I to say to the children?" Sir John's voice broke on the question.

"Tell them that the doctor has said that their Mamma will soon go to God. The older three know how it stands with her, but it is still a blow when the time comes."

"Should I still let them go to her room?"

"If they wish, but I would not compel them. They may want to say goodbye to her and should they choose to sit with her for some time, I would permit it, but one of us three should also be there. To watch alone would be too great a burden for a young person. Some of us should also sit with them at mealtimes. Doctor White is right about the need for us to keep up our strength."

The slow hours dragged interminably. Will and Helena sat in turn with Sir John and his lady; he had pulled a chair up to the bed and spent most of his time there, her small hand enclosed in his big one. The older children looked in and out and Miss Bowen brought Emily to wish her mother a last good-night. "She will sleep now and wake up in Heaven," she said quietly.

"Good night, Mamma, and sleep well," the little girl whispered, leaning over from where she was held in Will's arms to kiss her mother. She then looked at her father. "But you will not go to God, Papa?" she asked anxiously.

With a strained smile he got up to take her from Will. "Not for many, many years, Sweetheart. Not until you are a grown-up lady with children of your own, who will call me Grandpapa." He kissed her brow. "Good night, my pet. Shall I carry you to your room?"

She nodded and he left with her, Will moving to his seat and taking his mother's hand so that she did not miss the loving clasp. Helena came in a few minutes later.

"Sir John is sitting with the children; I have ordered some supper for him. Will you stay here later so that he can stretch out on the bed in the dressing-room for a few hours? You can wake him if necessary."

He nodded and reaching out his other hand pulled her to him so that he could rest his head against her breast. Her arms enfolded him and he felt her stroke his hair.

The following morning, about mid-day, surrounded by her family, Phoebe, Lady Malcolm, exhaled her final breath. After some minutes, her husband kissed her forehead and then her hand which he tenderly laid on her breast. He looked down at her for a moment and, his voice breaking, began to recite the twenty-third psalm.

"The Lord is my Shepherd, I shall not want, He maketh me to lie down in green pastures, He leadeth me beside the still waters."

One by one they joined in, at times faltering, but finishing together.

"Surely goodness and mercy shall follow me all the days of my life and I will dwell in the house of the Lord forever."

They sat with her awhile, weeping quietly but taking comfort from one another until at last Helena said gently, "Let Máire and me tend to her one last time. You may come back soon."

~~~

Two days later a much-loved wife and mother was laid to rest in the old churchyard. Her husband and three sons accompanied her on her last journey. Her daughters and daughter-in-law gathered together with Sir John's sister Mrs Harvey, Miss Bowen and the other women of the household to read the funeral service, taking turns to read as they so often had in happier times.

"Poor Mamma." Kate dried her eyes. "She suffered so much."

"Now she feels no more pain," Helena comforted her. "She is at peace."

Soon the gentlemen returned, accompanied by neighbours who had also paid their last respects. Supported by Helena and her aunt, Kate took her first shaky steps in her new role as the lady of the house. She was dignified and reserved in her black dress, and, with her hair up, looked older than her years. Will noticed more than one interested masculine glance cast in her direction. He drew Helena aside. "I think you and the other ladies could withdraw now. I shall explain to Sir John."

~~~

"Thank you, Miss Kate." Mrs Byrne, the housekeeper at Colduff, finished jotting down the instructions for the day's meals. "And what about after dinner? Will the family take tea together as usual? Where should we serve it?"

Kate looked flustered and glanced at Helena who, as had become her habit, sat to one side, quietly supportive of her sister-in-law as she had been since they had arrived at Colduff.

"Perhaps we should ask your father?" she suggested.

"Oh, Helena, would you talk to him?" Kate pleaded. "He is so sad and I don't know how to raise such things with him. He keeps to the library and will see nobody."

"It is understandable. Picking up the threads of life after bereavement is no easy matter." She looked at the housekeeper. "We shall ascertain Sir John's wishes and let you know, Mrs Byrne."

"Thank you, Miss Kate, my lady."

"What was the custom before your Mamma became ill?" Helena asked Kate when they were alone.

"I'm not really sure. Only Jack was used to dining with our parents when he was at home from Trinity. The rest of us took our meals in the nursery although they had said that once I reached my sixteenth birthday, I would join them. But by then Mamma could no longer leave her room and Papa decided we should all dine with him, even Emily, and later take tea with Mamma."

"Let us see what he wishes to do now."

Inwardly apprehensive, Helena tapped on the library door. After waiting a moment, she opened it slowly. Sir John sat at his desk, staring unseeing at the papers spread on it.

"May I have a word, Sir John?"

"Lady Rastleigh, of course." He gestured to a comfortable chair beside the fire. "Please be seated."

She obeyed and waited for him to take the chair opposite her. "What may I do for you, ma'am?"

"It's more—I do not wish to interfere—"

"You could not," he said simply. "You have been such a support these last weeks. Phoebe greatly valued your presence, as I do myself."

"I am so happy to have known her and most grateful to you all for making a stranger welcome at such a sad time."

He shook his head. "Rastleigh's wife could only be a stranger to us, if she wished to be. From the beginning, you opened your arms to us, and especially to the children."

"It is easy to love them."

"Yes." He sighed. "They need me now more than ever, but—" he broke off.

"It is hard to find the way back to everyday life, is it not?"

"That's it. It cannot be as it was before, and we have no notion of what it should be. We teeter on the brink of a vast pit, yet must cross it."

"At the beginning, all we can is skirt it, I think; deal with the small things that can or must be done. For example, Kate tells me that it is only recently that they all dine with you and that you take tea together. Do you wish that to continue?"

"Yes, of course." He suddenly looked broken-hearted. "But where? We used to meet in Phoebe's room for tea."

"Perhaps the ladies could withdraw while you remain with the gentlemen over a glass of port? Even if Alexander is too young for port, I am sure he would enjoy being allowed to remain with you and his brothers. You can then join the ladies for tea in the drawing-room. It will be good experience for Kate as well, for next year she will probably start to go out in society."

Sir John smiled wanly. "It is hard to think of her as being old enough for it, but she has had to grow up quickly this year."

"Some time ago, you said you would send the girls and Miss Bowen to your sister for the winter and take a house in town yourself. Do the children and the servants know of your intention?"

"No. I asked my sister to say nothing. She suggested taking Kate and Emily with her when they left, but I could not part with them so soon."

"And the boys? They risk falling behind if they do not soon resume their studies."

"That is true. What of you and Rastleigh? How long do you stay with us?"

"We haven't really discussed it yet."

Sir John got up and rang the bell. "Request his lordship to join us at his convenience," he said to the footman. "And bring some coffee." While they waited, he looked over at Helena. "I think you are no stranger to grief, ma'am. You have suffered loss yourself, if I may be so bold as to ask?"

"Yes."

"As did my Phoebe. Should I have less courage than she did? She will show me the way."

When Will entered the room a few minutes later, he found his step-father and his wife sitting quietly at either side of the fire. He could not have explained why, but he felt the miasma of despair that had surrounded Sir John had thinned a little.

"Ah, Rastleigh. We were just wondering what your plans are. How long do you stay here? Your wife has very properly reminded me that we must pick up the threads of life again."

"We should not delay here much longer. I have just read that Parliament was prorogued again until 29 November and I must spend some time at Rastleigh before then."

"How will you explain to Kate and Emily that they are to go to their aunt?" Helena asked. "Jack and Alexander expect to leave, but I am concerned that the girls might feel they are being sent away because you do not want them here."

"On the contrary, it is out of concern for them. Phoebe was anxious that we should not spend a gloomy winter here, just the three of us. The boys will be in Dublin and if I take a house there, Jack may visit me and we will not be too far from Alexander. My sister lives some ten miles north of Dublin and I plan to see my daughters frequently. They will not be abandoned."

"If you put it to them like that, I am sure they will understand. And Miss Bowen will be with them. They are considerably attached to her, I think."

"She has been a tower of strength to us this year. She was reluctant to take her usual holiday in August, but Phoebe insisted. We had not thought she would decline so rapidly."

"They will need some time to get used to the idea," Helena said.

"Supposing we all depart a se'ennight hence," Will suggested. "We could travel together until we meet the road to Dunleary; perhaps take a nuncheon at the inn before we part."

~~~

"I must send word to the yacht to make ready for our departure, and to the Castle to prepare for our arrival," Will said, as he and Helena strolled through a copse that was alight with autumn colours. "It has been a sad but not unrewarding sojourn here. I felt I was closer to my mother and brothers and sisters than ever before. I don't know why, but she spoke much more frankly about the past than she had previously. Maybe seeing me married revived old memories."

"She was a fortunate woman, for she made two happy marriages. Sir John was reminded that she too had suffered bereavement when we were talking earlier. He said that she would show him the way forward."

"I sincerely hope we shall only have the one marriage, and that a long one," he said, smiling down at her.

"If God wills." She slipped her hand into the crook of his arm. Richard had died before they could marry, of course, but they would have been happy together. She had not expected this second chance, but she was glad she had not rejected Will's proposal.

The days on the yacht as well as this time with Will's family had provided an opportunity for them to get to know each other more privately without the demands that would otherwise be made of the Countess of Rastleigh. But the respite was almost over and now she must take on all the responsibilities of her new role. Did the fact that the previous countess died a decade ago make it easier or harder? Had Will's households become used to being bachelor establishments? How would they react to having a new mistress suddenly sprung upon them?

"Tell me more about Rastleigh," she said to Will, "the people, I mean."

"The tenants, whether farmers, shopkeepers or tradesmen— they would simply say they are Rastleigh people; some families are there as long as we are. They are rooted in Rastleigh soil, good men and women, hard workers who also know how to celebrate. You will like them, I think."

"And the servants?"

"Generally, we like to employ people from the estate, but after I inherited, I sent down the butler and housekeeper from London."

"And they accepted such a move? I should have thought that London servants would find the country too slow."

He shrugged. "They were very set in their ways. I wanted someone younger, more flexible but I did not wish to turn them off—times were bad, after the war, if you remember. They were not young, but too young to pension off. This seemed a neat solution, especially as the previous butler and housekeeper, a married couple, wanted to retire."

"How did they settle in?"

"Well enough, I suppose. I don't spend a lot of time there—at most, two months in the year, compared with six months in London."

Helena wondered what they felt about the advent of an unknown mistress, but they must have expected their master to marry someday. At least she need not worry about ill-trained servants, she thought as they returned to the house.

~~~

"When shall we see you again, Will? Will you come again next year as usual?" Alexander broke the despondent silence after dinner.

"It's too soon to say." Will hoped that Helena might not be in a condition to travel the following year, or better yet, she might be occupied with a new baby.

Kate looked dismayed. "How will you write to us? We shall not be here—we shan't even be together."

"Write to you?"

"Yes, do say you will continue to do so. Mamma was always used to read your letters to us and we enjoyed them enormously."

Alexander laughed. "Especially the one about the coronation and the man throwing the capon up to his family. You can't write to us, for we'll all be in different places," he added mournfully.

"Stop pestering your brother," Sir John said.

"We can do it another way," Will decided. "You may each of you write to me and if you give me your address, I'll engage to answer any letter I receive."

"May we write to you as well, Helena?" Kate asked shyly. "I liked having an older sister."

"Of course you may, and if we are unable to visit you next year, you might like to come to us at Rastleigh. Will has already spoken to your father about it."

The prospect of this cheered them up to such an extent that Alexander proposed a final *table à toupie* tournament. "We shall have two teams and play three rounds of four games each," he announced. "Let's draw lots for teams."

It was a close-run thing, with Helena, Sir John, Miss Bowen and Alexander just defeating Will, Jack, Kate and Emily. To everyone's surprise, the governess demonstrated a cunning flick of the wrist that sent the top spinning cleverly down the board.

"I used to play a similar game with my brothers," she said in response to their applause, "only we called it Devil among the Tailors. But *table à toupie* is a much more genteel name. Now it is time for Emily to go to bed, for we have a long day tomorrow. Kate, you will retire at nine o'clock, if you please, and Alexander too."

"Father, Will, should you like a game of billiards?" Jack asked hopefully.

"Go and play, Will," Helena said. "I'll go up with Kate and Alexander."

"May I not come and play until bedtime?" Alexander said and on receiving permission left with his father and brothers.

"You know, Kate," Helena said when the door had closed behind them, "you have a good friend in Miss Bowen and I am sure you will deal famously with your aunt. But should there ever be something that is causing you concern, you may write to me about it at any time. Apart from your usual letters, I mean, for I shall look forward to hearing how you are all getting on."

"And you must tell me all about Rastleigh and your life in London, for I am sure you will see things differently to Will."

"You mean he doesn't report on the modish styles and entertainments?" Helena's mock amazement had her sister-in-law in giggles. "I shall try to do better."

When Will came to bed, having shared a last decanter of port with his step-father and brother, he found his wife sleeping peacefully. She automatically moved to make room for him and as he turned on his side to put his arm around her, he thought rather muzzily how pleasant it was not to have to seek out a lonely bed.

~~~

In Rastleigh Castle, the butler carefully opened the latest issue of *The London Magazine* at the listing of recent marriages. "'William Henry, Earl of Rastleigh to Miss Helena Dorothea Swift, elder daughter of the late Sir Thomas Augustus Swift'," he read. "Pray hand me the Baronetage, Mrs Miller."

Silence reigned in the cosy parlour as he turned the pages, peering through silver spectacles until he found the entry on Swift of Swift Hall in the County of Wiltshire. This he read carefully, then removed his eye-glasses and looked across the hearth to where his companion had drawn up her armchair at just the right distance to the fire that she could warm her toes without scorching her slippers.

"A country Miss of five and twenty."

The housekeeper shook her head, with a disapproving "Tsk, tsk. Why, she must have been at her last prayers. When I think, Mr Jenkins, that he could have looked as high as he liked, barring a royal princess. A duke's daughter, certainly."

"Be that as it may, Mrs Miller, this is better for us. Who knows what demands and requirements such a lady might have? As it is, we need not worry."

"That is true, Mr Jenkins. She will be so grateful to have caught him, that she'll be more than happy to leave things as they are."

The butler carefully smoothed the magazine and placed it on a silver tray, then pulled the bell-cord.

"Take this to Dr Thornton," he instructed the footman who answered the summons.

"And tell Cook to prepare one of her possets," Mrs Miller added. "There is a chill in the air this evening."

Book 3

Chapter Fourteen

Helena stretched luxuriously, unimpeded by a warm body next to her. Will must have slipped out earlier. Sunlight gleamed through her closed eyelids. It must be quite late. The cabin door opened quietly and Lennard peeped in.

"Good morning, my lady. His lordship said to let you sleep. Will you take breakfast here or in the day-cabin?"

"In the day-cabin." Helena threw back the bed-clothes and got up, taking a minute to find her balance as the yacht ploughed through the waves. They must be making good headway, as Will would say. "What time is it?"

"Ten o'clock, my lady."

"Good heavens! Come, help me dress quickly."

Will's face lit up when he saw her. "Good morning, Helena. I hope you are you feeling more the thing. You have been run ragged these past weeks."

"It is a long time since I slept the clock round, but I feel much better for it. Some tea and toast and I'll be as right as rain."

"You cannot but rest today and for most of tomorrow. I hope you won't find it too dull."

She laughed. "I have plenty to keep me occupied. You may also tell me more about Rastleigh and its people."

"I see you are already turning your mind to the next task ahead, but not today. Today we shall be lazy and indulge ourselves in idleness. I didn't like to see you so weary yesterday. Today is for you to recover in idleness. Or I can read to you, if you prefer. Here we have John Keats's verses and Byron's Don Juan. It is too cool to stay on deck for long, but we can take a turn about it if you wish."

The morning passed peacefully. There was something particularly soothing about the rhythm of the yacht and, after some time, Helena was embarrassed to find her eyes closing again.

"You need a nap," Will said and without further ado took her to their cabin. "Lie down for an hour."

"What will you do?" she asked drowsily.

"I'm going to take the helm for a while. I need to do something." He picked up a shawl and spread it over her, stooping to kiss her briefly before he left.

"I do not know why I am so tired," Helena said some two hours later. "You are not so affected."

"On the contrary, I crave movement. I'm used to at least two hours vigorous exercise each day, even when I am in London. At Rastleigh I spend a good part of the day on horseback. When I'm in town I ride before breakfast and frequently go afterwards to Angelo's or Gentleman Jackson for a bout. I find I need it to keep my head clear. The days at Colduff were too quiet for me in that respect. If we did go riding, it was not for long. Mostly I had Jack and Alexander with me, sometimes the girls as well. If we walked, it was the same. But otherwise there was little enough to occupy me."

He looked at her as she leaned on the railing beside him. "It was different for you, I think. You seemed always to be on the alert in case something needed to be addressed. You noticed when Kate was unwell or Sir John needed distraction. You helped him deal with Alexander. To a large extent you took responsibility for the household after we arrived and we all brought our problems to you. There was a general expectation that you would manage things, soothe fraying tempers, lift despondent spirits, ensure that, as my mother faded, the family adapted its routines so that she would not be distressed or overwhelmed by us. In military terms, you were always on duty and now the campaign is over you need to recoup your strength."

"I suppose you're right," she said thoughtfully. "I hadn't looked at it like that. I do seem to take charge in such circumstances. Maybe I should not," she added doubtfully.

"No, that is not what I meant. It is more that it is your nature to help if you perceive a need. And you are so calm and competent that people turn to you with relief. But you are not a busy-body and you're not officious. Such persons make a great stir and seem to exist in a sort of whirlwind, issuing instructions on all sides but really achieving very little." He smiled down at her. "Both Mother and Sir John mentioned to me how much they valued your kindness and thoughtfulness, and told me that I was most fortunate in my choice of wife. Kate is delighted to have an elder sister and Jack is half in love with you, I think."

"Oh no," she protested.

"It is just calf-love and will do him no harm," he said callously. "Indeed, I hope it may inoculate him against the charms of silly girls who do not have two thoughts in their head to rub together."

"You are terribly harsh," she said, laughing.

"I am not, I assure you. At least he is only heir to a baronetcy, not an earldom, although Colduff is a comfortable estate."

She stared at him. "Was it really so difficult for you when you came on the town?"

"I was one of the biggest prizes on the marriage-mart. I quickly learnt that any attention was much more likely meant for the future Earl rather than for Will Hall. You have met Stephen Graham. He is just as personable, just as intelligent as I. We share the same interests. However, at that time no one could foresee that he would receive a generous legacy from his godfather and become a wealthy member of parliament. It is not that people were impolite, but they didn't seek out his company, parade their daughters in front of him, hint that he might like to take them driving—you know the sort of thing. He was simply another young man new on the town. I envied him, because he was at liberty to invite a young lady to stand up with him without her mother preening herself on the fact that her daughter had caught his eye." He snorted. "My grandfather always pushed me to marry—I could have any girl I wished, he said—I had only to throw the handkerchief. Should I marry, I wanted a wife I could talk to, but it was impossible to converse with any female for longer than the briefest exchange of courtesies without subjecting her to gossip, and I was wary of raising expectations that I might not wish to fulfil."

"I never thought of it from the gentleman's perspective," Helena admitted. "A young lady must always wait for the gentleman to signal his interest."

"That is what the rules say and how a proper young lady behaves, but believe me there are plenty of less proper ones, or ones who are, shall we say, better schooled in tactics, who employ diverse arts to gain an unwitting or even unwilling gentleman's attention. I have suffered the whole gamut, from the full-frontal assault via her Mamma claiming an acquaintanceship and then sighing that her daughter just happens to be free for this dance, to the more subtle flirtatious glances and dropped fans. Not to mention the more blatant girls who suggest a turn on the terrace or try to arrange to be found together in a secluded room.

"And then there are the ones who agree with everything you say, even if you contradict yourself three times within five minutes." He fluttered his eyelashes and simpered, "Yes, my lord; no, my lord; indeed, my lord; I am quite of your opinion, my lord."

She laughed. "I can just picture you under siege. But they are no worse than the flirts, rakes and fortune-hunters who make up to young women and in fact do a great deal less harm."

"There are plenty of fortune-hunting women about too."

"That's true, but you must remember that there are not many ways a young lady may earn her living reputably—really only as a governess or a companion. And their lot is not always easy, for they frequently fall victim to unscrupulous gentlemen who think they are fair game. A man may be forgiven, or even applauded, for an indiscretion that ruins his female partner, even if she in no way consented to his attentions.

"In one thing we agree," Helena went on. "It is distressing to be sought not for oneself but for what one may bring the other person, in particular when the suitor has given no thought as to what he or she might offer in exchange. That, I think, is at the bottom of your argument; that too often the suitor behaves like a child in a shop—I want one of those, be it a husband, a title, a fortune, birth or beauty and the possessors of the desired qualities are interchangeable. If they do not succeed with the first, they move on to the next with nary a backward glance."

"That's it. They have made completely impersonal what should be the most personal thing in our lives."

"Yes, and while at the time they might not know what they are sacrificing, you have only to look at the number of couples who live separate lives once the all-important heir is born to perceive that many later realise what a poor bargain they have made."

He turned to her suddenly. "Don't let us be like that, Helena. I know we are no Romeo and Juliet, but there is something real and personal between us and we must cherish it and let it grow."

Richard's image flashed before her inward eye. She pushed it away. "I should like to try," she said to her husband and lifted her face for his kiss as his arms came round her.

~~~

"Come, I want to share with you one of my greatest delights," Will said after dinner, picking up a folded blanket. On deck, he moved a chair so that they had an unimpeded view of the sky and sat, tugging Helena onto his lap and tucking the blanket around them both. "Look up. I never tire of nights such as this."

High above them, myriads of stars flowed in a pale river of light across a vast expanse of night-blue sky.

"How beautiful," she whispered.

"The Milky Way."

He settled her against him, holding her close as they were rocked by the waves. It was a clear night with the slightest hint of frost in the air, just enough to make the nose tingle. The sounds of the water and the sails blended and faded, soothing their tired spirits and hushing the night. Helena felt she was no longer on the surface of the earth, but inside an infinite orb that extended far beyond the realms of imagination. She might have drifted away through the stars had Will not anchored her. She didn't know how long they sat there speechless. It was as if they had stepped out of time.

"Come," he murmured, setting her gently on her feet. He led her silently to the cabin and, without breaking the spell, swiftly removed their clothes and laid her on the bed. His touch was soft and tender, their need rose slowly and when he slipped into her, he lay motionless, embracing her closely. "Don't move," he whispered. "Let the sea do the work."

Helena felt the undulation bring him near and then away. Now and again a stronger swell pulled him deeper inside her and she tightened around him. The incessant languorous, movement of the water heightened the building tension by unexpected quickenings of pace, leading sometimes to a jerky drop that drove them even closer together. It became more and more difficult not to take over but just to respond to the boat as it rode the waters. Suddenly a larger wave lifted the yacht and held it poised for a moment before falling into the trough. They fell with it into long moments of bliss.

Chapter Fifteen

Helena appeared at breakfast in a dark grey travelling gown trimmed with black ribbon, its dullness barely relieved by small frills of white lace at her throat and wrists. Catching Will's surprised glance, she said, "I should not wish to show any disrespect to your mother by arriving at her former home without displaying some aspect of mourning. She was Viscountess Hall for over ten years, after all."

"You think of everything," he said admiringly.

"I must thank my mother and Lennard for this, for they packed some of the gowns I wore after my father died and Lennard made them over to suit the current styles while we were in Colduff. They will do until I can order some new ones."

"You mean to observe the usual mourning period then?"

"Don't you? I came to like and admire your mother and regret that she will no longer be in our lives. You will presumably place notices of her death in the journals."

"I hadn't thought of it," he said, startled. "But I must do so, of course." He looked at her. "Pray do not think harshly of me, it is not that I don't mourn her—she hasn't been a part of my life here for so many years. When we left Dunleary, in my heart of hearts I believed her to be still at Colduff, as she has always been." He seemed quite stricken, as if the loss of his mother had suddenly become real to him again.

What strange tricks the mind plays on us, Helena thought as she put her hand on his. "She will always live in your heart and in your memories."

He turned his hand to grip hers. "I shall send the notices tomorrow. Sir John only placed them in the Irish newspapers. Thank you. I must talk to Emmett about a mourning band for my arm."

"Lennard has plenty of ribbon, if he has nothing to hand."

Later he came to join her at the railing as she admired the passing scenery. They had rounded Land's End during the night and were now following the coast. "We shall put in at Weymouth—the carriages will meet us there. It is about an hour to Rastleigh."

"I believe Weymouth became quite fashionable under the old King."

"Yes, he liked to go there for the sea-bathing. There are some pretty little shops—I think you will like them."

~~~

Will leaned forward to peer out of the window of the travelling chariot. "It won't be long now until we reach the East Gate."

As he spoke the horses slowed and then they were passing a neat gate lodge, the keeper and his wife bowing and curtseying as they passed. "I'll take you to meet them one day soon."

They were going down an incline now, past wooded slopes and soon slowed again to cross a bridge over a stream. Will knocked to have the coachman pull up, then opened the door and urged Helena to stand on the step.

"Look there." He pointed to where crenellated walls and towers throned above the tree-tops.

Her eyes widened. "Is that the Castle? It looks very forbidding, like an ancient fortress."

"It was one, once. I suppose that is why it is quite small compared with more modern noble seats. We are constrained by the walls and the former moat, as well as the geographic situation. You'll see."

Soon they were out of the woods, driving uphill again, past well-tended, yellow-leaved orchards bare of fruit. Another turn, and they were on a wide avenue leading to a drawbridge and massive gatehouse. They drove under the arched entrance, emerged from the momentary darkness into a big, open space and continued up a central drive lined with neatly clipped box hedges that bordered geometrically laid out flower beds. Beyond these were buildings in the style of a hundred years ago. These must be the new wings Will had spoken of.

The carriage turned and stopped at the steps leading up to the front door of the centre building. Once Helena had stepped down, Will gently turned her to face the people that stood rigidly on the steps, men lined up on one side, women on the other.

"My lady, welcome to my home, which is now yours," he said, then raised his voice to proclaim, "I give you your new mistress, Helena, Countess of Rastleigh."

After a ripple of bows and curtsies, a plump, silver-haired man stepped forward. "My lord, my lady, may I offer our sincere congratulations on your nuptials and our good wishes for your future happiness."

His unctuous tones reminded Helena forcibly of the bishop on their wedding day and she had to bite the inside of her cheek to stop a laugh escaping.

"Thank you." Will turned to Helena. "May I present our butler, Jenkins?"

Helena gave her hand to the butler, who in turn introduced Mrs Miller, the housekeeper and together they presented the rest of the servants—he the men and she the women—in strict order of their position within the household. After she had greeted the scullery-maid, Will led her into the Castle while the servants silently filed down the steps and disappeared through a side door below.

What a stiff little ceremony she thought, but maybe things were done more formally at a noble seat. She remembered the beaming faces, the heartfelt congratulations and the flowers for the bride when Gus had brought Rosamund home to Swift Hall after their wedding trip. This reminded her more of a military parade.

A wide passage ran parallel to the front of the castle, apparently linking the two wings.

"This way." Will opened a large heavy oak door set in the wall opposite the entrance, a stone wall that looked as if it was the original exterior of the Keep. "The Great Hall."

Helena turned slowly, taking it all in. The room extended the full depth of the building and was so high that a man could comfortably stand on the elevated gallery at one end. Opposite it was a raised platform on which stood a table that would easily seat twelve. The high table, Helena thought, eyeing the two intricately carved throne-like chairs placed in the centre, against the wall. A large bay window admitted a diffused light through its small diamond-shaped panes; opposite it an elaborately carved overmantel sheltered an immense fireplace that was large enough to roast an ox, she thought fancifully. Heavy pewter candlesticks on the table and sideboards were the only ornaments.

Will caught her eye and laughed. "You look—"

"As if I have strayed into one of Mrs Radcliffe's romances," she supplied. "I have no doubt that if I open that," she pointed towards an arched door beside the dais, "I shall see a mad monk telling his beads as he brews a hideous potion."

"No," he said solemnly, "we have no wandering clerics, but there are some who claim to have seen a headless knight tumbling down from the gallery there. His head is thrown after him and he scoops it up and saunters out of the main door." He took her in his arms. "Never fear, my lady, I shall protect you though it cost me my life."

"My gallant saviour!" She swooned artistically and then gasped as he bent her back over his arm and kissed her deeply.

"Aye, my fine beauty. You might have escaped the dreaded knight but who will rescue you from the Wicked Earl? 'Twas he who decapitated the knight with one sweep of his sword when he found him in a tryst with the Countess."

"The monk is no doubt brewing his potion at the Countess's command so that she may have her revenge," Helena countered as her husband straightened up and, keeping his arm about her, led her to the arched door.

"I thought it fitting to bring you into the Great Hall first, but, apart from the library, we do not use the old part of the Castle anymore. I'll show you round it tomorrow." He hesitated. "For the moment we shall be in the wing my parents used—I have not made any changes since my grandfather died." He looked at her almost despairingly. "I didn't know where to start or even what I wanted. I thought we could use those rooms for now—they are the most recently renovated and I have lived in that wing all my life. Once you have found your way around the place, I hope you will make any changes you wish."

Although this was a very proper offer to a new bride, one that recognised that she was now mistress of the Castle, Helena wished he had allowed her time to familiarise herself with the Castle before making such a thinly disguised demand.

They passed through a narrow corridor and up a curved flight of stairs to a landing where he opened a door that led into a wide portrait gallery. "These galleries connect the new wings with the old. We use the one on the other side as a music room, but no one plays there now."

Helena looked with interest at the faces of past generations of Rastleighs as they passed. "Where is the Lawrence portrait of your mother?"

"In the drawing-room in our wing. There's a matching portrait of my father. She insisted that if she had to endure the tedium of sitting, he must as well. I believe they would only sit together and poor Lawrence must go from one easel to the other."

"I wonder why he did not just paint both of them on one canvas."

"My grandfather wouldn't have that. He insisted that they be painted individually as befitted the future earl and countess."

They had now reached the end of the gallery and went through another door to a spacious landing. Will ushered her into a pretty sitting-room decorated in blue and cream. Opening a connecting door, he said, "Your bedroom is here and," he pointed to a door on the opposite wall, "that leads to your dressing room."

The decoration and furnishings were old-fashioned but Helena could see how they would have suited her mother-in-law's fair prettiness.

"I hope you feel comfortable here for the moment," he said. "My rooms are opposite, but I should like it if we continue to share a bed. I think mine would feel very lonely without you now." As he spoke, he took her in his arms again.

He looks worried, she thought, nothing like as carefree as he was on the yacht. She reached up to put her hand on his cheek. "I would be lonely too," she said softly, "besides, who would protect me from the headless knight?"

He lifted her off her feet and swung her round, suddenly light-hearted. "So you will take your chances with the Wicked Earl?"

~~~

When her husband entered her dressing-room an hour later, Lennard was putting the last touches to her mistress's hair. It was piled on the top of her head, held in place by pearl combs. More pearls encircled her neck and her wrists. She smiled at him in the mirror as Lennard curtsied and withdrew.

"You look and smell delicious," he said, bending to kiss the nape of her neck. "What is that tempting fragrance?"

"Lily of the valley."

"My lady." He offered her his arm. Catching her stern glance, he added, "You must allow me to enjoy the novelty of having my countess under my roof."

"Do I get a dispensation too, my lord?"

"Absolutely not. You may defer paying your forfeit until later, however."

In the dining room, a number of dishes had been arranged on a table where twelve people might be seated comfortably. Two places had been set, one at either end.

"This will not do," Will said. "Set for her ladyship at my right." While the footmen laid the table anew under the butler's leaden supervision, he murmured to Helena. "Forgive me for keeping you waiting, but I have no wish to spend our meals shouting at one another."

"Nor I." She looked out the window. "Each wing seems to function as a separate use. They even have their own front doors."

"It is perhaps unusual, but it would be too awkward to have to go through the Castle itself whenever you wished to go from one wing to the other. In bad weather, of course, we do."

"And the servants?"

"There is another passage on the ground floor. The Great Hall is actually on the first floor of the keep. Originally the guard room and the armoury were below it, and the men-at-arms slept there. There were other buildings where the wings are now; judging by old drawings, rooms were built on higgledy-piggledy over the centuries."

"If you please, my lord."

Will looked up at the butler's comment. "Ah, we are served. No, not that chair for her ladyship, Jenkins. The countess's chair."

A footman immediately brought the armchair from the head of the table and set it at Helena's place, holding it while she sat.

Will inspected the dishes set before them. "Excellent. My favourite lobster pie. And here is chestnut soup with pigeon. And what have we there?"

"Crème Dubarry, my lord."

"Which would you prefer, my dear?"

"The crème Dubarry, if you please."

"You will take a glass of port with me, I hope," Will said an hour later, as the table was cleared of all but a bowl of walnuts. At her smiling nod he said, "That will be all, Jenkins."

"Please convey my compliments and thanks to Hope," Helena added as the butler departed, followed by the footmen.

Will raised Helena's hand to his lips. "All through dinner I have been thinking how beautiful you are." He touched one of her combs. "Your hair was made for pearls. All evening I have wanted to see what would happen if I were to remove these."

"You may find out later, sir," she answered sedately. "They were left to me by my grandmother—my colouring comes from her. It must run in her family, for the pearls are quite famous, I believe. She left them to me, Mamma thinks, because I was the one who looked like her. That reminds me; is there somewhere secure I may put them and the jewels your mother gave me?"

"I think there is a strongbox in your bedroom for your personal use. You will not wish to have to come to me if you wish to change a necklace." He smiled at her. "I haven't forgotten that I haven't given you a wedding gift, but as I was unable to present it in a timely fashion I should prefer to wait until I know you better and can find exactly the right thing for you."

Helena glanced at him in surprise. "You mustn't feel you should give me anything," she protested.

"I don't feel I should, I want to. But what I really want now is to find out how well those combs hold your hair and to see you clad just in your hair and your pearls."

"Will!" She blushed profusely at this suggestion.

He kissed the tip of her nose. "You have a deferred forfeit to pay, remember?"

Some two hours later Helena stirred and opened her eyes to look down at her husband's dark head which rested on her breast. He was so many different people, she thought. There was the coolly arrogant Earl who could keep others at a distance as he chose, the loving son and brother, the lonely, insecure child she glimpsed occasionally and, most surprising of all, the passionate husband who seemed to know no boundaries and would not permit her to set any either. He was obviously not without experience she thought idly and then mentally shrugged. The connections he may have had before they committed themselves to one another were no concern of hers. After all, she had not told him about Richard. Would it have been different with him, she wondered fleetingly and then chid herself for thinking of him when she was in her husband's bed. Almost as if to banish the thought, she lifted her

194

hand to brush his hair off his forehead. He must have been only dozing, for he immediately caught her hand and pulled it down to press a soft kiss in the palm. He sighed with satisfaction and nuzzled against her breast.

"To have you here in my bed," he said. "I don't know why it should make such a difference, but it does. You are the only woman ever to have shared it with me," he added.

"But you have shared other women's beds, I think?" she asked before she could stop herself and went on quickly, "I beg your pardon, it is none of my business what you did before we were wed."

He grinned. "You need not curb your disorderly thoughts on my account I assure you, and yes, there were other women, but I know now how insignificant and meaningless those episodes were. With you—there is a connection between us that makes it so much more."

Helena could not deny the connection but at the same time a small voice reminded her *there was love between you and Richard, even if it remained unfulfilled. You wouldn't say that what you had was insignificant and meaningless.* Did that make things worse or better?

Will didn't ask for love, she reminded herself, but affection and companionship and these she could give him with a willing heart. Turning in his arms she held him close.

"What would you like to do tomorrow?" Will asked as they settled to sleep. "I must spend some time with Thornton, but otherwise I am at your disposal."

"I should talk to Miller, and also look at the trunks my mother sent on from Swift Hall. Do you ride in the mornings before breakfast when you're here?"

"Sometimes, especially if I don't plan to ride out on the estate that day."

"When you go, may I join you?"

Will looked at her, surprised but pleased. "Should you like to? Would it not be too early for you?"

She shook her head. "I love being out of doors first thing in the morning, the world is so fresh and I would enjoy a long ride now after all the days travelling."

"Then let's go tomorrow. I should be delighted to have your company."

Chapter Sixteen

"The stables are on the other side of the moat," Will explained as he led Helena towards the gate house. "They were moved when the new wings were built."

She breathed a sigh of relief as they emerged onto the drawbridge, surprised at how shut in she had felt. "The moat is dry now?"

"Yes. I believe there was an ingenious system of sluices to divert the water from the two streams on the east and west so that it would flow around the curtain wall, but they were abandoned after the Restoration. Some trees grow there now as you see, but we keep it cleared from low-growing bushes so that it does not look too wild. It is a mass of flowers in the spring."

As soon as they had reached the handsome stable yard, a boy darted off, apparently to alert the head groom who emerged soon after, pulling on his jacket.

"Good morning, my lord."

"Good morning, Smithson. Lady Rastleigh wishes to ride. What can we offer her?"

"Honoured, my lady." The groom doffed his cap and bowed in response to Helena's pleasant, "Good morning."

"I first thought Nellie, but she may be too quiet," he said, looking at his new mistress in a considering but in no way offensive manner.

"What about Russet? He's a smooth goer, but has a nice turn of speed?" Will suggested.

Smithson nodded to the stable lad, who led out a gelding whose copper coat gleamed in the morning sun.

"Oh, you beauty!" Helena went to stroke his nose.

"He'll do," the head groom said. "We'll have him ready in a jiffy, my lady. Your maid had your saddle sent down, so you'll be properly turned out."

"Thank you, Smithson." Helena turned to Will. "Pray show me the rest of your stable while we are waiting. You have some fine animals here."

"Sir John keeps me well supplied and has done since he married Mother. He said to me once, there was not much he could do for me as a step-father, but at least he could do that."

"What a kind man he is."

"Yes. Before we left, he said he would send a mount for you as a wedding present. She should arrive any day now."

"How generous of him! Have you seen her?"

"No. A pretty grey mare, he said. Not too small and with a nice gait."

"She sounds lovely," Helena said, turning with a smile to address Smithson, who had been listening with great interest. "Will you have room for her, Smithson?"

"Indeed, we will, my lady, and we'll look after her for you, too. Russet is ready for you."

Will helped Helena into the saddle before mounting a rangy black who flicked his ears as if pleased to be on the move again.

"We'll go up onto the Downs," Will said as they cantered along the ride. "We can have a gallop there, if you are sure it will not be too much for you."

"Oh no. It is so good to be out and moving."

Once on the Downs, Will quickened the pace, turning to ride towards the sea.

"It is glorious," she exclaimed. "I have never before seen it from above like this. What a panorama!" She revolved to take the full view. "Is that the Castle? It's really impressive, but quite remote."

"You will not find it too dull here, I hope. You cannot see the village from here, but it is nearby. Weymouth is also quite attractive. We'll go in some day. You must also meet the Thorntons."

"Your secretary? He was at the wedding. Has he family near here?"

"His uncle, Dr Charles Thornton, who was secretary to my Grandfather and is librarian at Rastleigh. To my grandparents' surprise, he married my grandmother's companion, Miss Hannah Ainsworth when they were both about forty and since then they have occupied a suite of rooms in the east wing. After Grandfather died, he suggested that I look for a younger man to act as secretary and recommended his nephew, James. They worked together for about two years before James took over, but I asked Dr Thornton to stay on as librarian."

"That was kind of you."

"It gave them a good reason to remain here, for they could feel useful. He has lived here for nearly forty years and it has become his home. Grandmother was sincerely attached to Mrs Thornton, who took great care of her, especially in her last years."

"Do they have any children?"

"One daughter, Maria. She is about five years younger than I. I didn't see much of her once I went to school, but I know my grandmother was fond of her."

"Does she still live here?" Helena asked, wondering at this sudden mention of what appeared to be almost a foster family.

"She married two or three years ago, around the time Dr Thornton retired. She hadn't really lived here except for holidays since she was thirteen or fourteen. She was sent to school in Bath and then took up a position as governess near where James' family lives. It was there she met her husband, or so I am told." He laughed. "From something my mother said, I think the Thorntons were quite surprised to find themselves with a chick at such an advanced age and weren't quite sure what to do with her, apart from doting on her, of course, so it was probably just as well that her aunt took an interest."

They rode on in an amicable silence. I like that about him, Helena thought. You don't feel you have to be making conversation all the time.

~~~

"We'll call on the Thorntons this afternoon," Will said as they sat down to breakfast.

Helena looked at Jenkins who stood behind Will's chair. "Please enquire if three o'clock is convenient for them."

"We don't need to stand on ceremony with them," Will protested.

"Perhaps not in general, but I think the first time I meet them it is better to let them know we are coming. Older people are easily flustered and she may feel happier if she has had some notice of our visit."

"You are right as usual," Will said. "See to it, Jenkins."

"Very good, my lord. May I prepare you a plate, my lady?"

"Please, Jenkins."

Helena, who was quite hungry after their long ride looked with dismay at the selection of cold, shrivelled items the footman set in front of her. They had quite obviously been placed in chafing dishes some time previously, long enough for the coals to die and the food to cool.

"When was this set out, Jenkins?"

"At half-past nine o'clock, my lady, as is customary when his lordship is in residence."

"Was Cook not informed that his lordship and I would ride out before breakfast this morning?"

"I believe something of the sort was mentioned, my lady."

"Did Cook know when we would leave?"

"I am not sure, my lady."

"Well, this is inedible. Please remove it and tell her to prepare something fresh and hot as quickly as possible."

"At once, my lady," the butler said stiffly. He waved the footman to the sideboard with a rather dismissive gesture and left the room, presumably to go to the kitchen.

Will and Helena exchanged a few desultory words about their morning excursion until the footman had departed, then Will said, "You are taking up the reins at once, I see."

She flushed but said mildly, "I know it is a long time since the house had a proper mistress, but a good housekeeper should not permit this. I cannot abide waste and I will not tolerate people who do not accept responsibility or meet their commitments. It seems to have escaped Cook that she is employed to provide us with good meals when we want them, not when it suits her."

"What will you do?"

"I would not wish to be too hasty. I shall first talk to Jenkins and the housekeeper—Miller, isn't it? Once they have told me about the servants and the household routine, I'll see. Is there a suitable parlour in this wing?"

"The yellow one should do."

The door opened to admit the returning butler and footmen, the former supervising the latter as they put plates of bacon and eggs on the table as well as coffee, tea and toast.

"That will be all, Jenkins," Helena said. "I wish to see you and Miller in the yellow parlour at half-past twelve o'clock."

The butler stiffened. "Very good, my lady." He bowed and stalked from the room, the footmen on his heels.

Helena sighed with relief as she cut into an egg. "This is much better. And last night's dinner was excellent. She can do it properly if she wishes. How do you manage in London?"

"I take most of my meals out. If I do eat at home, I am content with something simple unless I am entertaining. Thornton discusses my plans for the week with Blaines each Monday, but I may look for food at any time. I don't follow a set routine."

"Do you entertain much?"

"Not formally. I am more inclined to suggest to a couple of friends that they come back with me for a late supper or to invite some gentlemen to dine with me at Brooks's, but sometimes I will give a small dinner, especially if my aunt is in town and can act as my hostess. I hope that next season we can do more. If you feel ready for it, perhaps we might do something here over the winter."

"Before I can do anything, I must see over the house. If it suits you, we might make a start after we have seen the Thorntons."

"Of course."

"More coffee? I want another cup of tea before I go in search of the yellow parlour."

Jenkins and Miller waited in the yellow parlour. They were neither of them young, both over sixty, and had a well-tended look to them, Helena thought. His silver locks were carefully pomaded and her white hair was beautifully arranged under a pretty lace cap that matched the collar on her gown of dove-grey silk. The white-on-white embroidered apron she wore over it was more ornamental than practical.

"You wished to see us, my lady?" Jenkins said frigidly, regarding his new mistress with an air of uneasy self-righteousness.

Helena sat at the writing-table. "I wish to gain an impression as to how the household functions—know more about the domestic routine and the servants' duties."

Miller bristled. "If you are not satisfied with the breakfast, my lady, I am sure that is nothing to do with me."

"You are the housekeeper, are you not?" Helena said mildly.

"Yes, my lady."

"And are therefore responsible for the running of the household, including the ordering of the meals?"

"Yes—no."

"Forgive me, my lady," Jenkins intervened patronisingly. "It is the practice at Rastleigh Castle that Cook manages the meals and the kitchen servants herself."

"Indeed? And who maintains the stocks and does the ordering?"

"Why, she does my lady."

"Does she also hold the keys?"

"Yes, my lady."

"Who checks the orders and the accounts?"

"Cook places them and checks the deliveries my lady. I believe she discusses the accounts with Mrs Thornton."

"Why is that?"

"I am sure I could not say, my lady."

"How do you spend your time, Miller?"

"I supervise the maids, my lady. It is a large building."

"So, you assign the maids their work and check each day that it has been done?"

"Not directly, my lady. The head maid in each area does that—the head housemaid, the head laundry maid and so on, apart from the kitchen and scullery maids—Cook is responsible for them. But of course, if I notice that the work is not properly done, I mention it."

"I see. And you, Jenkins?"

"I am responsible for the cellar and the footmen, my lady."

"Do you supervise them?"

"No, my lady. Parker, the under-butler does that."

"You cannot be overly occupied with his lordship away so much."

"We must be prepared. And of course, the servants' needs must be met."

"Servants' needs?"

"Meals, laundry and such."

"A building like this requires a lot of maintenance. Who ensures that repairs are carried out?"

"The estate carpenter, my lady."

"Who instructs him if something has to be done?"

"If anyone notices that something is in need of repair, they mention it to the under-butler. I understand smaller matters are dealt with directly, while larger ones are reported to Mr Hancock. His lordship's land steward," he explained condescendingly in response to Helena's look of enquiry.

"What about the cellars?"

"I have the oversight of them, of course, and am assisted by Parker."

"Who does the ordering and checks the deliveries?"

"I do, my lady."

"And do you pass the accounts to Mrs Thornton?"

"No, my lady. Being a woman, she would not understand them."

"I see. I wish to review all the household accounts and the books. Bring them, and all papers relating to them, to my sitting-room."

"I fear they may not be quite up to date, my lady. I can have them ready for inspection in a day or so."

"It does not matter if they are not up to date. I wish to see them now."

"But my lady—"

"Immediately, Jenkins. That will be all."

~~~

"Leave that for a moment, Lennard," Helena said to her maid who had started to unpack the trunks that had come from Swift Hall. "Tell me what you think of below stairs."

"Well, it's a bit odd, my lady. Not like anywhere I have been before. Mrs Miller and that Jenkins—they are not like any housekeeper and butler I have ever known. I know it has been only a day, but they don't seem to take any real interest in what has to be done—they behave as if they were the master and mistress. They take their meals separately, but not in the housekeeper's room, and Mr Emmett and I don't join them, as would be usual. Cook has to prepare special dishes for them. She has her own maid and he has a footman who also acts as his valet."

"And Cook?"

"Mrs Hope is different, my lady. She tries her best, but they keep her run ragged with trays of this and sips of that. And she gets no help from them. She was that anxious about the dinner she prepared for you and his lordship last evening, but they just said she should do whatever she thought fit. Master Will—for that is how they refer to his lordship—would not care what was set down to him. So she said even if his lordship didn't care, she had her pride and she was going to send up a nice dinner for him and his new countess."

"Did Jenkins pass on my compliments to her, do you know?"

"I don't think so my lady, for she was quite downcast this morning and then when you sent back the breakfast, she was so upset, although it is one of their rules that breakfast is to be served at half-past nine o'clock. It doesn't interfere with the servants' breakfasts and their elevenses, you see."

They were interrupted by a knock on the door, heralding a footman bearing an untidy stack of ledgers and papers.

"Mr Jenkins's compliments, my lady and these are all that is to hand."

"Thank you. Tell Emmett that I wish to see him."

The valet arrived speedily. "You sent for me, my lady?"

"Emmett, did you let anyone in the household know that his lordship and I proposed to ride out at nine o'clock?"

"I did, my lady. I told Jenkins and said that I did not think you would return before eleven, because his lordship had mentioned his planned direction to me."

"How long have you been with his lordship, Emmett?"

"Four years, my lady."

"What is your opinion of the way this household is managed?"

He hesitated a moment and then said, "It is the only gentleman's household I have served in that appears to function for the benefit of the butler and housekeeper. I will not say they are dishonest, my lady, but they seem to have forgotten that they are the servants and not the masters."

"What do you think of Cook?"

"She does her best, but is sadly lacking in direction. I was told that you were not satisfied with the breakfast and enquired whether she had been informed that you and his lordship would breakfast late. She said not."

"Do you think she was telling the truth?"

"Yes, my lady. She was really distressed by what happened."

"Thank you for being so frank, Emmett. Please tell Cook that I wish to see her in the yellow parlour. Lennard, I want you to stay here. I don't want these books to disappear."

When Helena went down again to the yellow parlour, she found Mrs Hope waiting for her in a high state of agitation. She was a buxom woman of about forty, her greying hair tied back in a severe knot. She curtsied immediately Helena came into the room.

"Oh, my lady, please forgive me. If only I had known you and his lordship were going out before breakfast. But Mrs Miller insists breakfast is to be on the sideboard by half-past nine o'clock because after that she gives me her orders for the day and she does not like to be disturbed."

"Orders for the day?"

"Yes, my lady, for the servants' meals and whatever little dainties she wants for herself and Mr Jenkins. Tonight, they want a lobster pie like I made for his lordship yesterday."

"Do they indeed?" Helena said dryly. "But you decide what to send up for our meals, I understand?"

"Yes, my lady. They say his lordship doesn't mind what he eats but I notice what he prefers and try to give him that."

"What about Dr and Mrs Thornton? Who decides what to serve them?"

"I discuss the menus for the week with Mrs Thornton when we review the accounts. They have small appetites. Dr Thornton just wants a 'neat dinner' as he calls it, three or four dishes, nothing too fancy but he does appreciate a well-made dish."

"As do we. I understand our compliments on last night's dinner were not conveyed to you, Mrs Hope. His lordship and I enjoyed it very much."

Mrs Hope blushed and curtsied at this.

"I will be making changes, Mrs Hope, as I am sure you will appreciate. For now, Miller and Jenkins will eat the same meals as the other servants and they will eat with them. They are not to be served separately. I leave it to you to decide what to send up for his lordship and me tonight. Lennard will let you know when we wish to dine and Emmett will tell you in the morning when his lordship wants his breakfast. If we have no guests, there is no need to set up a sideboard full of dishes—we prefer to have something freshly prepared, as it was this morning. Emmett can probably advise you on his lordship's likes and dislikes—I know he detests kidneys for example—and in a day or so I shall talk to you again."

"Thank you, my lady." Relief and hope were clearly visible in Cook's face.

"I shall speak to Jenkins and advise him of my instructions," Helena said, going to the bell pull. "If you encounter any difficulties in the meantime, please let Lennard or Emmett know."

Half an hour later, Will found his wife surrounded by a mass of loose papers and registers. "What on earth have you got there?"

"The household accounts. Jenkins fears they are not up to date, but I insisted he bring them to me at once."

"What a jumble," he said disapprovingly.

"They are not at all up to date, apart from the exception of the kitchen accounts. I understand Mrs Thornton reviews them each week."

"Mrs Thornton? I wonder why?"

"We shall have to ask her. From what I have discovered, Miller and Jenkins do next to nothing. With you away these past months, there can be no excuse for this disarray."

"Why don't you let James have a go at it? He can put the papers into some sort of order and report his findings to you. I'll ask Emmet to take them to him."

"That's a good idea." She looked at the clock. "I must change before we go to the Thorntons. Come and talk to me while I do so and I'll tell you what I have learned."

Chapter Seventeen

The Thorntons awaited them in a pleasant morning-room decorated in the style of the previous century. Helena liked them immediately. Mrs Thornton was a plump little woman with silvery hair simply but attractively styled and a pair of round, gold-rimmed spectacles perched on a snub nose. She beamed as she said, "Welcome home, my lord. It is indeed a good day when you bring home a bride."

"Thank you, ma'am." He turned to Helena. "May I present Mrs Thornton and Doctor Thornton?"

Dr Thornton reminded Helena of her father. He was tall, with stooped shoulders and untidy grey hair. He peered over his spectacles and supported himself with a walking-stick, which he immediately transferred to his left hand so as to shake hers and Will's fervently. "A warm welcome home, my boy, to you and your lady. Hannah and I wish you health, happiness and a long life together."

"Now," Mrs Thornton said when they had taken their seats and tea was poured. "Pray tell us all about the wedding. And about your poor Mamma, as well," she added to Will. "We were so sorry when the joyful news of your marriage was so swiftly followed by the notification of such a sad event."

"It was word of her illness that led us to marry so quickly," Will answered. "My Aunt Amelia suggested it so that Helena could accompany me to Ireland and I am eternally grateful to her, to them both for it."

"It cannot have been easy to arrange things with such little notice."

"No," Helena said, "but Mamma and Lady Amelia proved to be formidable generals. Nothing was lacking."

"Indeed, a true helpmeet is a wonderful gift," Dr Thornton said when they had heard all there was to hear about the wedding. "My lady, I understand that you are the daughter of my old friend and mentor Sir Thomas Swift."

"You knew Papa?" she exclaimed joyfully.

"From my first week at Cambridge. He was some ten years older than I but we worked closely together, especially later when I had completed my initial studies. The contact lessened of course once we had both left the university, but we stayed in touch. He even stayed with us here once, about twenty years ago. There was a folio in the library that he wished to consult. You grandfather found him a most interesting and amiable guest, my lord," he added to Will.

Helena found a peculiar comfort in the fact that her father had been a welcome visitor to her new home—it made it seem less strange, somehow—and the party fell into a further happy sharing of reminiscences and anecdotes.

"And what do you think of Rastleigh Castle, my lady?" Dr Thornton asked.

"I have hardly had a chance to see over it, for we were riding this morning and since then, I have been otherwise occupied." She briefly recounted her conversations with Jenkins, Miller and Cook, finishing, "I fail to see why you should be troubled with Hope's accounts, ma'am."

"It was no trouble at all to help her," Mrs Thornton assured her. "She is an excellent cook and a good-hearted creature, but has a simple nature and was not happy that there was no one to check her books. It was not what she was used to, she said."

"I cannot understand what duties if any are undertaken by the other two in the normal way," Helena went on.

"I have wondered that myself," Mrs Thornton confessed, "but Jenkins intimated that their return here was to be regarded as a sort of retirement in respect of their long service, with only nominal duties."

"Was that what you had arranged with them?" Helena asked Will.

"Of course not. I was never particularly partial to them for there was always a false note—some sort of lack of respect in their demeanour, or so it seemed to me."

"I don't think you were wrong," interjected Helena, thinking of their comment that Master Will would not care what was set down to him.

"But my grandfather seemed satisfied with them and I thought it unfair to dismiss them after his death. The old butler Higgs and his wife, who was housekeeper here, retired at that time and it appeared simplest to send Miller and Jenkins in their place." He looked at the clock. "If I am to show you more of the Castle, we should go now."

Helena rose to make her farewells to the Thorntons. "Once we have this sorted out, you must dine with us."

"We should be honoured, my lady."

"We'll start with the old Keep," Will said. "I suppose it is the most interesting, even if less comfortable than the new wings." He led her through the east gallery and into the transverse hall. "You have already seen the Great Hall, but there are two interesting suites of rooms behind it on the far side. Maybe the clerks worked there or the Lord would retire there when he wished to consult privately with someone. There is also a beautiful little chapel in the southwest corner. The lower rooms are not as bright as they once were," he added, reaching for the latch, "but as the gallery is only half the height of this floor, the upper rooms still have good light." He opened the door of a sizeable but dark room. "I suppose it's only good for storage now, as is the middle one." The end room, with a window in the south wall of the castle was sparsely furnished with a table and two chairs.

"Where does that door lead to?" Helena pointed to the outer corner of the room.

"The chapel," Will replied, drawing the huge bolts and pushing the heavy door which opened slowly with an ominous creak.

"The lair of the mad monk," Helena uttered in spine-tingling tones as she stepped over the threshold. "But this is beautiful!"

The small room with bare stone walls and a high vaulted ceiling was lit by three arched mullioned windows set with scenes from the life of Christ, exquisitely executed in richly coloured stained glass. Will drew her attention to the Nativity, set against an imaginary landscape. "Look at the castle on the hill."

"Surely that is the old Castle?"

"And here." He showed her a man and woman in medieval dress, humbly kneeling behind the shepherds. "We believe they are the builders of the Castle, Robert Hall and his wife Ann."

"You have a look of him." Helena stepped closer. "You have the same eyes and nose."

"It's a look you will find repeated over and over again in the picture gallery."

"How did this escape the iconoclasts, and especially Cromwell's army?"

"Some would say good luck, others by a special blessing. The roundhead troops never reached here for some reason."

"It would be nice to refurnish it. Could we use it for christenings? Would it have to be re-dedicated?"

"I don't know. You can ask the rector on Sunday. Let's go on."

They continued up an oak staircase onto a landing. "These are the upper rooms," Will said, opening the first door. "I always thought they could be made quite attractive."

"I am sure Jack and Alexander would love to stay in a real castle," she replied as she preceded him into the room. "This seems to be in use," she said in surprise, looking at the comfortably furnished bedroom. A fire was set in the hearth, ready to be lit. "A woman sleeps here," she added, noting the toiletries set out on a handsome dressing table. She opened a connecting door reveal a snug sitting-room with a glowing fire.

Two armchairs were placed either side of the fireplace and a dining table and two chairs stood at the window, with a fine tallboy opposite. A decanter and glasses were set hospitably on a silver tray.

Will removed the stopper and sniffed. "Excellent port," he commented, looking around at the tasteful selection of ornaments, silver and paintings. He pointed at one of some overblown roses arranged in a pewter vase. "That was always in my grandmother's boudoir."

He pulled the bell-cord vigorously then opened a second connecting door which led into another well-furnished bedroom, this one more masculine in its style.

A footman hurried in, tugging at his waistcoat. "You rang, my lord, my lady?"

Helena looked at him. "I do not think you were on the steps when we arrived yesterday, were you?"

"No, my lady."

"Why not?" Will demanded. "My instructions were that all the servants were to assemble to greet her ladyship."

The footman swallowed. "Mr Jenkins felt it would spoil the symmetry if there were not a matched assembly on each side of the steps, so he instructed some of us to remain indoors. I meant no disrespect, my lord, my lady."

"What is your position here?"

"I am Mr Jenkins's footman, my lord. Mrs Miller's maid and I assist them to dress, look after their rooms and clothes, serve their meals." He paused for a moment, obviously recalling that this had changed. "Answer their bells, pass on their orders and run their errands."

"Answer their bells? Are they occupying these rooms?"

"Yes, my lord."

"Did Miller's maid also remain indoors yesterday?" Helena asked.

"Yes, my lady."

"I see," Will said. "My compliments to Mr Thornton—he is in the library—and would he please join us here. You are to return with him and wait outside."

James Thornton arrived within minutes. "What's this?" he asked, looking around the cosy parlour.

"Jenkins and Miller appear to have set themselves here up in style," Will told him.

"They are not married, are they?" Helena asked.

"Not to my knowledge," Will said. "James, what have you gathered from the books?"

"I have only had a quick look through them. They are in total disarray but I think that that is more laziness than fraud. They have certainly made a well-feathered nest for themselves here. I imagine they have been availing themselves of your supplies rather lavishly as much more is purchased than my uncle and aunt would ever consume."

"Apparently we also employ a personal servant for each of them," Will said dryly. "They were not among the servants waiting to greet us yesterday."

James Thornton raised his eyebrows. "They tried to conceal their existence? That is a horse of a different colour."

"Indeed." Will had heard enough. He jerked open the door, startling the waiting footman. "Emmett and her ladyship's maid are to attend us here at once. The rest of the servants are to be in the Great Hall in fifteen minutes."

"Yes, my lord."

"Speak discreetly to Emmett and Lennard. Do not discuss what has happened here with anyone. If questioned, say I have instructed you to remain silent."

The low murmur on the floor of the Great Hall died away when Will and Helena took their seats on the dais, Emmett and Lennard stood behind the great chairs while Mr Thornton seated himself in a third chair that had been placed at the end of the long table.

Will surveyed the group below him. The servants had gathered together in the centre of the floor, well separated from the butler and housekeeper who stood to one side nearer the dais. With his usual air of condescension, Jenkins appeared to convey the impression that, although present, he was apart from his fellow-servants, and privy to his lordship's intentions. Miller appeared more agitated, twisting her fingers as she looked uneasily around the room.

"Are you all here?" Will asked

A ragged chorus replied, "Yes, my lord."

"It has been brought to my attention that not everyone was present on our arrival yesterday. This was contrary to my orders."

"If I might explain, my lord," Jenkins said smoothly, "it was thought it would be detrimental to the symmetry—"

"So I have been informed," Will interrupted. "As you and Miller were obviously unable to carry out this instruction yesterday, we shall start again. Not with either of you," he added as Jenkins opened his mouth. "We'll start with the kitchen. Hope, you are to present your subordinates by name and position. They should come forward one by one and then wait with you there." He pointed to the wall opposite the butler and housekeeper

When the cook had complied, Will said, "And now the head housemaid."

Group by group they moved to the appointed side until on the left there remained Jenkins, Miller, Jenkins's footman, a maid and another upper servant. Will lifted a brow at these last. "And you are?"

He listened stonily as they introduced themselves as "Parker, the under-butler, your lordship," "John, Mr Jenkins's footman, your lordship," and "Dorothy, Mrs Miller's maid, your lordship."

Finally, Will looked once more around the assembly. "I ask you all again, is every servant here? Is anyone missing?"

The under-butler came forward to say, "All the indoor servants are present, your lordship."

"Can you identify to Mr Thornton those who were not present yesterday?"

"Yes, my lord."

"Once you have done so, you are to escort Jenkins and Miller to the ante-room to the chapel and remain with them until I send for them. They are not to go anywhere else."

"My lord, I must protest," Jenkins said loudly.

"You will do as you are told," Will replied coldly and gestured to Parker to lead them out. He raised his voice. "The rest of you may return to your duties." He regarded the worried faces in front of him. "If you have been doing your work properly and conscientiously, there is no need for you to be concerned."

Will rubbed his eyes wearily as the door closed behind the last maid. "Bring your chair around here, James, so that we can confer. For a start, I had no idea we employed an under-butler and I would not have seen the need for one."

"While there could be no objection to the housekeeper and butler drawing on the services of the maids, I would not countenance their engaging personal servants reserved for their own use," Helena said.

"If all the servants were here this afternoon and none have left recently, we seem to be paying two footmen and two maids more than are officially employed. Certainly, none are marked as having left," Mr Thornton said.

"Who actually pays them?"

"Jenkins, as far as I know. He draws the relevant sum from Mr Hancock each quarter. But I wonder if he pays out the full wages or retains a 'tribute' as it were."

"Can you make some enquiries?" Will asked.

"I think you should also ask them for their keys," Helena said. "Parker will know whether they hand over all of them. We must check the cellars and other storerooms."

"What are you going to do with them?" Mr Thornton asked

"I don't want them here. If there is no evidence of fraud or theft, they may leave tomorrow with a carefully written character and whatever is owing to them."

"What about the rooms they have been using? There were some pretty ornaments and other items there that you said had come from the Castle," Helena said. "They should be cleared before we allow them back."

"An excellent suggestion. Thornton, please give your uncle and aunt my compliments. Explain the situation and ask them if they would be kind enough to remove anything that is not obviously personal, leaving only the most basic furniture. I imagine they will recognise many of the pieces. They should take a couple of footmen to carry things. If anything has been taken in error, it will be returned, provided it can be proven not to be Castle property."

"Very good, my lord."

"We'll leave them sweat for another hour or so before we send for them, but not here. In the yellow parlour, I think."

Will peered into the dark from the window of Helena's sitting-room. He had never been so mortified. Breakfast had been bad but these latest revelations were the outside of enough. At last, he faced his wife.

"I am indeed sorry, Helena, that your first day at Rastleigh should have turned out like this."

"It's not your fault," she said in surprise. "And, if it had to be done, it is better done at once."

"It is in some sort my fault for I have been neglectful. I am Rastleigh. If my servants have been able to take such advantage, some of the blame must be laid at my door. The truth is I have never really taken ownership of the Castle itself."

"Why is that?"

"I don't know. Perhaps because I resented it. Without the title, I would have been able to go to Ireland with my mother and Sir

John, would have known my brothers and sisters better, would not have been forced into taking on an adult's responsibility at so young an age. When I think of Jack—what a carefree life he has led up to this summer. Sir John couldn't be described as overly indulgent but his children are permitted to be children and to grow up in a more natural fashion. I don't think I was ever allowed to be young. When I was Jack's age I was at Oxford, it's true, but all the vacation time was spent learning about the estates and my duties to the earldom. My grandfather was a hard taskmaster and I had to work all the more to make up for the month at Colduff each summer."

"I see what you mean. But you must not be too hard on yourself because of what happened in the past."

"You shouldn't be required to clear up after me! I am ashamed of myself."

She got up and came to take his face between her hands. "I don't mind, truly," she said, kissing him gently. "In fact, it was worth it to see you suddenly transformed into the Lord of the Manor, enthroned in the Lord's chair, his Lady by his side, and his servants summoned to stand before him in the Great Hall."

He began to laugh. "I was, wasn't I? I didn't even think about it—it was instinctive."

"It was positively awe-inspiring. The servants were petrified, especially when you started separating the sheep from the goats."

"I suppose we must soon see our goats," he said with a smile. He lifted her hand and kissed it. "Thank you, Helena."

A tap on the door heralded Dr and Mrs Thornton.

"Come and take a glass of wine with us," Will invited. "I am sorry to have saddled you with such a task, but I thought you would be best placed to know what had been removed from other rooms in the Castle."

"Better ask what had not been removed," Dr Thornton replied dryly. "Their rooms are quite bare now. I also took the liberty of retrieving half a dozen of your best port that Jenkins had set aside for himself."

"It is disgraceful," Mrs Thornton said. "I am shocked by such presumption."

"What will you do with them?" her husband asked.

"Nothing before morning. James is carrying out some other investigations for me and my ultimate decision must depend on those. But they may not stay here after tomorrow. If they have merely been venial, I shall give them some months' wages when they leave, but it depends on what James discovers." He thought for a moment. "Parker may return them to their rooms where they are to remain until sent for tomorrow. Their bells are not to be answered and I want two footmen stationed in the passage the whole time. I am to be informed if they attempt to leave. Parker should set up a roster of those he considers most trustworthy."

"Will they have had dinner?" Helena asked Mrs Thornton.

"Yes. The servants' dinner is served at four o'clock."

"Parker should tell Cook she may provide them with a simple supper and breakfast. Not lobster pie, as Miller ordered this morning," she added caustically.

"Lobster pie? Surely not, my lady."

"Apparently the one served to us last night looked most appetising," Helena replied with what her husband could only describe as a grin.

"Again, my apologies and many thanks for your help," Will said to the Thorntons.

"We are happy to have been of assistance, my lord; you and your lady must know that you may call upon us for anything. Has it occurred to you that they may have removed objects not only to decorate their rooms but also to sell?"

"How should we be able to prove it, or even discover what was missing?"

"We took a full inventory after your grandfather died. He had been Earl for so long and as the Higgses and I wished to retire, we thought it best to have the ledgers up to date. We also put most of the more valuable items in the strong room and that is marked on the lists."

"I remember. We felt it would be wise as I would be here less often."

"There is a separate record of the silver in the butler's pantry. It should be quite easy to check that. Higgs and his wife still live in the village. He may be seventy-five but is as sharp as ever."

"I'll send a message asking them to come up tomorrow morning."

"Charles and I shall help too," Mrs Thornton said firmly. "We spent a lot of time with the old Earl and Countess and have a good idea of what should be where."

Dr Thornton drained his glass. "Well, I'm for my dinner. Good evening, my lord, my lady."

Chapter Eighteen

"Well, James, what have you to report?"

"It is as I feared. Apart from the wages of the four non-existent servants, Jenkins claims for higher wages than are actually paid to the other servants."

"And the others were happy that he took a share?" Will asked incredulously.

"It was not done that way, more as if he charged a premium on the wages so that if twenty pounds was agreed, he recorded twenty-four pounds in the wage roll."

"Take thy pen and write down fifty," Helena murmured.

"That was the opposite, but the intent was the same—to defraud the master. He also claimed top wages for himself."

"So he is clearly guilty of fraud and theft apart from his completely inappropriate conduct," Will said.

"It could be a hanging matter; he would be sentenced to transportation at the least," Mr Thornton replied.

"Let us see what tomorrow brings. Your uncle and Higgs are to check the inventory in the morning.

"I can have another go at the books tonight," Mr Thornton volunteered.

"What shall we do in the meantime?" Helena asked. "I am reluctant to promote anyone or bring in new people until we are sure that we have stopped the rot. I was wondering about your London butler. Are you satisfied with him? Could we get him down here temporarily at least?"

"That is a good idea. The house in London seems to be run much more efficiently—it is more comfortable at least. What do you think, James?"

"I think it should work," Mr Thornton replied slowly. "I have a greater insight into those accounts, and they seem in order, but at the end of the day we must assume that people are honest. Mrs Murray is well able to manage on her own in town, especially when you are not in residence. And I have never felt uneasy with her or Blaines as I have had on occasion with Jenkins. Regrettably, I put it down to the old retainer resenting what was a change of not one but two generations at the helm of the earldom."

"We'll do that, then," Will said decisively.

"The head housemaid—Susan is it? —strikes me as being very sensible. She might act as housekeeper for the time being. If she proves herself, we can keep her on," Helena suggested.

"Yes, she's Smithson's daughter and, I would have thought, reliable."

"Parker may continue as under-butler for the moment and, if Blaines considers him suitable, he could take over once Blaines has knocked things into shape."

"What about the personal maid and footman?" Mr Thornton asked.

"According to Lennard and Emmett, they are not popular with the other servants because they regard themselves as being above them. But they did do their work," Helena replied. "We have no need of them and I would prefer to make a clean sweep of things and let them go, but will give them a character and wages in lieu of notice, provided we uncover no evidence of their involvement in Jenkins's and Miller's schemes."

~~~

With the exception of a few small ornaments that might have been lost due to normal breakages, the check of the inventories revealed nothing untoward. Parker had been able to account for everything in the butler's pantry. A man in his mid-thirties, he had been delighted to have been offered his position some two years ago. He had been uneasy about the way some things were done but, as he confided to Higgs while counting the silver spoons, he had never worked in such a great house before and, being uncertain as to what was usual, had not liked to question his superiors. He was relieved to learn of Blaines's proposed arrival. Mrs Higgs, who was some years younger than her husband, had volunteered to come in each day to train Susan, who was honoured by the suggestion that she act as housekeeper but nervous at the responsibility involved.

"It all falls into place," Helena said to Will as they sat over a nuncheon the next day. "Have you decided how to deal with Jenkins and Miller?"

"I am reluctant to have my gullibility exposed in court," he confessed. "While they are guilty of a colossal breach of trust, it is only the fraud with the wages that is criminal. I propose to offer them a choice. They may take their chances, first in being handed over to the local constable and then brought to trial or, in exchange for a written confession, may take the next boat to America and try their luck there. I imagine they will opt for the latter. Lennard and Emmett will pack their things with Dr and Mrs. Thornton supervising. I have asked Blaines to bring a Bow Street Runner who will escort them to the boat and ensure they leave on it. He is to find one that will not put in anywhere else but sail directly to its destination."

The housekeeper and butler, though initially inclined to try and bluster their way out of the situation with tearful references to "your lordship's dear grandmother" and condescending reminders that, "your lordship may not recall what was customary, as you were just a child when we entered his late Lordship's service" were brought to a halt by Will's icy comment.

"If you imagine that my grandfather would have condoned for one moment such an egregious breach of trust, not to say outright fraud, you are sadly mistaken. You have abused your positions shamefully and I am seriously inclined to send for the constable immediately. I shall do so if you continue to deny your guilt. There is so much evidence that you have systematically defrauded the Estate of a sizeable portion of the sum you claimed each quarter to pay the servants' wages that I am convinced that at a trial you be found guilty and sentenced at best to transportation, at worst to hanging. I am prepared to have my opinion put to the test by laying information against you and having you arrested at once. You may await your trial in gaol."

"I'll tell you," cried Mrs Miller. "It was all his doing." She looked viciously at Jenkins. "He could not be content with the cosy life we had made for ourselves here, but must have more. His retirement nest egg, he called it. He wouldn't be satisfied with a cottage like Higgs. Oh no. He was going to move somewhere else and set up as a gentleman." She spat out the last word, prudently moving back from her fellow-accused, who had advanced on her, raising a threatening hand.

"Shut your mouth, woman. They can't prove anything." He staggered as Parker seized him from behind.

"Take Jenkins to the chapel ante-room and remain with him," Will ordered two sturdy gardeners who waited to one side. "If he gives you any trouble, you may restrain him."

"Now, Miller," he said severely once the little group had departed, "you may explain to us how the wages were handled."

"Why, my lord, Jenkins looked after it all. He received the money from Mr Hancock each quarter and called in the servants to pay them. What was left he kept for himself."

"Did he give you any of it?" Helena asked.

"No, my lady. That is, he did offer, but I wouldn't take it. That would be stealing," she added virtuously.

"And employing a personal maid to serve you at his lordship's expense was not?" Helena asked quietly.

Mrs Miller pleated her apron nervously. "No, my lady, I did not see it as such."

"How did you think of it then?"

"It was a-a-a perquisite," she replied truculently, "owing to me because of my long service and position."

"Mrs Higgs had no such maid and she had been here for over forty years."

The housekeeper tossed her head at this remark but did not reply.

"Miller, you are to write out a full account of your behaviour and your knowledge of what Jenkins did," Will said. "Do not attempt to conceal anything—remember we have also spoken to the other servants. Mr Thornton and Parker will remain with you. Mr Thornton, please bring it to the library when she is finished. Parker, you will stay here with her; she is not to be left alone." He turned to Helena. "Let us see what they have discovered upstairs."

The suite of rooms had already been cleared and the servants' personal belongings had been packed up.

"Nothing of any significance in Mrs Miller's room, my lord," Dr Thornton said. "She has some money but no more than you might expect a housekeeper to have saved. Jenkins, on the contrary," he indicated a large strongbox, "foolishly kept the key to this with the house keys, so had to hand it over yesterday." He opened the box to display some thousands of pounds. "Even allowing for the fact that he could save most of his earnings, I should say he was skimming elsewhere apart from the fraud with the servants' wages. I suspect he had come to an arrangement with your vintners."

"Shall we go to the library?" Will said. "Let me carry this," he added, taking the strongbox. "It will be too heavy for you, Doctor."

Helena followed her husband up an oak staircase to a book-filled room that ran the width of the Great Hall below, but was only half its depth. A spacious desk was placed in front of one large window and two smaller ones, presumably for the Thornton uncle and nephew, before another.

At the front of the keep, the library looked out to the Gate House and over the walls to the woods beyond. "What a lovely room," Helena said. "I particularly like that you can see out over the surrounding walls."

"The best vista is from the solar; it backs on to the library and looks out to sea. This way." Will opened a door.

She moved past him into a large, panelled room. It had the same high, beamed ceiling as the library but here the windows were deep bays allowing light to pour in on all three sides. Below, on the headland, green slopes dotted with sheep stretched to the craggy grey walls of the ruined Norman keep, and spread right and left to crown steep cliffs standing sentinel above a sparkling blue sea. A stately ship passed, sails billowing, completely dwarfing a handful of smaller boats that plied busily through the waves.

"What a magnificent prospect. It is wonderful to see it from a height, like this."

"Tomorrow, I'll take you up to the roof of the tower. The view from up there is even more spectacular."

A step sounded outside and Mr Thornton cleared his throat. "My lord, my lady?"

"Finished it, has she?" Will turned away from the window. "What is your impression, James?"

"She maintains stoutly that she did not steal anything. She seems to have a peculiar sense of honesty that made it possible for her to do as little as possible for her wages while making lavish use for her own comfort of goods and services paid for by your lordship, but would not permit her to pocket your coin. I sent for a footman and maid to remain with her while I stepped outside to talk to Parker. He agreed with me that she appeared to be telling the truth and had somehow convinced herself that she was entitled to her perquisites, as she calls them. Jenkins, on the other hand, he describes as a nasty piece of goods. He said that if they had not received word of your marriage, he would have left at Michaelmas, but hoped that the arrival of the countess might result in some changes."

"I see. Ask your uncle and aunt to join us, James."

"What are we to do with them?" Will said when the elder Thorntons had arrived. He looked at his wife. "My lady?"

"I think Miller will be punished enough if she is turned off without a character. At her age she will not find it easy to find another position in such circumstances. I should not like to condemn her to travel with Jenkins, for he would be quite vengeful I think, now that she has spoken against him. She may leave immediately. I shall even arrange for her to be taken to the coaching inn."

"If I may make a suggestion, my lady," Mrs Thornton said, "you might like to pay her coach fare to a place of her choice, as long as it is at least one hundred miles away. You will not wish her to remain in the neighbourhood."

"That is a good idea. Thank you, Mrs Thornton."

"And what of Jenkins?"

"He cannot escape punishment," Dr Thornton said firmly.

"I admit I have no wish to have my failings made public," Will said. "If he makes a full confession and restitution, I shall allow him to travel to America as a free man, otherwise he must take his chances with the law."

When confronted, Jenkins cursed and swore, refusing to answer any of the charges against him.

Will rang the bell. "Send for the constable to come at once and take a prisoner in charge," he instructed the footman who answered it. Addressing his former butler, he continued, "I shall personally place your strongbox in the custody of the magistrate. A Bow Street Runner will come in a day or so. You have until then to decide whether you will accept my offer of clemency, in which case he will escort you to a boat bound for America. If you continue to brazen it out, he will take you to Dorchester to await trial at the Lent Assizes."

The prospect of several months in gaol to be followed by a trial and, if he were fortunate, a sentence of transportation, proved daunting enough to do away with Jenkins's protestations of innocence. "I accept your offer," he cried desperately.

"Then sit and write your confession, including details of your dealings with the wine merchants and others. The Runner will release to you the balance of your funds and your belongings when you board the ship. Until then, you will remain in his custody. You will spend the intervening time in gaol, for I will not permit you to remain under my roof."

Once the constable had departed with his prisoner, Will handed James Thornton the butler's confession. "Consider this overnight together with your uncle, and let me know in the morning what is owed to the Estate. Please also prepare some sort of quit-claim for Jenkins to sign, in which he acknowledges that he pays this sum to the Estate in restitution of moneys fraudulently obtained from it. He must sign that as well as his confession before he is allowed to depart."

~~~

Two days later all was resolved. Miller had gratefully accepted the offer to have her fare paid to the village near Manchester where her sister lived. She had her savings and proposed to say that she had decided to retire with the arrival of the new Countess.

"If you behave yourself, no one need ever know of what happened here," Helena said, not unkindly. "You have been given a chance. Use it wisely."

"Yes, my lady, thank you, my lady," the former housekeeper replied, still shocked by the news that Jenkins had been handed over to the constable. "You won't regret it."

The personal maid and footman were happy to depart with a quarter's wages in lieu of notice. Blaines arrived and immediately took charge and when Will and Helena sat down to dinner, it was with the rewarding sensation of having successfully negotiated these unexpected shoals and reefs without running aground.

"And all because we went riding before breakfast," Helena sighed as she sipped her wine.

"Because you wanted to go riding," Will corrected her with a grin. "If I had been on my own, I would have left earlier and perhaps not ridden as far. Also, I wouldn't have delayed as long in the stables."

"If you were back sooner, the breakfast might not have been spoilt," Helena concluded. "My nurse used to recite a rhyme, 'for the want of a nail, the shoe was lost'."

"Mine too. It ends 'for failure of battle a kingdom was lost, and all for the want of a horse shoe nail'. Well, we didn't lose our kingdom. I might have regained mine and you have certainly laid claim to yours."

Chapter Nineteen

"Good morning, my lord, my lady," Smithson said, adding, "your new mount has just arrived, my lady."

Helena took one look at the elegant, leggy mare, her coat of soft grey set off by a silver mane and tail and a small black diamond between her dark eyes, and fell in love. "You're adorable," she whispered, stroking the soft nose.

"Here." Will put a piece of apple in her hand

Smiling she held it out and the mare lipped at it.

"What is her name?" she asked the groom who had brought her from Ireland.

"Silver Mist, my lady."

"It suits her perfectly. Do you go directly to Colduff or will you see Sir John on your return to Ireland?"

"I'm to go to Dublin first, my lady, to report to Sir John."

"Then I shall give you a letter for him and one for the young ladies as well."

"I shall have some letters too," Will said. "Byrne, isn't it? You will want to rest your horse for a day or so before you set off again.

Smithson here will look after you. Have you money enough for the return journey?"

"Yes, my lord."

"Take this, anyway." Coins clinked as he put them into the groom's hand.

"Thank you, my lord."

"I can't wait to try her," Helena said. "But she must settle into her new surroundings first and recover from the journey. Where will you put her, Smithson?"

"I thought in the paddock with Nellie for now, your ladyship. She'll like some sweet grass, I'm thinking."

~~~

A month later, Helena had become accustomed to life at Rastleigh. Accompanied by Will, she had ridden over the estate and met the tenants. Their neighbours had been introduced to her after church, although because of Will's bereavement they had only just started to call. The rector had announced the death of Lady Malcolm the Sunday after their arrival and notices had also appeared in the news-sheets.

The household was now functioning properly. Both Blaines and Mrs Higgs were satisfied with their protégés' progress and felt they could be confirmed in their new positions at the next quarter-day. Lennard reported that the pervading feeling below stairs was much improved. The servants were pleased that Miller and Jenkins, who had been inclined to lord it over them, had been dismissed and also that the earl and countess proposed to remain at the Castle for some months still. "They feel they have more of a purpose, my lady," she had explained.

Helena herself felt much more rested after all the upheaval of the preceding months. She had needed some time for herself. Will had been occupied in picking up the threads of the estate business he had perforce neglected over the late summer and into autumn and she had spent peaceful hours on her own, painting or working on her embroidery. She had written to her family, to Kate and Emily and also to Richard's sister Caro, who had received the news of her marriage with delight and heart-felt good-wishes 'for, as you know, Richard only wanted you to be happy, as do we'. She also received a kind letter from Lady Harbury, expressing the hope that they would meet in London when Parliament reconvened at the end of November.

Helena put down this missive. Did she really look forward to going to London? After the events at the Castle, she was apprehensive about conditions at Rastleigh House. How much would she see of Will once they were in town? Would he pursue the masculine round of sport, his clubs and the Lords? What place would there be for a wife in his life? She could not imagine that they would spend as much time with one another as they did here at Rastleigh where they had next to no engagements and usually shared all meals as well as sitting together in the evenings. Such would not be the case in London; in any event it was not customary for a married couple to live in one another's pockets. She would have to make her own life, she supposed, but then she must do that here too.

But how? She was restless, suffering from a lack of purpose, and missing the daily interaction with her mother, Rosamund and the children. She was aware of the ache in her lower belly that heralded her courses. She knew it was early days, but could not help being disappointed. With a sigh, she carefully folded the fine lawn fichu she was embroidering as a Christmas gift for her mother, wrapped it in a protective cloth and went to place it in her work-box—a handsome article made of mahogany with brass fittings and a stout lock that Gus had given to her the Christmas after their father died. When she had gasped and thanked him, secretly thinking it was a little excessive and she would have preferred something smaller and lighter, he had lifted out the fitted tray filled with useful implements, and another one below it to show her a third level. 'You may keep your money here, securely locked away, rather than leaving it in a drawer where anyone might come upon it.'

Biting her lip, she surveyed what remained of the coins and banknotes she had brought with her from home. There were few calls on her purse here at Rastleigh but thirty pounds would not take her very far in London, especially if she was to commission her bride-clothes.

Mamma had always received her allowance on Quarter Day, and so had Helena after she had made her come-out. That first year, Papa had given her thirty pounds a quarter but she had not had to pay for her London dresses out of that and it was more than enough to cover any little luxuries or fripperies she wanted to buy. After he died, Gus, who was her guardian, had increased it to fifty pounds a quarter which was also to cover her clothes. Each Quarter Day, Gus would call at the Dower House and ceremoniously hand his sister two purses, one containing forty gold sovereigns and the other holding ten pounds broken down into more useful coins.

She couldn't remember exactly what sum had been fixed for her pin-money in the marriage settlement, but it was generous, she knew. She remembered Gus saying to her in the carriage on the way to their way to her wedding 'You have chosen a good man, sister, one who will take care of you.' But Will had never once mentioned money, or asked her how she was fixed for funds. The last quarter day had been Michaelmas, but that had been just a week after his mother's death and he had other things on his mind. It was now almost a month since they had left Colduff, and he still had not raised the subject.

She was reluctant to do so, especially after all the fuss about the butler's accounts. It would put her on a par with his servants. But although not his servant, she was dependent upon him, she reminded herself. In marrying she had given up her independence. She had not thought the cup would be so bitter.

She would give him another couple of weeks, she thought, as she closed and locked the box. Surely, he would say or do something before they went to town?

The room darkened and heavy drops drummed against the window. Another wet and windy day. It was almost a week since she had been able to leave the Castle and the walls seemed to close in on her. This doesn't feel like a home, Helena thought; there seems to be no real heart to it. While the new wings were more comfortable than the medieval Keep, they felt more deserted than occupied. Looking down onto the formal knot gardens on either side of the approach to the Keep, she tried unsuccessfully to imagine children romping there with a dog or bowling a hoop. She shook her head. Time enough to think of that. More importantly, was there a room she could make her own, one that would be home to her?

She thought longingly of the solar. What would it be like on a day like this? She snatched up a warm shawl and wrapped it about her shoulders. She would go and see.

Even on such a gloomy day the solar was much brighter than any room in the new part of the Castle. Out to sea, roiling white-capped waves surged and ebbed. The play of the water was echoed in the clouds scudding across the sky. Helena felt exhilarated. A strong gust of wind rattled the windows, drawing her attention to the draughty frames, but surely the carpenter could mend them. She sent for Mrs Higgs and Susan Smithson.

"Do either of you know if it is safe to light a fire here? When was the chimney last cleaned?"

"In the spring, my lady," Susan said. "All the chimneys were cleaned then."

"Even in the rooms that have not been used?"

"Yes, my lady."

"I should like a fire lit here immediately. You worked here for over forty years, did you not, Mrs Higgs?"

"Almost fifty, my lady."

"Do you know what was done with the furnishings of the Keep when it was closed up? I am aware that it was long before your time, but you might have heard mention of it."

"I'm not exactly sure, my lady, but there is a lot of furniture and such in the storerooms beside the ante-room to the chapel and below that in the old guardroom and armoury. There are also chests and presses in the attics of the new wings that might contain some other items. If you wish to go up there, my lady, I'll just have someone check that it is dusted and swept."

"I should like to see if we could make this room more habitable; if it were suitably furnished, I would use it as my private sitting-room."

"I'm sure something can be done, my lady," Mrs Higgs said placidly. "I think some of the old furniture may be in the red parlour in the east wing. We can certainly find enough that you can start using this room at once, while you consider what else you may wish to do."

"Please ask the carpenter to see what can be done with the windows. The frames seem to be loose." Helena walked to the door. "This afternoon we shall see what we can find in the attics and other rooms."

"Very good, my lady. We must be sure that the chimney is drawing properly, for that fire-place has not been used in I don't know how many years. I'll send Philip up and some of the maids as well to give this room a good clean and polish all the wood-work and the floor."

"I am going to make the solar my private sitting-room," Helena told Will as they finished their nuncheon.

"What a splendid idea. I shall be delighted to have your company in the Keep, if you don't find it too uncomfortable."

"I'll try it at any rate. According to Mrs Higgs, some of the old furniture may be stored in the attics and elsewhere, so we'll start by looking there. But the gothick style is all the rage now and surely there is someone who can advise us as to how the keep might be made more habitable." She looked at him seriously.

"There is a—an emptiness at the centre of Rastleigh and I think it may be because the Keep is hardly used. It may sound fanciful, but I think the Keep is the head and the heart of the place; the galleries and wings are the limbs."

"You may be right. I have long felt there was something lacking here, but could not say what. May I join you in your explorations?"

Their searches led to a considerable trove of heavy wooden furniture: tables, chairs, sideboards and cabinets, some of it plain and some ornately carved. Two high-backed, upholstered settles were immediately pronounced perfect to be placed either side of the fireplace in the solar. Even more exciting was a long row of chests, presses and coffers that yielded a vast selection of leather, damask and tapestry wall-hangings, curtains and cushions, some in good condition, others faded and worn. In the storerooms of the keep itself, apart from tables and benches for the Great Hall, they found smaller benches, a lectern and two prie-dieu that must have come from the chapel. Heavy iron candlesticks and fire-irons were also discovered in the depths of these rooms.

"Well, there is enough here to furnish the whole place," Will said. "They must not have thrown anything away."

"We'll bring it down bit by bit," Helena said. "We can start with the solar and then the Great Hall unless there is anything you would like for the library. Will you need any extra help, Mrs Higgs?"

"Maybe for the lifting, my lady, but that is easily arranged. It will be just the task to keep the servants occupied over the winter.

I think they will all be excited by the idea of setting the Keep to rights."

"Do you think they are finished in the solar? If we could put a table in, we could have a cup of tea there. I am curious to see how warm it gets now that the fire is lit."

"I am sure we can manage something, my lady. Shall we say in half an hour?"

"That will be perfect, Mrs Higgs." Helena looked at Will and then at her gown and hands. "I think we shall need that just to get clean and tidy again."

A historian, Dr Thornton had always regretted the fact that the Keep was so neglected, and he was thrilled at the idea of restoring it. "We shall make good headway while you are in town. There are many smaller items scattered through the newer buildings which more properly belong in the Keep; portraits, mirrors, that sort of thing. I shall have a good hunt through the rooms that are not in use at present, if you permit."

Mrs Thornton was equally interested in the thought of Helena's new gowns, although she frankly admitted that she was not *au fait* with the current styles or even the fashionable modistes. "However, you must have a gown made for Wassail Eve. There I can help you."

"Wassail Eve? Will has mentioned it once or twice, and I always meant to ask him about it."

"It is Old Twelfth Night, which is the sixteenth of January. It has been celebrated here since time immemorial and nobody would ever agree to use the new calendar for it, for all that it is well over two hundred years since it was introduced. All the tenants and villagers come to the Great Hall for a feast. You will need something warm, for we go into the orchard afterwards. I find the best is to have two woollen gowns, an over-gown and one under it in a contrasting colour. No train, of course, and half-boots because we walk to the orchard. Oh, and this year you will wear your hair loose—all the brides do."

More confused than enlightened by this muddled flood of information, Helena asked could she see Mrs Thornton's gown.

"It is quite medieval in character, is it not?" she said, as she inspected the pale blue gown worn over a darker under-gown. The neck and sleeves were beautifully embroidered and a woven girdle was decorated with the same embroidery.

"I suppose it is. I took the idea from the old Countess and she had it from her mother-in-law, or so she told me."

"I shall make a sketch of this for the modiste, and of the embroidery too. I do not think there will be time for me to do it myself before January."

Book 4

Chapter Twenty

Helena shifted restlessly on the seat of the carriage. Will sat sprawled in the corner opposite her, immersed in the Morning Chronicle. They would reach London in less than two hours. There was no help for it, she would have to talk to ask him about her pin-money. She was mortified, and also annoyed that he had not seen fit to broach the subject himself.

She took a deep breath. "Will?"

He looked up at once. "Yes, my lady?" When there was no smiling rebuke, he peered at her more closely and came to sit beside her, taking her hand. "What is it, Helena?"

"Oh dear, this is exceedingly awkward." She closed her eyes, swallowed, opened them again and said determinedly, "Will, I need to talk to you about money."

"Money?" he repeated blankly.

"My pin-money. You have done nothing about it. I know we signed all those papers before the wedding, but it was such a rush and I did not really need any up to now, and anyhow I still had some funds of my own, but now we are going to London and there I shall need more and how am I to know how much I may spend?"

Her voice trailed away and she felt her face grow hot as he looked at her, horrified.

"Dear God! Helena, my dear Helena, please forgive me. That I should have let it come to this! I must be the poorest excuse for a husband that ever lived. Pray don't be distressed—it is all my fault and my only, weak excuse is the confusion in which we were wed and in the following weeks, well, we had other concerns. Then, when we came back to the Castle, I never thought of it. I am so sorry, my dear." He lifted her hand and kissed her fingers.

"I thought, no hoped, it might be something like that," she replied, turning her hand so that it gripped his.

He squeezed it and said with a rueful grin, "But you could not help wondering if you were married to the greatest skinflint in history?"

"Never that," she protested, "but I did wonder if perhaps you intended to be a controlling husband."

"Controlling? Ah, as in making you come to me for everything?"

"I am sorry for thinking so badly of you."

"It is only what I deserve for being so careless. I can only plead that I never had a wife before. Let me put your mind at rest. First, you may spend what you like on the household and your bride-clothes; I have no idea what you will need or what it might cost. Over and above that, you will have pin-money of two hundred pounds per quarter. I am told that is a reasonable sum, but if it is not enough you have just to tell me."

"Not enough," she said weakly. "That is eight hundred pounds a year. A family could live quite comfortably on that."

"This is solely for your personal expenses of course—all bills for household expenditure will come to me."

"But you cannot just give me *carte blanche* to buy what I like."

"I trust you, Helena, and your word shall be my bond. There will be a good deal to be spent on our homes, both at Rastleigh and in town and you are to order whatever you wish."

She was silenced by this demonstration of his confidence in her.

He smiled at her wryly. "I am a wealthy man. In addition, don't forget that your father left you well-dowered. Do not let money come between us, despite my folly in not explaining sooner how matters stood."

"No," she said, both relieved and apprehensive. Clearly the demands on the countess and her purse would be much greater than those made on Miss Swift.

~~~

Rastleigh House was a plain stone building, its only ornament the sweep of curved stone steps that led to the wide front door, a door that opened immediately their carriage drew up. Blaines, who had travelled ahead of them, stood ready to receive them. The housekeeper, Mrs Murray waited beside him, with the rest of the staff arrayed behind them in the large hall. As she made the rounds to murmurs of 'welcome, my lady', Helena felt none of the constraint that had been so apparent on her arrival at Rastleigh. The servants here seemed glad to have a mistress again, she thought as she accompanied Will up the broad, oak staircase.

The countess's apartments were spacious and well-appointed in the style of the previous century, the furniture gleaming from decades of elbow grease. Although the rooms had not been occupied for ten years, there no fusty smell; indeed, the faded curtains looked as if they had been recently cleaned and rehung. Fires burnt in all the grates, and bowls of aromatic potpourri lent a pleasant scent to the air.

"Some correspondence has arrived for your ladyship," the housekeeper said. "It is on your writing-table. Would you like some tea, after your journey?"

"I had a note from Lady Harbury," Helena said to Will half an hour later as they drank a reviving cup of Pekoe. "She will call on me tomorrow, and will be delighted to advise me on my new wardrobe."

"I hope you will not feel obliged to continue in strict half-mourning all winter. My mother would not have expected it of you and I should like to see you in colours again."

"If we go into company, I think I must. But when we're private at home, I need not be so meticulous."

"Once you have made your plans with her ladyship, I'll arrange for Mr Lawrence Owens to call. He is an expert on all things gothick and can advise us about the keep."

"What shall we do about the rest of the Castle? Whatever about sleeping in the Keep in the summer, I think it might be cold and uncomfortable in the winter. Should we move to the Earl's and Countess's apartments in the east wing, leaving the west wing for guests or would you prefer to stay in the heir's accommodation?"

"No," he said slowly. "It is time I moved. They must be refurbished, of course."

"I should like to have the Keep ready first, and the east wing could follow when we're in town next season. The west wing won't need as much work. We must also look at the kitchens, for they have been sadly neglected. Cook was talking longingly of a Rumford fireplace that a Mr Thompson has adapted for use in large kitchens. And of course, we mustn't forget the nursery and schoolroom."

"Helena! Do you mean to tell me—?"

"No, no," she replied, blushing. "But it is only sensible to think of these things when we are making changes. If I am going to use the solar, I should like to have a day nursery near me in the Keep and I thought the rooms that Miller and Jenkins were using might make a nice schoolroom."

"You're full of plans."

"Wait until I start on the grounds," she teased.

"What do you want to do in the grounds?"

"I don't know, yet. Maybe it will look better in the spring, but within the walls they strike me as being overly formal and beyond them there is no garden apart from the kitchen gardens, just the woods, the orchards and the stable paddocks. I couldn't see where children might play, or even roam safely."

"There are plenty of trees to climb," he pointed out, "and two streams to fall into."

"I think we could do better than that," she said. "I don't mean to emulate Capability Brown, but surely the woods near the Castle could be made more pleasant, with pretty walks laid out, a space cleared near the stream where we could sit, maybe even a summer house? We could plant some interesting trees as well. I would not want it too ordered."

"Just help nature a little?"

"Exactly."

"I had been thinking of making more paddocks. That new mare of yours is too good not to breed. I'll talk to Smithson."

"And perhaps enlarge the succession houses."

"Why not? But we have all winter to make plans for the Castle. First you must consider what needs to be done here before the Season. You will have noted how sadly outmoded it is. The main reception rooms have not been redecorated for I don't know how many years; as far as I know there has not been a ball since my father died. I don't want to throw everything out, but it must be refreshed. And your own rooms as well, of course."

Charged with completing such a task in less than five months, Helena's little bubble of delight in making plans for the Castle burst. She put down her cup, opened her mouth to speak, then changed her mind. "I must write a quick note to Lady Harbury about tomorrow," she said, getting up. "When would you like to dine?"

Blaines knew from the Castle that Will wished his wife to be seated on his right when they dined alone so that they might converse with ease, but she was rather silent that evening.

"You did not eat much," he said as they sat later in the small drawing room. "Are you unwell or tired from the journey, perhaps?"

"Neither. I do not know whether I am more angry or appalled."

"What do you mean? What is the matter?" He sighed inwardly. What was upsetting her now? After their earlier conversation about money, he had little inclination for a further discussion about his shortcomings.

"Appalled by the idea that I must bring this house up to date in just a few months, and angry at the way you simply tossed the task into my lap without a by-your-leave. I have had very little experience of your style of life and you just assume I will know what to do. I haven't been in London since before Waterloo and have led a quiet country life since then. You know that."

"I want things to be right for you," he protested.

"But you expect me to arrange it all for myself. Why have you never done anything about the state of the house? After all, it is the one you spend most time in, is it not?"

"I wouldn't know where to start."

"And I should? You are used to visiting the great houses of the *ton*. You clearly have some expectations, for otherwise you would not be so sure that so much needs to be done."

Will looked at her, astonished to see his capable Helena so upset. "Ladies have a much better understanding of these matters."

She swept him an ironic curtsey. "Well this lady doesn't," she snapped. "Perhaps your lordship would be so kind as to give me more detailed instructions in the morning? It has been a tiring day and I wish to retire. Good night, my lord." Turning on her heel, she stalked out of the room without giving her indignant husband a chance to reply.

He stared after her, annoyed that she had walked away from him. What maggot had got into her?

An hour later and no clearer in his mind, or indeed his head, he followed his wife to bed. For the first time since their marriage he was unsure of his reception. Hesitantly he opened the door to her bedchamber. All was dark and she seemed to be buried under the bedclothes. He paused for a moment and then, with a shrug and a strange ache he could not place, stepped back and closed the door quietly.

Helena, equally miserable, held her breath as his figure appeared in the doorway, silhouetted against the candlelight in the room behind him. When he disappeared and the door shut between them, she rolled onto her back. She lay wide-eyed for a long time in the dark, before falling into a heavy, uneasy doze and woke late, with a headache and an aching throat.

Will finished his breakfast and crossed the hall to his desk in the library, where he sat making a pretence of considering the piles of paper that had built up on his desk.

"The post, my lord."

He automatically sorted through it, setting aside a letter addressed to Helena. On an impulse he took it and went up the stairs. He had not thought her the type to sulk and what the devil had she meant by requesting "his lordship" to give her "more detailed instructions in the morning", as if she were his servant, for God's sake, or some tradesperson employed to do his bidding. His pace slowed. Was that how she thought he was treating her—detailing his requirements and assuming she would take over from there? But to walk away from him like that!

He found her sitting at a table in the window, a cup of tea in her hand, a plate of untouched toast in front of her. A Kashmir shawl was wrapped around her shoulders; over it her hair hung in a heavy plait down her back. She was staring out the window but turned her head at the sound of his step. She was paler than usual and her eyes looked strained. She regarded him gravely.

"Good morning, Will." Her knuckles white as she gripped the cup. It shook slightly and she carefully set it down.

"Good morning, my dear." He bent to kiss her cheek almost automatically. "Helena, what the devil happened between us last night?"

She raised her brows. "I am not accustomed to being addressed in such language or that tone, my lord."

He sketched a bow. "I beg your pardon, my lady."

She nodded graciously but said nothing.

"There is a letter for you."

She put out her hand to receive it. "Thank you."

Will walked to the other window and stood looking out, his back to the room. "Helena," he said again, despairingly. "What happened?"

She got up and went to stand beside him. "I don't know, Will. Something snapped inside me."

"What and why? If you could tell me, I would try to understand."

"I don't really understand it myself. I tried to work it out for hours last night. I couldn't sleep." She shivered suddenly.

"You're cold. Come over to the fire." He sat her down in an armchair and drew another up beside it. Her tea had gone cold and he emptied the cup, refilling it from the pot. She had eaten nothing, he noticed. There could be no denying that he had upset her, even if inadvertently. But she had upset him as well. "Now, explain," he commanded.

Helena glanced fleetingly at her husband. His shoulders had slumped and he ran his hand through his hair. He no longer sounded quite so annoyed, she thought. Maybe it would be worthwhile trying to get him to see things from her point of view.

"I had been looking forward to coming here," she started slowly. "I thought it would be a way to ease into town life as your countess, especially as we would not be able to go much into society, but I would see Lady Harbury again, and she offered to give a little dinner party for us. It would be a beginning. And I was delighted to be able to visit the best modistes, for as Miss Swift I could not afford to, you know, or at least not for all my gowns. Then there is Hatchard's and I thought too that we could perhaps visit places like the British Museum. It would be a holiday."

"Yes."

"Talking about what we might do at the Castle, was mostly speculation still, was it not—almost like building castles in the air—a fancy in which anything is possible."

Her eyes had been fixed on his face but now she looked down and began to pleat her shawl. He put his hand gently over her restless fingers.

She looked up and went on. "And then you inform me that before we do anything, the main reception rooms and the ballroom here must be refreshed, as you put it, before the Season. I must consider them and decide what I wanted done. Pouf! My cloud castles vanished.

"Later, I said to myself, first you had to get married in a hurry, then there was his mother's illness, then his thieving servants, then the refurbishment of his principal seat and now he wants you to redecorate his town house before the Season starts." Her voice rose. "We have only been married for three months, Will. What will you ask of me next, I wonder? When do we journey to your other properties to ascertain what needs to be done there?"

Helena stopped and caught her breath. "I'm sorry. I know all these things fall within the purview of a wife, and pray believe me that I was happy to do what I could for you and your family. You probably think it is unfair and unreasonable of me to complain now, but it is too much, one thing after the other. Country life at Rastleigh was not too dissimilar to the way we lived at Swift Hall, but here in town I must enter into a new world and one that can be unforgiving to someone who is almost unknown and especially if that someone has married one of the most sought-after bachelors in society." She smiled sadly at him. "You have frequently complained about how pursued you were. How do you think the Mammas will accept a nobody who snatched the prize from under their noses?"

Lennard knocked just then to announce that Mr Graham had called to see his lordship.

"Give him my apologies, Lennard," he began.

Helena interrupted him. "No, go down and see him. If I am to be in a fit state to receive Lady Harbury, I must rest before dressing."

"Come, let's get you into bed." Seeing her come to her feet rather shakily, he put his arm around her and led her to the bed. "You're all done up, aren't you? Shall I send a message to Lady Harbury that you are unwell?"

She shook her head. "I want to see her. It will be good to see someone who knows Helena Swift rather than Lady Rastleigh. I shall be better in an hour or so, if only I can rest." She lay back on her pillows and closed her eyes.

Chapter Twenty-One

"**B**enedick, the married man! How goes it, Will?" Stephen Graham said as he dropped into an armchair in Will's library.

"Until last night, I should have said wonderfully. Now I don't know."

"A rift in the lute, eh? Nothing to worry about; it happens a lot in the first months or so I'm told. An apology and a pretty bauble will set you right."

Receiving no response to this, Stephen abandoned his air of levity. "Do you care to talk about it?"

Will ran his fingers through his hair. "I must, I think, if you don't mind. Strictly between ourselves, Stephen."

"Don't worry, I'll keep mum. Pour two glasses of your excellent Madeira, sit down, and tell me all."

Mr Graham listened in silence as Will described the events of the previous evening and this morning's subsequent conversation.

"She's nervous about facing the *ton*," he said bluntly. "Can't say I blame her. You know as well as I do how some of those tabbies can be. Is there an older lady who could help her? Her mother, your aunt?"

"Not her mother, I think. Her sister-in-law is expecting another child in the spring. And my aunt rarely comes to town and not for the whole Season. Helena is close to Lady Harbury, I understand. Perhaps she would help."

"I know her. A pleasant woman, but not one of the leading hostesses. From what you say, your bride doesn't want for backbone—she just needs some encouragement. She's right too; she has had a lot to deal with. In the normal way of things, she would still be choosing her bride-clothes—you wouldn't even be married yet. She would have had a chance to return to society as Miss Swift. Now she must take centre stage as Countess of Rastleigh. There would have been a lot of interest in her, once the betrothal was announced, but she would have had her mother and your aunt to assist her."

"And I haven't been much support," Will said ruefully. "She is so accomplished in all things that it did not occur to me that she might need some. Hell, I even forgot to provide her with funds."

"What?"

Mr Graham shook his head at Will's confession of his neglect in this important matter. "Poor girl. I trust you have rectified the matter."

"Yes—damn it, no! How the devil am I to do it, Stephen? Do I open a bank account for her, and deposit her allowance there each quarter?"

"That won't do. She would not be the sole beneficiary of it. As her husband, you could draw on it or close it at any time."

"But I wouldn't," Will protested.

"That is not the point," Stephen said patiently. "The point is that you could."

"What should I do? Hand her rouleaux of guineas or a roll of soft?"

"Better a combination of both. And somewhere secure to store it."

"It seems damn mercenary," Will muttered. "She's my wife, not my mistress."

"A mistress would have haggled with you before you laid a hand on her. And demanded a payment up front. This is completely different. How would you have liked it if, instead of giving you an allowance, your grandfather had made you come to him for everything? No matter how indulgent he might have been, you would rather have had control over your own money."

"When you put it like that—" Will said slowly.

"It strikes me, Will, that she is trying her best to be a wife, but what sort of a husband are you?"

"Not much of one, I fear."

His friend regarded him keenly. "You keep people at a distance. It is the way that old devil, your grandfather, trained you, I suppose. But it also means that you are not attuned to the needs of others. You must lessen that reserve of yours if you want to be a husband to your Helena. Try and look at your life together through her eyes for a change." He paused for a moment. "I remember my mother saying that marriage is easy for men, our lives are not really different afterwards, except perhaps improved. We remain in our own world. A girl gives up everything—her family, even her name."

Will looked up at this, but did not interrupt.

"If, as in Helena's case, her husband does not live in the same part of the country, she has to leave her old life behind her. No one knows her except as a wife. It is all strange to her. And for your wife, the change has been extreme. Society will not expect anything more of you now that you are married, but much will be expected of her. The positions of the Countess of Rastleigh and Miss Swift, who lived retired with her widowed mother, are completely different. If she gets off on the wrong foot—"

Will held up his hand. "Enough, Enough! Thank you, Stephen. You've given me a lot to think about—more than enough for the moment."

"Very well. Do you feel up to looking at these papers or would you rather leave them for now and go to Lady Rastleigh?"

"She is resting before Lady Harbury calls. I don't want to disturb her before then. I'll talk to her afterwards. Try and mend my fences."

"You don't need to mend your fences, Will, you need to tear them down."

Some hours later, Mr Graham rose to leave. "We have a plan of action, now. On that other matter, it occurred to me that my godmother is the person we need."

"Your godmother?"

"Lady Neary. Her younger daughter was married in the summer and she is bored, or so she was telling me the other day. I'll bring her to call on Lady Rastleigh, see if they take to one another. She couldn't have a better guide through the pitfalls of the *ton*."

"I'm much obliged, Stephen. I'll walk with you. I don't like to buy jewellery as an apology—it smacks of dealing in indulgences to me; too much like purchasing forgiveness, but Helena loves flowers."

"That's the way to do it."

~~~

Helena waited in the small drawing-room for Lady Harbury. She hoped her ladyship would ascribe her dull pallor and drained complexion to the grey bombazine of her high-collared, long-sleeved gown. Lennard had trimmed it with plaited black gauze and added a full ruff and wrist-ruffles of white crepe, but these could not alleviate the effect of a disturbed night. Perhaps the heat of the fire would bring a flush to her cheek.

The room was small only when compared to the drawing-room proper from which it was separated by double doors. Together, they would easily hold upwards of one hundred persons. Helena found the dark red, greens and golds oppressive. She would prefer something lighter, also lighter furniture, although she had to admit that these heavy, wide-seated armchairs were more comfortable than many modish chairs.

"Lady Harbury."

Helena jumped up and went to Richard's mother, hands outstretched. "How good of you to come and see me so soon."

"As if I could stay away. My heartfelt felicitations on your marriage, my dear. A small trifle, with love from us all."

"Thank you. Do come and sit down." She led her ladyship to a sofa she had had drawn up near the fire and took a seat beside her before opening the little parcel. It held a delicate shawl in hues of lavender and silver wrapped around a painted fan. Helena spread it open. "How beautiful. Thank you, ma'am."

"I had it from my mother. I thought because of the subdued colours—you see it is all shades of black, grey and silver—you could use it now, but the scene of children playing is not at all melancholy."

Helena's blinked resolutely to clear her eyes. "You are too kind, Lady Harbury. Thank you so much."

"Not at all, my dear Helena—I hope I may still call you so?"

"I should be offended if you would not."

"Now, tell me how you go on. So much has happened to you in so short a time. Harbury and I were so happy when I received your letter that you were to be married. We had quite given up hope that you would."

"I don't quite know how it happened," Helena said with a smile, "but suddenly I was considering it seriously."

"From what I hear, he seems to be getting more like his stiff-rumped grandfather as the Seasons go by. I hope he is good to you?"

"Indeed, he is."

"And are you good to him? No missishness, I trust? It is out of place in marriage."

Helena blushed and laughed.

"I see you deal well together," her ladyship said indulgently. She looked at Helena more closely. "Kindness is important. As long as you are kind to one another, you will weather the little storms that beset every couple, especially at the beginning."

"I am sure that is true, ma'am."

They were interrupted by the arrival of servants bearing the tea equipage. Helena dismissed them once everything had been set out and made the tea herself.

"Thank you, Helena." Lady Harbury accepted a cup and a little cake. "Now, tell me about your gowns. I have arranged with Madame Colette that we shall visit her premises tomorrow morning. She would have been more than happy to come here, for to dress the new Countess of Rastleigh will be quite a triumph for her, but I thought you might like to see how she is set-up. Anthea will join us—she and Michael come up tonight. A change before the winter sets in, she said."

"My mother had some mourning gowns made up and sent to me, but I need something more modish, especially if we are to dine out, either here or at Rastleigh. And then there is half-mourning. Rastleigh does not wish me to wear it, he prefers me in colours, but I think I must, in company at least."

"I was saddened to read of Lady Malcolm's death. I did not know her well; she was younger than I—but I remember how beautiful she was when she made her come-out. Hall was quite dazzled by her. As to half-mourning, you are quite right, my dear. However, you are fortunate that the permitted colours suit you and much may be done with accessories such as shawls and fans. Touches of cream, white and silver will also serve to lighten it. At least you will be out of mourning by the time the Season starts. And of course," Lady Harbury added with an intriguing smile, "there are all manner of things you may order to wear when you are alone with your husband, especially as you had no opportunity to purchase any bride-clothes."

"Not even a wedding-gown," Helena said regretfully. "We made do with my new summer gown and a silk spencer over it."

"I am sure you looked charming. Now, are you and Rastleigh free to dine with us tomorrow evening?"

"That would be delightful. I shall send a note to confirm, once I am sure that he does not have another commitment. Thank you for your kindness, Lady Harbury."

"Nonsense, my dear. I shall call for you at eleven o'clock tomorrow morning." Lady Harbury hesitated and then ventured, "Dearest Helena, your mother is not in town. If there is ever anything you are unsure of or on which you need advice, you know you may always apply to me."

"Is Mr Graham still here, Blaines?" Helena asked when the footman had shut the door behind her ladyship.

"No, my lady. His lordship went out with him but he said, should you enquire, to inform you that he would not be long."

Comforted by Lady Harbury's unqualified offer of assistance and support, Helena repaired to her own apartment. She would have another look at the latest modes in preparation for the morrow.

She was contemplating a particularly hideous example of this year's deep-brimmed bonnets when Will arrived, carrying a sumptuous posy of dark red roses interspersed with some cream buds, the stems wrapped in a lacy paper cup and tied with red and cream ribbons. He looked both repentant and concerned as he offered them to her.

"I beg you to forgive my thoughtlessness, Helena. I have not been trying to see our life together through your eyes and I failed to realise the demands I was making of you. I am truly sorry and promise you I will do better."

She took the roses from him. "They are beautiful, and such a wonderful scent. Thank you, Will."

"They reminded me of pearls in your hair. Can you forgive me, Helena?"

She put her hand on his. "Of course, I forgive you. I knew, even at the time, that it was not intentional."

He sat beside her on the sofa. "I do not think that that makes it any better. I should be thinking of you as well as of myself. To hurt you so out of carelessness! It is as terrible in a different way as if I had known what I was doing. Though I promise that I will never hurt you knowingly."

"Lady Harbury said that there are little storms that beset every couple at the outset of their marriage. I did not say anything to her. She was talking in general. She said that it was important that we remained kind to one another, for then we could weather the storms."

"She sounds like a woman of sense." Will took a breath and said, "I have other reparations to make. We did not discuss yesterday how you are to receive your pin-money."

"I am used to receiving my funds quarterly, but it is a lot of money. I will need somewhere to keep it safe—I doubt if my work-box will suffice."

"Your work-box? The one on the table in the window?"

"Yes. Let me show you."

"It is quite ingenious, isn't it," he said when she had unlocked it and lifted out the two trays. "I agree it will not be large enough."

"Is there a strongbox in these rooms as well? I didn't look last night."

"Probably. Let's see."

They found one in a heavy armoire but it was locked and there was no key.

Will frowned. "I wonder—come with me, Helena."

Curious, she followed Will across the linking saloon to his apartments. Like hers, they consisted of a withdrawing room, a bedroom and a private room that would originally have been called a closet but now served as a dressing-room. He took a key from his pocket and opened a large oak armoire, showing her the large strongbox inside.

"I seem to remember—" he said as he unlocked it. "Yes, here it is."

He handed Helena a little chatelaine that held a bunch of keys.

"The countess's keys. Just don't ask me what they open. I always thought they were more decorative than anything else. Shall we try your strongbox again?"

One of the keys fit. "Excellent," Helena said. "This will take my jewellery, and most of the money. I'll continue to keep some at hand in the work-box."

"I was thinking—if you prefer, you could receive it monthly rather than quarterly. You are owed several months now and that will start you off, but it might be better afterwards to have it in smaller, more frequent increments."

"It would be worth trying. Thank you, Will."

"Have I made good my fault?"

"You have, very practically too. I should not have been so reluctant to mention it to you."

"Was it really so hard for you to talk to me about it? I didn't think I was such an ogre."

She was silent, her eyes on her hands as they pleated and smoothed the end of her shawl. "I think because having to ask you for it brought home to me that I am now nothing in the eyes of the law, dependent on you for everything, with no rights of my own."

There was a bitter note in Helena's voice that Will had not heard before. It was on the tip of his tongue to insist that she had nothing to fear from him, to reassure her that he would never forbid her anything, on the contrary he would refuse her nothing. But, as Stephen had pointed out, he could. Legally he could forbid or refuse or permit as the humour took him and she had no choice but to comply. It meant that their marriage was of necessity between two unequal partners. Her freedom and liberty would be what he allowed her and, in the most extreme case, she was dependent on his whim.

Even if all husbands were good to their wives, and he was not so naive or ignorant to suppose that that were the case, it still left the women trapped in a supplicant and subordinate situation. Many men, he knew, would justify this by quoting the bible or simply by claiming that any man was innately superior to any woman. He was too honest to do this. He thought of his widowed mother, whose father-in-law had had the final say about her only child.

"The situation is unfair and unjust, I agree. However, it is based on the law and for the moment we must live with that. I promise you here and now that I shall use any opportunity I have to improve the rights of women." He took both her hands in his.

Catherine Kullmann

"For now, we must work with what we have. We have just agreed that we shall not let money come between us. Let us rather say, instead of money, all the power which the law gives to a husband. I know I am asking a lot of you, but can you find it in your heart to trust me not only not to abuse that power, but also never to use it?"

"Not even if you thought it was for my own good? Frequently men try so to justify the restrictions or demands they put on their wives."

"Not even then. I shall always speak my mind to you, just as, I hope, you will speak your mind to me. Just as good friends speak freely to one another, advising and counselling at times but never forcing their own opinion on the other. But I promise you that I shall never forbid or refuse or even permit you to do something. Your decisions will always be your own, freely made, and I shall respect them, even if I do not like them."

"Are you saying you abjure the power the law gives you over me?"

"In so far as I can. Where you may not act for yourself, I must act for you but it will be as you wish, and never without first ascertaining your wishes."

"I see what you mean. Perhaps we cannot yet change the law but we can do our best to circumvent it in our dealings with one another."

"That's it. Will you give me your trust?"

She looked deeply into his eyes, then her features relaxed and a beautiful smile spread from her eyes to her lips. "I will trust you, Will," she said solemnly, "and I thank you."

He caught her to him and held her close, feeling as if he had evaded a hidden pitfall to reach a secret treasure. "You will never regret it, I promise you." He kissed her gently. "I missed you last night."

Helena leaned back against her husband's arms so that she could into his eyes. "Then why did you not come to me?"

"I did not know what reception I would get after that superb curtsey to my lordship and the way you swept out of the room."

"I suppose I did." She had to smile, despite remembering how sorely his withdrawal to his own room had wounded her. "I felt you were not listening to me, so I had no hope of making you understand."

"Another time simply say, 'Will, you are not listening'," he recommended dryly.

She considered him thoughtfully, imagining how her brothers would have reacted if she had retreated from them in such high dudgeon.

"Why do you look at me so intently?"

"You are not really used to family life, are you? At least not apart from the time you spent each year at Colduff and even there you said it was different this year to other years. Besides, your brothers and sisters cannot be considered your contemporaries."

"I suppose not. From the time I was twelve I lived only with my grandparents, who maintained the old-fashioned, more formal ways."

"Have you ever lived with a woman?"

"Helena! What a question to ask of me! But no, I have not," he replied curtly.

"I am sorry if I am intruding," she said remorsefully, "but I think I have been unfair to you, too. I forget that this whole world of feelings is almost as strange to you as the life of a countess is to me. I don't mean that you are unfeeling," she added hastily, "but I think you haven't shared your life with someone before, the way I did with my family. You have not known that closeness and security, neither the bonds of absolute affection and trust nor the arguments and differences of opinion that can arise and may be quite hefty, but cannot ever shake those bonds."

Will held her away from him and looked down into her face. "Is, that is, do you think that maybe such a bond could grow between us? Is it not something for parents and children or brothers and sisters?"

"Why should it not also be for husband and wife? If they do not set the example, how are the children to learn?"

"Yes, of course, you are right."

"Is that not what you meant when you spoke of a deep and abiding affection developing between us?"

"I suppose it is."

He looked quite shaken, she thought.

Later that night, after they had made love with a new tender intensity, she rested her head on his shoulder. "This is what distinguishes the bond between husband and wife from other family bonds."

"Does each bond have a distinctive element?"

"I think so." She yawned. "Maybe it is also different from couple to couple. It depends on what you put in, I suppose."

Chapter Twenty-Two

When the three ladies arrived *chez Colette*, they were escorted to a private salon where Madame awaited them. An elegant, well-corseted Frenchwoman with dark hair and bright, dark eyes, curtseying deeply she professed herself enchanted to be afforded the opportunity of making gowns for the new Countess of Rastleigh. She was honoured to be permitted to assist Milady, who would be a pleasure to dress—her unusual colouring, her height, her poise and a figure to be envied. Yes, certainly, she could make some black gowns immediately—there is a good choice of fabrics and styles to set off milady's creamy skin and superb figure and she would have all the ladies wishing for an opportunity to wear black. Some discreet embroidery, jet beads and pearls, for example, would be permissible. She would take measurements and start her girls immediately

This done, the ladies turned to the happier task of selecting fabrics for the period of half-mourning.

"You will need at least one ball-dress," Lady Harbury insisted. "There will be some entertainments between Christmas and the start of the Season."

A selection of day and evening gowns followed, a new riding habit and, to Helena's blushing surprise, an intriguing range of nightwear and wraps, "for you are a new bride, my dear."

"Indeed, Milady," Madame Colette put in, "and your petticoats need not be in mourning!"

Madame engaged to come to Rastleigh herself before Christmas for the final fitting of the half-mourning gowns. For the rest, she would do herself the honour of calling on her ladyship as they were ready, if she might call each morning. Helena readily agreed. "If you were to come at half-past ten o'clock, Madame, that would be most suitable."

"We shall take some refreshments at Gunter's," Anthea announced as they prepared to leave. "We must also look for shoes, bonnets and all the little fripperies that make shopping such a delight."

"Not today," Helena protested. "I have borne the burden of this morning's labour, standing to be draped, pinned, twisted and turned, while you merely were required to sit on a comfortable chair, sip tea and provide your opinions. Gunter's sounds delightful and perhaps we could visit Hatchard's, but the rest can be left until another day."

Madame, who had been listening with interest, now volunteered to bring a selection of hats, gloves, shawls and other items with her for Milady to choose from when she called in two days' time with the morning gowns. She could also arrange for an excellent shoemaker to call, if Milady wished. "I often work with him and once he has your measurements, he can make shoes and slippers to match your gowns, Milady."

"A splendid suggestion, Madame," Helena said. "If you can assist us in this way, we may then visit the shops to look solely for those particular pieces which appeal especially. I do not wish to spend all my time in the shops, or at least not in pursuit of a new wardrobe," she amended.

~~~

As the carriage rolled towards Harbury House that evening, Helena could not but look back at her first visit there. Then I was a young girl, excited and apprehensive at once, but eagerly looking forward to what life might bring. I never thought I would be returning here as the Countess of Rastleigh. Suddenly she began to laugh. In response to Will's enquiring look, she said, "My coming-out ball was held at Harbury House. Lady Harbury kindly offered to give a dance for me as the house Mamma and Papa had taken for the Season had no ballroom. I just remembered discussing the guest list with Mamma and her ladyship. Your name was mentioned and Lady Harbury said it would be a triumph indeed if you were to attend and solicit my hand for a dance, but it was too much to expect. You rarely accepted invitations to coming-out balls and never danced with girls. I think she still sent you a card, just in case, but you escaped her trap, my lord."

"How foolish of me," he sighed, leaning in to press a long kiss on her lips. "If only I had known the trap was baited with such a tempting morsel."

"But not for you, at least not now," she said, staying his roving hands. "I cannot arrive looking like a doxy who has just entertained her favourite in the carriage."

"As long as I am your favourite," he murmured, releasing her and sitting back to watch her straighten her gown and run her hands over her hair. "With whom did you dance?"

"At my ball? Jonnie and Richard, although I never did know how they contrived to be there, for the regiment had not yet returned home from France. But I didn't think about that at the time. It was only later that I wondered. Papa, of course, Michael and Lord Harbury; Gus, though he was far more interested in Rosalind. They had met some weeks previously, and he had prevailed upon Mamma to invite her to visit us in London. In fact, by the time the gentlemen from both families had danced with me, there was little opportunity to stand up with new acquaintances, although Jonnie made a point of presenting some other officers who were already in London."

"Certainly, my recollection of you during that season is of seeing you surrounded by a rapture of regimentals."

"They were most attentive, and indeed I was grateful for it, for to make your bow to society like that is quite daunting. Just consider what your mother had to endure."

"Regrettably, the facts of her fortune were well known. I think her uncle and aunt wanted to get her off their hands as quickly as possible. Your father did not make that mistake. I was quite taken aback when I learnt the extent of your inheritance."

"Yes. He didn't discuss it with me at the time, but explained to me later that he did not want to run the risk of my being married for my money. Here we are."

As they mounted the steps, Helena was seized by the memory of another evening towards the end of that first season. Conscious of her age and innocence, Richard had been careful not to overwhelm her with his attentions or to make her the subject of unwelcome talk. They had moved in a fluctuating set of officers and their families, all bent on extracting the maximum enjoyment from this first, carefree season after the long war with France. He always solicited her hand for the supper dance but as they went into supper as part of a group that changed each evening, this had not attracted undue public attention.

He borrowed Michael's curricle to take her driving but Michael understood this as an act of friendship towards Jonnie's sister. The Harburys and the Swifts had frequently made up a party for outings or visits to the theatre and other entertainments. However, as other eligible bachelors and young ladies were also invited, Richard and Helena were able to spend time together without anyone thinking anything of it. When he started calling her Nell as Jonnie did, no one was surprised.

That evening they had discovered their shared love of Mr Moore's Irish Melodies. They were a great favourite of Richard's mother and she had importuned her son to sing, calling upon Helena to play for him. When he became tired, she enquired if Helena sang and had them switch places. They must have performed for over thirty minutes. Now, once again at his parents' door, Helena wondered if shadowy echoes of their voices were still to be heard in the drawing-room, perhaps 'at the mid hour of night'. That night was the first time he kissed me, she remembered, when we went into the garden once the music was over. She glanced at her new husband and then deliberately banished thoughts of the past and what might have been.

Lord Harbury made Helena a correct, formal bow, addressing her as Lady Rastleigh, which made her giggle inside, before holding out his arms to her. "Come and give an old man a hug, Helena, it does my heart good to see you again."

"And mine to see you, sir," she said, embracing him fondly.

"You must forgive us, my lord," Harbury added to Will. "We look upon your countess as one of our own. She was an angel to our son Richard after Waterloo."

"She has told me of your son's death. I do not think it can ever be too late to offer my heartfelt condolences on his loss. If Helena is part of your family, may I hope that that honour will also be extended to her husband?"

"Delighted, Rastleigh, only too delighted," Lord Harbury said bluffly, then turned to introduce his son and daughter-in-law to the earl.

Astonishing, thought Lady Harbury. I never thought to see Rastleigh so at ease; not at all on his high horse. She was charmed by his rarely-seen smile and quiet words of appreciation for her kindness to his wife. He does not seem to know the depth of her involvement with Richard though. Aloud she explained to Helena that it was to be a small family party. "Just the six of us, for we have not seen you for an age, though you are a faithful correspondent."

"As are you and Caro, ma'am," Helena replied.

Dinner was announced and they went in, soon to be immersed in an exchange of family news, interspersed with discussions on the latest political issues as well as a goodly selection of society gossip.

When the ladies had withdrawn, Lord Harbury signalled to his son and guest to come closer.

"You are a lucky dog, Rastleigh," he said pouring himself a glass of port. "You could not have found a better wife in all of England."

"Indeed, I think so too, sir," Will said quietly. "I know how fortunate I am."

The conversation soon moved to agricultural and equine matters and Will mentioned his idea of breeding Helena's new mare.

"Take my advice," Michael Harbury said, "don't do it until you have purchased her another one equally as good, for she will not thank you if she has no horse for several months while the mare is in foal. With two, you can breed each one every other year."

"An excellent idea, sir." Will raised his glass to him. "I shall write to Sir John Malcolm immediately. The mare was a bridal gift from him to Helena and he may have another ready next year. As I recall he also had a well-built young stallion. If he does not wish to part from him, he will talk to his neighbours for me."

"You are well acquainted with Sir John?" Mr Harbury was visibly impressed. "He has a small stud, but absolutely top class and will sell only to a select few."

"He is my step-father. Should you like an introduction?"

"Above all things! Do you know if he is looking to sell any hunters?"

"I am not sure, but if not, he would be happy to see what is available in the vicinity. A lot of the farmers there keep one or two horses, you know and you may be sure that any mount he selects for you will be sound."

"If you are writing to him, perhaps you would put in a word for me. I would take up to three."

Lord Harbury pushed back his chair. "We had better join our ladies, God bless them."

~~~

Mr Owens presented himself the next day and professed himself delighted to advise on the restoration of Rastleigh Keep. "We shall make the best use we can of the original pieces my lord, my lady. It is fortunate that due to the recent fashion for all things gothick, other pieces are now being offered for sale and there is also a good range of fabrics in the gothick style available for curtains, hanging, cushions and that sort of thing." He looked around the library. "I notice some older pieces were obviously brought here as well—that table for instance. Do you wish them to stay here?"

Will looked at Helena.

"I think not, Mr Owens," she said. "I shall request the housekeeper to show you over the house, so you may see what is here. There may also be something in the attics."

~~~

"The Dowager Lady Neary and Mr Graham have called, my lord, my lady. They are in the saloon."

"Thank you, Blaines." Helena looked at Will in surprise.

"She is Stephen's godmother. He said he would bring her to call on you."

She raised her eyebrows. "And you didn't think to mention it?"

He shrugged. "I wasn't sure she would come. She's a bit of a Tartar. You will get on well together if you stand up to her."

Helena rose. "Let us brave the Tartar then."

"My lady," Will said as they entered the saloon. "What a pleasure to see you here."

"Rastleigh." An elderly lady, severely but stylishly dressed, inclined her immaculately coiffed head graciously. She appeared to be taller that the average, but this may also have been due to the upright manner in which she sat and the deep purple turban which provided some additional inches. Her dark blue eyes, magnified by a skilfully wielded lorgnette, peered intelligently at Helena. "So, this is your bride?"

Helena's spine stiffened as she extended her hand. "How kind of you to call, ma'am." Having touched fingers with her visitor, she smiled at Mr Graham. "It is very good of you to bring your godmother to see me." Cadence and word choice left her meaning open to debate—was Lady Rastleigh to be honoured by the condescension of such a call or was Lady Neary to be pleased by the outing her godson had indulgently arranged for her?

"My pleasure, ma'am."

Lady Neary graciously accepted a cup of tea and commenced a refined inquisition of her hostess. Helena quietly parried each thrust with ease, replying calmly and politely without revealing her inner nervousness. In fact, she quite enjoyed it, she thought, remembering how such an encounter with one of the dowagers of the *ton* would have petrified her at the time of her come-out.

"Will you take some more tea, ma'am?"

"No, I thank you." Her guest handed her cup to her godson to be returned to the tea tray. "You may give me a glass of that excellent Madeira of yours, Rastleigh, if you will."

"Of course, ma'am." He poured a glass and brought it to her. Her ladyship sipped approvingly, turned to her hostess and said, "Well done, child. If you can hold your own with me at my most haughty, you have nothing to fear in the *ton*."

"I beg your pardon, ma'am?"

"No need to poker up. I wish to support you. I have seen many a young bride worried about facing society in her new position and you have no mother or mother-in-law to stand by you, for your parent does not come to town much, I understand."

"Not since my father died. She prefers the quieter round of country life and of course there are her grandchildren. My sister-in-law is expecting another happy event in the spring, so Mamma will probably go to stay at the Hall for some weeks then. She lives in the Dower House."

"Well, if you would accept me as a—" Lady Neary paused.

"—Wicked godmother?" suggested Mr Graham.

"Hold thy peace, Sirrah or I shall turn thee into a...a...badger!" Her ladyship brandished her lorgnette as if it were an epée.

He flung up a hand to defend himself. "Not the lorgnette! Anything but the dread lorgnette!"

"Pray spare him." Helena's voice quivered with laughter. "I should be delighted to be your honorary goddaughter."

"I wonder if there may not in fact be a relationship between you," Will put in.

"What do you mean?"

"Your eyes are similar, both in colour and setting. In addition, there is a general resemblance in your profiles."

"You're right, Rastleigh," Mr Graham said. "I always thought your wife reminded me of someone, but could not decide whom."

"Forgive me, ma'am, but when you were younger, was your hair a very dark red like mine?" Helena asked cautiously.

Lady Neary nodded. "No one knew where it came from for neither my mother nor either of my grandmothers had it."

"Was one of these ladies perhaps a Falconer? I am told that my colouring comes from my father's mother who was Helena Margaret Falconer."

"My maternal grandmother was Amanda Falconer. Well, we can work out the exact details another time, but it is obvious we are cousins. In which case there can be no need to stand on ceremony. You gentlemen may take yourselves off to the library or the billiard room while we ladies get to know one another better."

Will cocked an eye at his wife, who was again trying to repress her laughter, and at her nod, got to his feet, collected his friend and withdrew thankfully. "I only hope Helena will forgive me," he said as they took their accustomed places in the library.

"I am sure she will. Godmamma's bark is much worse than her bite and Lady Rastleigh seemed to be vastly entertained by her."

Indeed, Helena felt as if Pallas Athena herself had descended, aegis raised to protect her whether she wished it or no. As she discovered, this was not far from the truth.

"I have been suffering from ennui since Judith married," her guest confided. "You cannot have two mistresses of one estate and Neary's wife does quite well. They would not hear of me removing to the Dower House while Judith was unwed, but I insisted once the celebrations were over."

"It was the same with Mamma. We stayed with my brother until my younger sister married but then she and I removed to the Dower House."

"You?" Lady Neary was surprised. "Did she not think to find a husband for you, too?"

"She knew I did not want her to try. I had two Seasons, then there was Waterloo and afterwards Papa became ill. When it was all over, I was a different person. Like Mamma, I preferred the pace of country life."

"Until Rastleigh appeared like Hades, to snatch you away?"

"I suppose he did," Helena said, laughing. "It happened so quickly because of his mother's illness." She explained how Lady Amelia had urged them to marry at once.

"And you agreed? Bravely done, indeed. Have you come to town to purchase your bride-clothes?"

"In a way. Now I need more mourning and to make provision for half-mourning. I thought to wait until spring to see about clothes for the Season."

"A sensible decision. Now," Lady Neary went on briskly "I know you do not wish to go much into society while you are in mourning, but there is to be a benefit performance of Mr Handel's

Messiah next week. I shall get up a small party—it would be quite unexceptional for you and Rastleigh to attend, and return to me for supper. And you must call on me, of course. We must explore the connection between our two families."

"Would it be permissible for us to give a small dinner—just family and close friends?"

"Why not? You have to eat," her ladyship replied acerbically.

"I shall talk to Rastleigh then, to arrange a date."

"Well, this has been delightful. I shall take my leave of you now, Cousin Helena."

"Thank you for calling, Cousin," Helena said equally gravely. "Indeed, I am most grateful to you and to Mr Graham for bringing you to me."

"You know," Lady Neary said, "Stephen must be just as much a Falconer as I am, for his mother and mine were sisters. Clemency was much the younger and, as my mother was dead before Stephen was born, she asked me to be his godmother. Therefore, he is your cousin, too."

Helena smiled. "I wonder what he and my husband will make of that."

Chapter Twenty-Three

How long could it take to try on a few gowns? Will was losing patience. After several wet and windy days, November had finally favoured them with crisp, sunny weather. They could take a drive in the Park, or perhaps further afield. Helena's modiste was to call that morning, but surely, they were finished by now.

Opening the door to her dressing-room, he found his wife, clad only in a chemise and light stays, installed on a pedestal like a goddess surrounded by hand-maidens. He watched unnoticed as an older, almost excruciatingly stylish woman handed something to Lennard who stood on a higher platform. The maid dropped a garment over Helena's head and the older woman drew the skirts down. She then stood back to scrutinise the effect of a petticoat made in the palest silver silk, embroidered with delicate, multi-hued flowers and leaves. At the hem a double ruffle frothed gently.

"Well, my dear," he drawled, moving into the room, "if this is what you have been doing all morning, I can only approve."

At the sound of his voice everyone jumped. Helena blushed and looked reprovingly at him, the maid and seamstresses bobbed and scurried to obey Madame Colette who, having curtsied imposingly, commanded them to clear a chair for Milord. Feeling rather like a pasha, Will obediently sat and stretched out his legs, wondering how quickly he could remove the whole pack of them from his wife's presence.

"Now the gown," Madame snapped. This time it took two acolytes to drop it over Helena's head. It was like a secret present, one only he knew to unwrap, Will thought, as embroidered silver slowly yielded to black silk.

The modiste twitched the skirts into place and then assisted Helena to step down from the stool. "Would Milady be so good as to walk to the window and back?" Helena complied and the skirt swayed enticingly, revealing every so often a flash of silver ruffle.

"Excellent," Madame said again. "For half-mourning we shall use silver ribbons and lace. And now the cloak." She snapped her fingers at one of the seamstresses who hurried to bring a dark, hooded mantle, trimmed with pale fur.

"From Russia," Madame said reverently. "Midnight blue velvet with the finest arctic fox." She held it open, revealing it to be fully lined with the fur, and put it around Helena's shoulders. It fell beautifully. "I knew Milady was tall enough," Madame approved. "This is not for little girls." She pulled up the hood, arranging it so that the silvery-blue fur framed Helena's face. Helena slipped her hands through the wide sleeves and Madame handed her a matching muff then turned her to face the mirror.

"Perfection."

"Is it not very expensive?" Helena asked.

"No," Will said. "You may send the bill to me, Madame."

Madame Colette curtsied. "As you wish, Milord."

He smiled at Helena. "When will you be finished here? I came to enquire if you would like to go for a drive."

"We are finished for today, are we not, Madame?"

"Yes, Milady."

"A drive would be delightful, my lord. Shall we say in twenty minutes?"

Helena took a deep breath as they turned into the Park. "This was an excellent idea. We have been cooped indoors for too long."

"We must make the most of these fine days. That reminds me, you were used to drive yourself in Wiltshire. I don't think there is anything suitable at Rastleigh apart from the old gig that the Thorntons use. What sort of carriage would you like? A phaeton? Though not a high-perch one, I think," he added, eying the equipage swaying towards them, the spirited white pair guided by a dashing female dressed all in white.

"Good heavens, no!"

"We'll look for a suitable low-to-middling one that you find easy to get in and out of. Will one horse be enough?"

"Of course. I shall only be tooling around the neighbourhood. You are too generous, Will."

He turned his head to smile at her. "No arguing about money, Helena, remember?"

"I may thank you, at least, may I not?"

Before he could reply, they were confronted by a slim young man on a fine black horse who had pulled up when he reached their curricle.

"Cousin." He bowed gracefully from the saddle. "I did not know you were in town."

"How should you, Hall?" Will replied curtly and then to Helena. "My dear, may I present Harry Hall, my heir. Hall, my countess."

"Lady Rastleigh." The young man bowed again. "Your servant, ma'am. How long do you remain in town? If you permit, I shall do myself the honour of calling upon you."

"Please do. I am not sure how long we shall be here. It depends on Parliament."

"Of course. I shall not delay you any longer, ma'am, Rastleigh." With a flourish of his whip, he moved on.

"A pleasant young man," Helena commented.

"You have not yet had the pleasure of encountering him in a ballroom. On horseback he is not such a fribble, I grant you."

"Many young men go through a dandy phase before they settle down. I often wondered if it was the only way they could compete with the officers' dress uniforms, for you must admit they can be dazzling. Things may have changed now that the wars are over, but when I made my come-out the girls all sighed for a military admirer."

"You did not lack them yourself."

"No, but I was to some extent protected, having a brother in the army. A bit like Mr Jenner's vaccination, I suppose."

To Will's surprise and annoyance, Mr Hall called the next day while he and Helena sat in the drawing-room with Stephen Graham and his cousin Hester, Lady Neary's widowed daughter whom Helena remembered from Brussels.

Her husband, Major Matthew Dunford, had sold out after Waterloo. His constitution had been weakened by being left lying wounded on the wet ground for over two days after the battle and Helena had been sorry to learn that he had succumbed to an inflammation of the lungs some two years previously, leaving Hester with three children: two boys and a girl. The two ladies had been delighted not only to renew their acquaintance but also by their newly discovered relationship and Will was about to suggest to his friend that they withdraw to the library when Blaines announced his heir.

"I wish to offer in person my felicitations on your recent marriage and also," Mr Hall turned to Will, "to express my condolences on your recent loss, Cousin."

He spoke sincerely, without any of his usual flourishes and Will's, "Thank you, Hall," had a shade more warmth to it than was usual when he addressed his cousin.

"Pray sit down, Mr Hall," Helena said. "Are you acquainted with Mrs Dunford and Mr Graham?"

"Indeed, my lady. I hope you are enjoying your stay in town?"

"To be frank, I find the combination of November fog and all the fires extremely unpleasant."

"You are spoiled by the fine country air," he said with a slight smile. "But I agree, London is not at its best, now."

"How long do you remain in town, Mr Hall?" Mrs Dunford enquired.

"Not beyond the end of the month, ma'am. I go to join my mother and sister in Norfolk." He turned to Will. "I believe you were in Ireland in September, Rastleigh. Did you happen to encounter the King? I understand he greatly enjoyed his day at the races—left his whip as a prize for future generations."

"I suppose you have to respect the fact that he was not hypocritical enough to make much of pretence of mourning his wife for all that court mourning was prescribed for several weeks," Mrs Dunford said. "I believe he wore a black armband, but that is all. A sad end to a sad marriage. We shall see you on Friday, Cousin Helena?"

"Yes indeed, I am looking forward to it immensely, Cousin Hester. I have never attended the performance of such a large work before."

Not long after, Mr Hall also took his leave. "Delighted to have made your acquaintance, Lady Rastleigh. I shall do myself the honour of bringing my mother to call on you next year, if I may. She is not in the habit of coming to town, but I hope to encourage her to bring my sister Rachel out next Season. She should have come out this year, but with my father's illness and death, it was not possible."

"Pray do," Helena said with a warm smile, "and your sister too, of course. I should be most happy to meet them."

~~~

The resounding chorus of Amens reverberated around the church until Helena felt the building swayed in unity with the echoing voices, about to take flight and soar into the heavens free of all earthly restraints. The solo singers had been unable to resist and had joined in Mr Handel's paean to the defeat of death. She moved closer to her husband and slipped her hand into his, both to share her pleasure with him and to anchor herself amid the exhilarating sounds of the choir and orchestra. Will's hand closed over hers and he moved so that their shoulders touched as they listened to the final notes of the great work.

"I cannot thank you enough, Cousin Verity," she said later to Lady Neary as they waited in the portico for their carriages. "It was wonderful—I have never heard anything to compare with it. The words and music are in such perfect harmony and create a sublime expression of faith."

"Who is that talking to Lady Neary?" Lady Westland asked her companion. The burning torches high on the walls illuminated animated features that were admirably framed by the stunning silver fox trimming of the stranger's hooded cloak. Her hands were concealed in a matching muff.

"I have no idea. I saw Stephen Graham earlier. Lady Neary is his godmother, I know. I'll warrant she has selected a bride for him. See, there he comes with Rastleigh."

As the ladies watched, Mr Graham offered his arm to Lady Neary, while the Earl of Rastleigh angled his towards the mysterious stranger, who slipped one hand from her muff to tuck it into the crook of his arm. He closed his arm to draw her to his side, covering her hand with his free one as he smiled down at her so fondly that Lady Westland was silenced by a mixture of astonishment and ire.

"Well! She must be the new Countess," her friend said. "He would not squire another interest to such a party, if indeed he has one, for he seems very *épris*."

Lady Westland swallowed the scorching words that rose to her lips and with a glittering smile cried, "Ah, there are our escorts!"

Without a further glance towards her erstwhile lover she swept down the steps of the church exclaiming, "What kept you so long? Where shall we go? I vow I am parched."

Chapter Twenty-Four

Parliament duly met on the twenty-ninth of November, only to be prorogued again, and Lord and Lady Rastleigh returned to their principal seat in comfortable amity. Their trip to London despite, or perhaps because of its inauspicious beginnings had been most successful.

Helena felt much more assured in her role as Countess of Rastleigh. The renewal of her friendship with the Harburys and the surprising revelation of a relationship with the Nearys had given her additional confidence. She had enjoyed her ventures into society and had been warmly received both at Lady Neary's and at Lady Harbury's who, true to her word, had given a dinner for them at which she had met some other peers and their wives. Her own quiet dinner party had gone well and she had taken the opportunity to discuss with the assembled ladies what needed to be done with the public rooms of Rastleigh House.

Her table had been completed, surprisingly, by Mr Harry Hall. Will had not been too happy at Helena's suggestion that his heir be invited to dinner, but she was able to prevail by pointing out that it was to be a family occasion and there was no other bachelor to balance her table. Mr Hall had accepted the invitation with gratifying alacrity and his behaviour on the night had been unexceptional.

"What is Mr Hall's mother like?" Helena broke the lazy silence that had descended on the carriage after nuncheon.

"I don't really know," Will replied. "A quiet lady, I gather. The only time I spoke her was after her husband's funeral. He was one of the Carlton House set, but I had the impression she preferred to remain in the country."

"Is there only one daughter?"

"I think so. I've never met her. I hope she is better to pass than her cub of a brother."

"He's young and probably a bit adrift. From what you say, he cannot have received much good advice from his father and now he is responsible for his mother and sister."

"Then he should spend less time at the tables and more on his acres," Will said trenchantly.

"It is easy for a young man to go astray. Does he have any relatives on his mother's side who might guide him?"

"Not to my knowledge. She was an only child and, I believe, an heiress."

~~~

It was nearly dark by the time the carriage passed under the Gatehouse arch and golden lamplight spilled out from the main door to the keep. Footmen bearing torches emerged to light them up the steps.

"Welcome home, my lord, my lady." Parker bowed.

"Thank you, Parker."

Dr Thornton and his wife appeared in the door to the Great Hall. "Welcome home," they said in unison, then stood back, gesturing to Will and Helena to enter. "We thought to surprise you with the results of our endeavours," Mrs Thornton added.

"This is truly splendid," Helena exclaimed. "I feel as if I have stepped back in time. When I think of how cold and barren it was when I first saw it."

She turned in a circle to take everything in. Slightly faded multi-hued hangings covered the bare walls, with the Rastleigh arms displayed to great effect behind the Lord's and Lady's seats. Candles in holders of polished pewter lit the high table and a round, oak table that stood in the middle of the room, surrounded by chairs. Carved wooden screens sheltered high-backed, cushioned settles placed near the glowing log fire in the huge hearth, creating a snug space to sit. More candles on chests either side of the window and on a side-board between the chimney piece and the top table, cast light on an array of pottery and pewter vessels.

"You have worked wonders," Will added. "And this was all hidden away?"

"Say rather, preserved," Dr Thornton said.

"It is more welcoming, is it not?" Mrs Thornton said. "Much more could be done, but we wished to give you a first impression."

"Welcome home, my lord, my lady." Susan Smithson came in with a rich apple cake, followed by a footman bearing a tray set with a steaming punch bowl and glasses. "I thought some mulled wine might be welcome after your journey."

"Indeed, it would." Will gratefully inhaled the aromas of apples, nutmeg, cloves and cinnamon that wafted across the room.

Smithson, as she was now called following her promotion to housekeeper, served the wine and set the punch bowl on a trivet near the fire.

This is the way coming home should be, Will thought—spicy, warm and welcoming, not cold and lonely.

~~~

Helena had reached the end of her long letter to Kate and Emily, describing her new wardrobe and the refurbishment of the Keep.

Mr Owens was vastly excited by the discovery of three suits of armour and a collection of swords, halberds and I don't know what else in a small room at the back of the armoury. He entered into deeply technical discussions with Will and the blacksmith and is to return in January with an expert to consider how they might be restored and displayed. The solar is now most comfortable with new curtains and cushions. Will frequently joins me here for our nuncheon or for tea as we love to sit looking out to sea.

You will be happy to see your father and brothers when they join you at your aunt's home for Christmas. This first year without your dear Mamma will be rather melancholy for all of you at times. Do not attempt to repress such feelings, but rather accept them as part of your grief. At the same time, you will also enjoy some of the festivities and may be reminded of happier times spent with your Mamma. Do not feel guilty when this happens, but welcome these gentle intimations that it is natural that acute grief passes. This does not mean that we forget those we love. They continue to live in our hearts.

With fond remembrances to your father and brothers and my compliments to your aunt and also Miss Bowen, I remain, dear Kate and Emily, your affectionate sister,

                          Helena Rastleigh.

   Post Scriptum. Will has just come in and desires me to send you his love.

She folded, sealed and addressed the letter and handed it to her husband for franking. "I imagine you have written to Jack and Alexander, telling them about the armour and the weapons."

He nodded. "They love to hear about the Keep, Alexander especially. We shall have no choice but to have them all here next summer."

"Should you mind?"

"Not in the slightest. It would be nice to see the Castle full of life. I thought we might invite the Waltons and your family as well."

"Mrs Thornton has told me about Wassail Eve, but how do you celebrate Christmas?"

"Quite simply. The Grahams come to dine on Christmas Day and sometimes the Thorntons are here. The servants get their boxes on the twenty-sixth, of course."

"I have spoken to Mrs Graham about families that might be in need, and intend to call on all the houses. Not just the needy ones. Hope has been working hard making cakes and preserves so that I can take a gift to each family and also books for the children. Mrs Graham has given me a list of names and ages and I have sent an order to Hatchard's. Mrs Thornton will come with me. She has been doing her best to keep things going since your grandmother died. Your grandfather just told her to continue, apparently."

"That's right. She asks me every year if she do the same as before. You are going to be busy."

"I am not used to being idle, as you know. I also want to see what needs to be done in the kitchens, dairy and stillroom and make up some of my favourite salves and potions."

"The Castle is yours, my lady, just as long as you remember that I have a strong aversion to eyes of newt."

"That leaves me plenty of scope. I must see have we enough toes of frog."

"I have been wondering should we not invite Mr Hall and his mother and sister for Christmas," Helena said later.

"Why should we? I can't abide him."

"Do you really know him? From what you have said, you and your grandfather had very little to do with that side of the family."

"That is true. They were never invited here, probably because Grandfather hated the idea that a cousin was the heir presumptive after my father died."

"You are the head of the family. I think Mrs Hall would welcome our acknowledgement and support in bringing out her daughter but it might be no harm to take their measure, as it were, before deciding how involved we wish to be." She paused and continued carefully, "Besides, should we not be blessed with a son, Mr Hall or his son will inherit so it is better that he knows the estate. Even if your grandfather had good reason not to invite the father, we should at least get to know the son before deciding to follow suit."

Will did not look happy at the idea and Helena put her hand on his arm for a moment. "I shall not press you if you do not like it."

"I don't, but I can see the merits in what you say. But I am not having a rowdy house party," he declared forcefully.

"That is out of the question, for we are still in mourning, they are not long out of it and we can explain that it will be a quiet, family occasion."

"Let us invite them but—perhaps they will decline."

Chapter Twenty-Five

Will was astonished by how much he enjoyed Christmas. What had previously seemed like an especially dreary Sunday now was full of colour and celebration. For the first time in living memory a Yule log was lit in the Great Hall. On the morning of Christmas Eve, the younger members of the party had gone to collect greenery in the woods and the ladies fell to decorating, sending the gentlemen off to find ladders so that the higher regions of the Hall could be reached.

There had been considerable discussion regarding the revival of the Yule log ceremony, especially as there was no remaining part of a previous year's log available from which the new one could be lit. In the end it had been decided to light it from the kitchen fire as this fire burned all year round and was never extinguished. The entire household assembled in the Great Hall and the youngest and oldest members—Dr Thornton and a scullery maid, who was nearly overcome by the honour, carefully brought a pan of live coals from the kitchen. The log was lit to great acclaim and was followed by the distribution of mulled cider and mince pies.

"Thank you for all you have done these last months," Will said before the servants dispersed. "May this new fire bring us warmth and light in the coming year."

~~~

On Christmas morning Will slipped out of bed, returning to hand Helena a small packet. "Merry Christmas, my dear Helena."

She carefully unwrapped it to reveal a charming necklace of coloured gemstones set as flowers. "It's beautiful—and matches my wedding brooch."

"Yes. I had it made so that you can attach it here in the centre as a pendant. It should look well with your black, silk gown."

"How ingenious, and how thoughtful of you." She pulled him back down beside her to thank him with a kiss.

"I have a gift for you too," she said sometime later as they breakfasted rather hastily so as not to be late for church. "But you will not get it until tonight."

~~~

Will looked down the long table that had been brought down from the dais so that diners could sit on both sides. His wife sat at the other end, his gift sparkling at her throat. The rector and Dr Thornton were on either side of her, while Mrs Hall and Mrs Graham sat to his right and left. Helena had chosen to mix the three families rather than adhere to the strict rules of precedence. "There is nothing more dispiriting than being seated beside one of your own family when you are invited elsewhere. I must put

Stephen Graham beside his mother, he does not live here the rest of the year and he has Rachel on his left."

Mr Hall sat between Mrs Paul Graham and Miss Graham while Mr Thornton sat between Miss Graham and Mrs Hall. Opposite, the Graham brothers Paul and Stephen were either side of Rachel Hall. Once the soups were removed and Will and Dr Thornton had begun to carve the turkey and sirloin of beef that replaced them, plates were passed up and down the table together with instructions for 'just a couple of sausages, please' or 'no oyster sauce' or 'some red cabbage and a slice of neat's tongue'. Plum pudding was much in demand, as were the mince pies. Glasses were filled and conversation became general as company manners were replaced by a more cordial fellowship.

Christmas dinner was at the old-fashioned hour of three o'clock. The last garnet gleam of a winter sunset was fading in the west when the whole party withdrew to the solar for carols, charades and cards, the elder Grahams and Thorntons good naturally interrupting their game of whist to join in the singing or hazard a guess as to a sought-after word. Several hours later, an aromatic bowl of smoking bishop provided, as the rector put it, a parting glass for the Grahams.

When Helena and Will were finally on their own, he pulled her into the curve of his arm. "You are a miracle-worker," he whispered, his cheek resting against her hair. "When I think how dismal previous Christmases here were, formal, dull and dreary." He shifted to look down into her face. "And you? Did you enjoy it? It is your first Christmas away from home, is it not?"

"I loved it. I did miss my family of course, but there is something special about being the mistress of my own home."

"You certainly were that, saying to one 'go' and she goeth and to another 'come' and he cometh—"

"Because there were hardly any—really no Christmas traditions here. I had a free hand. But now my lord, it is time to start a new Christmas tradition."

"That the Lord must make love to his Lady before the day is out?" he asked with a kiss.

"No, or at least not yet. He must receive a present from his lady. But first you must change your clothes; you will need to dress more warmly."

His warmest garments had been laid ready for him in his dressing-room. He quickly changed and sought out Helena who now wore a heavy cloak over a woollen gown.

"Now, my lord."

Bemused, he followed her back into the Keep. At the foot of the tower stairs, she handed him a lantern and took another before heading upwards, past the solar, past the top room in the tower until, she opened a door to step onto the roof.

"Is everything ready, Paul?" she asked a waiting footman, who was well wrapped up against the cold night.

"Yes, my lady."

"Thank you. That will be all."

Helena took her husband's hand and led him to where a large telescope had been set up in a sheltered corner. She stood on tiptoe to press a kiss on his mouth. "Happy Christmas, Will."

"What is this?"

"The first day you took me up here, I thought it would be the perfect place to study the stars. I know you love the night sky." She placed both lanterns on a table against the wall beside a bench piled with blankets. "I ordered this from Dollond's when we were in town and arranged to have it delivered and set up here. Paul has been shown how to take care of it, but I have the instructions and some books about astronomy for you downstairs."

"Helena!" Will was unbearably moved by the thought that someone, not just someone, no, she—his wife—had gone to all this trouble to arrange the perfect gift for him. His arms locked around her; all he could do was mutter, "Thank you," as he drew her down to the bench, rocking her gently against him.

"I don't know why I never thought of this," he whispered, looking up at the star-strewn sky. It was as if they were in another world. After some minutes, he got up, tucked a blanket around her and sat before the telescope, adjusting the sight until the stars seemed to leap to meet him, inviting him to walk among them. At last he stirred and rubbed his eyes. "You must come and look." He settled Helena on the stool and helped her to focus the instrument.

After some time, she sat back and looked up at him. "It's truly magical."

"Yes, but I think we should go down now. I don't want you to freeze. What do we do with the telescope?"

"Paul is waiting below. He'll see to the fire as well. There is a cover for it, in case it rains, but I understand it is reasonably weather-tight."

"It's a most amazing gift. Thank you, again, Helena."

~~~

"What do you make of young Hall?" Will asked James Thornton a couple of days later. "The two of you seem to go on quite well together."

"Yes, to my surprise. The impression I had acquired of him in town was not very favourable. He's inclined to run with a ramshackle crowd."

"Plays rather deep, or so I thought, but I have seen no evidence of it here."

"I think he may be a bit lost—not quite sure what to do with himself or even how to behave. It cannot be surprising that he chose to model himself on his father, I suppose."

"Lady Rastleigh mentioned that the girl said their father had taken little or no interest in them until the boy came down from Oxford. Presumably he then introduced him into his own circles."

"A father like that is worse than no father at all. I'm not sure what size his estates are, but from things he let drop, he has received little or no training in how to manage them. He is very close to his mother and sister, however. It's clear that it is not merely a sense of duty that connects them but a deep affection."

"That is true," Will said, remembering how, despite his previous rebuff, Mr Hall had sought Helena out on his mother's and sister's behalf.

~~~

"Hall, my steward tells me there is a problem with the mill. It is upstream, some miles north of the village," Will said the next morning. "Do you care to accompany me there? It's a perfect day to ride out."

Harry Hall tried to conceal his surprise at this invitation, but said at once, "I should love to, Cousin."

He was interested in everything to do with the estate; the interaction with tenants and workmen, the way Rastleigh stopped to exchange a few words with a labourer trimming hedges or complimented a farmer's wife on her ale. He watched and listened as the earl consulted with his steward and the miller about the best way to effect the necessary repairs. They dropped in to an inn on the way back and here again Rastleigh seemed completely at home despite his usual reserve.

"How do you know what to do?" Harry asked.

"What do you mean?"

"With the tenants and the mill; looking at the fields, you could talk about the crops. How did you learn all that?"

"My father died when I was six and from then on, I spent all my free time with my grandfather and his secretary or his steward, learning everything about Rastleigh and my role as the prospective earl. Grandfather wanted me to be able to step into his shoes at an early age, if need be. You received no such training, I take it?"

Harry snorted. "My father took no interest at all in the estate—on the contrary, he appeared to despise it. About once a year, he invited some friends to a house party, but once Rachel was thirteen, my mother always ensured that we went to stay with friends while they were there. It is one of the few times I remember her arguing with him. He insisted that he needed a hostess and she replied that he managed well enough without her for the rest of the year and she was not going to risk having her daughter accosted by some libertine in his cups." He grinned. "I don't think he ever realised that the most elderly housemaids and menservants in the neighbourhood were swapped into Lambert Court for his parties."

"And yet he persisted in going there."

"I imagine he liked to give the impression that he was master there, but it comes from my mother's family and, I think, is administered by trustees. I don't know the details."

"But you are the heir, are you not?"

"I believe so, but not until my twenty-fifth birthday, which is at the beginning of February. The thing is, I should like to be more involved but don't know how to go about it, and I haven't liked to raise it with my mother in case she thinks I am eager to depose her. But it is awkward when people refer to me as 'the young master'. I am always afraid they will ask for something and I won't know what to say."

"I understand. I ride out most days, although not always as far as we went today. If you wish to go with me, be ready by half-past nine o'clock."

"Thank you, Cousin, I should like that." Harry went on rather awkwardly, "That business with the heir's allowance—I didn't mean to presume, but some of the fellows assumed I was in receipt of one, so I thought I should ask."

"How are your finances? Are you badly dipped?"

"No, thank God. I had a run of good luck and came about—in fact I'm now quite plump in the pocket. Frankly, I don't really have a taste for gambling, but it was something to do."

"You will need to make some changes in your acquaintance if your mother and sister are to come to town next Season."

"I am aware of that," Harry said stiffly.

"You don't appear to be a weakling. Do you box?"

"I've no taste for it. Got knocked about too often at school. I am not very tall and grew late so the first few years I was among the smallest."

"What about fencing?"

"While I was at Oxford, but not in recent years."

"Would you like to try it again? We can have a bout if you like. I have a set of foils here."

"That would be splendid."

They rode on in amicable silence. As they neared the Castle, Rastleigh said, "I would be happy to accompany you when you speak to your trustees and your man of business after your birthday, should you wish me to. I don't mean to imply that you cannot deal with them on your own, but sometimes it does not harm to have someone at your back."

"Cousin, I should be most grateful," Harry said sincerely.

"Are they in London?"

"I believe so. My mother will know."

"Once we have arranged a date convenient to both of us, I suggest you write to them to say they may call on you at Rastleigh House. But first you should go through whatever papers may be at Lambert Court and bring them with you. Copies of deeds, settlements, your father's will—that sort of thing."

~~~

"Poor boy," said Helena when Will recounted this conversation to her. "I am glad you are going to help him."

"How were things here?"

"We walked in the woods this morning; Cousin Anna had some good suggestions about how they might be improved. Then Lady Purfoy called with her daughter and daughter-in-law to invite us all to their Twelfth Night party. I said we would go—it will be a nice end to the Hall's visit. Mrs Thornton says these evenings are always most enjoyable."

"I can't say. I've never stayed over Twelfth Night. Yes, Parker?"

"Mrs Hall requests a private word with you, my lord, my lady. She asked me to enquire when would be convenient."

"Show her up here, Parker."

"Very good, my lady."

"I do apologise for disturbing you, Cousins," Mrs Hall said as she came in to the solar.

"You do not disturb us," Helena replied. "Come and sit here at the fire."

"Will you take some refreshment, Cousin Anna? A glass of Madeira or some ratafia?" Will enquired.

"A small glass of Madeira if you please."

"Now, how may we serve you?" he asked kindly. She was inclined to flutter around him, as if not used to the company of tonnish gentlemen.

"Oh, not precisely serve me. I would not so presume. I wanted to thank you for your kindness to Harry—he was in alt after he came back from your ride—but also to explain some things to you. I have never spoken to him about it—it is not the sort of thing a mother wishes to discuss with her son, but I feel I should tell someone, especially now that his birthday is so near." She paused and took a sip from her glass.

"Would you prefer me to leave?" Will asked. "You could just tell Helena."

Mrs Hall shook her head. "You must know, too."

Helena came to sit beside her and took her hand. "Just start at the beginning," she said encouragingly. "The words will come."

Mrs Hall closed her eyes for a moment as if summoning strength. "I was an orphan," she began abruptly, "the last surviving child of two well-known Norfolk families and, as such, a great heiress. Although I was just seventeen, I had several suitors, but none of them, I felt, wanted me as much as they wanted my money. I met Anthony Hall at a house party given by his mother's sister. I think she—his aunt, I mean— picked me out for him.

"When I did not respond to his courtship, he contrived to have us stranded one night at a cottage in the woods. We had journeyed out as a group and 'somehow'," her voice turned on the word, "become separated from the others and got lost. His aunt arranged it so that our return the next morning was witnessed by the whole party who had assembled at the stables at an unusually early hour." Her voice trailed away. "On the way back, he had been insisting we must become betrothed. I refused of course, but on seeing the crowd he cried apologies to his aunt for alarming her, but no harm done and she may wish him happy, for Miss Lambert had consented to be his wife."

"Had he forced himself upon you?" Helena asked quietly.

"No, but that made no difference. Being away together overnight was enough. He made it quite clear that I did not really appeal to him in that way; my money was the attraction, although that did not stop claiming his husbandly rights from time to time over the years," she added bitterly. She was looking into the fire as she spoke and did not see the appalled and pitying glances exchanged by Helena and Will.

"One of my trustees was Sir Peter Drummond, an old friend of my grandfather's, and of your grandfather too, I believe." She looked at Will, who nodded. "He felt he could not in good conscience advise me against the marriage, as Hall's aunt emphasised that only so could my reputation be saved. She was so sorry, but too many people knew what had happened for it to be hushed up.

"However, he was determined that Mr Hall should benefit as little as possible from the marriage. He and Lord Rastleigh devised a settlement which allowed him half the interest from my capital, but no voice in how it was to be invested, nor was he permitted to realise any of it. All the landed property remained in trust; my husband was to receive half the income remaining after all expenses of the estates, including generous provision for me and any children, had been deducted. On their coming of age, a quarter of my husband's income through his marriage was to go to any sons and a quarter of the capital was to go as dowry for any daughters."

Will whistled. "So he stood to lose half of his income to his children."

Mrs Hall smiled. "I believe he was not happy when Harry turned twenty-one. He could not influence the payment of his allowance, for it was all done by my trustees. He would not benefit in any way from my death, for my interest would revert to my children or, if I did not have any, to charity. If he predeceased me, then everything returned to me and the trust would be dissolved."

"They boxed him in neatly. I am surprised he went ahead with the marriage," Will said.

"He had little choice, having made such a public announcement. He was still left with quite a respectable income, even if he had no control over it. And your grandfather told him that if he baulked, he would disown him and have him thrashed on the steps of his club. I was not supposed to know that, but Sir Peter told me." She smiled again and continued, "As a result, my husband took no interest in Lambert Court or the other properties, nor indeed was he allowed to. The estates have been managed by my agent together with my trustees and of course they consult me as to my wishes. But since he died, I have not known what to say to Harry who assumes he has inherited the estates. I fudged things with the story of a trust until his twenty-fifth birthday, but there is none, of course."

"Did he inherit anything from his father?"

"My husband left everything to him—I believe there is a town-house, a hunting-box near Melton and some money in the funds. Harry lives in the house when he is in London. I have never seen it."

"Did he make any further provision for your daughter?"

"No. I did not encourage any closeness between them. He was not fit company for her."

"What a tangle," Will said. "You have my deepest sympathies, Cousin Anna, and my admiration for the way you have dealt with such a difficult situation. But now you need to devise a way out of it."

"That's it. I know Harry would not hold it against me, if I could but bring myself to explain the circumstances to him."

"Would you permit me to do that, man to man?"

"If you would, my lord, I should be most grateful. I hoped I would have the courage to raise this with you while we were here and I brought the relevant documents with me."

"Excellent foresight. What do you wish to do now? I would not advise leaving things as they are."

"No. I must make proper provision for Harry and Rachel, and I should like him to start learning about the estates. I had feared he was falling into his father's way of life, but I think that was more by accident than design."

"I'll keep an eye on him," Will promised. "He will take more of an interest in the estates if he has a say in how they should be run."

Mr Hall was horrified to learn of his parents' history and readily forgave his mother for her deception, especially when he learnt that she had already planned to seek Will's advice. "Poor Mamma," he said. "I remember Sir Peter; he died about ten years ago. He was always kind to Rachel and me. As for my father's aunt," he added venomously, "she may not look for me to acknowledge her again."

"What, is she still alive? Who is she?"

"Lady Georgina Benton. I think she is not long turned seventy—she was considerably younger than my grandmother. She never married and seems to have regarded my father as a substitute son. She never came to Lambert Court, of course, but he introduced me to her when I came on the town. She is inclined to treat me like a grandson," he added with an air of revulsion, "and hints she has made me her heir."

"You cannot give her the cut direct, much as you may wish to; it could rebound on your mother and sister. But you may certainly keep her at a distance. I'll warn Helena as well in case Lady Georgina should try and presume on the connection by calling on her."

"Will," Helena said after he had reported on his conversation with Harry, "I think we should invite Cousin Anna and Rachel to stay with us during the Season. It would give them a lot more protection and standing, especially if this Lady Georgina tries to get up to any mischief. I would not bring Rachel out, precisely, Cousin Anna would do that, but I could support her."

"Would you mind? It would mean doing something with the house before the Season begins. Would we give a ball for Rachel? I don't want you to have to do more than you are happy with."

"I'm sure I shall manage. I'll consult Lady Neary about the house—she will know the best places to go. Anne and Lord Philip will be in town for the Season as well; Amelia is the same age as Rachel and they are cousins, too."

"What about Harry? Is he to stay with us?"

"I should think he would prefer to remain in his own house. But I'll make it clear that he may visit his Mamma and sister as he pleases and need not stand on ceremony."

"Be sure to give them a suite well away from our apartments; so that I can have you to myself."

"That shouldn't be a problem. I intend to make one of the rooms opening on to the garden my private parlour, where only you will be admitted. However," she went on with a mischievous twinkle in her eyes, "I must warn you that with two young cousins making their come-outs, you will not be able to avoid at least one visit to Almack's."

"With you to protect me, I can brave even that."

Chapter Twenty-Six

"What do you think?" Helena asked as Will came into the room. She nodded towards the two garments laid out on the bed—a long-sleeved, dark green tunic and the shorter, gold-embroidered, ivory gown to be worn over it. An elaborate ivory, green and gold girdle lay beside them,

"They are beautiful, and perfect for Wassail Eve," he replied. "Why do you ask? Are you having second thoughts?"

"They feel so different, not at all confining except for the girdle and that rests on my hips more than my waist. And it seems very strange to go into company with my hair just hanging loose down my back."

"Perhaps this will help." He opened the box he carried and took out a chain of fretted gold set with emeralds and pearls. He did not put it around her neck but set it on her head so that it circled her brow and held her hair in place. "Perfect," he said and then carefully lifted her hair to put a long matching chain around her neck.

His voice deepened as he turned her back, towards the long pier-glass. "My lady."

"Oh, they are wonderful. Wherever did you find them?" she said in an awed whisper.

"In the strong room." He framed her face with his hands and took her mouth in a deep kiss.

"Will," she gasped, even as her fingers slid through his hair.

He tugged at the ties that fastened her loose wrapper. The garment fell from her shoulders and slipped to the floor leaving her in her stockings and fine lawn chemise.

"We do not have much time and where? I do not want to crush my gowns or my hair." Her voice fell away as he backed her to a low, wide chair, turning her so that he could sit.

In a trice, he had opened the fall of his breeches and arranged her on her knees astride him, smiling wickedly as he pulled her down on to him. "Now your gowns and hair will be undisturbed, my lovely dragon, provided you are willing to ride St. George."

~~~

Helena was still blushing as she waited with her husband at the top of the steps to the Keep. For how many centuries had the Lord and Lady watched the people of Rastleigh come down the torch-lit path to the Keep to celebrate this night? This was no solemn procession, but a gathering of friends and families. There was a perceptible air of excitement as people drew near; greetings were called and answered and soon the different groups had merged into a steady procession. Bows and curtsies were made to murmurs of 'My Lord' and 'My Lady', and the guests hurried indoors to find their seats.

A long horn-call sounded from the parapet of the gate-house. "That's the warning to any stragglers to hurry," Will said. "Once the gate is barred, no one else can gain entrance."

The trumpet's triumphant blare sent a shiver down Helena's spine. Lennard lifted the cloak from her shoulders and slipped away. It was time. Helena's heart skipped a beat as she placed her hand on Will's wrist. The Thorntons and Mr Hancock, the land steward, and his wife took their places behind them. Another fanfare sounded from the gallery. Every eye was upon them as they paced slowly to the dais and took their seats at the high table.

It was like a scene from an old romance or one of the Flemish paintings she had seen in Brussels, Helena thought, as she looked at the smiling faces bright with anticipation. Everyone wore their best, the men breeches, serge coat and coloured neck cloths, and the women woollen gowns set off by carefully trimmed fichus and caps.

Soon, willing hands passed tankards of cider and ale along the tables. When all had been served, Will held his tankard aloft. "My friends, people of Rastleigh, we have come together to celebrate the end of the old year and the beginning of the new. Tonight, we forget our sorrows and remember our joys, for life is fleeting and to be lived to the full. Wassail!"

"Wassail!" The rafters rang with the full-throated reply as tankards were raised, then drained with alacrity.

"Tonight, we feast and make merry! Wassail!"

The doors under the gallery were flung open and a procession of servants appeared, headed by footmen, two to a charger, bearing whole roast boar wreathed with rosemary and bay leaves.

They were paraded down the hall to further fanfares, presented to Will for inspection and removed to the sideboards for carving. Their decorative garlands were hung on pegs on the wall, from which other, faded ones were removed and flung on the fire, filling the hall with a spicy, aromatic scent.

"They are from last year," Will said, in answer to Helena's questioning look.

Platters of succulent pork soon graced the tables along with dishes of roast fowl, spicy sausages and puddings, bowls of baked roots and onions, and loaves of fresh bread, all interspersed with dishes of apples, pears and nuts.

As platters and bowls were emptied, the hum of conversation grew louder, punctuated by the giving of toasts and intermittent bursts of laughter.

Helena glanced sidelong at her husband. He sat at his ease in the great carved chair, his long fingers curved around the handle of his tankard, the heavy gold ring he always wore glinting in the candlelight. He looked lordly, she though suddenly. Much more so than on the day they had confronted Miller and Jenkins. This was his place, and his people.

Almost as if he had felt her gaze, he turned to smile at her. "Well, what do you make of us?"

She shook her head, baffled. "I've never experienced anything like it. It feels as if I have been transported back to the Middle Ages."

"I suppose it must. I've known it all my life. I remember standing at the window to watch the wassailers go out. I must have been only three or four, for my father and mother were among them, and my grandparents, of course."

"How old were you when you first took part?"

"Sixteen. But my grandfather kept a strict eye on me."

"Why?"

He laughed. "You'll see later."

Below, the replete revellers drained a last cup as all was cleared away and the tables removed, the benches being set around the walls to leave the dance floor free. A group of musicians struck up a brisk tune.

"My lady?"

Helena took Will's hand and together they went down to join the dance.

They lined up in rows, men and women facing one another, not long ways as was usual, but across the room. When all were assembled the music stopped and started again, each side, men and women, linking hands and advancing towards and then retreating from the row opposite, before separating to take their partners.

"It's wonderful," Helena said to Will as they clasped hands. She twirled away from him to link arms with his neighbour and swing around him before returning to her own partner.

"It's an old custom here, I'm glad it has survived."

They were separated by the dance and each side again linked hands to dance towards one another, the men lifting their joined hands to form arches that the women passed under to face another set of partners. On and on they went, turning at the bottom of the Hall to dance up again.

When the music stopped, Helena curtsied to her latest partner, the son of one of the tenant farmers. "What now?" she wondered, but he proudly offered her his arm and escorted her back to the dais where her husband waited to claim her.

A cry went up. "The Brides' Dance!"

Again, a fanfare sounded. Escorted by their husbands, five women, their hair, like Helena's, flowing loose down their backs, came to stand before the dais where six wreaths woven of ivy, mistletoe and red holly berries had been placed on the table beside six leather purses.

Dr Thornton rose. "My friends, it is part of our tradition that last year's brides dance for us on Wassail Eve. His lordship rewards each of them with a purse of gold and in one of these purses is a token. She who finds that token is the Queen of the Wassail. There is however one exception and one that we at Rastleigh have waited over one hundred years to see again." He paused dramatically. "Not since Henry, fifth Earl of Rastleigh brought his lady to the Castle in the year of Our Lord sixteen hundred and ninety-eight has the new wife of the Lord of Rastleigh danced the bride's dance. On this auspicious occasion, she, our new Lady, is also Queen of the Wassail."

Will held out his right hand to Helena. When she placed hers in it, he raised her to her feet. Retaining her hand, he held up a gold ring. "My lady, receive the ring of the Lady of Rastleigh. By it, all shall know that where I am master, you are mistress." He placed it on her finger and bent to kiss her hand to renewed trumpet fanfares and loud cheers and applause.

Helena curtsied deeply to her husband. Rising, she took both his hands. "I accept the ring of the Lady of Rastleigh and shall wear it with pride. Your people shall be my people and where I am mistress, you are master." Turning to those assembled in the hall, she added simply. "Thank you, good people. I am honoured by my lord's trust and by your welcome, not only tonight but since my arrival here. I hope to be worthy of them."

Smiling proudly, Will took one of the wreaths and set it on her head to renewed cheers. The other brides now came forward to receive their wreaths and Will and Helena stepped down from the dais, she to dance with the brides and Will to stand proudly with his fellow bridegrooms. It was a simple circle dance, finishing when the circle opened so that each bride could claim her husband and dance around the hall with him to the applause of all. At the end they mounted the dais, the brides to receive their dowries and all to watch the remaining dances.

"It is the greatest day of all for the women of Rastleigh, the day they dance the Brides' Dance," Mrs Thornton had explained to Helena, "even more important than the wedding day itself. The wreaths will hang in their homes until the next Wassail Eve. Traditionally his lordship's purse belongs to the woman—the husband may not claim it and woe betide him who tries."

The pace of the music picked up. "The Maidens!"

At the call, all the unattached women formed a circle, facing out. The single men followed in another circle facing them and, as the music quickened, both groups linked hands and started to dance, each one circling to their right. The pace got quicker and quicker until it suddenly stopped. Each man seized the woman opposite him and, as the music started again with a pronounced, uneven rhythm, the couples circled the floor with a peculiar jigging step until the music stopped again. The circles reformed and repeated the dance twice more before everyone took to the floor in a wild dance that left everyone gasping for breath when the music stopped.

There was a quick hunt for outdoor garments. Warmly attired, the company formed a long line of couples, starting with Will and Helena at the dais, then the other brides and grooms, then the maidens and their partners followed by the remaining pairs until the double row stretched past the musicians playing at the door of the Great Hall, down the steps and along the drive.

"Wassail! Here we go a-wassailing!"

As the shout went up, great steaming cups redolent of spices, apples and toast were carried in. They were presented first to Will and Helena before the bearers proceeded down the rows offering the cups to each person as they passed. When they reached the door of the hall the musicians changed to a capering tune and all the couples lifted their joined hands to form a long archway. Will took Helena's hand and led her under the tunnel of linked hands followed in turn by the other couples. Out of the hall, down the steps, out to the gatehouse and over the drawbridge they went, following the cupbearers and musicians to the orchard, singing and dancing, some bearing torches and many banging pots and pans as well.

It was wild, even manic, Helena thought, now understanding why the rector and his family were not to be seen. "He thinks it wiser not. You will see why," was all that Will had said when she had wondered why they were not to be among the guests.

Once at the orchard they spread out among the trees, some couples falling into each other's arms. Will pulled Helena close as he caught his breath. He adjusted her wreath and smiled at her, saying, "We'll make a beautiful pagan of you yet," before he kissed her. She flushed but then noticed that the other brides were embracing their husbands just as enthusiastically. She lifted her hand to put back his hair and her new ring gleamed in the torch light.

"To your duties, my Queen," Will said when the last couples had reached the orchard. He took her hand and led her to a big apple tree, the oldest in the orchard. "Take a piece of toast from the cup and put in the fork of the tree," he said, lifting her high in his arms as around her all burst into song.

> *'Here's to thee, old apple tree*
> *Whence thou mays't bud,*
> *And whence thou mays't blow*
> *And whence thou mays't bear apples enow!*
> *Hats full! caps full!*
> *Bushel!—bushel!—sacks full!*
> *And my pockets full too –huzza!'*

The Rastleigh people sang lustily and made even more noise with their improvised instruments. Will twirled Helena around, then paused while she rested her hands on his shoulders, looking down into his face. He laughed exuberantly, then slid her down against his body. "A kiss for luck," he said, taking her mouth to loud cheers. The roots of the tree were sprinkled with wassail and they went on to other trees.

By the time they reached the last tree, Helena was dizzy from the movement, the smell of the wassail and Will's kisses. The musicians struck up the strange, uneven tune again, but at a slower pace, the rhythm driving the dancers who spread out over the grass beneath the old trees. The moon had risen to cast a silvery glow, creating mysterious shadows and as Helena danced, held steady and close by Will's strong arms, she noticed some of the couples slipping away into these shadows.

"Time for us to leave." His voice was a husky whisper in her ear as he led her to a clearing where horses waited patiently. He lifted her to his saddle and swung up behind her, holding her cradled against him.

She rested her head on his shoulder, tipping it back to luck up at the stars. "Never in my most fanciful dreams have I thought to experience an evening like this."

His arms tightened about her. "Did you like it?" he asked, before kissing her softly.

"It was wonderful, splendid, magical, pagan—oh, I don't have the words."

"It is not over yet, my lady." He raised a hand to caress her breast. "You have one last task to perform."

"Gladly," she whispered, reaching up to trace his lips with a finger, "how can I refuse the Lord of Rastleigh?"

Their loving had never been wilder or more exuberant. They rejoiced in one another—the sight of her silken breast and thighs, of his muscular limbs and heavy arousal, the feel of all the different textures and sensations—crisp, smooth, soft, hard, skin and bone, lips and ears, moist, sinewy, all the different curves, nooks and crannies their bodies offered each other, the sound of gasps and moans, whispered words and cries, the scent of perfumes overlaid by that of desire, the taste of wassail, salty perspiration and secret spices—until they reached a final peak together and collapsed into one another's arms, after some minutes rousing enough to pull up the covers and tuck themselves into one another to sleep, more one person than two.

The next morning Helena lay against Will's shoulder, her hand lifted to examine her ring. It was chased with apple leaves, blossom and fruit. "You have one too," she said, turning his right hand to compare.

"Yes, it was given to me the first Wassail Eve after my grandfather died."

"Who presented it to you?"

"Jim Sykes, the oldest tenant farmer. Dr Thornton held it until then. As librarian he is also keeper of the annals and knows how these things are to be done. Mine is plain. Only yours is decorated. You must wear it always now, as I do mine."

"How old are they?"

"No one seems to know. The most ancient annals record the rings of the Lord and Lady. Dr Thornton thinks the reddish colour of the gold means that they were made with gold from Britain or Ireland." He looked over to the dressing table, at the coronet and necklace. "Can you put your hair up in a style that will permit you to wear the coronet?"

"I'm sure Lennard will contrive something. Why?"

"So you can wear it each Wassail Eve. You looked magnificent last night. I should like to have your portrait taken wearing those gowns and your hair down. We shall have a more conventional one painted in London, but I think I'll bring a painter to Rastleigh and have the other one done here. I should like to have a remembrance of last night, although I shall not forget it as long as I live."

Book 5

Chapter Twenty-Seven

"**H**aving ignored the summons for the third of January, I feel I must attend Parliament on the fifth of February," Will said a few days later. "Shall you come to town with me or wait until we know whether it is another false start? I don't know what the King is thinking of, with four successive prorogations since July."

"I imagine he couldn't face the thought of all the bickering and currying for favour," Helena replied. "But, Parliament or no Parliament, there will be a Season. And since we have invited the Halls, or the Hall-Lamberts, I should say, to stay with us, I had better come with you so that we can see what must be done in Rastleigh House before they arrive. Did Harry consult you about the family's change of name?"

"He did, and I told him I had no objection."

"It is a symbol of his coming into his own. It was wise of his mother to make Lambert Court over to him. She could live another thirty years or more, and it would have been intolerable for both if he remained tied to her apron strings. Now they are both free to live their own lives."

~~~

Rastleigh House, 24th April 1822

To Mrs Caroline Thompson

My dearest Caro,
*Well, it is done! We have been to Court and returned to put off
our finery and relish our triumph. I had been wondering how His
Majesty would manage presentations when he has no queen, but
he simply holds the Drawing-Rooms himself.*

*You may imagine my delight when I learnt that not long after
ascending the throne, he had decreed that ladies need no longer
wear hoops to Court. As you know, Queen Charlotte was most
insistent upon these and you will recall how cumbrous and
difficult to manage they were. One still must have lace lappets,
plumes and a train, but otherwise may dress modishly and hope
to wear one's gown elsewhere without the court trimmings. The
fashion for ostrich plumes is such that I am surprised that there
are any of these birds left to survive on this earth. Each lady
yesterday had what may be fairly described as a full bonnet of
plumes upon her head.*

*Rachel looked extremely pretty. It is fortunate that her
colouring is not insipid for we saw many girls in white who looked
as if they had been too long in the wash! This was partly due to
an excess of sensibility, I suppose, and also to the extreme heat,
for the King likes his apartments so very warm. His Majesty was
most gracious to Rachel, recalling, "his old friend Hall." He was
a trifle puzzled at the change of name but Mrs Hall-Lambert just*

said with quiet dignity that it was fitting on her son's coming into his inheritance and he accepted this without further demur.

Mr Hall-Lambert frequently squires his mother and sister to their engagements and has become quite the protective brother, glowering at any rake or roué who might edge into his sister's orbit. I have heard some of the older ladies commenting on the change in him, but it is all favourable and no little credit is given to Rastleigh for having taken him in hand. Now that he is Hall-Lambert of Lambert Court he is starting to attract the Mammas' interest and I believe is looking to my husband for instructions on how to repel them without alienating them as far as his sister is concerned. As Rastleigh's way of dealing with the importunate is to look forbiddingly down his nose and stalk away, I don't think he will be of much assistance to him, Mr Hall-Lambert I mean. His Mamma and I have advised him to spread his favours and not to ignore the wall-flowers, for many a shy girl blossoms with a little attention. The important thing is for him not to let himself be entrapped into having to offer more than he wishes to give.

My own gown was of jonquil silk, with ornamentations of the palest green on the bodice, sleeves, hem and train. The wide neckline and sleeves were trimmed with lace and I wore a diamond parure that is part of the Rastleigh jewels.

When we arrived in town there was waiting for me a new barouche, exquisitely fitted out in shades of sapphire blue and silver, with the most beautiful team of grey horses. R. is so taken by Sir John Malcolm's Silver Mist that he has decreed that all my horses are to be grey. He has also arranged for a special sapphire and silver livery for my coachman and footmen. We make a fine sight, especially in the Park and I look forward to taking you up when you are come to London.

The Season is now fully underway. Mrs Hall-Lambert and Rachel have got to know the other girls and Mammas by first attending the small parties which are designed to ease the debutantes into the social round. Some evenings we all dine together but more frequently Rastleigh and I dine elsewhere. I am getting to know more people as well as renewing my acquaintance with others.

I am finding tonnish life less difficult than I had feared. Ladies Harbury and Neary have quite successfully "fired me off" as they say. I have found the change to town hours quite wearying and am no longer able to rise early to ride with R. We have agreed that we need not accept every invitation and try not to have more than two engagements each evening with perhaps one other during the day. Lady Neary approves of this, for it makes us more sought after, she says. But even with that, between shopping and calls, drives in the Park and the rest of the fashionable round, the days fill up quickly.

I have made myself a lair in a sunny parlour that opens to the garden here at Rastleigh House. Here I can attend to my correspondence and my embroidery as I am working on a grand scheme at present. Once I have retreated here, I am not at home to anyone except R. I must be grateful that he is not in the Cabinet, or otherwise too involved in politics although he conscientiously attends the debates in the House of Lords and his contributions, as reported in the Morning Chronicle, are thoughtful and concise. I should like to hear him speak one day.

The gardens here are pretty and well-maintained but quite old-fashioned. There is a good herb garden and I have started making some salves and simples for the still-room. I shall take some of these as well as some cuttings back to the Castle, for the still-room there was in a dreadful state and it will be some time until my new physic garden is productive. I have arranged for a new still-room and am taking advantage of our time in London to equip it properly. I ran into Surgeon Phipps and his wife last week in Bond Street. This was most fortunate, as he was able to give me the direction of an excellent apothecary from whom I may obtain supplies.

We have already given a couple of little dinners. We find nine other couples, making twenty persons with us, a good number. The other evening Earl and Countess Benton were among the guests. His father was brother to Mr Anthony Hall's mother, so he and Mrs Hall-Lambert's husband were first cousins, tho' there doesn't seem to have been much of a connection between the families and I had to make her known to his lordship and his wife. They acknowledged her very properly and Lady Benton said she would call so that she could make the acquaintance of Rachel who was elsewhere that evening, chaperoned by one of the other Mammas with whose daughter she has struck up a friendship. The evening went well; the conversation was intelligent and interesting.

Lady Benton called the following day with her daughter-in-law Viscountess Marfield. The latter is a pleasant woman who invited me to attend a meeting of a ladies' literary society of which she is a founding member.

Catherine Kullmann

I am so pleased, my dear Caro, that your mother has persuaded you to come to town for at least part of the Season. I long to see dear Amanda and Davy and to sit down for a comfortable coze with you. From time to time I see old faces from our army days. There is a Highlander who plays the pipes outside Fortnum and Mason's and I always give him something in memory of the Duchess of Richmond's ball.

I met Wellington the other evening at a ball. When introduced, he looked at me keenly and asked what my name had been before I was married. He then professed to remember me and spoke kindly of Jonnie, Richard and Major Thompson. I know he called to your parents' house after Waterloo to enquire about the wounded, but would not have thought he would remember in such detail. He asked me to stand up with him for a waltz, an invitation not appreciated by R, for you know of the Duke's reputation with the fair sex. He behaved correctly, however, perhaps because R remained at the side of the ballroom, his eyes fixed sternly on me throughout.

There is so much more to tell you that it is as well you are to join us soon. But now I must leave you as I have engaged to go to the Park with my guests.

I remain, dear Caro, your affectionate friend
Helena Rastleigh

Helena and Mrs Hall-Lambert strolled in the Park with a cluster of matrons and their daughters, accompanied by a bevy of attendant young men who cleverly contrived, as they thought, to separate the girls from their Mammas. They walked across the grass, Helena and her guest falling behind the other ladies as they

338

discussed the final fitting of Rachel's gown for her own ball which would be given at Rastleigh House the following week.

"I had never thought to see her so pretty," Mrs Hall-Lambert said fondly. "The coiffeur has devised a charming style which tames her locks so that they curl beautifully and I have found some pretty combs topped with little jewelled flowers—not too much, you know, just right for a girl in her first Season."

"That faint blush of pink in the gown is lovely with her dark hair."

"There you are at last, niece."

At the strident call, Helena looked up to see a plump, well-corseted elderly lady, fashionably dressed, her hair concealed by an amber turban and her face rouged in an older style, inspecting them with disfavour through a lorgnette.

Helena raised her eyebrows. "You are surely mistaken, ma'am."

"Not you. I mean my niece here." The lorgnette pointed at Mrs Hall-Lambert.

"You have the advantage of me, ma'am," the latter said calmly.

"What! Do you deny your dear husband's aunt?"

Mrs Hall-Lambert said nothing more and, as people turned to look, she hurried to catch up with Rachel.

"I will not be denied! I am Lady Georgina Benton."

"Lady Georgina." Mrs Hall-Lambert looked back and made the smallest possible inclination of her head.

"My card for my grand-niece's come-out has gone astray," her ladyship announced grandly. "You will kindly request the Countess of Rastleigh to have another one sent to me at once."

She dabbed at her eyes with a lace handkerchief. "My dear Anthony would have been devastated if his aunt were not present at his daughter's come-out."

"The card did not go missing. No invitation was issued and none will be sent. Good day to you, Lady Georgina."

Maintaining her calm air, Mrs Hall-Lambert turned to Helena. "We have fallen sadly behind, Cousin." It was only when they had collected Rachel and were seated again in the barouche that she began to tremble.

"Home, please, John." Helena took Mrs Hall-Lambert's hand as the coachman eased the barouche out of the line and turned to leave the park. "Well done, Cousin. You were magnificent."

"I didn't think. She made me so angry with her talk of my dear husband. Oh dear, no doubt there will be a lot of talk."

"I should not worry about it. Benton acknowledges you and if there should be an issue with his aunt, people will assume the fault is on her side, not on yours."

"Do you really think so?"

"Shall I ask Rastleigh to have a word with him in confidence? He can explain why you do not wish for the connection."

"I do not like to put him to the trouble."

"Nonsense. He will be only too pleased to help."

So it proved. Earl Benton looked disapproving when told of the episode and said, "I am not surprised. I never liked my aunt's relationship with Hall, and always wondered what the true story of that marriage was. Tell my cousin not to be alarmed."

He made a point of seeking out Mrs Hall-Lambert at the rout they both attended the following evening, making it clear that she was not out of favour with his family, and the talk died down, despite Lady Georgina's ostentatious cutting of the Hall-Lambert family whenever their paths crossed. She had contrived to be introduced to Helena but Helena's manner had been so reserved that she had not raised the question of an invitation to the ball, perhaps fearing another public rebuff.

~~~

Will got up from his desk and looked out the window. It was raining heavily, he saw with no little degree of satisfaction, and the ladies would not be taking the air in the park today.

"Where is her ladyship?"

"She is in her parlour, my lord."

"Excellent." Whistling, he went down the passage to enter a large room that even on this grey day was bright thanks to the French doors and windows and the cheerful primrose colour of the drapes and upholstery. Helena sat at her writing-table, obviously just finished with her correspondence. She smiled when she saw him.

"You're very cheerful."

"Yes, for I think to have an unplanned hour or so with my wife. You won't be driving in this weather."

"Shall I ring for fresh tea?"

"If you wish. I should prefer a glass of Madeira." He helped himself and went to the window and looked out. "How are you coping? I hope it is all not too much for you?"

"Oh no, but I wasn't made for this life. I don't know how some ladies manage to attend so many events."

"And yet at Rastleigh you are fully occupied all day."

"It's the late hours, I think. After midnight all I want is my bed."

"Very proper," he commended her. "After midnight all I want is your bed too."

She attempted to frown reprovingly at him but could not resist his wicked grin. "We are sadly out of fashion," she remarked. "From what the other wives say, it is most unusual for husband and wife to share a bed each night and even when they do, it would not be for the whole night."

"Oho! So that is what the ladies discuss when they withdraw after dinner. And they look down on us for telling improper stories over our port." He looked over at her. "I hope that you are content to remain out of fashion, my dear, for I should be most reluctant to leave you each night or not come to you at all."

Helena rose and curtsied. "As my lord insists."

"Now what are you thinking of?" he demanded, pulling her into his arms. "I have learnt not to trust you when you are all sweetness and light."

"How am I to take that?" she protested. "Would you rather a shrew for a wife?"

"Peace, I will stop thy mouth." He suited the action to the words and drew her down to lie with him on the day-bed. "What would those other wives say if they could see us now?"

"Some would be envious, some appalled, I think. Not everyone has made as amiable a match as we did."

"So you are content with your lot, my lady?"

She nodded and lifted her face for his kiss, sinking into his embrace.

"Am I welcome in your bed, Helena?" he asked more seriously.

"Always," she whispered, untying his cravat. "I would be lonely without you, Will."

"There are too few of these opportunities," he remarked later, stroking her back as she rested against him.

"Yes," she agreed regretfully, looking at the clock on the mantelpiece, "and we may not delay much longer."

"Are the preparations all made for our ball?"

"Almost. The invitations have all been sent, the orchestra has been engaged and the theme decided upon. It is to be a spring garden."

"What will you wear?"

"My gown will be mainly blue so that I can wear your mother's sapphire parure. I think she would have been pleased to know I wore it for our first ball here. For most people, the earldom passed simply and directly from your grandfather to you, but this will be a reminder of your parents."

He smiled at her, touched by this thought. "I hope Madame is providing some of her delicious undergarments," he purred.

"You will just have to wait and see, my lord."

"I shall have to lead Rachel out for the opening dance, I suppose, but the supper dance is mine, my lady."

"Will, we cannot. We must look after our guests and not dance with one another."

"I am allowed one dance with my wife and it will be the supper dance," he declared in a tone that brooked no contradiction. And the last dance as well, he added silently to himself.

~~~

Despite the fact that, or perhaps because it could not be described as a sad crush, the Rastleigh ball was a great success. Will had refused to invite more than his rooms could comfortably hold so the guests could easily mix and mingle, moving from the ballroom to one of the card rooms or on to the terrace for a breath of air as they wished. Helena ensured that no young lady who wished to dance was left without a partner, Harry Hall-Lambert doing Trojan work here.

"He has changed immensely," Will commented to Helena as they waited for their waltz to begin. He was filled with pride and satisfaction. To be here in his own home, his beautiful wife a regal hostess at his side, presiding over the come-out of a charming cousin—how his life had changed since the previous Season. His arm tightened around Helena's waist. "It's a pity that none of your family could be here."

"I know, but Rosamund and the baby are more important. I am so glad that we received word yesterday that all had gone well. Otherwise I would have been wondering the whole night. At least your aunt and her family are here. I am sure that she will call on Mamma as soon as they are home."

"Without a doubt. She takes all the credit for our match, you know. I believe she is using it to pay off some old scores among the tabbies."

"I can just imagine it." She gasped as he gathered her closer to whirl her around the corner of the dance floor, lifting her off her feet.

"Remember that first day with little Sally?"

"The only credit your aunt can claim for that is that she drove you and the others out of the house in advance of the ball."

"Ah, but what about the outings to Salisbury and Stonehenge? They did not happen just by chance, you know."

She looked up at him, astonished. "What do you mean?"

He turned her so that they were dancing side-to-side and back-to-back. "Once I indicated my interest in you," he said over his shoulder, "she immediately offered to create some opportunities for us to spend time together, semi-privately, if you will."

"Do you mean the two of you conspired against me?" she asked when she came back to face him.

"With success, you will own, for here you are, Countess of Rastleigh."

"Certainly the last thing I expected to be this time last year."

The musicians ended with a final flourish and Will led Helena towards an old lady who was following the proceedings with great interest.

"I should like you to meet old Lady Needham properly. She was a great friend of my grandmother's. She seems frailer this year. This is the first party I have seen her at."

Her ladyship looked up as they approached. "Well, young man! I thought you had engaged my services for this Season and then you go and do the job yourself."

"My apologies, ma'am. But how could I run the risk of losing my chosen lady? Will you do us the honour of taking supper with us?"

"Nonsense! You should be paying attention to your bride."

"No indeed, ma'am," Helena intervened. "We cannot hope for privacy tonight. Pray come with us and tell me all about this arrangement you had with Rastleigh."

Nothing loath, Lady Needham accepted Will's proffered arm. Offering the other to his wife, he led them to a small round table in the supper room where, having seated his ladies, he departed in search of sustenance.

"I wish dear Mary could have lived to see this day," her ladyship said. "She would have found you a worthy successor, my dear. And to see Rastleigh so happy! It is a kind thought on your part to wear his mother's jewels tonight. That brooch is different, though. It is not part of the set."

"It was Rastleigh's wedding gift. I thought it fitted well to our Spring theme."

"It is pretty, but is that the best he could do?" Lady Needham raised her eyebrows. "I had not thought him a skinflint."

"You wrong him, ma'am. He is most generous," Helena protested. "There was so little time and he had other things to think of."

"And why was that?" Lady Needham demanded.

Helena looked at her in surprise, a polite set-down hovering on her lips.

"There is no need to poker up, my dear. I have known Rastleigh all his life and his grandmother most of mine. I am an inquisitive old lady, but I mean you no harm."

Will returned to the table just in time to hear this comment. "Now, ma'am, I cannot have you putting my wife to the question."

Lady Needham accepted a glass of champagne but returned to the fray. "I just want to know why you got married in such a havy-cavy, secretive manner."

"Did we do so?" Will asked coolly. "I was not aware of it, were you, my dear?" He raised his glass to Helena in a silent toast.

"On the contrary my lord, the important members of our families were there and the ceremony was conducted by my brother-in-law."

"Assisted by Sarum. I was not aware that we had to apprise all and sundry of our plans in advance. However, I have no objection to telling you, ma'am," he said to a chastened Lady Needham, "that I was most grateful to my bride when she agreed to bring the date of our wedding forward so that she might be a support to me during my mother's final illness. Her presence at my mother's bed-side in Ireland was greatly valued, not only by me but also by the whole family." He took Helena's hand and kissed it gently. "It is not without significance that she chose to wear my mother's gift to her tonight, a happy memento of the affection that quickly grew between them in those last weeks."

Her ladyship cleared her throat. "I beg your pardon, my dear, and yours too, Rastleigh. Will you allow me to drink to your happiness?"

"Gladly," said Helena.

"Now tell me how you found things at the Castle. Sadly neglected I have no doubt."

She listened with great interest to their account of the bringing back to life of the Keep. "Excellent," she pronounced, "and I note this house has been spruced up too. You have achieved wonders in so short a time. You must not work her so hard, Rastleigh. Now it is time I went home, if you would be so kind as to call for my carriage."

Will looked at Helena ruefully as her ladyship departed. "The old vixen! I had no idea she would go for you like that!"

She laughed and took his arm. "I think she was satisfying herself that you had not fallen prey to a designing harpy. She is very fond of you."

"She may keep her affection to herself if she is going to attack you. Now, where may I conduct you, my lady?"

"To the Harburys. I need something gentler after Lady Needham."

"I like your Mrs Thompson. But I shall have to leave you with them—it's time I took another look into the card room."

They paused to watch Rachel dance with Stephen Graham. "Isn't he too old for her?" Helena asked.

"Perhaps. He's probably just doing the pretty after meeting her at Christmas."

"I see Cousin Anna is dancing too." Helena watched her turn gracefully under the raised arm of a kind-looking gentleman of about fifty, neatly turned out but not in the first stare of fashion.

"Mr Dyer, is it not?"

"Yes. He is a widower—his daughter is being brought out by his sister, Lady Martin. There are two sons, I believe—one at Oxford and one at Eton."

Once the last guests had departed, the Rastleighs and the Hall-Lamberts withdrew to the library to review the evening. Will went to the decanters and raised an eyebrow at his wife.

"Pray ring for champagne," she said. "I can enjoy it now."

Blaines returned speedily, accompanied by a footman bearing a platter of delicacies. "I had thought you might like something to eat, my lady."

"An excellent idea, Blaines. Thank you. That will be all. Tell the servants to go to bed."

"Thank you, my lady."

"That was thoughtful of Blaines," Mrs Hall-Lambert said. "Generally, the lady giving a party rarely has the opportunity to have any supper."

"That is true," Helena said as she helped herself to some lobster patties. "They must have held these back, for they are quite fresh."

"I cannot thank you enough, Cousin Will, Cousin Helena, for all you have done for me," Rachel said. "Not only tonight, which was wonderful beyond my dreams, but for everything else—the whole Season."

"Well said, my love," her mother agreed. "We are deeply appreciative of your support, Cousins."

"Yes, indeed," added Mr Hall-Lambert. "We are much obliged to you both. Allow me to compliment you on a most successful evening, Cousin Helena. I have heard only the highest praise."

Will raised his glass to her. "To your first ball as Countess of Rastleigh."

Mrs Hall-Lambert looked up at this. "In a way this is a first Season for you, too. You deal with everything in such a sovereign fashion that one tends to forget how new it must be for you."

"For Will too," Helena remarked to general laughter. "I don't think he has ever given a ball before."

"And is now exhausted," Will exclaimed, theatrically putting the back of one hand to his brow. "Come, my lady."

For the next few days, the Rastleighs' ball was the talk of the *ton*. Due to the exclusiveness of the invitation list, those who had been there enjoyed weaving little anecdotes describing the evening into their conversation, while those who had not been so privileged eagerly snapped up these morsels and repeated them in the hope that they might be supposed to have belonged to the inner circle. Rastleigh House was besieged by callers and the number of bouquets brought for Rachel and Helena was such that it was necessary to receive callers in the grand drawing-room.

Rachel was generally agreed to be one of the successes of the Season. She did not let this go to her head and continued to show a friendly impartiality towards all her suitors and was as likely to be seen strolling with her brother or another young lady as with a swain. She had struck up a friendship with Arabella Dyer and they frequently attended events together, Rachel's mother and Arabella's aunt sharing the chaperoning. If this meant Mrs Hall-Lambert spent more time in the company of Mr Dyer, no one thought anything of it.

Not everyone sang the young Countess's praises however. Lady Westland and her particular friend Mrs Logan were heard to wonder what "poor Rastleigh" saw in her, Mrs Logan relating that he had not appeared particularly *épris* when they were at the same supper table during Lady Amelia's dance the previous summer.

"And not four weeks later they were wed," she would add, before saying, "one cannot but wonder," and break off, with a sad shake of her head.

Lady Westland, having failed to renew her connection with the earl, was doubly chafed to have lost the interest of his heir, the more so as it emerged Mr Hall-Lambert, "as we must now call him," was in possession of a handsome independence.

Match-making Mammas, who had set their sights on Rastleigh in previous Seasons or who had had hopes for this one, also resented the capture of one of the chief prizes on the marriage mart by an unknown, who then had the temerity to introduce a rival to their own daughters to society.

"Miss Hall-Lambert has an unfair advantage," they were wont to sigh.

Chapter Twenty-Eight

With the hurdle of her own ball behind her and Rachel's footing in society secure, Helena was happy to take things more quietly. She no longer felt obliged to drive in the park each day, preferring to meet her friends more privately. She enjoyed literary salons and *conversaziones*, where the *entrée* was gained more by intelligence and wit than by birth and fortune, but was not so fond of musical *soirées* and, if asked to perform, always refused.

Will's political interests now took up more of his time and if he was unable to escort her, she went with either Caro Thompson or Lady Marfield. If not required by his mother and sister, Mr. Hall-Lambert also proved to be a willing escort. In some ways he was more up to snuff than Will, who was inclined to hold himself aloof from the more rakish elements of society, and on occasion had steered her away from a particular lady or gentleman. She saw Ladies Neary and Harbury regularly and had become good friends with Lady Needham despite the inauspicious beginning to their acquaintance. She tired easily and was now sure she was with child, although she had not yet said anything to Will and was curiously reluctant to do so.

Will, for his part, was bedevilled by a niggling unease that he could not readily define. He had come fully into his inheritance. His wife was universally admired and acclaimed; he was tired of receiving compliments about her beauty and accomplishments. She managed his home, graced his table and welcomed him to her bed. All of this was genuine, he knew. There was nothing false or feigned in her. She had established her own court—this was maybe too strong a word, but she was usually to be found among the same group at balls and parties. Most of the gentlemen, he came to realize, had served in the campaigns against Napoleon.

She sometimes sat out a dance with a former officer whose wounds no longer permitted him to take to the floor, and accepted from time-to-time invitations from select gentlemen to a quadrille or a country dance, but never to a waltz. He did not know when he noticed that she only waltzed with him, but the mere idea of her twirling in another man's arms made him tense with anger. On the thought, the musicians struck up for yet another waltz and he crossed the floor of the ballroom to bow before his wife.

"My lady?" He held out a commanding hand and, curtseying, she put hers into it, letting him lead her on to the dance floor. Once in his arms, she appeared content to remain silent, giving herself up to the dance. It was an easy silence and he enjoyed the unity of movement but found himself looking at her face, serene and somehow remote and wondering, what she was thinking about.

If he had asked, the answer would have been "nothing." Helena had learnt to live in the moment. The past was too painful and who knew what the future might bring. Here and now, she had this. The music came to an end and when her husband announced, "I think we can go now, don't you?" she readily agreed.

The one custom that remained unchanged between them was that of sharing a bed. No matter how late they came in, no matter how early he got up, they slept together. Frequently Helena was asleep when Will returned home from a political dinner and he slipped quietly into bed beside her.

One evening however he had returned unexpectedly to find no wife waiting for him. Not knowing what to do with himself, he retired to his library where he brooded over a glass of cognac until he heard her voice in the hall. Rushing out, he found her taking her leave of Harry Hall-Lambert. He was barely able to be civil to his cousin and thank him for escorting his wife, and then did not know what to say to Helena. How to explain that something was eating at him, when he did not know himself what it was? If only she would once ask something of him, he thought, or show him that he was as indispensable to her as she, he realised, had become to him. But no, she was always kind, always generous, always giving. She made no demands. The only time he had seen her out of temper was that first night they had spent in London. So, what had he to complain about? Nothing. Nothing at all.

"I'll wait for you downstairs," Will said the following evening. Helena sat at her dressing table while Lennard put the finishing touches to her toilette. "I promised Benton some papers—they are in the library."

She smiled at him in the mirror. "I'll only be a few minutes."

The papers were not where he thought them to be. As he sorted through the pile of documents on his desk, he heard the sharp rat tat of the door knocker, followed by men's voices—Blaines, answered by the deeper tones of a stranger. Who could be calling at this hour? There was a cry from Helena, followed by the rustle of skirts and the patter of evening slippers across the floor. Will came into the hall just in time to see his wife in the arms of a strange officer who lifted her off her feet and exuberantly spun her around. The look of joy on her face and her happy laughter froze his heart. She had never looked or sounded like that for him. The stranger put her down and Helena leaned her head against his shoulder.

"Oh, Jonnie! To see you again after all these years."

"Nell! What a fine lady you are. Let me look at you." Over her shoulder he spotted Will in the doorway and said, "You must be Rastleigh. I'm Jonnie Swift." He held out his hand with an engaging smile and Will grasped it, only able to think, 'Her brother, not a lover'.

"What are you doing here? Why did you not let us know you were coming? How long can you stay?" The questions tumbled from Helena's lips.

"One at a time, little sister. I'm on furlough; I didn't write because I would have been home as soon as the letter was and I don't know how long I will stay. I plan to go down to Swift Hall tomorrow, but had to spend the night in London—I had despatches to deliver—and thought I would see if you were at home."

"You will stay here tonight," she decreed.

"But you're going out," Jonnie said, looking at her finery and the light shawl over her arm.

Her face fell and Will could not bear to see her so disappointed. "You are not feeling well," he said solemnly. "You are suffering from a sudden megrim."

She grinned at him impishly. "Now that you mention it," she let her voice trail away, "I don't feel at all the thing."

"Shall I make your apologies to Lady Benton?"

"Please, Will." She smiled gloriously, her happiness shining in her eyes. It took another man to put it there, he thought, bereft, and bent to kiss her goodbye.

~~~

"Tell Cook we'll dine in an hour, Blaines. And where shall we put Major Swift?"

"The blue bedchamber, my lady?"

"That will do excellently. Where are your trunks, Jonnie?"

"Outside, with my batman."

"I shall see to it, my lady."

"Come, Jonnie, I'll show you to your room."

"May I send up some refreshments, Major?" Blaines enquired as they turned towards the stairs.

"Some good English ale, please, Blaines."

Major Jonathan Swift followed his sister up the stairs, still with a slight sensation that the ground was swaying under him. After six months on board, it would take him some time to get used to solid land.

"Here you are." Helena opened the door to a large, comfortable bed-chamber. "Just pull the bell if you want anything.

I'll see you downstairs when you are ready." She hugged him again. "Welcome home, Jonnie."

The door closed behind her and soon reopened to admit his batman with Blaines, who was supervising a fleet of footmen, some bearing his trunks, others hot water for a bath and the all-important ale.

"Looks like we're home at last, Major," his batman said as the door closed behind the last one.

"That's right, Coombes. Help me out of these clothes and lay out my evening kit, then see to your own quarters. And remember that this is a respectable household. No seducing the housemaids," he added with a grin.

"As you say, Major. How is Miss Nell, if I may be so bold?"

"Stunning. Every inch the countess. She has grown up a lot."

"Ah, we've been away too long. And for what? Fighting Boney was one thing."

"But this was a horse of another colour," Jonnie agreed.

Bathed, shaved and refreshed, Jonnie returned to the hall.

"Her ladyship is in her private parlour, Major," the butler said. "Allow me to show you the way."

Jonnie followed him down a long corridor to a wide room with tall windows and French doors opening on to a terrace.

The room was light and airy, scattered with evidence of his sister's occupations—a writing table, books, an embroidery frame, even an easel. A group of comfortable looking chairs was set at the hearth. An elegant day-bed stood against one wall and inviting window seats were piled with cushions. A small dining table had been placed at one window and on another table nearby an array of dishes had been set out so as to appeal to the eye as well as the palate.

"Thank you, Blaines. We'll serve ourselves. Here we can be quite private," Helena said. "Will's cousins stay with us for the Season and if you only have one night, I want to hear all your news without interruption. Come, pour yourself some wine. What would you like to eat? We have a cold soup, a dish of asparagus, a platter of ham, a fine salmon and salads, and here is a beefsteak pie. And sweetmeats, of course. Some strawberry tarts— "

"Enough, enough!" he said, laughing, and poured two glasses of hock. He handed her one and raised his own to her. "To happy reunions."

"I want to hear all about it—the flowers, the elephants, the tigers, the Rajahs and the palaces—the way people live."

"The damn thing—excuse me, Nell—is that we don't try to find out the way people live; we want them to live our way. In the past it was different to some extent, I understand, but now—I don't know why we have to send an army half-way around the world so as to keep some merchants and investors happy. It's not like the war against the French. But I don't mean to prose on about such things. There is so much that is beautiful in India; yes, some is savage and wild, but there are also ancient cultures and elevated thoughts and ideas."

"Start at the beginning. We had your letters, of course, but it is not the same."

"First you must tell me how the rest of the family does."

"All are well. You will see for yourself tomorrow. Did you receive Gus's letter telling you of the birth of another daughter last month—Rose Helena or Rosie as they call her?"

"No. All went well for Rosamund?"

"I think it was not as difficult as the previous times. I had a letter from her the other day; she seems in good spirits. But you will have three new nieces to see tomorrow, and Tom of course. He's a big boy now—almost seven."

"I have been away too long." Jonnie helped himself to poached salmon with asparagus and salads and set to, expressing his appreciation of the excellent English fare.

"Come and see the gardens," his sister said, when he had finished eating. "I love the long summer twilight."

He got to his feet. "So do I. In India there is practically no twilight—darkness drops like a curtain. It is quite disconcerting at first."

~~~

When Will came home, the parlour was empty and the French windows ajar. He was just about to step out onto the terrace when he heard Jonnie's voice.

"And what about you, Nell? We've talked about me all evening and never a word about you. I was delighted to hear that you had wed, but also surprised. You swore never again to consider marriage."

"Nor did I," she replied. "It just happened—suddenly he was there and I was thinking about it."

"And such a match—a countess, no less!"

"That argued more against him than in his favour. But we deal very well together."

"Is he good to you?"

"He couldn't be kinder."

"It all seems dashed prosaic to me. Do you love him, Nell? Love him the way you loved Richard?"

The ensuing pause seemed to Will to last forever. Then, he heard:

"I could never love another man the way I loved Richard. That Nell is gone—as he is gone. They were young, gay, and heedless, sure they would live forever. But they didn't."

She was silent and then Jonnie asked gently, "What of the new Nell? Does she love her husband?"

Will's nails cut into his palms as he waited for her answer.

"He doesn't want me to. He offered a marriage based on affectionate companionship and that is what I accepted. He liked, admired and respected me, he said."

"It sounds too deuced flat to me; I should want some passion in my life. Otherwise you might as well marry your aunt."

"Oh, Will doesn't treat me the same way as he treats Aunt Amelia," Helena said lightly.

"Aunt Amelia? We don't have an Aunt Amelia."

"You may not, but I do. Have you forgotten that Lady Amelia Walton is Will's aunt? But tell me, were there no pretty women in India?"

"That is something I am certainly not going to discuss with my sister," he retorted. "Take my arm as we go up the steps."

Will eased away from the window. His hand shook as he lit more candles.

"You're back." When he turned at his wife's comment, she smiled at him. "Was it a useful evening?"

"So-so. I have all manner of messages for you, wishing you a speedy recovery."

"Oh dear! I should feel guilty, I suppose."

"Nonsense! You are entitled to at least one such indisposition each season. A cognac, Swift?"

"Thank you."

"And you, my dear?"

"Some orange wine, please. Mamma and the others really have no idea that you are coming, Jonnie?"

"None at all, Nell."

"How I wish I could see their faces when you suddenly appear."

Jonnie looked from husband to wife. "Why don't you both come with me?"

Helena turned to Will hopefully. "What a wonderful idea. Could we?"

He shook his head. "I really should be in the House this week—there is a discussion about the state of Ireland."

"Couldn't Nell come down with me?" Jonnie asked. "You may be sure I would take good care of her. You could follow us once the debate is over and spend a few days with Gus and Rosamund. Nell says she hasn't yet seen their new baby."

"What do you think, Will?" Helena asked softly.

He felt a dull ache in his chest. He had wanted her to ask something of him, but to seek his agreement to leave him for some days? And yet, he could not find it within him to deny her.

"Of course, you must go, but in our carriage, with your own coachman and footmen. And you must break the journey. Jonnie might manage it in one day, especially at this time of the year, but

I shouldn't care for you to travel at such a pace. If you take a suite at The George you need not set a foot outside your apartments."

"My batman will travel with us. He is armed and can sit on the box beside the coachman," Jonnie put in.

"Lennard will go with you of course," Will said. "You will need to make an early start, so you should get to bed now."

She nodded and went to kiss Jonnie goodnight. She smiled at Will, who walked with her to the door. "I shall not say goodnight to you yet," she whispered, rising on her toes to kiss his cheek. Slightly comforted, he walked with her to the foot of the stairs.

"I shan't be long. I just want to go over the arrangements for your journey and let Blaines know when you will want the carriage. He should also send ahead to The George so that all will be ready for you."

"At nine o'clock?" she suggested.

He nodded. "I have an early appointment so I shan't be able to see you off, but I'll make sure all is in hand before I leave."

Will had wondered should he go to his wife's bed, but really nothing had changed between them, and she had made it clear that she expected him. She was almost asleep when he came, but moved into his arms with a sweet intensity, whispering her pleasure at being able to visit her family and her anticipation of their joy when they caught sight of Jonnie. He silenced her with a deep kiss and joined as intensely with her. Her welcome was no different to that on any other night, and yet he did not fall asleep as easily as usual, but lay awake holding her and trying not to think of the conversation he had overheard.

When he came into Helena's room the following morning, she was writing the last notes of apology for cancelled engagements. "I must be off. The coach is ready and I have impressed upon Jonnie and the coachman to take great care of you."

She came into his arms for his kiss. "When shall I see you?"

"By Saturday evening at the latest. It depends on how long the debate goes on." He smoothed back a stray wisp of her hair. "Enjoy yourself, and give my compliments to your family, and mine, too if you should see them."

"Thank you for not making any difficulties, Will. I think you didn't wish me to go, but you keep your promises."

"What do you mean?" He did not deny that he would have preferred her to stay at home.

"Remember when you promised never to forbid or refuse or even to permit me to do something—that you would respect my decisions, even if you did not like them? This reassures me that you really meant it."

"Have you ever doubted it?" he asked, almost angrily.

"No. In fact I had nigh forgotten it, probably because we have never really disagreed about my plans and intentions. But when I went up to bed last night, I remembered it and thought all the more of you for it. It is one thing to promise something in the abstract and another to act on that promise when the occasion arises."

"I suppose it is," he said shortly, still irritated.

She looked at the clock. "You must go. I'll walk downstairs with you."

Jonnie came into the hall however to bid Will farewell and he had to content himself with a brief, final kiss before setting off to stride briskly towards St James's Street.

~~~

Rastleigh doesn't look too happy, Lady Westland thought as she peered at his lordship from the discreet carriage that was bringing her home after a rather disappointing night with her latest *inamorato*. "Why, my lord, is the gilt already off the marital gingerbread?"

When she saw the travelling chariot and four drawn up in front of Rastleigh House, she rapped on the roof of the carriage.

The coachman peered through the trap. "My lady?"

"Go slowly around the square until I tell you to proceed."

When they returned to Rastleigh House, she was gratified by the sight of the countess, in her best looks and attired for travelling, being handed in to the carriage by a handsome officer, and a stranger at that. The man sprang in after her, the steps were put up, the door shut and the chariot moved away.

Well, Lady Westland thought, when the cat's away! She rapped again. "Home!"

Now, how might she best make use of this interesting piece of information? With whom would she first share it? Nothing would please her more than to see Lady Rastleigh cast down from her pedestal, and her husband's horns revealed.

Chapter Twenty-Nine

Dorothea Swift turned white when her two "lost" children suddenly appeared in her parlour door. Tears of joy in her eyes, she did not know whom to embrace first or longest, unable to release one so as to enfold the other.

Clasped in her son's arms while she clung to her daughter's hands, she exclaimed, "Oh, my dear, dearest ones, to see you again, and both together! What a wonderful surprise. I am sure I do not know if I am on my head or my heels. Of course I'll come to the Hall with you. Jonnie, you wait here while Helena helps me select my gowns."

"Take your time, ma'am. I'll take a turn outside," Jonnie replied. "You cannot imagine how I have missed an English garden."

"It is like old times," Lady Swift said happily as she and Helena inspected the contents of her clothes-press. "I have missed you sorely, my love, and look forward to hearing all about your life since you left us. Letters are not enough, you know."

"I agree, Mamma." Helena hugged her. "Is this a new dinner gown? How elegant. I should take it with you—it is most likely that we shall see the Waltons once Will is here."

"Has Amelia returned home? She sent me a splendid description of your ball—I was so sorry I could not attend."

"I quite understood. And Rosamund looks so well. I can't wait to see the baby."

Later that evening, Dorothea looked around her daughter-in-law's dinner-table. "What joy to see all my children together again. I had quite given up hope of it."

~~~

The next days were all holiday. Jonnie, still restless after the long sea voyage, spent much of his time riding with his brother, enjoying the English countryside in all its fresh summer beauty while Helena sat with the women or played with the children. Above all, they talked, filling one another in on all that had happened since they had last been together. Enthralled as the family was by Jonnie's stories of India, they were as interested in Helena's account of the events in Ireland and at Rastleigh, not to mention her tales of the current Season.

"She has acquired a new polish, is more worldly-wise," Rosamund said privately to her husband one evening. "She is completely the countess."

Happy as she was to be at her girlhood home, Helena found that she missed her husband. It would have been more pleasant to tell their stories together; she constantly wished to appeal to him for corroboration or additional explanation. Without him, her bed felt empty. And she felt guilty. Jonnie's voice echoed in her mind.

"What of the new Nell? Does she love her husband?"

"He doesn't want me to."

Had her answer been fair to Will? Had he ever implied that he did not want, would not value her love? He had offered her 'affectionate companionship' but when she thought about how he behaved towards her, other words came to mind—tender, considerate, ardent—in one word, loving. What did he know of love? Not a lot, at least when it came to the expression of it. He hadn't grown up in an affectionate, openly loving family as she had. And she had loved before—she had loved Richard. Will had offered her the best he knew, while she had given him second-best.

What did she really feel for him? It was more than mere liking, she knew. Could she not love him or would she not? "Love is dangerous, love hurts," she whispered into the night. "It is safer not to love. If you love someone they die, like Richard and Papa, or leave you, like Jonnie."

Could she honestly say that she would have preferred not to have loved them? Love might bring pain, but it also brought great happiness. She looked back over the months of her marriage. If she could go back to that day at Stonehenge, would she decide differently? Did she wish to return to shallows? There could only be one answer. And the answer was Will. Suddenly she had a vision of him raising his cup on Wassail Eve, proclaiming, 'life is fleeting and to be lived to the full'. *Am I too ungenerous to offer him my love, just because he did not know to ask for it? Am I a coward, afraid to risk love again?*

~~~

Left behind in London, Will was short-tempered and lonely. He slept in his own bed for the second time since his marriage; tempted to go to the familiar comfort of his wife's, but unwilling to give in to this need, especially when she had duped him so. Why had she not told him that she loved Richard Harbury, had apparently planned to marry him? He felt a fool when he thought of the Harburys—it explained why they were so close to her. And then to say he didn't want her to love him! That was of all possible accusations the cruellest, the most unfair.

He might not have been able to name it, but he had realised that something was missing between them although she did not appear to have any such concerns. She would never love another man as she had Harbury. 'Never love another man.' The words reverberated in the hollow chambers of his heart.

Leaving the Lords, he brusquely brushed past a small group of his fellows, ignorant of the glances exchanged behind him. It was unlike Rastleigh to be so ill-humoured. Arrogant, yes, but not discourteous.

"He must be missing his wife," one lord said slyly.

"He says she is visiting her family," another responded to knowing laughter.

Will's steps led him home and, almost compulsively, to Helena's parlour. The air was scented by the flowers in a vase on the table but also, he thought, faintly of her lily of the valley. He poured himself a large glass of cognac and sat in "her" chair, tiredly closing his eyes. Phrases tumbled through his mind. 'He doesn't want me to.' 'I could never love another man.' 'That Nell is gone.'

'I accepted a marriage based on affection.' 'He doesn't want me to.' 'He liked, admired and respected me, or so he said.' Then he heard Jonnie. 'You might as well marry your aunt.'

He remembered the joy on Helena's face when she saw her brother. She had never looked like that for him, so open and free. She had kept so much from him—now he realised that she had always retained a part of herself, separate and inviolate. He had answered all her questions—even the one about previous women in his life. He looked into the glass. What would she have said if he had asked her a similar question? Would she have confessed all? He tossed back the remains of his drink.

About to pour another, he froze, the decanter poised over his glass. What would she have said? Helena was truthful. He recalled her trying to explain her feelings about being a wife, dependent on her husband for all things. She might not have furnished him with unsolicited information about her past life, but she would have answered him—if he had asked. Had he ever asked her about herself, tried to get past the hidden barriers? He had felt them, known they were there. Had he said, "Why do you never ask me for anything?" Or, "I want something more?"

He knew now that that something more was love. Again, he heard her voice. 'He liked, admired and respected me, or so he said.' What a tepid litany. But she had accepted it. 'That Nell is gone, as he is.' On the way to Colduff she had relived her experiences of Waterloo, of Richard Harbury's injuries and death. She had been extremely distressed, but he had not thought to ask what Harbury had been to her. *More than Hecuba*, he now thought gloomily*, but I was too taken up with my own worries to see it.*

Was he being unfair? Perhaps Helena did not want to risk love again. Was it too much to ask of her? Or, worse, was she unable to? Could one only love once? He shuddered and then thought of his mother. She had loved both her husbands. If he accepted that Harbury's Nell was gone, would it be too much to ask his Helena to change the basis of their marriage? He had won her hand but not thought to seek her heart. What could he offer her? All he had was his own heart. Was that the answer? 'By just exchange, one for another given'? Maybe that would be enough. But first he must talk to her, shake gently at those barriers. He felt like trampling them down, but that might injure her. He must be careful, take his time.

The debate in the House of Lords finished unexpectedly early on Thursday. Leaving Parliament, Will met Stephen Graham.

"Are you coming to Brooks's?"

"No, I'm going to retrieve my wife. I was just waiting until the debate was over."

"Poor lady," a gentleman behind him murmured to another.

"She deserves whatever she gets," his companion responded. "Females—they're all the same!"

"Poor, dear Rastleigh," Mrs Logan cooed that evening when she heard the latest developments. "Of course, it was an incredibly rushed marriage—but in less than a year to look elsewhere—and before she has borne an heir."

~~~

Gus emerged, blinking, from the library to greet Will when he arrived at Swift Hall the next afternoon. "Welcome, Rastleigh. We didn't look to see you before tomorrow."

"The debate collapsed yesterday and I left at once," Will said as they clasped hands. "Where is Helena?"

"Resting. You are both in the blue suite." Gus nodded towards a footman. "Thomas will take you up."

Will eased open the door that led into the bedroom from the suite's sitting-room. Blue-sprigged curtains billowed gently at the open window while the matching bed curtains were tied loosely back, framing his sleeping wife who lay on her side, one hand half open on the pillow, and the sheet just covering her breast. He crossed to the bed, looked down at her for a moment, then continued as quietly to the dressing-room where he stripped and washed away the dust of the road. Returning to the bed, he gently raised the covers and slipped in beside Helena. As the mattress dipped beneath his weight, she rolled towards him and he caught her to him. Without waking, she put her head on his shoulder and completed their embrace. Her breathing changed, she exhaled deeply and her body relaxed against him as she sank into a profound slumber. Immensely heartened by this silent, instinctive welcome, he held her to him, quietly resting his cheek against her hair. His breathing slowed to match hers and his eyes closed. *I'm back where I belong* was his last thought before sleep claimed him.

Helena woke to feel a firm male body against hers. She opened her eyes to see her husband looking at her with such love that her eyes filled with tears.

"What is it? Don't cry, Helena."

"I'm just so happy to see you. Oh, Will, I've missed you so!"

A pleased smile lit his face. "Did you, Helena? Really?"

She nodded, sniffed and fished under her pillow for her handkerchief. "Nothing was the same without you. Even being here—well, it's no longer my home, is it?"

"I felt home was not home without you. Nothing was right, it was like a song sung out of tune." He paused and then said, "Helena?"

"Yes, Will?"

"I must talk to you. I must tell you I overheard you and Jonnie talking that evening—just before you came in from the terrace."

She made no pretence of not understanding him but blushed in horror and embarrassment. Moving away, she sat up and turned to face him.

"You said nothing. Are you angry—about Richard?"

"I was," he confessed, "but then I remembered that you didn't know I was listening. It wasn't said to hurt me. And if you did not tell me some things, well it was partly my fault because I never asked about," his voice faltered, "about other men or your feelings for Richard Harbury or even your feelings for me."

Her heart turned over. "I thought about that night too," she admitted. "I thought I had not been fair when I said that you did not want my love."

"When I asked you to marry me, I did not ask for it, I know. I was too ignorant or perhaps too afraid—or maybe too proud. I don't know. But now I would value your love above all things. I just don't know why I did not realise it sooner. Love makes you vulnerable, I suppose."

"Yes. I realised that after I avoided Jonnie's question. I was afraid to risk love again, and so refused to think I might love you."

"And now?" He had been lying propped up on one arm but now he sat up, his eyes focussed on hers.

She looked down. "The first time—young love—is easy. Perhaps that's why they call it falling in love. You're taken by surprise and there are no difficulties. Well, there weren't for us, at least. And then, when it all went wrong—it wasn't only Richard, but also Papa and even Jonnie. He didn't have to go to India, you know. He had sold out and did not need to seek another commission."

"You said, 'that Nell is gone'."

"Jonnie was the only person to call me Nell—Richard picked it up from him. I couldn't properly mourn Richard, for our engagement had not been made public as we thought to wait until after Bonaparte had been defeated. When we came home here, well Brussels was another world, and Nell was another person. And Jonnie didn't want to talk about him. I suppose he was mourning too, not only Richard but all the others." She met Will's eyes. "Richard gave me a ring just before he died. I wore it on my right hand until the day I said I would marry you."

He lifted the hand that now wore the Lady's ring and kissed it. "Did you find it difficult to take it off?"

"Yes and no. I think I knew in my heart it was time. He must have had an intimation that he wouldn't recover because, after he gave it to me, he made me promise that I wouldn't mourn him too long. He said he was not such a selfish brute that he wouldn't wish me to love again and find happiness with another man."

"That was true love, indeed. And was he right? Can I make you happy? Can you—do you—love me, Helena?"

"He was. You do. I love you, Will," she said simply. "And what of you? Do you love me?"

"With all my heart." He quickly drew her down to rest against him so she would not see the tears stinging his eyes. "Feel how it beats for you. I didn't recognise it at first, but I think I must have loved you from the beginning. I only wanted to be with you."

"Be with me now," she whispered. "Love me now."

"I have something for you," she murmured much later, as they drowsed in one another's arms, their hands sweeping lazy caresses along their sated bodies.

"Mmm? There is nothing more I want in all the world."

"Not even this?" She placed his hand on her belly, shaping it to her new roundness. "A little boy or a little girl?"

"Helena!" He shot up in the bed with a huge smile, not unlike her nephew when he was presented with his first pony. "Are you sure?"

"I have been for some time, but I could never find the right moment to tell you."

"Why not? What was the problem?"

She flushed. "It seems so silly now, but I thought it was the final point in our agreement."

"Agreement?" he repeated, puzzled.

"When you proposed. Affectionate companionship and my own home and child were what you offered."

"Why did this so-called agreement mean you were reluctant to tell me about the baby?"

"It did not seem enough anymore," she said seriously. "I did hint once and you just said there was time enough for that and turned away. And you are out so much when we are in town. I thought I would see even less of you. Perhaps you would stop coming to my bed."

"What foolish notions you have," he said severely. "But I am indeed sorry if I have been neglecting you. I will do better in future."

"Now that I think about it, you also promised me pleasure and comfort in bed."

"You didn't tell Jonnie that," he pointed out smugly. "If you had, he might not have been so quick to say it was like marrying your aunt. I think I owe it to myself to put him right."

"Will! Don't you dare!"

He fell back on the pillows, laughing. "Have you told anyone about the baby?"

"No. That is, Lennard and Madame Colette guessed."

"While I just thought you were more deliciously rounded than previously. When do you think he or she will be born?"

"October."

He gave a whoop of joy. "A wassail babe! What a splendid Wassail Queen you are." He chuckled unrepentantly at her affronted look. "That is what we call October babies—and it brings the greatest good fortune if the Wassail Queen bears one."

Helen blushed even more brightly at the thought that everyone at Rastleigh would be making precisely the same calculations.

"Ours will probably not be the only one," Will consoled her. "There are usually several babies born in October, and sometimes to girls who dance the brides' dance the following Wassail Eve."

At this Helena gave up all thoughts of modesty and propriety. Wassail Eve obviously had its own rules.

~~~

"You are happy now," her mother said as the ladies sat in the drawing-room after dinner.

"He loves me," Helena said simply.

"And you?"

"I love him too."

"And a baby as well. It is all I ever wished for you. Now, if I could just find a bride for Jonnie."

"Matchmaking already, Mamma?" Jonnie said as the gentlemen came into the room. "Let me decide what I want to do with my life first, I pray you."

"Don't you intend to stay in the army?" Gus enquired.

"As to the army, I cannot say. But I have no wish to return to India. Now that I'm home I see what an unreal life it is."

"You are on furlough, aren't you?" Will asked.

"Yes, for six months."

"Then you need not make a hasty decision but can take some time to look about you. Why not stay with us in London? I can make you known to people, put you up for Brooks's if you wish. You've been in military society for so long that it will be a while until you find your place here."

"Thank you," Jonnie said gratefully. "I'd like to do that, but I think I'll remain here for another couple of weeks."

~~~

Every week, subscribers all over London eagerly awaited the new issue of *The Ladies' Universal Register*. Most readers ignored such useful and instructive items as 'A new Method to Remove Mould from Linens' or a receipt for 'A Savoury Dish of Pickled Neat's Tongue with White Turnips', turning immediately to the centre pages which were headed *'Tonnish Topics and Society Secrets'*.

Lady Westland was no exception. A satisfied smile played on her lips as she read: *Which titled Lady, not even wed one year, was Recently seen departing London with an unknown, gallant escort. Having Rashly maRRied in haste, it seems she has now had sufficient leisure to Repent.*

"We shall see how you like being the butt of scurrilous gossip, my lady. And you, your arrogant lordship, for whom no society female was good enough, what do you think of your little nobody now?"

Chapter Thirty

Returning to the Hall from a couple of hours at the river, Will came in through the back door, handed four fine trout to a kitchen-maid and continued on to the front of the house. He had not known that Rosamund played the pianoforte. He paused for a moment to listen to the smooth scales that modulated into swift arpeggios that tumbled down the stairs as he began his ascent.

As he crossed the first-floor landing, he was astonished to see his sister-in-law and Helena's mother huddled together in the corridor outside the drawing-room. At the sound of his steps, they looked over as one and put their fingers to their lips. Puzzled, he stole over to them and peered through the half-open door. Helena placed some music on the stand and sat at the instrument. While he watched, she began to play a simple melody which developed into a series of variations, each one more subtle that the last. Occasionally, she seemed to falter, but always found her way through the intricate labyrinth.

Lady Swift's eyes were wet. "She hasn't played since she came home with Jonnie after Waterloo," she whispered. "About an hour ago, we heard the first scales. This piece by Handel was always a favourite of hers."

The music came to a close and Will stepped back, taking the two women with him. "It may overset her if we all rush in together. Let me go to her now."

Helena sat at the pianoforte, her hands in her lap. At the sound of the door she turned a tear-streaked face to him and he hurried to kneel beside her.

"What is it, Sweetheart?"

She smiled through her tears. "It's everything and nothing. I haven't played since Richard died. He loved to listen to me and his mother had the pianoforte moved into his room. During those last weeks I played so much for him. Afterwards I couldn't play or sing any more. But today I felt suddenly that I wanted to try."

"And succeeded splendidly. I was lost in admiration. How do you feel now?"

"Lighter." She rested her head against his shoulder. "Now I can remember the happy times as well."

"That's as it should be."

She sat up and smiled at him. "I must have the pianoforte at Rastleigh House tuned. Do you think we could order one for the Castle? I don't remember seeing one in the music-gallery there."

"Of course. Maybe two? One for the solar as well? I should like you hear you playing when I'm working in the library."

"I wonder will you say that when you hear me play the same phrase ten, twenty times in succession," she retorted teasingly. "But now, I think, I shall play some more."

~~~

The Rastleighs returned to London in complete harmony with one another and the world in general. The weather had become unseasonably warm and as Helena was suffering more than usual from the heat, she remained at home during the day, resting in a shady part of the garden. Will accompanied her on a walk during the cooler, early morning, but as this was outside the fashionable hours, it went unremarked.

On Friday evening they dined with Lady Neary, but the party was made up of a carefully chosen group of her ladyship's intimates and no question of scandal raised its head, Helena merely replying in the affirmative when asked if she had enjoyed her visit to her family. Her attention was then distracted by another guest and she did not supply any further information. It was observed that although she seemed tired, both the Earl and his wife were in great good humour and there was no evidence of any constraint between them.

Late on Monday, Lady Rastleigh drove in the Park in her new barouche. Mrs and Miss Hall-Lambert accompanied her. They did not stop either to chat with the occupants of another carriage or to stroll on the lawns but made a couple of gentle circuits and departed.

The following evening Stephen Graham encountered a flushed, agitated Rachel in Lady Martin's ballroom.

"Miss Hall-Lambert, you look distressed. Has someone offended you? May I be of assistance?"

She hesitated. "I am probably making too much of things, Mr Graham, but—"

"But?" he asked encouragingly. "Come, let us stroll on the terrace."

The wide terrace ran the width of the ballroom, with stone steps leading down from it to the garden below. Stephen led Rachel to the balustrade; here they could talk without being overheard, but remain in full view of the company in the ballroom.

"Now, tell me what has happened."

"It is hard to describe, but something is wrong. I do not know what precisely. A group of the girls are not as friendly towards me as they were at the beginning of the Season; some turn away when they see me while others put their heads together and whisper or giggle. Just now, I went into the ladies' retiring-room. Lady Westland was there together with other ladies and several debutantes and they all stopped talking when I came in. I didn't say anything, but Lady Georgina Benton, she is my great-aunt, you know, but Mamma will have nothing to do with her, said nastily. 'Not so proud now, are you, girl?'—and they all laughed."

"The wicked old hag! What did you do then?"

"I was not about to let them frighten me away, so I went to the mirror to tidy my hair—I had been waltzing with Mr Ponsonby— and then left without saying a word."

"Well done."

"Oh, well, from time to time, people at home would pass remarks because my father was never there and Mamma taught us to pay no heed to them. His mother was Lady Georgina's sister."

"Is there anyone who might recently have taken against you? Have you rejected any suitors or anything like that?"

She flushed. "Well, one, no two really, I suppose, though I was able to prevent the second from proposing outright. But I don't see them causing the ladies to be so spiteful. Indeed, we remain on perfectly good terms—they both asked me to stand up with them tonight."

Making a mental note to find out who her partners had been that evening, he asked, "Are the Rastleighs here tonight?"

"No. Cousin Helena has been feeling the heat—she was like to swoon this afternoon—and he wouldn't permit it." She looked up at him. "We should go in, I think."

"Will you drive with me tomorrow?" he asked as they strolled back to the ballroom. "I shall give some thought to what you have told me and you must do the same. There is something smoky going on, but I don't know what. Should you object if I spoke to my godmother, Lady Neary? Little escapes her—she is always *au fait* with the latest *on-dits*."

"Would you, Mr Graham? I should be much obliged."

As soon as they returned to the ballroom, Miss Hall-Lambert was claimed for the next dance. Stephen took a turn about the room but could get no inkling of what might be behind the change in attitude towards her. He didn't think she was imagining it—she had always struck him as being well-balanced and more mature than her contemporaries. From what he could see, she had not let her success go to her head and she obviously wasn't hanging out for the next best husband if she had already rejected two suitors. Of course, with her parents' example before her, it was understandable that she might not wish to rush into matrimony. We make women very vulnerable, he thought and what is excused in us ruins them. We claim our laws and customs are for their protection, but who can protect them against a husband?

The following day, it was his godmother who was in a high state of agitation. Barely acknowledging his greeting, she snapped, "Look at this," before slapping a journal down in front of him. "Judith brought it around this morning."

Mr Graham peered curiously at the sheet. "*Tonnish Topics and Society Secrets.* Not like you to be immersed in a scandal rag, ma'am."

"Read that," she ordered, pointing at a paragraph.

"*We understand that a certain Peer has Retrieved his eRRant wife. The lady, who does not seem to be Repentant has not been seen in Recent days.*"

"What has that to do with anything, ma'am?"

"Fool! It refers to the Rastleighs of course." She handed him another journal. "This was in the previous issue."

He read it, frowning. "They were away, of course," he said slowly. "Her brother arrived unexpectedly from India. He hadn't been home for over five years and she travelled with him to visit their family. She wanted to be there when he arrived, to see their surprise. Will couldn't get away immediately, but followed afterwards. In fact, I recall him telling me that he was going to retrieve his wife, in those very words. They are back in town now, but I understand she is suffering in this hot weather."

"A young bride? I should hope she is," came the tart rejoinder. "Obviously someone got wind of her travelling with her brother and could not wait to make something scandalous of it. Judith told me that her husband said there had been talk in the clubs. She is not one to gossip, so was not aware of what might be being said among the ladies."

"I can guess by whom. It leads me to the reason for my call. Not that I need a reason to call upon you," he added hastily in response to her glare before recounting his conversation with Miss Hall-Lambert. "I have her permission to discuss it with you, so do not break her confidence."

"A sensible, well-behaved girl, and attractive too. You could do a lot worse."

"I can give her ten years, ma'am," he replied without thinking, and to his own surprise.

"Nonsense. With that apology for a father, I should think she would relish the security of a husband who is slightly older, one on whom she may depend. And a man who is demonstrably neither a wastrel, a rake nor a fop! However," Lady Neary continued trenchantly while her godson blinked at this encomium, "that is for another day. I suspect you are right to be suspicious of the Ladies Westland and Georgina. What an unholy combination—a match made in hell, in my opinion."

"Both of whom would be pleased to do Will a disservice."

"And Helena too. What is to be done? I doubt if they have heard—the subjects of infamous rumours are usually the last to become aware of them. They must be informed, and we are the best people to do it. Then we must devise a strategy to deal with this malicious tittle-tattle. You may escort me to Rastleigh House."

He looked at the clock. "I should be happy to, ma'am, but I am committed to take Miss Hall-Lambert driving."

"Excellent. She is staying with the Rastleighs, is she not? Then we may request to speak to the three of them. There is no time to waste, Stephen. Others will have read that scandal sheet as well.

And Heaven knows what will be in the next issue if this is not stopped quickly and completely."

If the Rastleighs were surprised to find their presence requested by Lady Neary, and Mr Graham and Rachel waiting with her in the drawing-room, they did not show it. Once the courtesies had been exchanged and refreshments served, Lady Neary took the floor. She displayed the two items from *The Ladies Universal Register*, repeated what she had heard from her daughter-in-law, and then asked Rachel to recount what she had told Stephen the previous evening.

Helena was both horrified and concerned that Rachel had been made to suffer because of the rumours while Will, incandescent with rage, alternated between threats to horsewhip the editor of the Register and offers personally to throttle the traducers-in-chief.

Lady Neary clapped her hands. "Silence! You are upsetting your wife, sir. We know what is happening. Now we must decide what is to be done."

"I think Rachel, forgive me, Miss Hall-Lambert, had the right approach yesterday, when she behaved as if nothing was amiss." Stephen smiled at her approvingly. "It cannot have been easy."

"And we must all continue to do that," Helena said. "I understand that people are linking these items to me and to Will as well, but we must continue to behave as if they do not exist. By referring to them, or taking any sort of action in relation to them," here she looked at Will, "we give them credence."

"That is true," Lady Neary conceded, "but we must also whip the carpet from under the scandalmongers' feet, by subtly making the truth known."

"I should like to know how the story started." Will had calmed down and begun to address the problem in a more rational manner. "Jonnie was only here that one evening and the two of you left quite early the next morning. It must have been someone who saw you leave—the only other time you might have been noticed is at one of the stops on the road and if you had been recognised there, I don't think there would have been time enough to have had the first piece printed."

"Put the servants on it," Stephen advised. "They can find anything out. Have you grooms you can trust? I'll put mine onto it as well."

"And Lennard," Helena said. "She and your Hannah," she looked at Rachel, "can buy ribbons or try to match a button. It will give them the opportunity to talk to other maids."

"Jonnie is coming up on Friday," Will put in. "If we can find out who is behind this, we can make sure that they, and the rest of the *ton*, know who he is."

"A good notion." Lady Neary nodded approval. "In the meantime, we behave as usual. If there is an opportunity to refer to your brother—what is his rank, by the way?"

"Major, Major Jonathan Swift."

"We should do so, but only if it can be done completely naturally. We do not wish to appear on the defensive."

"I think we should warn my mother and my brother," Rachel said. "If people are bringing me into it, they may do the same with them. Indeed, Lady Georgina is more than likely to do so."

Will looked at Helena. "Would you talk to Cousin Anna, my love? I'll have a word with Harry. We are meeting at Gentleman Jackson's tomorrow."

"I thought he didn't like boxing," Helena said, surprised.

"He has changed his mind," Will replied with a grin. "He has a neat right too, and is extraordinarily quick on his feet. The Gentleman is always holding him up as an example of brains as opposed to brawn."

They all smiled at this and Lady Neary and her escort got up to take their leave. Stephen seized the opportunity to have a quiet word with Rachel.

"We did not have our drive today. May I hope you are free tomorrow?"

"If you wish."

"Above all things. Shall I call at the same time?"

"If you please."

He smiled at her and went to bid farewell to Helena.

"Thank you," she said. "It can't have been easy to come here with such a tale."

He nodded towards his godmother. "I brought the big guns to protect me."

"Will you both dine with us on Friday?" Will asked. "You will meet Jonnie and we can devise a plan of action."

"If there is an important ball on Saturday, we should all attend," Lady Neary said. "I am sure the hostess will not object to the addition of an eligible young man to her guest list."

"It's the Armstrongs'," Rachel said. "Sophia Armstrong and Arabella Dyer are close friends. They have not behaved any differently to me since all this started; if anything, they have been especially cordial."

"I shall send Lady Armstrong a note asking if my brother, who is but newly returned from India, may accompany us," Helena said.

"Now we really must go," Lady Neary said firmly. "Do you go out this evening?"

"To Lady Harbury. They will be pleased to know that Jonnie is home; he was a great friend of their son Richard from their schooldays. They bought a pair of colours on the same day and for the same regiment."

"And you, my dear?" She turned to Rachel.

"To Lady Holton's ball, my lady. I go with Mamma."

"Then I shall see you there," Stephen said. "May I have the honour of the supper dance?"

"I should be delighted, sir."

~~~

"Will you not play for us, Lady Rastleigh?" Lord Harbury said that evening. "I remember your playing with great pleasure. There was one piece in particular—it was called a sonata but described as 'almost a fantasy,' and indeed the first part was like a dream."

"I know the one you mean—it is by Herr van Beethoven. I no longer know it by heart, I fear. Do you have the music here?"

Caro Thompson quickly produced it, and without further ado Helena seated herself at the pianoforte and began to play a series of quiet, steady successions of notes that were soon overlaid by a soft, sonorous, drawn-out melody that cast her listeners under a spell.

One of them, a gentleman who was more a connoisseur of the fair sex than of music, thought idly that the lady's choice reflected her personality, serene and somehow distant. Was it true that she had sought amusement elsewhere? It seemed unlikely, especially in so blatant a fashion. But when her ladyship launched into the passionate final movement, he revised his opinion. There were fires there indeed, and they were not at all banked. He listened with greater enjoyment, admiring the forceful elegance and intensity of her playing. If she were like that in the bedchamber—

He glanced at the lady's husband, whose attention was fully focussed on his wife, an expression of fond, proud possession on his face. As he watched, Lady Rastleigh played the final chords and lifted her hands to rest them on her lap. Ignoring the applause that broke out around her, her gaze met that of her husband and a smile of extraordinary intimacy illuminated her face. So that's the way of it, the gentleman thought. She must indeed have been visiting her family. No wonder Rastleigh was in such a hurry to retrieve her.

"I started playing again when we were at Swift Hall," Helena later said to Lady Harbury. "It is fortunate that your husband requested that piece for it is the one I have been practising."

"I did not know you had visited your old home. I trust all is well there?"

"Yes, indeed. Jonnie is there. He came quite unexpectedly and I wanted to see my mother's face when she saw him. In fact," she added reflectively "she was as moved to see me. It has been a lonely winter for her, I think."

"Jonnie is home? What wonderful news. Will he come to town before the end of the Season? I long to see him again."

"We expect him on Friday. He will accompany us to Lady Armstrong's ball on Saturday."

"Then we shall be sure to go. We must meet next week for a private coze and you shall tell me all your news." She looked meaningfully as she said this and Helena blushed.

~~~

The air at Lady Holton's was much frostier.

"Your cousins do not accompany you?" one matron said pointedly to Mrs Hall-Lambert.

"Not this evening," she replied tranquilly and moved on.

An encroaching widow, who liked to give the impression of a closer connection to persons of title than was the case, was transfixed by Lady Neary's gimlet eye when overheard in the card-room to observe with a titter, "Poor dear Rastleigh. And, of course, the wedding was so sudden, was it not? Almost secretive one might say."

Raising a minatory lorgnette, her ladyship intervened. "Might one indeed? I was not aware, Mrs Crome, that you were on such terms with his lordship that you would expect him to keep you informed of his most private family affairs."

"No doubt you know all about it, my lady," a gentleman who had been listening lazily put in cheerfully as the unfortunate widow turned puce with mortification.

"Not that it is anybody's business but their own," Lady Neary returned awfully, "but the earl and countess brought their wedding date forward last August so that she could accompany him to

Ireland where his mother lay dying. They remained there for several weeks—until the End, in fact. She was a great support to the stricken family, I understand."

A respectful silence was broken by the gentleman saying sincerely, "A treasure of a wife, indeed. Rastleigh is to be envied."

Mr Graham made it his business to be aware of Miss Hall-Lambert's whereabouts at all times. She stayed close to her mother and Mr Dyer's sister, Lady Martin, between dances but seemed to have no difficulty in finding partners. As he came to claim her for the supper dance, she was saying to Miss Dyer and a number of other young ladies, "I am all agog to meet Lady Rastleigh's brother, Major Swift. He will be here on Friday. He returned from India just two weeks ago, without letting anyone know he was coming. You may imagine her surprise and delight at seeing her brother again after over five years. Nothing would do her but to accompany him to Wiltshire on his first visit to their family. She says he tells the most thrilling tales of India—tigers and riding on elephants and wonderful temples. And the Indian women—would you believe some of them don't wear gowns but just a long shirt over a sort of trousers." Her voice fell on the last word and Miss Dyer's eyes rounded.

"What! I wonder if he has sketches. They must be very comfortable," she added wistfully.

"Well done," Mr Graham said as they joined a set for a quadrille. "Nothing like a slightly naughty tit-bit of information to make sure it will be repeated."

"I thought gentlemen never gossip."

"Of course not. At times it may be important to share information, but only when required by the exigencies of the prevailing circumstances."

"What exigencies might these be?"

"The imperative requirement to assuage one's burning curiosity," he said promptly, provoking a head shake accompanied by a pursed-lip smile. Fortunately, the music started and he was not called upon to defend this outrageous statement.

At supper they shared a table with some of his friends and their partners, and he was pleased to note that Rachel was at ease in this society, quick-witted and light-hearted, but also able to join in when the conversation changed to a more serious topic.

"I shall call for you at five tomorrow afternoon," he said as he returned her to her mother.

"I shall look forward to it." She gave him an unusually sweet smile and he walked away thinking, in his godmother's words, that he could indeed do a lot worse.

On the other side of the ballroom, Lady Westland murmured into Mr Hall-Lambert's ear. "And what do you think of your fine cousins now?"

He coldly looked her up and down, and gave her the most abbreviated of bows. "Pray excuse me, ma'am," he said and walked over to invite Miss Dyer to stand up with him.

He didn't know what her ladyship was hinting at, but was sure it was nothing good. He was doubly irate when Will told him the whole story, with the result that when one of his old acquaintances twitted him at Jackson's the next morning on, "Lady R's jaunt out of town. Quite military, I hear," he floored him with a neat right and knocked him down again after he had scrambled to his feet.

"I say, old man. What was all that about?" a bystander enquired.

"Nothing," Mr Hall-Lambert said firmly, holding his opponent's gaze; "nothing unless one is eager to have a dawn appointment."

"Nothing at all," the unfortunate agreed through the handkerchief held to his nose. "Beg pardon. Can't think what came over me."

Mr Hall-Lambert nodded sternly to his erstwhile cronies. As he departed, he heard one to mutter, "Whew! Was that old Harry Hall?"

~~~

As the tide of gossip ebbed and flowed, Helena was not without her supporters. Lady Needham was heard to animadvert on the spiteful behaviour of ill-bred females who sought to spread calumnious reports of ladies whose reputations were beyond reproach. "But hell hath no fury like a woman scorned, as they say and there are those who cannot tolerate the idea that another may succeed where they have failed."

On Thursday evening the Earl and Countess of Rastleigh were to be seen at the opera as the guests of Lord and Lady Thornbury and on Friday it was reported that they had spent some hours on the premises of Messrs Broadwood in Great Pulteney Street, his lordship listening indulgently and with obvious pleasure while her ladyship tried out a number of the finest pianofortes.

Where Lady Westland, having launched the arrow of scandal, was content to let it fall where it would, Lady Georgina Benton was more consequent in her actions. She bitterly resented the earl's alienation, as she put it, of the affections of her grand-nephew and his countess's failure to invite her to her grand-niece's come-out ball. The wishes of Mrs Hall-Lambert were irrelevant to her; to her mind her niece-in-law had fulfilled her purpose by marrying her nephew—though in contriving to withhold so much of her fortune, she had been sadly lacking in her duty—and bearing him a son.

If her ladyship could now spoil sport for the Rastleighs and the Hall-Lamberts, she would do so. Her threat to tarnish the young Anna Lambert's reputation had not been an idle one, and it would not have been the first time she had resorted to such means to achieve an advantage or avenge a slight. Imperious by nature, she was fully aware of her consequence as the daughter, sister, and aunt of successive Earls Benton and her arrogance and sense of entitlement had increased with age, growing bitter as she saw her sphere of influence waning.

Lady Georgina was an avid keeper of journals—no item was too small to be noted down, for one never knew what might later prove to be significant. Having overheard one young matron recall that she had made her come-out the same year as dear Lady Rastleigh, with a false smile of interest Lady Georgina ascertained the year and sat down to review her volumes for 1814 and 1815. Surely, she must have noted something about the chit!

Chapter Thirty-One

Jonnie Swift arrived at Rastleigh House mid-afternoon on Friday, to be greeted by his brother-in-law. "Helena is resting. Come into the library for some ale and a sandwich—there are matters we need to discuss."

Ten minutes later, his air of relaxed boredom had given way to fury. "What the devil! Nell is supposed to have run away with an officer! What mischief-making, ill-begotten son of a mongrel bitch had put that about?"

"It is more likely to be a daughter than a son," Will said dryly. "We have our suspicions and shall discuss them at dinner, which is to be a council of war, so to speak."

Jonnie shuddered. "There is no point in looking to me for ideas on how to deal with it if there is a female behind it. I'd as soon stumble over a nest of scorpions. Sooner, in fact."

"The ladies have their own way of coping," Will replied, telling him appreciatively of Lady Neary's masterly set-down to Mrs Crome, the report of which had quickly reached Rastleigh ears. "And all done with an icy smile. The unfortunate lady has not been seen in society since, I believe."

The door opened to admit Helena who smiled at Will before going to embrace her brother. "What are you plotting?"

"I believe you have become a most notorious lady," he teased. "Eloping with an officer, no less."

"It is your fault, for the only officer I left town with was you."

"And that is how we are going to annihilate them," Will remarked. "Are you ready to appear in society, brother?"

"Yes, you will need your full-dress uniform tomorrow evening," Helena agreed, then intoned portentously, "You, too, are going to the ball."

"I'd better have a word with Coombes."

"Tell him to talk to Emmett if he requires anything or if you need to make some quick purchases."

"I had heard that Waterton was Lady Westland's latest interest and my groom contrived to bump into his coachman last night," Stephan Graham began once the company had assembled that evening. "He drove her home one morning last week—it was after nine o'clock. There was a travelling chariot drawn up in front of the door here and she instructed him to drive slowly once around the square. As they passed again, he saw the countess and an officer get into the coach."

"Lennard and Hannah happened to meet Lady Westland's maid at the drapers," Helena said. "She was quite chatty and Lennard mentioned that she could pass on some interesting snippets to *The Ladies Universal Register* if only she knew how. The girl said it was quite easy—you went to a Mr Poole, not at the Register's office but at another address in Soho. She went on to warn Lennard that she should be careful that an item could not be traced back to her as she knew maids who had lost their place that way. It was different for her, because she delivered notes at her mistress's command. There had been one last week and one the week before, and her mistress had permitted her to keep the sovereign she received each time."

"Despicable!" Lady Neary looked as if there were a bad smell under her nose. "Now, the question is, do we keep my handsome new cousin," she favoured Jonnie with an approving nod, "out of sight until tomorrow evening when we may present him to the *ton* with great effect, or should we provide a few tempting glimpses of him in advance?"

"Lady Neary's grandmother was a Falconer; a sister of our great-grandfather. Mr Graham is also descended from her," Helena explained in a hasty undertone to her brother, trying to stifle her laughter at the look on his face as he contemplated the prospect of being paraded captive before the society lionesses by one so obviously at the head of the pride.

"Major Swift could drive with Cousin Helena in the park tomorrow," offered Mrs Hall-Lambert.

"That would be too blatant," Lady Neary objected. "We must be subtle."

"Helena must rest tomorrow afternoon if she is to attend a ball later." Will's voice brooked no contradiction. "She and I usually stroll in Green Park in the mornings, before it gets too warm. What if Jonnie were to accompany us?"

"Much better. There is a good deal less company, but there is bound to be someone who thinks to comment on it," her ladyship approved.

"Think you should also behave normally, Swift," Mr Hall-Lambert interjected. "Go to your club, that sort of thing. Not just hang out of your sister's apron-strings. No disrespect, Cousin," he said to Helena who smiled back at him.

"The thing is," Jonnie said, "I don't have any normal behaviour. Not in London, I mean," he continued, with a stern glance at his sister, who again seemed about to succumb to her mirth. "I have never lived here. My father put me up for White's and I've kept up the membership, but I have hardly ever been there, apart from your Season in 1814. Richard and I were glad to have the opportunity to withdraw there, away from all the giggling females."

Helena made a face at him and he smirked at her as the other gentlemen nodded sympathetically.

"We can call there later on," Stephen Graham said. "Do you care to accompany us, Hall-Lambert?"

"Much obliged, but I am committed to my mother and sister this evening."

"Do you fence or box, Swift?" Will enquired.

"I prefer to fence. Some of the chaps in the regiment were good and we regularly had a bout together."

"Excellent. We can go to Angelo's later tomorrow. Shall we see you there, Harry?"

"Very likely, Coz."

"That should do it," Lady Neary pronounced. "Do you have any foreign orders, that sort of thing, Major?"

Jonnie laughed. "I do in fact have an immense ruby and diamond star, a gift from a Rajah, but I shall not be wearing it here."

~~~

"May I present my brother, Major Jonathan Swift, who is newly arrived from India? Jonnie, Lady Armstrong and Sir Howard Armstrong."

"Welcome home, Major." Lady Armstrong held out her hand, thinking the success of her ball was already assured. An accomplished hostess, she had had no difficulty in resisting the temptation to which a lesser woman might have yielded of revealing in advance Lady Rastleigh's request to be permitted to bring her brother to her ball, rightly considering that the astonishment would be all the greater if he were to appear unheralded.

"Thank you indeed, my lady, and for your gracious invitation."

"I do hope you enjoy yourself," she said now, noting the sidelong glances already being cast his way. "Pray do not hesitate to seek my assistance if you require a partner for dancing."

She watched as the Rastleigh party began their progress around the ballroom, followed by a susurration of comment.

"Is that her officer?"

"Surely not, with Rastleigh there?"

"Isn't her necklace magnificent?"

"Too old-fashioned for my taste."

"Her brother, you say? How odd that we have never heard of him before."

"Let us see where they stop—we might be able to pause near them."

"Jonnie!" Lady Harbury came forward, both hands outstretched. "Welcome home, my dear boy!"

He took her hands and bent to kiss her cheek. "Thank you, ma'am."

"You remember my daughter, Mrs Thompson?"

"Indeed, I do. How delightful to meet you again, ma'am."

The dark-haired woman shook her head, smiling. "Caro, please. I refuse to be ma'am or even Mrs Thompson to you, Jonnie."

"Caro, then. You have a daughter, if I remember correctly. How is she?"

"Very well, thank you. Amanda is nine now."

"Is she the young lady type, like my younger sister or more like Helena was?"

"A bit of both, I think. Of course, as the elder, she must give a good example to her brother."

"Her brother?"

"Davy was born in January 1816."

"I had no idea. My dear Caro! I am sure his birth was a bitter-sweet moment for you."

She nodded tearfully. "I'm sorry, Jonnie. Seeing you has brought it all back."

"I feel a bit the same. I expected people to look the same, but of course they are all older, even Nell."

"She is very happy now. I'm so glad for her. She looks wonderful tonight."

"There is Lady Needham," Helena said. "I'll sit with her for a while. Will, you need not hover around me so—go and play cards or find someone with whom you can talk politics."

He led her to the sofa where her ladyship sat enthroned. "You may safely leave her with me, Rastleigh," she said, adding to Helena as he sauntered off. "If you do not take a firm hand, he will have you demented with his fussing. When is the babe due?"

Helena blushed and looked around to see if anyone could hear. "October."

"Are you feeling well? Not ill in the morning?"

"No longer and it was not too severe. I was just tired all the time."

"Another few weeks and you may go to Rastleigh for the summer. Now, who is this excellent dancer?" She nodded towards Jonnie who waltzed past with Caro.

"My brother, Major Jonathan Swift; he is just returned from India."

"Is he indeed? You may present him to me," she ordered, beckoning imperiously when the music stopped.

Jonnie obeyed the unspoken command, bringing Caro with him.

"Over five years in India?" Lady Needham said. "No doubt your mother was delighted to see you home in one piece."

"Yes, my lady. I shall never forget the look on her face when my sister and I walked into her parlour. Helena came with me to Wiltshire, for she couldn't bear to miss the excitement."

"Swift, is it not?" a hearty male voice said behind him.

"Colonel Macintosh." Jonnie turned to salute an older, ram-rod straight gentleman. "Do you remember my sister, now the Countess of Rastleigh, and Mrs Thompson, Major David Thompson's widow?"

"My lady, Mrs Thompson. I think we have not met since before just Waterloo."

The group around the sofa grew larger. After some time, Helena began to feel the need for some fresh air. "Pray excuse me, ma'am," she murmured to Lady Needham. "Jonnie, would you give me your arm, if you please."

"That's better," Helena said after some minutes on the terrace. "I felt as if I would melt into a puddle, just like the candles. Would gas lights emit less heat, do you think?"

"Probably," Jonnie replied. "You would need fewer for one thing. But it is a harsher light, not as flattering to the complexion, I should say."

"I suppose not."

"It was good to meet the Harburys again. I have been away too long, Nell."

"Far too long," she agreed. "It is time you got to know your own country. You can start by visiting us in Dorset."

He touched his brow in salute. "Yes, Milady. When do you return there?"

"I'm not sure. It will depend on when Parliament rises."

He looked carefully at her. "Are you feeling more the thing? I should go in—I am engaged to Miss Hall-Lambert for the next dance."

"And after that?"

"I don't know. You may find me some partners, Nell, but not too many debutantes, I implore you. I'm out of practice when it comes to talking to them."

She laughed, and tucked her hand into his arm. "First, we must brave the eye of the needle." She nodded towards the animated group at the door to the ballroom. "Why must people congregate in the most awkward places?"

"I have no idea. Let me go ahead. Stick close to me, Nell."

He turned sideways, easing through the crowd until his progress was blocked by a vivacious lady clad in bright green who was too busy plying her fan to notice her surroundings.

"I beg your pardon, ma'am."

She let the fan collapse as she looked up into his face "Oh, think nothing of it—Major?"

When he did not immediately respond, her gaze went past him to his sister. "Will your ladyship not make your—escort known to us?"

Nell pokered up at the insinuating tone, reminding Jonnie of a colonel's lady confronted with a befuddled subaltern.

"My brother, Major Swift," she said icily. Over a general intake of breath, she added to him, "This is Lady Westland. You must forgive her impetuousness. She is always eager to know the latest topics and secrets in circulation in the *ton*."

He nodded stiffly. "My lady."

Her ladyship turned first white, then red, then white again. Fist clenched on her fan, she opened her mouth as if to say something but obviously thought the better of it and turned on her heel. A passage opened in the silent crowd to permit her departure.

"What effrontery," one matron remarked to another, "but I can't say I'm surprised. And we may now guess where all the rumours started."

Conversation started up again, even more animated than before, but Jonnie and Helena did not linger.

"She obviously thought she had caught us out," Helena said when they had left the group safely behind them. "She was waiting for us, together with that coterie of her bosom-bows."

"I can't understand why she would challenge you before all in such a brazen way. Have the two of you crossed swords in the past or does she just enjoy stirring up a hornet's nest?"

"I don't know, but I think she had hopes of Will at one time. From something Lady Needham said, I gathered there may have been an episode some years ago while she was still married and, once she was widowed, she thought to improve on the previous interlude. He was a tempting catch, you know," she added with a self-deprecating grin.

"Nell!"

"Now, Jonnie, you cannot expect me to be ignorant of these matters. And what he did before we were married is really no concern of mine. After all, he has had to accept my connection to Richard. We loved one another. One could say that that would be much more of a threat to a subsequent marriage."

"But it is no longer?"

"No. I have at last learnt to put it behind me and not to be afraid of loving again. Richard will always be part of my past, but Will knows he is my present and, I hope, my future."

"I'm glad, Nell. Now, where is that champagne?" He lifted two glasses from the tray of a passing footman and raised his to her. "To your happiness, Nell. I didn't get a chance to drink your health at your wedding. And Rastleigh's too. I think he has changed his view of marriage as well."

She smiled gently and just said, "We are very happy, Jonnie. There is Mrs Dunford. You will remember her from before. I shall go and sit with her while you search out Rachel."

"How nice to see your brother again," Mrs Dunford said. "We lost so many at Waterloo that it is wonderful to see a half-forgotten face after all these years. He has changed, of course, as we all have."

Helena saw Jonnie glance over to them. Once he had returned Rachel to her mother's side after their dance, he came to join them.

"What a pleasure to see you again, ma'am. Is Dunford here with you?"

She put a gentle hand on his arm. "He died three years ago, Major, from an inflammation of the lung. He never really recovered from the drenching he got at Waterloo, not to speak of his wounds. It was some time before he was found, you know."

He looked at her, shocked. "I am exceedingly sorry to learn of it, ma'am. He was a good man and a good officer."

"That battle continues to haunt all of us, does it not? But I'm delighted to see you safe and well, Major. What have you been doing all these years?"

The Rastleighs' table in Lady Armstrong's supper room that evening was the object of general and undisguised interest. The countess was in glowing looks and it was whispered that she was in expectation of a happy event, which explained his lordship's proud and protective stance. The story of how Lady Westland had been routed was conveyed to those unlucky enough not to have been in the vicinity of that thrilling encounter and Major Swift, who was escorting Mrs Dunford, was pointed out to the inquisitive.

It was noted that Mr Stephen Graham had danced the supper dance with Miss Hall-Lambert for the second time that week. They had been spotted driving in the park as well. And Mrs Hall-Lambert was again in the company of Mr Dyer. Both mother and daughter appeared to be having a successful Season. Mr Hall-Lambert, who had changed so much for the better this year, was squiring Miss Armstrong. Even though he may not be Rastleigh's heir for much longer, it was understood that he had come into a pretty inheritance from his mother's family and Hall-Lambert was a well-sounding name; it could not be denied that Hall-Lambert of Lambert Court had a ring to it.

Making his way through the room, the Duke of Wellington, now a cabinet member and Master-General of the Ordnance, paused at Major Swift's chair, causing the major to leap to his feet and salute his former commander-in-chief.

"Glad to see you again, Swift. You must call and tell me the latest about India. I am always grateful for good intelligence."

"Your Grace." Jonnie saluted again as the Duke bowed to the rest of the table and moved on.

This was the final straw for Lady Georgina Benton. Her baleful eye had missed none of the comings and goings and her resentful nature seethed at the admiration and approbation accorded to Lady Rastleigh. Sitting with an impoverished cousin, who had had the misfortune to accompany her, she made no secret of her feelings.

"Look at her, sitting between poor Rastleigh and that Major, as if butter wouldn't melt in her mouth. And what if he is her brother? She was always surrounded by officers. A flighty miss, if ever there was one. They weren't all her brothers—you may be sure of that. Always flirting with one or the other—shameless. There was one in particular—a Captain Harbury. I wonder what has become of him. And then she disappeared from society. She had many a green gown before tonight, I'll warrant. Who is to say that he didn't tap her first? No one has heard any more of him if it comes to that."

It was unfortunate that these rantings grew louder just as an inexplicable lull fell in the rest of the room.

Lady Harbury stiffened at the mention of her son's name. "You wicked old harridan! How dare you!"

She collapsed back in her chair, gasping for breath. Her husband immediately went to her side, urging her to be calm.

At this, Will rose and strode down the supper-room, pausing to say to Lord Harbury, "If you will permit me, my lord?"

Harbury waved him on and Will continued to where Lady Georgina sat, a look of false innocence on her raddled face, as if to say what had she to do with anything.

"Lady Georgina, in your malicious and intemperate utterances you have not only cast aspersions on the most virtuous of ladies, but have impugned the honour of a beloved son, both of his family and of England, one who gave his life at Waterloo. I do not ask for an apology, madam, for an apology from such as you can only be a further insult. I take leave to tell you that you are a disgrace to your name and station."

Patches of rouge appeared out on her ladyship's cheeks as she attempted to stare down the surrounding onlookers. A murmur of "hear, hear" died away as Earl Benton came forward. He looked contemptuously at his aunt and bowed to Will, the Harburys and Helena, who had joined them. "My lords, my ladies, I beg you will accept my profound apologies for the insult offered by one of my house."

Lord Harbury did not hesitate to offer his hand. "I accept your apology and I thank you, my lord."

Lord Benton turned to the Armstrongs. "Sir Howard, Lady Armstrong, pray excuse us. My aunt has overly exerted herself."

"Of course, my lord," Lady Armstrong said, murmuring to a footman to send for the Benton carriage.

"Come, Aunt!"

Surrounded by her nephew and his countess as well as their son, Viscount Marfield and his wife, Lady Georgina rose sulkily, barked at her companion to follow and was ushered out of the room in grim silence.

"We shall send the carriage back for you," Benton said to the Marfields. "You must remain and try to smooth things over here."

"I think you have already paved the way, sir. It was a lucky chance that had you so near and able to intervene at once."

The carriage drew up and the earl followed the three ladies to it. "We'll get her to her room now. Tomorrow we must discuss what is to be done."

Lord Marfield nodded and offered his arm to his wife as they went back into the house. "Did you hear it all?"

"I had just come into the room. She was raging and ranting as if poor cousin Cassandra were the only other person there. It was disastrous that there was one of those odd hushes that occur sometimes in a crowded room and everyone could hear her. Once she started, of course, they were all ears."

"I'm sorry for Lady Armstrong. To have this happen at her ball cannot have been pleasant."

"Nonsense," Lady Marfield said robustly. "She will be the envy of the other hostesses for her ball will be talked of at least to the end of the Season. But I think we should go and have a word with her now. Your mother and I will need to call on Lady Harbury and Lady Rastleigh tomorrow and renew our apologies."

Lady Harbury had withdrawn to a small parlour with her family, Will and Helena. Reposing on a chaise-longue, she patted her eyes with a lace-trimmed handkerchief. "I am so grateful to you," she said to Will, "for defending my boy like that. How could she attack him so? And to use him to defame Helena! He would have been beside himself with anger."

"I don't think she meant it personally; it was more part of her attack on me," Helena said reflectively. "I suppose she recalled having seen me with Richard—maybe the sight of Jonnie caused her to remember us together—and the rest was her wicked imagination and venomous supposition. I know you will not let it go any further, but I think you should know why she is so resentful of me."

"Ruining reputations seems to be a habit of hers," Caro said when they had heard the story of Mrs Hall-Lambert's marriage and the more recent episode regarding the lack of an invitation to Rachel's ball. "In one way it was fortunate that things turned out the way they did this evening. She was so extreme that it was clear that what we heard were the ravings of a bitter old woman and Rastleigh's devastating rebuke will ensure that no one will dare repeat what she said. It would have been far worse if she had confined herself to scurrilous mutterings that might have acquired a life of their own. It is a sad reflection on our society that there are always those who are willing to repeat and elaborate the most appalling and unfounded gossip."

"I trust Benton will now put a halt to his aunt's gallop," Lord Harbury said. "Are you feeling more the thing, my dear?" he asked his wife. "Would you like to go home?"

"No. I think it is important that we all remain for a while longer. Let us stroll first on the terrace and then we should behave as usual, just as if nothing had happened."

~~~

"Thank you for standing up for Richard," Helena said later that night as she lay in Will's arms.

"How could I not? If he was worthy of your love, he was worthy of my defence. It may seem odd, but I've come to think of him as a younger brother. Maybe it is because his parents look on you as a daughter and have welcomed me as your husband."

"It does sound unusual, but I know what you mean."

"Harbury was quite properly more concerned for his wife just at that moment; his elder son was not there and so it fell to me, as a son-in-law if you like, to act."

"Other men might be jealous or resentful of Richard."

"How could I be when I now have your love? And not only that, I love you. This—what is between us—is something I never thought to have, did not even know to ask for. You would not be the Helena I love without him. So, I could not wish he had never been part of your life or even that you had not loved him."

Helena was moved beyond words, beyond tears by this declaration of devotion. She kissed him softly and then lay without speaking, her head on his shoulder. "I did not know to look for it either," she said at last. "I thought my heart was silenced, but you have made it sing again."

He rested his hand on the sweet curve below which their baby grew. "Sleep now, my dearest love," he whispered. "My heart sings with yours."

Epilogue

It was a week past their wedding anniversary. Will sat at his desk in the library, catching up with the work that he had neglected during the past weeks. Sir John Malcolm had brought his family to stay with their brother for a month and he and Helena had also welcomed the Waltons and the Swifts. The Castle had come to life in a way he had never previously known, with young voices echoing from the walls as their eager guests had explored it from the dungeons to the battlements. The new pianoforte had been delivered and, for the first time he could remember, music was heard in the east gallery.

There was an air of contentment about Rastleigh these days. Once his people had become aware that the Countess was carrying a wassail babe, there had been no stemming the flood of congratulations and good wishes. She had been the recipient of a stream of well-meant advice, while many a glass of ale had been raised to congratulate the father-to-be. The harvest looked to be promising and a good crop of fruit was ripening in the orchards.

"She's brought luck back to Rastleigh, she has," he had heard more than one person murmur. The additional employment created both within the Castle itself and outside was also much appreciated. Word had spread and sons and daughters, some with families of their own, who had had to seek employment elsewhere, were able to return home. Disused cottages had been refurbished and were once again inhabited. The rector was talking about the need for another teacher at the little school while Will was hoping to encourage a good physician, one of whom Helena approved, to settle in the village.

He laid down his pen with a happy sigh. Time to join his wife in the solar. She looked magnificent these days, proudly carrying her babe before her. Her veneer of calm had finally shattered; now she was quicker to show her feelings.

Today, she leaned against the cushions on the window seat, enjoying the afternoon sun and admiring the play of light on the gentle waves below. She looked up at his entrance. "Finished?"

"With the most urgent, at any rate." He came to sit beside her, sliding his arm around her and bending to kiss her, his other hand caressing the swell of her pregnancy. "How are you feeling? Are you both well?"

"Exceedingly so. I have a surprise for you." She took his hand and led him to the opposite wall. "All those old hangings we found gave me the idea to put my embroideries together in one piece. It is a record of our first year together."

"What a wonderful idea. And it looks magnificent. I knew you were talented with your needle, but this surpasses anything I have seen." With increasing appreciation and delight Will studied the large, colourful hanging that was suspended by broad linen loops from a pole. It consisted of a series of embroidered panels, some of them sub-divided, that had been stitched together and backed with heavier linen.

Amused and touched, he saw little Sally swinging from Helena's and his hands; their breakfast of grilled fish by the stream, the two of them standing hand in hand at Stonehenge and then leaving the church on their wedding day. They were on board the *Sweet Mary*, he high in the rigging while she sat below at her easel, and here they were on deck at night, the starry sky spread above them. Another scene depicted the family gathered around his mother's day-bed as Kate read to them and in another he sat alone with his mother, holding her hand. He had to smile at the divided panel where, on one half, Helena curtsied to him, her head held defiantly high and in the other he was standing scowling with his arms folded, glaring at the agitated hem and skirts of her gown, the back of her head just visible in the doorway, her indignant departure captured forever.

Here they waltzed, there they rode together, she on her grey mare. On Wassail Eve he gave her the Lady's ring and later they danced in the orchard in the moonlight. In the last one, she sat at her pianoforte, while he stood beside her, ready to turn the page.

"The only one I don't understand is this one." He pointed to a small panel depicting a sleek lioness that seemed to purr smugly. "Why a lioness? And come to think of it, she looks like a cat that has got the cream."

"Or the cheese?"

He burst out laughing. "You little devil! How are we to explain that to people?"

"Very few people will have the opportunity to study it closely, but if they ask, we shall simply say that it is a classical allusion. You may sigh and say that your wife is a blue-stocking, if you wish."

"You left out Lady Georgina and Jenkins and Miller."

"I don't want to remember the ugly things. Sad ones, yes, like the loss of your mother, but we do not wish to forget her. You brothers and sisters were so happy to see her portrait here."

"You have given me so much this year," he said, suddenly serious, framing her face with his hands and looking deep into her eyes.

"And you me." She reached up to pull his head down to her for a kiss. "We are no longer bride and groom now, and by this time next year, God willing, we'll be parents. Who knows what the future will bring, but with you I am not afraid to face it."

"And with you, I will live it, not stand aloof from it." He kissed the finger that wore his wedding ring. "In thee, my choice, I shall rejoice as long as we both shall live."

Background Note

This is a work of fiction but set in a real place and time. While it would not be possible to list all the sources consulted, I wish to mention the following:

- *An Authentic History of the Coronation of His Majesty, King George the Fourth* by Robert Huish, Esq., London 1821.

- Coronation Oaths: According to Huish, George III swore *to confirm to the people of England the true profession of the gospel established in this kingdom*, while George IV's oath bound him *to maintain and preserve inviolably the settlement of the united Church of England and Ireland as by law established within England and Ireland*. For a long time, George IV refused the Royal assent to the Catholic Emancipation Act (which was finally passed in 1829) on the grounds that it would violate his coronation oath.

- Twelfth Night or the Feast of the Epiphany or the Feast of the Three Kings is celebrated on 6 January, the twelfth day of Christmas. The Calendar Act of 1750 which provided for the change from the Julian to the Gregorian calendar, resulted in the 'loss' of eleven days at the introduction of the new calendar in 1752 when 2 September was immediately followed by 14 September. In parts of England, including the south-west, the old calendar was still adhered to for some things, including wassailing, which traditionally took place on 'Old Twelfth Night' or 17 January, a tradition that continues in some places to this day.

- The verse sung by the wassailers is quoted by a 1791 correspondent of The Gentleman's Magazine. The full Rastleigh Wassail Eve celebrations are, however, a figment of my imagination.

- For those from other latitudes, according to The Year Book of 1832, twilight in England on 22 May ended at 11.37 p.m. On 23 May, the compiler notes, 'No REAL NIGHT during the remainder of the month.

- The Beethoven sonata 'quasi una fantasia' played by Helena at the Harbury's in Chapter Thirty is his Sonata No. 14 in C-sharp

Minor, Op. 27, No. 2. First published in 1801, it received the nickname 'Moonlight Sonata' in the 1830s when a reviewer compared the first movement to a boat floating in moonlight on a lake.

- If you go out to Poulaphuca today, you will find a big lake, known locally as Blessington Lake. The Liffey was dammed here in the 1940s to supply Dublin with drinking water. It is still beautiful, but the wildness that Helena spoke of is gone.

The Duchess of Gracechurch Trilogy

Set in Regency England from 1803 to 1816, *The Duchess of Gracechurch Trilogy* celebrates friendship, family and love.

Wed before she was seventeen in a made match to a duke's heir, heiress Flora Hassard quickly learns that her new husband has very little interest in getting to know his new wife. Supported by her mother-in-law, she creates a happy home for herself and her children while 'donning the Duchess' in society where she uses her position and influence in the *ton* to befriend young wives *"whose husbands are, well, distant, shall we say? They are safe in that circle, or as safe as they want to be. The older women keep an eye out for the younger ones, warn them of the worst rakes, that sort of thing; keep them out of harm's way." (*Perception & Illusion*)* Flora is content, but her contentment has come at a high price—she has had to turn her back on love.

Books One and Two of the Trilogy tell the stories of two of the brides Flora befriends while in Book Three Flora herself takes the lead. *Note: While Books One and Two can be read in either order, The Duke's Regret contains spoilers for the first two books and should be read last.*

***Book One:* The Murmur of Masks**

Eighteen-year-old Olivia, daughter of a naval officer is desperately in need of security and safety, following the sudden death of her mother. Unaware that his affections are elsewhere engaged, she accepts Jack Rembleton's offer of a marriage of convenience, hoping that love will grow between them. When Olivia meets Luke Fitzmaurice at a ball given by the Duchess of Gracechurch, Luke is instantly smitten but Olivia must accept that she has renounced the joys of girlhood without ever having experienced them.

An unexpected encounter with Luke at a masquerade ten years later leads to a second chance at love. Dare Olivia grasp it? Before she can decide, Napoleon escapes from Elba and Luke joins Wellington's army in Brussels. Will war once again dash Olivia's hopes of happiness?

Reviewers said. *"I read it very quickly as the story was very compelling and the characters really came to life and engaged me." "Depicts both the harsh reality of the battlefield and the pleasures and challenges of society life in England."*

***Book Two:* Perception & Illusion**

Cast out by her father for refusing the suitor of his choice, Lallie Grey accepts Hugo Tamrisk's proposal, confident that he loves her as she loves him. But Hugo's past throws long shadows as does his recent liaison with Sabina Albright. All too soon the newly-weds are caught up in a comedy of errors that threatens their future happiness.

Lallie begins to wonder if he has regrets and he cannot understand her new reserve. She resolves to find her own sphere, make her own life and is delighted to be welcomed into the circle of the Duchess of Gracechurch. When a perfect storm of confusion and misunderstanding leads to a devastating quarrel with her husband, Lallie feels she has no choice but to leave him. Can Hugo win her back? Will there be a second, real happy end for them?

Award winning author Nicola Cornick said of Perception & Illusion: "*It was a real pleasure to read a book so well-rooted in the manners and mores of the period. I also loved your protagonists and the depth you gave to their emotional journeys and to the rest of the characters and story. Bravo! It was a lovely read.*"

Book Three: The Duke's Regret
A chance meeting with a bereaved father makes Jeffrey, Duke of Gracechurch realise how hollow his own marriage and family life are. Persuaded to marry at a young age, he and his Duchess, Flora, live largely separate lives. Now he is determined to make amends to his wife and children and forge new relationships with them.

But Flora is appalled by his suggestion. Her thoughts already turn to the future, when the children will have gone their own ways.

Divorce would be out of the question, she knows, as she would be ruined socially, but a separation might be possible and perhaps even a discreet liaison once pregnancy is no longer a risk.

Can Jeffrey convince his wife of his sincerity and break down the barriers between them? Flora must decide if she will hazard her heart and her hard-won tranquillity when the prize is an unforeseen happiness.

"Well-researched and strongly recommended." The Historical Novels Review

All three books are available as eBooks and paperbacks; there is also a box set of the whole Trilogy.

Amazon UK https://amzn.to/2xhAe1t:

Amazon US https://amzn.to/2KKfdVY

A Suggestion of Scandal

If only he could find a lady who was tall enough to meet his eyes, intelligent enough not to bore him and had that certain something that meant he could imagine spending the rest of his life with her.

As Sir Julian Loring returns to his father's home, he never dreams that 'that lady' could be Rosa Fancourt, his half-sister Chloe's governess. They first met ten years ago but Rosa is no longer a gawky girl fresh from a Bath Academy. Today, she intrigues him. Just as they begin to draw closer, she disappears—in very dubious circumstances. Julian cannot bring himself to believe the worst, but if Rosa is innocent, the real truth is even more shocking and not without repercussions for his own family, especially for Chloe.

Driven by her concern for Chloe, Rosa accepts an invitation to spend some weeks at Castle Swanmere, home of Julian's maternal grandfather. The widowed Meg Overton has also been invited and she is determined not to let such an eligible match as Julian slip through her fingers again.

When a ghost from Rosa's past rises to haunt her, and Meg discredits Rosa publicly, Julian must decide where his loyalties lie.

"A smooth read; providing laughs and gasps in turns. Readers will enjoy the cool-headed Miss Fancourt, while hoping that Sir Julian puts the pieces of the puzzle together quickly! A host of other loveable and detestable characters keep the entertainment moving through the trials, tribulations, and victories of love." Historical Novels Review

https://amzn.to/2NE7J4A Amazon UK,
https://amzn.to/2LPrzb7 Amazon US

The Potential for Love

"There is an essential something that calls us to another, something that we recognise or that resounds within us on the most intimate level."

"Love, you mean?"

"Rather the possibility or potential for love." Her father shook his head. "It's impossible to describe, Arabella, and it may take us some time to recognise it, but we do know when it is not there.

When Arabella Malvin sees the figure of an officer silhouetted against the sun, for one interminable moment, she thinks he is her brother, against all odds safely returned from Waterloo. But it is Major Thomas Ferraunt, the rector's son, newly returned from occupied Paris who stands in front of her.

For over six years, Thomas's thoughts have been of war. Now he must ask himself what his place is in this new world and what he wants from it. More and more, his thoughts turn to Miss Malvin, but would Lord Malvin agree to such a mismatch for his daughter, especially when she is being courted by Lord Henry Danlow?

As Arabella embarks on her fourth Season, she finds herself more in demand than ever before. But she is tired of the life of a debutante, waiting in the wings for her real life to begin. She is ready to marry. But which of her suitors has the potential for love and who will agree to the type of marriage she wants?

As she struggles to make her choice, she is faced with danger from an unexpected quarter while Thomas is stunned by a new challenge. Will these events bring them together or drive them apart?

"The heroine is brave and resourceful, the hero gallant and willing to learn, and the insights are perceptive. Very satisfying. Strongly Recommended."

Historical Novels Review http://mybook.to/ThePotentialForLove

About the Author

Catherine Kullmann was born and educated in Dublin. Following a three-year courtship conducted mostly by letter, she moved to Germany where she lived for twenty-five years before returning to Ireland. She has worked in the Irish and New Zealand public services and in the private sector. Widowed, she has three adult sons and two grandchildren.

Catherine has always been interested in the extended Regency period, a time when the foundations of our modern world were laid. She loves writing and is particularly interested in what happens after the first happy end—how life goes on for the protagonists and sometimes catches up with them. Her books are set against a background of the offstage, Napoleonic wars and consider in particular the situation of women trapped in a patriarchal society. She is the author of *The Murmur of Masks, Perception & Illusion, A Suggestion of Scandal, The Duke's Regret,* and *The Potential for Love.*

Catherine also blogs about historical facts and trivia related to this era. You can find out more about her books and read her blog (My Scrap Album) at www.catherinekullmann.com Her Facebook page is https://www.facebook.com/catherinekullmannauthor

Lightning Source UK Ltd.
Milton Keynes UK
UKHW012258120421
381871UK00002B/543